Marianne Aucoin was a stranger, even if she had been married to Hilary's brother. *If.* Like Stephen, even when faced with a marriage certificate and a boy who looked so much like her brother, Hilary still wanted some ultimate proof.

'I'll go now,' she said coldly, and went to the door. Before opening it, she turned and looked at the two foreigners.

'I don't want you to feel unwelcome,' she said quietly. 'I'm sure you knew this would be a shock for us. But as long as you're staying here, we'll make you as comfortable as possible.'

Marianne inclined her head, and Robert met Hilary's eyes for a moment. As they regarded each other, Hilary felt a brief tremor of disquiet.

The boy *must* be Baden's son, she thought. Such a likeness could surely not be explained any other way. Yet there was something in that face, in those eyes, which was not Baden, something that made her deeply uneasy inside, and she felt a sudden intense wish that he had not come, that they could return to their lives as they had been an hour ago. For now that he had, nothing would ever be the same again.

Lilian Harry's grandfather hailed from Devon and Lilian always longed to return to her roots, so moving from Hampshire to a small Dartmoor town in her early twenties was a dream come true. She quickly absorbed herself in local life, learning the fascinating folklore and history of the moors, joining the church bell-ringers and a country dance club, and meeting people who are still her friends today. Although she later moved north, living first in Herefordshire and then in the Lake District, she returned in the 1990s and now lives on the edge of the moor with her two ginger cats and black miniature schnauzer. She is still an active bell-ringer and member of the local drama group, and she loves to walk on the moors. Her daughter and two grandchildren live nearby. Visit her website at www.lilianharry.co.uk

An Heir for Burracombe

LILIAN HARRY

An Orion paperback

First published in Great Britain in 2010
by Orion
This paperback edition published in 2011
by Orion Books Ltd,
Orion House, 5 Upper St Martin's Lane,
London WC2H 9EA

An Hachette UK Company

7 9 10 8 6

A CIP catalogue record for this book
is available from the British Library.

ISBN 978-1-4091-2012-4

Typeset by Deltatype Ltd, Birkenhead, Merseyside

Printed in Great Britain by Clays Ltd, St Ives plc

The Orion Publishing Group's policy is to use papers that
are natural, renewable and recyclable products and
made from wood grown in sustainable forests. The logging
and manufacturing processes are expected to conform to
the environmental regulations of the country of origin.

www.orionbooks.co.uk

For Rosie and David

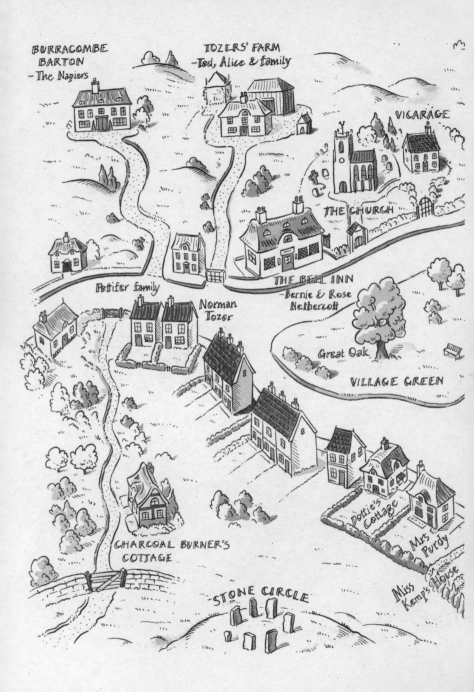

BURRACOMBE
BARTON
- The Napiers

TOZERS' FARM
- Ted, Alice & family

VICARAGE

THE CHURCH

THE BELL INN
- Bernie & Rose
Nethercott

Pettifer family

Norman
Tozer

Great Oak

VILLAGE GREEN

CHARCOAL BURNER'S
COTTAGE

Pottie's
Cottage

Mrs
Purdy

Miss
Kemp's House

STONE CIRCLE

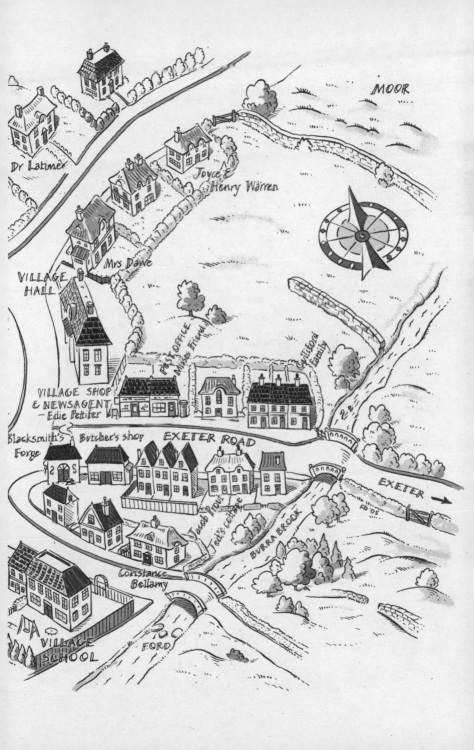

Chapter One

June 1953

An heir for Burracombe.

The phrase circled in Hilary's mind as she lay in bed that night, unable to sleep. So much had happened that day; so much that would change her life – all their lives – for ever.

It was as if Baden himself had returned.

Robert Aucoin's face swam before her eyes. The face of a young boy, barely into his teens, a boy she had never seen before but felt she knew with the familiarity of a sister. Which was nonsense, of course – she was almost twenty years older than he. But she had known a brother so like him they could have been twins, could have grown up together here, in this very house, playing, squabbling, laughing and crying together.

But this boy wouldn't be at all like Baden. How could he be? He was born in Occupied France at the beginning of a long war, and brought up with no knowledge of Burracombe, of his English heritage. How could he be at all like Baden?

And yet ... There was that flash in his eyes. That sudden lift of his chin. That directness in his gaze.

All those were Baden. Her brother.

Once again, her mind went back to the moment, only a few hours ago, when she had entered the drawing room to find the two strangers waiting for her. A young woman, perhaps two or three years older than herself, small and dark, with flashing eyes in a vivid face, wearing a red costume that was clearly not new but was of unmistakably French cut and well cared for. And the boy. The boy whose first glance caught Hilary with a flicker of recognition, so unbelievable that it was gone before she knew it.

He was about thirteen, his smooth hair as dark as his mother's, his eyes a bright, deep blue. Yet although he resembled her in colouring, there was nothing else about them that was alike. He was slim, long-legged without being lanky, and promised to be well-built when he reached manhood. His features were of a cleaner, more sculpted cast, and even though he sat quite still, there was a composed air of grace about him that was in subtle contrast to the half-concealed challenge of the woman's expression as her eyes met Hilary's.

In that first bewildered moment, Hilary had been at a complete loss. Her mind still full of the Coronation celebrations the day before, she had been quite unprepared for visitors, and even less prepared for the shock of the Frenchwoman's words.

'I am Baden's widow, Miss Napier – Marianne.' A tiny pause. 'And this is our son, Robert.'

'Your *son*?' She had stared at them, unable at first to take it in. Then she'd looked once more at the boy's face and that flash of recognition came again, more strongly. Those dark-blue eyes ... those straight brows ... 'But ... I don't understand. Baden wasn't married.'

'He was,' the young woman said quietly. Her English was remarkably good, Hilary thought, her dazed mind catching at brief impressions as the words flowed by. 'He was married to me.'

The story needed to be told more than once before Hilary could fully understand it. The meeting of the couple while Baden Napier's regiment was positioned near Marianne's home; the swift falling in love, the colonel's permission to marry before

2

the regiment moved on two days later. And then the news that the entire unit had been killed.

'It was very quiet, a civil ceremony only, just a few days before the retreat to Dunkirk. I scarcely had time to be a wife before I became a widow – but it was not long before I knew that I was also to become a mother.' She had cast a swift glance at her son, sitting quietly beside her, his dark-blue eyes taking in his surroundings but returning again and again to Hilary's face. 'It was not an easy time for me,' she said quietly. 'A woman alone, with a child on the way.'

'It couldn't have been.' Hilary tried to imagine it. 'But you *were* married, I mean, there was no reason—'

'I was married, but only partly. You see, in France we have two ceremonies for the marriage – the civil one, which is carried out by the mayor, and the religious one in the church. Baden was not Roman Catholic, so we could not be married in church until he had been prepared, and, in effect, my marriage was not recognised. It was as if it had not happened.'

'But it was legal.'

'*Mais oui,*' Marianne said. 'It was legal. But I was still, in most people's eyes, an unmarried woman, and soon to have a child. And even in war-time, in a small town such as ours, these things mattered.'

'There would have been money,' Hilary said. 'From the Army. You were a British citizen as soon as you married Baden. There would have been a pension.'

'It was discussed. But where were the papers to prove this? The whole unit was gone. And our town was badly damaged – the town hall itself burned to the ground, with all the documents it contained. There was nothing except the papers I had been given after the mayor married us' – she took a slip of paper from her bag and handed it to Hilary – 'and I could not let this go. Who could I send it to, after all? We were an occupied country. We had no communications. The Germans were hardly likely to forward letters to the British Army for

3

me. If they had known I was married to an English soldier, they would have imprisoned me.'

'I see.' Hilary stared at the paper. Although unlike an English one, she could see that it was a marriage certificate, and she had little doubt that it was genuine. But Marianne was probably right; it would not have been enough, even if she had been able to get it to the right authorities.

'So what did you do?'

The Frenchwoman shrugged. 'I did the only thing possible. I married again.'

'You – you *married*? But—'

'Remember, in the eyes of the Church my first marriage had not happened. Legally, I was a widow anyway, although there were no records of the civil ceremony – except that.' Her eyes went to the certificate, and Hilary handed it back. 'You must understand,' she went on, leaning forward a little, 'that it would have been very hard to bear a child as an un-married woman. My father would not have been able to keep me at home. There was nowhere to go, and the town was full of Germans. What do you suppose would have happened to me?'

Hilary met her eyes and understood what she meant. A town full of Germans, a woman with no reputation and no home. The only life open to her would have been a life on the streets. She thought of Baden, who must have loved this girl, who had married her and then died, leaving her pregnant.

'If only we'd known.'

'There was no way to let you know,' Marianne said simply. 'If Baden had written, his letter was probably with him when he died. And I could never write.'

There was a moment's silence. Hilary tried again to imagine what it must have been like for the young girl, who could have been no more than nineteen or twenty.

'So you married again,' she said slowly.

The Frenchwoman met her eyes. 'It was the only way.

Jacques was the son of a friend of my father. We had been sweethearts once, before I met Baden. I went to him when I knew, and told him, and he said he would marry me. He said he would bring up Baden's child as his own.'

Hilary glanced at Robert, who had been sitting perfectly still, only his eyes moving as he followed the conversation. She said, 'You speak very good English.'

Marianne nodded. 'My father taught English in the local school. We used to come to England every year, before the war, and stay for a month. And I have always spoken English to Robert, too, so that when the time came ...'

When the time came for what? Hilary thought, and a tiny finger of chill touched her heart. Why had they come now? What did they expect? She looked at Robert again, still feeling that small shock of recognition. Certificates meant nothing when the likeness was so strong.

The door opened suddenly, and Stephen looked in. 'Is everything all right, Hil? Only Father's getting a bit ...' His voice trailed away as he stared from Marianne to her son, his eyes widening. 'Hilary?'

'Come in, Steve, and shut the door.' She waited until he had done so, and then she said quietly, 'This is Marianne' – she looked helplessly at the Frenchwoman, uncertain now whether she had been told the surname – 'and ... and Robert. Her son.' She hesitated again, wondering if Stephen saw the resemblance. He was several years younger; would he remember what Baden had looked like at this age? 'Baden's son,' she finished at last, hardly able to believe that she was saying the words.

Stephen stared again, and then sat slowly on a chaise longue, facing the two newcomers. He started to speak, stopped, ran his fingers through his fair hair, opened his mouth again and looked bemusedly at Hilary.

'I ... I don't understand. Did you just say what I thought you said?'

5

'Yes,' Hilary said.

'But ... but Baden didn't ... He never ...' The idea was beginning to percolate through Stephen's shock. 'Is there any *proof*? I mean, anyone could come here claiming—'

'Look at him,' Hilary said, feeling some discomfort at using the child in this way, yet not knowing what else to do. 'You may not remember Baden at that age, but I do. They could be twins. And you know the portrait in the breakfast room. He's not so very much older in that.'

'Yes,' Stephen said, staring at the boy, who returned his gaze with composure. 'But ... I still don't see ...'

'They were married,' Hilary said. 'A few days before Baden was killed. Robert is his son, his *legitimate* son. He was brought up as another man's child, but he is still a Napier.'

Stephen shook his head slowly. 'I can't take it in ... I need some coffee ...'

Immediately, Hilary felt a stab of guilt. She turned to the Frenchwoman. 'And so must you. I'm so sorry – I should have thought. I'll go and ask Mrs Ellis to bring some in. And you must be hungry, too. Have you had breakfast?' Her mind grappled with a new problem. It would be simplest to take them to the breakfast room, and simply ask the housekeeper to cook extra bacon and eggs. But her father was there, reading peacefully through the newspaper reports of yesterday's Coronation and Edmund Hillary's achievement on Everest. She couldn't risk the shock such a sudden appearance would cause him.

'Coffee would be welcome,' Marianne said. 'But nothing to eat for me. Perhaps some bread for Robert; boys of his age are always hungry.'

'Yes. I'll see to it.' Hilary left the room, thankful for the respite, and leaned for a moment against the door. Then she went to the kitchen, where Mrs Ellis was stacking dishes.

'Could you make us some coffee, please, Mrs Ellis? Enough for four. And some toast or something. Bring it into the sitting

6

room.' She pressed her fingertips against her forehead, trying to think what to do for the best. 'I'd better go and see Father, too – I don't want him coming to look for us.'

'Is everything all right, Miss Hilary?' the housekeeper asked anxiously. 'The foreign lady hasn't brought trouble, I hope?'

Hilary looked at her, wondering how much she suspected, and trying to remember if she had known Baden. She was a village woman, so of course she would have seen him about the place as a boy, but would she have made the connection? Did she ever bother to glance at the portrait, and even if she did, would she notice the resemblance? Perhaps only the family would be so sensitive to it. The family, and those who had known them well all their lives, like Charles Latimer and Basil Harvey. Even they ...

'I hope not, too,' she said, answering the housekeeper. 'No, I'm sure she hasn't. It's just a little complicated, and I don't want my father upset. I'll go and have a word with him now. If you'll just take the coffee and toast to the sitting room ...' She turned and hurried to the breakfast room, where her father was still going through the pile of newspapers. He glanced up as she came in, his mane of silver hair glinting in the early-morning sunshine.

'Marvellous news about Everest,' he said. 'The British right on top of the world, and on the day of the Coronation itself. Who was that at the door? And where's young Stephen gone?'

Hilary sat down in her place. 'Father, we've got a visitor. Two visitors, really. But I don't want you to worry about them. I need to find out a bit more first, and then I'll—'

'Visitors? Worry?' He stared at her, his cup halfway to his mouth. 'What on earth are you talking about? What visitors? And why in God's name should I worry about them?'

Hilary cursed herself for her clumsiness. 'No reason at all,' she said, knowing that there might be every reason. 'It's just a little bit ... well, complicated. Look, you finish your breakfast and then ... then go out for a bit. See what Travis is doing, go round the estate with him, something like that. I'll tell you all about it at lunch-time.'

Gilbert's eyes narrowed. 'You want to get rid of me. You want me out of the house. What's going on? Who the hell *are* these visitors?' He started to get to his feet. 'It's Stephen, isn't it? He's in trouble of some kind. They're police.'

'No!' Hilary jumped up and caught his arm, as he began to make his way to the door. 'No, it's nothing like that, I promise. Please, Father ... please don't go in there. I'm not trying to get rid of you. I just need some time.'

'Time for what?' He paused and glowered at her. 'Look, Hilary, you ought to know by now that I don't like being kept in the dark. I still happen to be the head of this family, and what happens in this house is *my* business. And I don't take kindly to being treated like a child. Now, I'm going to see these visitors for myself, and you can either tell me who they are first, or I'll find out for myself. Which is it to be?'

Hilary sighed. 'All right,' she said, letting her hand drop from his arm. 'I'll tell you. But sit down, please. It's going to come as rather a shock ...'

In the small sitting room, Stephen sat facing the visitors. They looked back at him – Marianne calmly, Robert with dark-eyed inscrutability. So far, the boy had not said a word.

'So you're Baden's wife,' Stephen said at last, aware of a need to break the silence. There was something in her gaze that gave him an odd, but not unpleasurable, sense of discomfort.

Marianne nodded and related her story once more. He stared at the marriage certificate, not really taking it in, then raised his eyes to hers.

'We never had the slightest idea. Why didn't you contact us before? Why wait till now?'

'Perhaps,' she said, 'it would be better if I told everyone together. To save repeating it.'

'Yes. Yes, I suppose so.' The door opened, and Mrs Ellis came in with a large tray on which stood a pot of coffee, its aroma filling the room, a pile of toast, a dish of butter and two jars, one of honey and one of marmalade, together with plates, cups and saucers. The housekeeper carried the tray to a table in the window, and began setting the things out.

'It's all right, Mrs Ellis,' Stephen said. 'We'll do that. Er ... Madame ...' he glanced at the Frenchwoman, as uncertain as Hilary had been as to what he should call her. 'Let me give you some coffee. And some toast.' He looked at Robert. 'You'll have something to eat, won't you?'

'You can sit at the table,' the boy's mother said. 'Coffee will be enough for me.'

Robert went to the table, as Mrs Ellis made her way out. He sat down, pulled a plate towards him, and began to spread the toast with butter and honey. Then he dipped it into the coffee that Stephen had poured him.

Stephen blinked but said nothing. He took a cup of coffee to the Frenchwoman and sat down again. They regarded each other in silence.

'Perhaps', Marianne said, 'you would tell me a little about your family. Your mother and father. Baden spoke of them often.'

It took Stephen a moment or two to remember that Isobel had died some years after Baden. 'Our mother's dead,' he said. 'After the war. And Father's not well – he had a heart attack a couple of years ago. But my sister, Hilary, still lives here and helps to run the estate.'

'And she is married?'

'No. Her fiancé was killed in the war. She came home when Mother was ill, and she's ... well, just stayed here. Looking after things. Looking after Dad.'

The Frenchwoman nodded. It was clearly a concept she could understand. 'And you, you will take over. The estate will be your responsibility.'

'Good God, no!' Stephen exclaimed. 'Nothing I'd hate more! No, I'm in the RAF, and when I come out I'm going to emigrate to Canada and start a flying business. That's my plan, anyway.' He wondered if he ought to be telling her all this. But none of it was exactly a secret, and if all she said was true, she was part of the family – his sister-in-law. It seemed a strange idea.

He glanced at the boy, sitting at the table in the window and eating his way steadily through the pile of toast. His nephew. Baden's son. And then, rather later than it had struck Hilary, the possible truth hit him with a jolt.

Baden's son. Baden's *heir*.

The door opened, and Gilbert Napier came into the room, slowly, his great head jutting forward a little, like a lion stalking its prey. He stopped, as Hilary closed the door behind him, and stared, first at the little Frenchwoman and then at the boy in the window.

Robert put down his toast and stood up, straight and slim, one hand resting lightly on the table. The light was behind him yet, even in silhouette, the likeness was unmistakable.

'Good God,' Gilbert said slowly, and put out his own hand as if seeking for support. 'Good … *God* …'

Chapter Two

In the village of Burracombe, the day was one for clearing up.

'That were a good do last night,' Ted Tozer remarked, leaning on the wide broom from the village hall, as he considered the remains of the celebration dance in the big marquee, 'but it takes a master lot of tidying up afterwards.'

'It's not too bad,' Luke Ferris said cheerfully, swinging past with a wheelbarrow. 'We'll just shove everything in here and have a big bonfire in the corner of the field. That greasy pole will get it going.' He bent to scoop up a pile of empty crisp packets. 'I'll pick up the bottles when I've dumped this lot.' He grinned. 'There'll be a few sore heads this morning, I reckon!'

'There's all they chairs and trestle tables to be took back to the hall, too,' Ted said. 'I'll bring the cart down, and us can collect 'em all up together. Some of you other chaps had better see to taking down that bunting. And my Alice and the other women will be down soon, to sort out the crockery and glasses. They'll need a hand getting it all back home.'

'Every cup and saucer in the village must be here,' his son Tom said, surveying the array of china on the long tables. 'I hope they can all recognise their own stuff.'

'Us only had a couple of old chipped mugs to drink our tea out of this morning,' Jacob Prout said, coming up with another armful of rubbish for Luke's barrow. ''Tis a good job us has got today to get all this done. A do like a Coronation you needs three days for – one to get ready and one to clear up, never mind the day itself.'

'It won't take long,' Luke said, wheeling his barrow away before any more could be piled into it. 'There are nearly as many people here today as there were last night – give a hangover or two.' He strolled off, whistling, and turned the barrowload out on to the heap at the end of the field.

'Us'll have a bonfire nearly as good as there were up on the tor last night,' Ted observed. 'Well, it were a good start for the young Queen. I bet she's feeling a bit tired this morning, after all the shenanigans they must have had at the Palace.'

As Luke had said, almost the whole village had turned out to clear the field, and on the other side of the river the inhabitants of Little Burracombe were doing the same. The rivalry between the two villages, set aside for the celebrations, was already resurfacing as they called jibes across the swiftly-flowing stream.

'Don't know how you can get yourselves in such a mess,' a burly young worker from one of the outlying farms jeered, as he wielded a pitchfork to gather up the straw bales that had been used for seating. 'Us is all tidy again. But then, we didn't lie abed half the day – down here at first light, us was.'

'And if you had been,' Tom Tozer retorted, 'you'd have seen us still dancing. Only difference between us and you Little'uns is that we knows how to enjoy ourselves proper! Why, I reckon half Little Burracombe was tucked up in bed with a cup of cocoa while we were just getting started.'

'Oh, we saw you all right,' another young stockman chipped in. 'Thought it was the pixies from up Crazywell Pool, come down to see what all the row were about.'

'Us always did say you lot was pixie-led,' Tom scoffed, and they all laughed and went on their way.

The women, led by Alice Tozer, arrived at the field gate just then, carrying baskets, and set about collecting their own crockery and glasses. The village hall owned two or three sets, but not enough to cater for the numbers who had attended the celebrations last night, and everyone had brought at least a few cups and saucers. Not their best, Alice had warned them, for some were sure to get broken, but she was pleased to see that her own set was intact.

'I don't reckon many got smashed at all,' she said, swiftly separating her china and packing it carefully into her basket. 'Put them all over there, in that corner, and my Ted'll take 'em back up to the village in the cart.'

Ivy Sweet picked up a cup, turning it over in her hand. 'That's pretty. I wonder whose it is? Your Joanna was looking a bit better last night, I thought, Alice. She's been real peaky these last few weeks.'

'Well, and it's not surprising, is it?' Alice said a little tartly. 'Losing her baby like that. Enough to make anyone look peaky.'

'Oh, I know, I'm not *saying* anything. Just that it was nice to see her here, enjoying herself. I thought she was very brave. I'm not sure I could have been out dancing, not three months after my babby had died in its cot.'

Alice turned and gave her a straight look. 'You might not be *saying* anything, Ivy Sweet, but it sounds to me as if you *mean* something. Us have all been trying hard to help poor Joanna get over her loss, and it wouldn't have done her no good to have stopped at home on her own last night, brooding. She's got two other little ones to think about, in case you've forgotten, and they need their mother to be bright and cheerful, if her can be. And what *none* of us needs is nasty, spiteful remarks about being "*out dancing*", as if she was down in Plymouth's Union Street getting off with sailors. Come to that, I'm quite surprised that you'm here yourself – I'd have thought you'd have been keeping it up till all hours in that pub you work in, in Horrabridge.'

'I don't know what you mean by that,' Ivy began, bristling. 'I'm not sure I know myself. But you can't help hearing things, and that place got itself a bit of a reputation a few years back, what with all those airmen from Harrowbeer. Polish, some of them, weren't they? And Czechoslovakian?'

'And what if they were?'

'Proper Romeos, from what I heard,' Alice said, turning away again. 'There was quite a few young girls had their heads turned by those young men, so I believe.'

Ivy's face coloured. 'I don't know what you'm implying, Alice Tozer. Anyway, they're all gone now – went the day the war ended and the airfield was shut down.'

'Left a few bits and bobs behind them, too,' Alice said. 'But there, you've no cause to worry, Ivy. That little Eddie of yours – why, he's the image of you, right down to that red hair of his.' She paused, then went on thoughtfully, 'Funny how yours only turned red the past few years; you were always a bit mousy as a girl, if I remember right.'

Ivy flushed a bright crimson that clashed badly with her coppery hair. She stepped forward, but Alice had already moved out of reach and was busy sorting through a tray of glasses. Ivy hesitated, pressed her lips tightly together, then stalked away to the other end of the long table.

'Goodness me,' said a voice at Alice's elbow, 'that was coming on a bit strong, wasn't it, Mother? I knew you and Mrs Sweet didn't get on, but I didn't realise it was that bad.'

Alice turned and saw her daughter Val gazing at her in astonishment. She sighed, and said, 'Maybe I did go a bit far. But I didn't like the way she was talking about Joanna, as if the poor soul's not entitled to any enjoyment. And it's the way she always promenades round the village as if she owns the place. Why, she's nearly as bad as Mrs Warren, the airs she gives herself. And if you'd known her as long as I have ...'

'So I gather,' Val said. 'What was all that about Polish airmen?'

'Nothing,' Alice said, colouring a little. 'I shouldn't have said it. I dare say she's always been perfectly respectable, and working in a pub don't make no difference to that. Look at Dottie Friend. A more respectable woman never walked this earth, and *she's* lived in London, too. Anyway, it was just talk, that's all, and as long as George Sweet wasn't worried, 'twasn't nobody else's business. And if she chooses to dye her hair, that's her business as well. But you'd better not mention it, Val, to either of them. Mabel Purdy told me that her Fred said something to George about it once, just for a joke, like, and got his head nearly bitten off for his pains. It's a sore point with both of them.'

Val chuckled. 'So much for peace and goodwill on the first day of the new Elizabethan age. Anyway, how is Joanna this morning? She didn't stay very late last night.'

'No, her wanted to get home to the baby. It was the first time she'd left Heather, you know, and even though Mother was with her she was still on hot bricks till she could see for herself that the little mite was all right. And she seems quite a bit brighter today – it did her good to get out.'

'She needs time to herself,' Val said. 'I'd offer to stay with Heather so she could have an hour or two – go to Tavistock, or see her friends – but I'm not sure she'd take all that kindly to the idea. I don't think she's really blaming me any more, but she needs to take her own time.'

'Maybe not.' Alice looked at her daughter thoughtfully. 'But you could offer to go out with her one day, and leave the babby at home with me. That might be better – it would help the two of you to get back on your old footing, too.'

'That's not a bad idea,' Val said slowly. 'I'll suggest it sometime. Has Jackie gone back to Plymouth?'

'Oh, yes, she was off at first light – couldn't wait to shake the dust of the village off her shoes. I was surprised she came home at all, to tell you the truth.' Alice finished sorting the glasses and carried her basket to the corner. Her lips were tight, and when she came back to the table and began on the cups and saucers, Val said mildly, 'We can't all be the same,

Mother, and it seems to me we've just got to accept that Jackie's a city girl.'

'But *why*?' Alice burst out. 'She's had a good life out here on the farm. We've never made her do too much about the place, just given her a few jobs to do, same as the rest of you. How does she come to like being in a place like Plymouth all the time? All that noise and bustle, all those strangers. You could walk the streets for weeks and never see a face you know. And working in a hotel? You know your father and me have never been happy about that. You don't know who she's going to meet, and with nobody keeping an eye on her . . .' Alice picked up a cup and stared at it.

'Jennifer Tucker keeps an eye on her. She makes sure Jackie's in at a decent hour, and she has a pretty good idea who her friends are.'

'She has a pretty good idea who Jackie *says* her friends are,' Alice corrected her. 'Once that girl's out of the house, who can tell for certain what she's getting up to? Oh, I know your dad and me were pleased enough when she offered to take our Jackie as a lodger, but she can't be expected to take the same care as we would. And it's not going to last for ever, is it? You saw them together last night – Jennifer and that Travis Kellaway. It's obvious there's something going on there, and if they get wed, she's not going to stop in Plymouth, is she? And Jackie's already started to talk about living in at the hotel, like she did to start with.'

'There's not much you can do about it if she does,' Val pointed out. 'And the hotel housekeeper sounds a sensible woman. I'm sure they look after their girls.'

She began to pick out her own crockery, but her mind was more on Travis and Jennifer than on her sister. She had also noticed they seemed particularly friendly last night, as if it was a friendship that had been developing for some time. Obviously, they had kept it quiet, but had now decided to make it more public. She wondered what that meant. Would they marry?

They were both in their thirties, and at that age people didn't usually go in for long engagements. And if they did marry, they would be wanting somewhere to live. Travis was hardly likely to take a new bride back to the farmhouse lodgings he had been living in since he first came to Burracombe.

They might want Jed's Cottage, the little house Jennifer's father had left her, which Val herself had moved into when she married Luke. And where would that leave *her*?

We can't go back to the charcoal-burner's hut, that's for sure, she thought, packing cups and saucers into her own basket. It was fun living there for the first few months, but we've got used to proper running water and electricity now, and we've got a baby coming. But where else is there to live in Burracombe?

They might even have to move to Tavistock.

By three in the afternoon, the field was clear. The marquee had been taken down and folded into its big canvas bag, and all the poles and pegs had been bundled together. Ted had made a number of trips with the horse and cart, taking baskets of crockery and glasses to their various owners, and returning the trestle tables and chairs to the village hall. All the litter had been burned, and what couldn't be burned had been loaded on to a lorry to be taken to the rubbish dump. On the Little Burracombe side of the river, the task had been equally well accomplished, and you would never have known that the day before, the two fields had been the scene of races, competitions, a pig roast and a dance that had gone on until well after midnight. On his last trip, Ted brought a few sheep down in the cart and turned them out into his field, where they put their heads down and began to graze as if they had been there for weeks.

Jennifer Tucker had gone back to Plymouth on the early bus with Jackie, so as to be at Dingle's, the big department store where she worked, by nine o'clock. They sat together in the front seat upstairs, gazing out over the moor towards Cornwall and Plymouth Sound. On a clear day, from the Hoe, you could see the thin pencil shape of the Eddystone lighthouse, but the grey clouds and drizzle of Coronation Day hadn't yet cleared away, and there was only a faint glimmer of pewter from the sea.

'It was a lovely day,' Jennifer said. 'A shame about the weather, but it didn't seem to spoil things. It sounds as though it was worse in London – I wouldn't have wanted to be one of those people camping on the pavements all night.'

'Oh, I would!' Jackie said. 'I'd have gone like a shot, only I didn't have anyone to go with, and Mum and Dad would have had a fit. Honestly, they're so old-fashioned; they treat me as if I was five years old instead of nearly twenty.'

'Well, they're still responsible for you until you're twenty-one,' Jennifer said. 'I expect you'll worry about your children just the same, when the time comes.'

Jackie snorted. 'At the rate I'm going on, I won't have any children! Dad'll never let me get married, and by the time I can do it without asking, I'll be too old.'

Jennifer laughed. 'Don't be silly! It's not much more than a year till you turn twenty-one, and you haven't even got a serious boyfriend yet. Not as far as I know, anyway,' she added with a sideways glance. 'Though you have been out a few times just lately and been rather mysterious about it.'

Jackie coloured and turned her head away. 'You don't expect me to tell you everything, do you?'

'Of course not. As long as you're being sensible.' There was a short pause, then Jennifer added quietly, 'You *are* being sensible, aren't you?'

Immediately, Jackie flared up. 'What do you mean? Of course I'm being sensible! I don't know what you're talking about.'

'All right, no need to get up in the air about it. I didn't mean anything. But you know your parents expect me to keep an eye on you.'

'Yes, I do,' Jackie said, a little sullenly. 'It doesn't mean you have to watch me every moment of the day.'

Jennifer glanced at her thoughtfully. The conversation, which had started so pleasantly, had taken a sour turn. She said, 'I don't think I do that, Jackie. I like to see you having a good time.'

Jackie said nothing for a moment, then she turned back and gave a wry smile. 'Sorry, Jennifer. I didn't mean to get snappy. It's just . . . oh well, to be honest, I've been thinking lately that it's time I thought about moving out.'

'Oh. I see.'

'You know Miss Millington said I might be able to live in, when a room came up,' Jackie said, speaking eagerly now. 'Well, I think there might be one soon – one of the housemaids is leaving to get married. There is another girl who'd like the room, but I'm more senior than her, and I think I'd get it if I applied.' She hesitated. 'Would you mind?'

'Mind?' Jennifer said. 'Of course not. I'd miss you, but we always knew this arrangement wasn't going to last for ever. I knew you really wanted to live at the hotel. And now that you've had this time staying with me, I shouldn't think your parents could object too much.'

'Oh, yes, they could,' Jackie said, gloomy again. 'Dad could object to *anything* without even trying. They never wanted me to go and work in Plymouth in the first place.'

'Well, you have, and you're enjoying your job and doing well in it,' Jennifer said briskly. 'I think you should apply for the room. And besides . . .' She stopped, and Jackie glanced at her curiously.

'Besides what?'

'Nothing. Never mind.' But Jennifer had turned pink, and Jackie's face spread into a grin.

'I bet I know! It's Mr Kellaway, isn't it? I saw you dancing with him last night. Are you engaged?' She picked up Jennifer's left hand and looked at it, disappointed to find it ringless. 'Well, has he asked you? He has, hasn't he? What did you say? Are you going to marry him?'

Jennifer laughed, flushing and embarrassed. 'Jackie! What a question! What do you expect me to say?'

'I expect you to say "yes", of course!' Jackie gave a squeal of delight. 'You are, aren't you! Oh, that's smashing! I mean, old people do get married, don't they? You don't *have* to be young, like me. Where will it be – in Burracombe or in Plymouth? Can I be bridesmaid?'

'Jackie, stop it! And not so much of the "old people", if you don't mind. And nothing's been said yet, so please keep it to yourself. I mean it, Jackie,' she added firmly, as the bus arrived at their stop and they got up and started down the stairs. 'Not a word. Not to anyone at all. Is that understood?'

'Sure,' Jackie said in an American accent she had picked up at the cinema. 'Not a word.' Halfway down the stairs, she turned and grinned wickedly up at the older woman. 'But I *can* be a bridesmaid, can't I?'

Chapter Three

Gilbert Napier sat down heavily in the wing chair by the fireplace, his eyes fixed on the boy in the window. There was a long silence until at last he turned his silver head and let his gaze settle on the Frenchwoman. Hilary and Stephen watched anxiously as the two considered each other.

'Is this true?' he demanded at last, his voice harsh. 'Is this true, what my daughter tells me? You were married to my son?'

Marianne inclined her head. She held out the certificate, and he took it and scanned it carefully. In the window, Robert finished his toast and sat quietly, his dark-blue eyes missing nothing.

'This is dated three days or so before his death.'

'*Oui*,' she said. 'The order to retreat came very soon.'

'I believe some officers who had married in these circumstances made an attempt to bring their wives with them. Some even succeeded in getting them home.'

She moved one shoulder slightly, as if to say that she hadn't known this, but in any case it was not what Baden had done.

'You stayed in your village. With your parents?'

'*Oui*. Until I married again.'

His head, still bent over the certificate, shot up. 'You married again?'

'It was necessary.' She cast a brief glance at the boy.

'Yes,' he said, looking down at the paper again. 'Yes, I

suppose it was.' He turned his eyes back to the boy. 'Have you finished your breakfast?'

'*Oui*, monsieur.'

'Then come over here, to me.' The boy rose and came slowly towards him, stopping about a yard away. 'Do you speak English?'

'He speaks it almost as well as he speaks French,' Marianne said. 'My father and I spoke it with him as much as we could. With all the children,' she added, and Gilbert shot her another sharp glance.

'You have other children?'

'But of course. A daughter and another son: Philippe and Ginette. They are in France with my sister,' she added, when Gilbert looked round the room as if expecting them to step out from some hiding place.

Hilary watched her father anxiously. He had taken the startling news more quietly than she had expected, but that didn't mean it hadn't been a shock. She thought of his face when she had told him, the ruddiness draining from his cheeks, the harsh intake of breath, the swift, involuntary look towards Baden's portrait. It was something nobody had expected – a son to appear from nowhere, unannounced, years after his father's death. And she had wondered if the same thought had crossed her father's mind as had immediately thrust itself into hers; that this was an heir for Burracombe.

But her primary concern was her father's health. A shock like this could bring on another heart attack, and Dr Latimer had warned her that it could be fatal. Yet she could not, for the life of her, see what else she could have done. Marianne and Robert were here, in the house. Their presence could not be hidden.

As yet, though, Gilbert seemed to be handling it well. All the same, she would watch him carefully over the next few days.

He looked at the boy. 'So you are Robert Napier.'

'Robert Baden Napier Aucoin. I have my' – he hesitated and glanced at his mother, who nodded – 'my father's name.'

Gilbert frowned. 'But your mother says that my son was your father.'

'My husband brought him up as his own,' Marianne said. 'He was born within our marriage, and of course he took his surname. My husband – my *second* husband – was Jacques Aucoin. But he always knew the truth and had no objection to Robert bearing his real father's names as well.'

Gilbert shook his head, as if finding it all too hard to accept. Then he asked, 'And where is your husband now?'

'He died six months ago. He never really recovered from the war, you see. He and his parents, they worked for the Resistance. Their house was a *safe house*, I think you call it, where Allied airmen and soldiers were hidden before being brought back to England. In the end, they were discovered, and Jacques and his father were taken away, to Buchenwald. His father died there. Jacques was released when it was all over, but he was nothing but a shadow. He was never the same again.'

Hilary stared at her in shock. The Frenchwoman's voice had been quiet, almost unemotional, and somehow this made the story even more appalling. She looked at Stephen, whose face was pale, and at her father, and then the boy. Marianne was talking about his stepfather and grandfather. And Baden, his real father, had been killed only a day or two after he had been conceived. How did it make a child feel, to know that this was his history?

'And what happened to you?' she asked. 'Were you living in the same house? Did they suspect you as well?'

Marianne shook her head. 'I was a woman with young children. They did not consider me a danger. I went to live with my own parents then, and Jacques' mother came, too. She is still alive but very – what is the word? – frail now. My father died last year and my own mother lives with my sister and me, and my children, of course.'

Hilary nodded, trying to take it all in. She wondered what her father was feeling, but he only said, 'I see', before turning back to the boy.

'Do you understand what this means, Robert? Do you understand that if Baden was your father, I am your grandfather?'

Robert met his eyes steadily, and once again Hilary felt a stab to her heart. How many times had she seen her father and brother together like this, their eyes meeting as if in perfect understanding? Yet how *could* there be understanding between these two? They had never met before; they were not even of the same nationality.

'Yes,' Robert said, his voice quiet and tinged with his own accent, a strange sound to come from the mouth that looked so like Baden's. 'Yes, I understand. You are my *grandpère*, my grandfather. And this is where my father grew up.'

For the past few moments, Hilary had been aware of Stephen becoming increasingly restless by her side. Now he broke in. 'Just a minute. Let's not go so fast. Dad, we can't just accept this, not without any real proof. We've got to look into it. Just because he looks a bit like Baden—'

'A *bit* like him?' Gilbert echoed. 'Stephen, it could be the same boy. You probably don't remember your brother so well at this age, but *I do*. And so does your sister. Don't you, Hilary?'

'He looks very like him,' she admitted. 'But Steve's right, Father; we can't go any further without more proof. Though I'm not sure what,' she added. 'There'll be no regimental records, and this certificate—'

'That could have been forged,' Stephen said curtly. He glanced at the Frenchwoman. 'Look, I don't want to be rude, but you must see that we can't simply accept your word for it. There are all sorts of implications.'

'Very well,' Gilbert said, waving him to silence. 'You may be right, but first it seems to me that we need to find out just why Madame Aucoin has decided to bring her son here now. Can you tell us that?' he asked, turning back to Marianne.

She lifted her chin a little. Hilary, watching her, thought that she must have been very pretty when she was younger – small, with curling black hair and flashing dark eyes. She was still an attractive woman with a good figure, and she was, after all, only in her early thirties now, not much older than Hilary herself.

'I hoped that you would give us a little help,' she said. 'I told you my husband has died. He had been ill for some years and not able to work. My mother and I have been running a small *pâtisserie*, but she is ill and will not live very long. I have Jacques' mother to care for as well. My sister is helping, but I have two other children, both younger than Robert, and the *pâtisserie* will not keep us all. Baden told me that if anything happened to him I must come to you, but when it did happen that was not possible. And by the time the war ended, I had my family and my husband. Now' – she shrugged – 'things are different. And I thought that you should know your grandson.'

'Yes,' Gilbert said after a silence, 'so I should. You owe me that.'

At this, the Frenchwoman's face changed a little. Her eyes narrowed, and she lifted her chin and looked the Colonel straight in the eye.

'I owe you nothing,' she said. 'Until now, I have asked for nothing and I owe nothing.'

'It's not a question of asking,' he said tersely. 'The boy is my grandson.'

'Dad . . .' Stephen broke in, with a quick glance at Marianne. 'Dad, we've got to talk this over properly. We need advice—'

'Advice? What kind of advice?' Gilbert made a quick movement with his hand, as if brushing aside his son's objections.

Stephen gestured helplessly. 'I don't know. Legal advice, maybe medical advice. How to go about proving this. In any case, we can't do anything in a hurry.'

25

'Steve's right,' Hilary said. 'It's come as a shock. We can't make snap decisions about something as important as this.'

Gilbert grunted. He subjected the Frenchwoman to an intense look. She returned it steadily, and he shifted his gaze to her son, who remained as composed as he had been throughout the discussion.

'We need to talk as well,' he said at last. 'You'd better stay here at the Barton. Hilary, see that rooms are prepared for them.'

'But—'

He lifted his head and glowered at her. 'For God's sake, Hilary, do as I say, will you? Where else are they to stay? Aggie Madge's front room?' He turned back to the Frenchwoman. 'I take it you came with the intention of staying? You're not planning to go straight back to France?'

'I can stay for a week, perhaps two.'

'That ought to be enough.' He jerked his head angrily at Hilary. 'Well? Why haven't you gone to tell Mrs Ellis?'

Hilary stood up, as angry as he. She wanted to say, *Because I'm not your servant, to be ordered about*, but she bit her tongue. This was not the time for family squabbles, in front of strangers. And Marianne Aucoin was a stranger, even if she had been married to Hilary's brother. *If.* Like Stephen, even when faced with a marriage certificate and a boy who looked so much like her brother, Hilary still wanted some ultimate proof.

'I'll go now,' she said coldly, and went to the door. Before opening it, she turned and looked at the two foreigners.

'I don't want you to feel unwelcome,' she said quietly. 'I'm sure you knew this would be a shock for us. But as long as you're staying here, we'll make you as comfortable as possible.'

Marianne inclined her head, and Robert met Hilary's eyes for a moment. As they regarded each other, Hilary felt a brief tremor of disquiet.

The boy *must* be Baden's son, she thought. Such a likeness could surely not be explained any other way. Yet there was something in that face, in those eyes, which was not Baden, something that made her deeply uneasy inside, and she felt a sudden intense wish that he had not come, that they could return to their lives as they had been an hour ago. For now that he had, nothing would ever be the same again.

'What do you think?'

Hilary was in the middle of making the bed in the small guest room, and hadn't heard Stephen come in. She stood up and motioned to him to close the door.

'Where are they?'

'In the breakfast room. Dad's got Mrs Ellis cooking them bacon and eggs. He's found out they came on the early train to Tavistock and got a taxi here, and he says they've to be fed.'

'Well, I dare say they are hungry,' she admitted. 'She wouldn't have anything before, but the boy, Robert, tucked in as if he hadn't eaten in a month.'

'But what do you *think*?' he repeated. 'Is it true? Is that boy really Baden's son?'

Hilary spread the counterpane and sat down on the bed. 'He does look very much like him.'

'He doesn't look a bit like *her*.'

'Well, he wouldn't, would he? Not if he's like his father.' Hilary looked at her brother. 'Don't you believe she's his mother, then?'

'I don't know what to believe. It's all so bizarre. I mean, look at it, Hil: Baden marries this girl three days before he's killed, all the proof goes with him, except for that certificate she keeps brandishing about, nobody's left alive who could confirm any of it, and to top it all, she doesn't even contact us for thirteen years. Why not? Why didn't she write, once the war was over, and tell us about it then? Why wait all this time?'

'Because her husband was still alive,' Hilary said doubt-fully.

27

'But he knew about it, or she *says* he did.'

'Yes, but if he brought Robert up as his own, he might not have wanted the boy coming over here to see his English relatives. He might have been afraid he'd lose him. And he could have done, too. Can you imagine Father, presented with a grandson, *Baden's* son, letting him go back to France? He'd have moved heaven and earth to keep him here.' And once again, the words 'an heir for Burracombe' slid into her mind.

Stephen grunted, sounding so like his father that Hilary almost laughed. But the situation was too serious for laughter. She shook her head and picked at a loose thread in the counterpane.

'Well, all right. Suppose that was it. We still don't have any proof that she's telling the truth, or that she's the boy's mother. Or that he's not illegitimate.'

Hilary turned her head towards him. 'What difference would that make?'

'All the difference in the world, surely. If he's not legitimate, he'll have no claim on us at all. No claim on anything.'

'So you've thought of it, too,' she said slowly. 'The estate, the inheritance. If Baden had lived, it would have been his. And then his son's. And even if he hadn't lived ...'

'It would still be his son's,' Stephen finished. 'But only if he was "legitimate issue".'

There was a long silence. Hilary turned it over in her mind. If all that Marianne said was true, Robert was Baden's true and legitimate son, conceived in wedlock. But in law, he had been born to another man, who had claimed him as his son. What difference did that make?

'And it's all under French law as well,' she said, rubbing her forehead. 'Oh, Stephen, it's all so complicated.'

'And that's why I said we've got to get advice,' he said grimly. 'You saw the way Father looked at that boy. He was ready to accept him there and then, just because he looked like Baden. He's not thinking straight about this at all, Hil.'

Hilary nodded thoughtfully. 'You're right. We've got to persuade Father to take his time *and* some advice. But it may not do any good, you know.'

'Why? What d'you mean?'

She sighed and got up, smoothing the rumpled counterpane. 'Because whatever advice he's given, he doesn't have to take any notice. There's no entail on the estate – he can leave it to whoever he likes. If he decides that Robert is Baden's son, legitimate or not, he can make him his heir. And there's not a thing you or I, or anyone else, can do about it.'

Chapter Four

Once Travis had helped to take down the marquee, he strolled along to the Bell Inn. Dottie Friend was behind the bar, and she drew him a pint of ale and made him a corned beef sandwich with plenty of pickle. He sat on a high stool at the corner of the bar to eat it.

'Burracombe put on a good show yesterday,' he observed.

Dottie nodded. 'Us knows how to celebrate, I'll say that. I don't reckon we missed much by not going to London, though I wouldn't mind seeing all they decorations in the Mall. Proper handsome they look in the pictures.'

'You could always go up for a day during the summer,' he suggested. 'They're going to keep them for a few weeks. And there'll be the film they made of it, too – it's bound to be on at the Carlton sometime.'

'*And* in full Technicolor,' Dottie said, polishing the handles of the beer-pumps. 'Better than that tiny little television Mrs Warren's so proud of. Waste of time, that was, if you ask me.'

Travis grinned. He had been invited to watch the procession and ceremony on the television that Gilbert Napier had had installed in the sitting room at the Barton, but he'd declined. Jennifer hadn't been invited – there was no reason why she should be, since nobody had been aware of their increasing friendship – and he'd wanted to spend the day with her. Instead of sitting cooped up in a darkened sitting room, they'd gone to the church to hear the service broadcast there and take part in the hymns, and Travis had joined the bell-ringers in several of the peals they had rung throughout the day.

As if reading his thoughts, Dottie paused in her polishing and said, 'You and Miss Tucker seem to be getting on pretty well.'

'Yes, we're quite good friends,' Travis said non-committally. 'She's a nice person.'

'She is. And she've been very good to old Jacob. Like a daughter to him. Funny thing she's never married.'

Travis said nothing. Jennifer had told him about her disastrous marriage, to a man who had no interest in women but needed the protection of domesticity. The marriage had been quietly annulled once Jennifer had realised the truth, but she had suffered a good deal before then, and not even Jacob knew that it had happened. Since then, she had put up a protective fence around her emotions, and Travis was the first person, apart from her mother and sisters, that she had ever told.

He had wondered at first if she would ever be able to bring herself to love him as he wanted. But when he'd asked her to marry him, as they watched the sun set over Tavistock one evening a few days before, she had accepted as if hardly able to believe that he could love her.

'Even after what I've told you?' she had asked, with a tremble in her voice.

'Why not? None of it was your fault.'

'That's not what some people thought,' she said a little bitterly. '"Soiled goods" is what one of my so-called friends called me. It was awful, Travis. I was too ashamed to tell anyone the real truth, and nobody could understand why my marriage ended so soon. And what made it worse was that he was so good-looking. He'd had any amount of women ready to fall at his feet, and there was a lot of jealousy when he chose me. And then when it all fell apart ...' She shook her head, unable to go on.

Travis gathered her against him. 'You're not to worry

31

about that any more,' he'd said quietly. 'Whoever called you "soiled goods" isn't worth another thought. And nobody at Burracombe knows anything about it. You can start afresh with me, in a place where everyone loves you for the person you are.'

She nodded, and said, 'But can we keep it a secret for a little while? I need time to get used to it.'

Travis had agreed. But a few nights later, at the Coronation night dance, he had slipped outside the marquee, holding Jennifer's hand tightly in his.

'Let's walk down to the river.'

'I hope you're not going to try the greasy pole,' she'd said with a smile. 'I don't fancy diving in to save you when you fall off.'

Travis drew her towards one of the benches that had been placed around the field for the day's festivities. 'Sit down for a minute, Jennifer. There's something I want to ask you.'

They sat down side by side. He turned towards her and took both her hands in his. 'There ought to be moonlight,' he said. 'Or at least stars. But it's been grey and drizzly all day.'

'It hasn't mattered, though, has it?' she said, her voice trembling slightly. 'It's been just as good as if the sun had been shining. So perhaps it doesn't matter that the moon's not out now.'

'Perhaps not,' he said, and leaned forward a little and kissed her. 'Jennifer, I know we agreed to keep our news secret. But I'm finding it very hard. I want to tell everyone. I want to shout it from the rooftops! I want us to get engaged properly, with a ring and everything. What do you say? Do you really want to wait any longer?'

'No,' she said. 'I don't want to wait, either. Let's make it official. But I don't want a lot of fuss, Travis. No big party or anything.'

'That's fine by me,' he declared. 'So long as everyone knows you're mine.' He pulled her into his arms. Half laughing, half crying, she returned his kisses, and then rested her head on his shoulder. 'We won't have a long engagement, though, will we?' he asked. 'We're not twenty-year-olds. We want to get on with our marriage – at least, I do.'

'Yes,' she said. 'So do I. But … well, I'd like to be engaged for a *little* while. It's not something that's likely to happen to me again.'

'I certainly hope not,' he said with a grin, and kissed her again. 'All right. We'll have a proper engagement, with a notice in the *Tavistock Gazette* and the *Tavistock Times*, and we'll go in to town and buy a ring. And then we'll set a date for the wedding.'

'Yes,' she said, but there was a hesitation in her voice, and he glanced at her enquiringly.

'What is it?'

'The wedding,' she said. 'I'm not sure about the church. I don't know how they feel about a marriage like mine. I mean, I know it was annulled, I wasn't actually divorced, but … I don't want to have to explain it all, not even to Mr Harvey.'

'Well, we can get married in the register office,' he said. 'I don't mind. I'm not a particularly keen churchgoer – I ring the bells and go to the occasional service, but that's all. You won't have to explain anything then, just show them the papers. They won't ask questions. Will you be happy with that?'

'Yes,' she said, and he could hear the relief in her voice. 'Yes, I'll be very happy with that.'

Now, sitting on a stool at the bar of the Bell Inn and munching his sandwich, Travis was tempted to tell Dottie the news. But he and Jennifer had agreed that it should be announced first in the two newspapers in Tavistock, and in Plymouth's *Evening Herald*. It would spread quickly enough round the village then, and nobody would be scoring points off their neighbours because they had known first.

There were three people who must be told, however, before it was in any of the papers: Jacob Prout, and Gilbert and Hilary

Napier. Travis hadn't seen Jacob yet, as he'd left the field before Travis had arrived, but he and Jennifer had agreed they would tell him together. He would tell the Napiers himself, though, and he wanted to do that soon. It wouldn't do for the news to come to their ears by way of village gossip.

He wondered where Hilary was that morning. He had expected her to have been in the field with the rest, lending a hand to clear up and generally making herself useful. It wasn't her way to remain aloof from the more mundane part of any village celebration. Stephen should have been there, too, he thought, washing down his sandwich with a long draught of ale. Odd that neither of them had appeared. He hoped nothing was wrong at the Barton.

He would soon find out, however. Once he left the inn, that was his next port of call. Apart from telling them his news, there were a number of estate matters to be discussed with Hilary and her father. The holiday was over.

Once ensconced in her room, Marianne declared her intention of having a rest. 'We have had a long journey,' she said in her prettily accented voice, 'I am very tired.'

'Yes, you must be.' Hilary felt some relief. She had been wondering exactly what she could do with her unexpected visitors. Already feeling rather guilty at not having put in an appearance to help with the clearing up, she hadn't been looking forward to showing Marianne and her son around the village. How should they be explained? How could you begin to introduce them to curious neighbours?

'Don't even try,' Stephen had advised as he helped get their rooms ready. 'We don't have to explain anything. Just say their names and leave it at that. They're friends staying for a while, and it's nobody's business but ours.'

'It *will* be their business, though,' Hilary pointed out. 'A lot of them are our tenants, and if they notice how like Baden—'

'We'll cross those bridges when we come to them. *If* we

come to them.' Stephen arranged a row of books on a shelf. 'Let's not jump any guns. D'you suppose he reads English? Will he like Arthur Ransome?'

'Baden's books,' Hilary said, touching their spines. 'I've no idea, Stephen. But he might like to have them there.' She hesitated. 'What do you make of him? Of them both?'

'Not a lot, yet. She's rather attractive; I can see why Baden might have fallen for her when she was about eighteen. As for the boy, well, he's so quiet you hardly notice him.'

'Hm. There's a lot going on inside that head, though. Perhaps he's just shy and will open up when we get to know him.' She looked round the room. 'I think that's all we can do here. There's a tin of biscuits and some fruit, a few books, clean towels ... I can't think of anything else, can you?'

With Marianne safely in her room, at least until lunch-time, there was then the problem of what to do with Robert, who didn't seem to want to rest. Eventually Stephen offered to take him for a walk, and Hilary saw them off with some relief. Perhaps her brother could draw out the quiet French boy – *half*-French boy, she reminded herself. She hoped they wouldn't meet anyone who would remember Baden at that age and see the resemblance.

I need to let this sink in before I can start to talk to other people about it, she thought. People will have to know some-time, but not just yet. Let's keep it to ourselves for a while, at least.

She went to look for her father and found him in his study, his desk littered with unfamiliar papers. He looked up as she came in, and gestured towards them.

'Baden's school reports and letters. There are some photo-graph albums, too, amongst your mother's things.'

'They're in the cabinet in the drawing room.' She came to stand beside him, looking down at the reports, covered with the various handwriting of Baden's masters, and the letters with her brother's schoolboy scrawl, developing later into a

35

more mature copperplate. 'He had nice writing, didn't he?'

'Once he got out of the habit of giving as little information as possible,' her father agreed. 'Look at this one: *"We had shepperds pie and appel crubble for dinner."* And that was the sum total of his letter home for the week! He was about nine then.'

'I'm amazed he got away with it,' Hilary commented. 'Our teachers read our home letters before they were posted. I suppose they thought we might say something we shouldn't. Why have you got these out now, Father?'

He lifted his shoulders, and she thought that she had seldom seen him so much at a loss: Gilbert Napier had always seemed in command of any situation. She wondered if he might suffer some kind of delayed shock, and felt a quiver of concern for him.

'It's seeing her,' he said at last, speaking slowly, as if he didn't know quite how to express himself. 'Finding out that Baden was married and had a son – and we knew nothing about it. I thought looking at all this might help to tie it together, somehow.'

'And does it?'

Again, he moved his big shoulders. 'I don't know, Hilary. I just don't know.' He looked up at her, suddenly vulnerable. 'The boy's Baden's son. My grandson. It changes everything.'

'Only if you want it to,' she said. 'And I don't think—'

'What do you mean,' he interrupted, *'only if I want it to?* Of *course* it changes everything. Didn't you hear what I said? He's Baden's *son.*'

'I know. At least, that's what we're told. But—'

'D'you mean to say you don't believe it?' He turned and looked up at the photograph of Baden, taken at Oxford University, which hung on the wall behind his desk. Hilary followed his gaze and saw the smiling face, the smooth dark hair, the bright, intelligent eyes. Even with six or seven years between them, the resemblance to Robert was still unnerving. 'How could anyone look at that boy and doubt it for a second?'

'I know,' she said again, 'but we still need proof before we go any further. We really do, Father. People have been known to have doubles before.'

He stared at her, his heavy brows lowered and his lips pushed out, then grunted and turned back to the papers on his desk. 'And just how do we go about getting that proof? She's got a marriage certificate. I don't see what else can be done.'

Hilary moved round the desk and sat down in one of the leather armchairs. 'Can't they do blood tests or something?' she asked, with a vague idea that this might prove something. 'There must be some record of Baden's group.'

'Don't suppose it would tell us much. And why should it matter anyway? If I'm prepared to accept him, I don't see why anyone else should be concerned.'

'It depends what you mean to do,' she said. 'This is about Stephen and me, too, you know.'

'Oh yes,' he said, 'Stephen. Well, *he* certainly doesn't want to inherit. And as for you ...'

'Yes?' she said, feeling a bubble of anger rising in her breast. 'As for me?'

'Well, you've made it perfectly clear that you have no intention of continuing the line. Not interested in marriage, no desire to have children of your own to carry on the estate—'

Not interested in marriage! Hilary thought. When she'd been engaged once, to a man who had been killed in the war, and had felt herself drawn to at least two other men. As for having no desire for children of her own, how many times had she lain awake at night wondering if she would ever become a mother, longing to feel the warmth of her own baby in her arms?

'Oh, I know what will happen,' her father went on more loudly, waving down her attempts to interrupt. 'I know exactly

37

what will happen when I go. The estate will be broken up, sold off to anyone who's got the money to pay for it – incomers, with no feeling at all for the land and the traditions – and that'll be the end of the Napiers of Burracombe. It'll be the end of Burracombe itself. But now,' he said in a lower tone, leaning forward across the polished wood with its litter of old school reports and childish letters, '*now* there's a chance for it. This boy should have been heir – *would* have been, without question, if Baden hadn't been killed. There's a chance to bring him up here, give him the education and the breeding he needs – he's still a child, it's not too late – and see him raise his own family here, so that Burracombe can continue as it always has done, as it *should*.'

Hilary stared at him. She had stopped worrying that he might have a heart attack, and was beginning to think that she might have one herself. Her heart was beating so hard she felt it must wound itself against her ribs. She tried to speak, swallowed and tried again.

'Father ...' she said, and then stopped, not knowing how to go on. To her fury, she felt hot tears in her eyes. 'Father, you can't make a decision like that in just a few minutes. We have to take advice, legal as well as medical. We don't even know what this woman wants, why she came here.'

'I should have thought that was obvious. She wants her son to have what is rightfully his.'

'She allowed another man to bring him up.'

'That's irrelevant.'

'I don't think so. Look.' She rubbed her hand across her eyes and took a deep breath. Arguing with her father now would solve nothing. 'I don't want to make these two unwelcome. If the story is true, then of course we must do something for Robert. But we have to be careful. Let's at least talk to John Wolstencroft and find out what the legal situation is. After all, we don't have to be in any great hurry, do we?'

Gilbert grunted again. 'Very well, if it makes you any

38

happier. I'll ring him up and ask him to come over. And in the meantime ...' Whatever he had been about to say was lost as someone knocked on the door. 'Yes, who's there?'

The door opened, and Mrs Ellis put her head round it. 'It's Mr Kellaway, sir.'

'Oh, yes,' Gilbert said. 'He'd better come in.' He gave Hilary a sharp glance. 'And not a word about this, understand? They're visitors, that's all.'

Hilary bit back her own retort, that this was just what she would have said anyway, and looked up as the estate manager came in. 'Hallo, Travis. Have you been helping clear up after the party? I would have come down myself, but we've been rather busy here this morning.' She heard the stiffness in her voice, and cursed it. He was bound to notice an atmosphere between her and her father.

Travis, however, seemed to notice nothing. He was smiling, and she had a sudden premonition that he was about to tell them something else she didn't really want to hear.

'I'm glad to find you both here,' he said cheerfully. 'I've got some news for you.'

Chapter Five

At midday, Val and Luke went back to the farm and sat down with the rest of the Tozer family for their dinner. Alice took a large meat pie out of the oven and set it in the middle of the big table, and Joanna fetched bowls of vegetables. Minnie, who had peeled most of them, sat in her chair at the end of the table.

'That looks good,' Luke said appreciatively. 'The food at the party was all very nice, but however much you eat, you don't always feel as if you've had a proper meal after ham salad and trifle, do you?' He accepted a large slice of pie and helped himself to potatoes, new carrots and spring greens.

'Well, you certainly did your best to feel full,' Val observed. She looked at his lean body. 'I don't know where you put it all. You must have hollow legs.'

'That's what my mother always said. She also said I'd grow out of it, but I never have.' He glanced at her in sudden alarm. 'I wasn't being greedy, was I? There seemed to be plenty for everyone.'

'Don't you worry about it,' Alice said, sitting down after serving the pie. 'It's good to see a man with a healthy appetite. Not that there's many of the other sort round here,' she added, with a look at Tom's heaped plate.

'We'm farmers,' Tom said with righteous indignation. 'We work hard, and we need feeding up. I don't know what Luke's excuse is,' he added slyly. 'Sitting on a stool with a paintbrush all day isn't exactly hard work.'

'Some of those paintbrushes are very heavy,' Luke said with dignity, and they all laughed. 'Well, all right, maybe I am just greedy. But the cooking here is so good, anyone would be.'

'Go on, flatterer,' Val said. 'You're just trying to keep in Mother's good books.'

'You're not doing so badly yourself,' he remarked, looking at her plate. 'Still, I suppose you've got some excuse since you're eating for two now.'

There was a sudden silence. Luke glanced around, realised what he'd said, and turned scarlet. Val tried not to look at Joanna, and Alice began hastily offering the vegetables around again.

'It's all right,' Joanna said, a little too loudly. 'You don't have to be tactful. I do *know* Val's expecting.'

'Oh, Jo,' Val said miserably. 'I just don't want to upset you.'

'I'm not upset. I admit I was a bit to start with, but I've got over that now.' Joanna looked at her sister-in-law with determination. 'What's happened is bad enough without making it worse by being silly. It's not your fault that Suzanne ... that we lost our baby, and I can't expect you not to want your own family. I was being stupid.'

'No, you weren't.' Val laid her hand on Joanna's arm. 'It just came at the wrong time for you. Anyone would have been upset. I was, too.' There was another brief silence, then she added in a low voice, 'I'd been looking forward to sharing it with you.'

Joanna looked down at her plate. Then she lifted her head and looked at Val again, her eyes bright with tears. 'Well,' she said, 'we can still do that. As a matter of fact, I was looking through my cupboard the other day. There are my maternity things – I won't be needing them again. You might as well have them.'

Val drew in her breath. 'Are you sure? I was going to make myself a couple of smocks. I didn't like to ask you ...'

'That's all right. They'll do for everyday, and you can still make something new. They're not all that wonderful, mind; I had them for Robin as well.'

'I'd love to have them.' Val glanced at Alice, who was watching with tears in her own eyes. 'Actually, I was wondering if you'd come into Tavistock with me one day and help me find some material and a pattern. We could have a cup of tea while we're there.'

There was a breathless pause. Then Joanna said, 'Yes, all right. If Mother and Gran would look after Robin and the baby.'

'Of course we will,' Alice said warmly. 'Been wanting to get them to ourselves for a bit, haven't us, Mother?'

'That us have,' Minnie agreed. 'You two go off and have an afternoon out together. 'Tis time Joanna had a bit of time away from the farm.'

It was as if the whole house had relaxed. Everyone smiled, and the men, who had been keeping their eyes on their plates, began to discuss farming matters. Luke, who still felt left out of this kind of talk, pressed Val's knee under the table, and she turned her head and smiled at him. The long months of bitterness, which Joanna had seemed unable to overcome, had finally passed. The sadness would never entirely leave, but at least the family had come together again and the two younger women were taking the first steps to renewing their friendship.

It seemed like a new beginning.

Over the river, the villagers of Little Burracombe had also finished clearing up after the celebrations. Felix Copley, who had been vicar there for only a few weeks, had been working hard in the field, and had now gone back to the vicarage to have lunch with his fiancée, Stella Simmons.

'It's lucky the school's closed today as well,' he remarked, as they strolled up the drive through a blaze of brilliantly coloured azaleas. 'You've been a godsend, helping us this morning.' He thought for a moment, then added, 'Come to think of it, I mean that quite literally. You've been a real God-Send to me. I just wish you didn't have to go back to Burracombe every night.'

'It's only until Christmas,' Stella said, giving his arm a squeeze. 'And even that's sooner than we first intended. We meant to have a two-year engagement, remember?'

'I can't imagine how I could ever have thought it would be possible to wait so long. But now the Coronation's out of the way, we can start to make proper plans.'

'You've got a lot to do in your new parish first,' she reminded him. 'Your parishioners need to get used to you before they have a wife to contend with as well.'

'Nonsense! They're as eager as I am to have you installed in the vicarage. And you'll be able to protect me from all the predatory females who see an unmarried vicar as fair game,' he added slyly.

'Oh, I don't think you'll have any problem there,' Stella said unconcernedly. 'Nobody will be interested in you.' In fact, she knew that there was already a good deal of interest in Felix. Still barely thirty, with fair hair, very blue eyes and a winning, little-boy smile, he was a considerable and very attractive change from old John Berry, the previous vicar, and she'd caught several pairs of eyes fixed on him in speculation at his induction on Easter Day. It didn't worry her, for her trust in Felix was absolute, but privately she thought it would be a good thing when they were married and she was living at the vicarage.

They came to the top of the shrub-lined drive, and stood looking for a moment at the rambling house that was to be their home. Vicarages like this had been built when vicars were expected to have large families, and although Stella and Felix had agreed they wanted at least three children, there would still be quite a few rooms unused. Mrs Berry had left quite a lot of furniture, however, and it did mean there would be plenty of room for guests. Although Stella had no relatives apart from her sister Maddy, Felix was one of a large and sociable family.

'I'd like to invite the Budds to stay sometime,' she said, thinking aloud. 'You remember, the family in Portsmouth who looked after Maddy and me after our mother died during the war.'

'Of course I remember them. We went to their daughter Rose's wedding in January. It was where Maddy and Sammy met again.'

Stella looked at him in consternation. 'Oh, Felix! I hadn't forgotten – it's just that it seems so much longer ago than that. Such a lot has happened since then: Sammy and Maddy falling in love and getting engaged, and poor Sammy being killed. I can't believe it was only six months ago.'

'A lot's happened to us, too,' he said, slipping an arm round her waist and drawing her closer. 'It's all too easy to forget that it's still very early days for Maddy. She seems to be managing very well, though, all things considered. And Stephen Napier is being very tactful.'

'He's a good friend,' Stella said. 'You know, I think he may be genuinely in love with her, but he's just waiting. He may have to wait a very long time, though.'

'I didn't see him down at the field this morning,' Felix said thoughtfully. 'Nor Hilary, either. That's odd; I'd have expected them both to be pulling their weight. I hope nothing's wrong at the Barton.'

'Perhaps I'll call in on the way home,' Stella said. 'And we'd better go in and have some lunch now, Felix, because I've got quite a lot to get ready for school tomorrow. We'll be doing more work on the Coronation – the children's essays and pictures, of course, and our own tidying up after the Procession of Monarchs.'

'That was good, wasn't it? And the Crocker twins were very

effective as the Princes in the Tower. Nobody could doubt why anyone would want to wall them up, especially when they got into the tea tent and stole a whole plateful of Dottie's cream scones!' He chuckled, then asked, 'How soon will Miss Kemp start to look for your replacement?'

'Fairly soon, I think. I don't give my official notice in until the first day of next term, so the governors can't advertise yet, but she may start to ask around unofficially. Other head teachers often know of people who want to move, or newly qualified teachers looking for their first position, like me.' She sighed a little. 'I shall be sad to leave, though.'

'You can still do supply teaching if you want to,' he said encouragingly, rooting about in the kitchen cupboards. 'I'm not going to insist on you being a dutiful vicar's wife all the time. You can have a few hours of your own every now and again.'

'Thank you very much.' Stella took a loaf from the bread-bin and began to slice it. 'It won't be the same as seeing the children every day, though. You don't really get to know them if you only go in occasionally. I shall miss Shirley Culliford and little Betty. And Robin Tozer will be starting in September, and he's such a dear little boy. And there are all the others – Jimmy Field and Tom Bellamy and ... oh, all of them.'

'Even the twins?' Felix asked wickedly, and she grinned.

'Well, maybe I won't miss *them* quite so much! And some of the children would be going up into Miss Kemp's class anyway, and others, like Micky Coker and Henry Bennetts, will be leaving altogether and going to "Big School" in Tavistock. There are always a lot of changes in the September term. Is that a tin of Spam you're getting out for these sandwiches?'

'Yes, and there's a jar of Dottie's green tomato chutney to go with it, as well as a few early tomatoes from one of my parishioners, and a cake for afters from another. You see, they've already started to look after me.'

'So long as they're not being predatory as well,' Stella observed, opening the larder door. 'Good heavens, look at all this! A sponge, a plate of rock buns and a fruit cake! You'll be as fat as Humpty Dumpty if you eat everything.' She carried the tray of sandwiches through the back door to the garden, where a rickety table had been set in a patch of sunlight. 'Bring some water as well, will you, please?'

They settled down at the table with the little meal in front of them. The sun, so conspicuously absent from the celebrations of the day before, had struggled weakly through the clouds, and the kitchen garden, which had been Mrs Berry's pride and joy with its beds of herbs and salads and vegetables, looked neat and productive. Felix had kept the gardener, Bill Madge, and his wife Peggy, who acted as housekeeper, and, as he said, he was well looked after. All the same, no matter how welcoming the villagers had been and how much in demand his services were, he was lonely in his big house when Stella wasn't there, and he spoke the truth when he said he was finding it hard to wait for their wedding.

'I really do think we ought to start making plans,' he said. 'There's the guest list to start – that'll take ages to do. It's so easy to forget some aged aunt you haven't seen for years who will be mortally offended if she's not asked. And you know what an enormous family I've got.'

'Your side of the church is going to look a lot fuller than mine,' Stella said ruefully. 'The only relative I know of is Maddy. Both our parents were only children, and our grandparents died years ago. We don't have any cousins or uncles or aunts, not even aged ones we haven't seen for years.'

Felix put down his sandwich and reached across the table to take her hand. 'Then the sooner you're officially part of my family, the better,' he said. 'But there are plenty of friends who will want to see you married. The Budds, for a start, and the Hodges and some of the other people from Portsmouth and Bridge End. And all the children from school, and Miss Kemp and Dottie, of course, and Val and Luke and the Napiers and ... well, almost all Burracombe.'

46

'We can't invite everyone!' Stella said in dismay. 'Where could we possibly hold the reception? And we'll never be able to afford it.'

'Well, perhaps we couldn't invite them all to the reception,' he agreed. 'But they'll all want to come to the church to see you married. You're a very popular person in the village, darling.'

'And so are you,' she said. 'You were their curate. They'll be coming for you as much as for me.'

'Maybe, but if my side of the church is full of my relatives, everyone else can sit on your side. It won't be empty. They're your friends, after all. And don't worry about the cost – my mother wrote to me the other day saying she and Father want to pay for the reception. It's only fair, seeing as we've already agreed it'll be almost all my relatives. As for where we'll have it, what's wrong with here?'

'In the vicarage?' Stella said dubiously. 'Will there be room?'

'Of course there will. We've got that huge drawing room and the dining room, and we can open those big doors in between to make one big room, and it'll be just family and close friends, so if we borrow some extra tables and chairs we should be able to seat them all. We can get caterers from Tavistock to do the meal.'

'I don't know,' she said. 'It'll be an awful squeeze. And there'll be all the tidying up and clearing away afterwards.'

'Which we won't have to worry about. We'll be off on our honeymoon. And that's another thing we need to decide.'

'At the beginning of January?' Stella said. 'I can't think of anywhere I'll want to go then. Can't we just stay at home?'

'Can you really see my parishioners leaving us alone? You'll have to get used to sharing me with a stream of callers soon enough, my darling, so I refuse to make you start during the one time in our lives when we'll be forgiven for wanting to be entirely alone together.'

Stella finished her sandwich. 'Well, I'm afraid we're going to have to discuss it some other time. I really must go back now. I've got heaps to do, and I'd really like to call in at the Barton and see Hilary on the way.'

'You can't go without having a piece of cake,' he said, cutting two large slices. 'Come on, eat this, and I'll walk down to the Clam with you. I might stroll up to the Barton, too, although I've got quite a lot to do myself after taking yesterday off. It does seem odd that neither Hilary nor Stephen put in an appearance this morning. I hope Colonel Napier isn't ill again.' He sighed. 'But perhaps I shouldn't go. You know, it's really rather hard to forget that Burracombe isn't my parish now; I still feel I ought to keep an eye on the people there.'

'I expect you'll soon get used to it. Your own parishioners will keep you too busy to worry about anyone else.'

They took the plates and glasses back to the kitchen, and Felix gave her a hug and kiss; even though they were officially engaged, they still desisted from public displays of affection. Then they walked together down the lane to the wooden bridge which spanned the river between the two villages, and said goodbye. Stella crossed to the other side and turned to wave before setting off up the narrow, twisting path that led between high Devon banks and hedges to the bigger village.

It would seem strange, she thought, to live on the other side of the river. Although the two villages were barely half a mile apart as the crow flies, they were different worlds. Once she lived in Little Burracombe, she would only return to Burracombe itself as a visitor. She felt a sudden stab of dismay at the thought that Dottie, Val, Joanna and all her other friends, not to mention Miss Kemp and the children in the school, would continue with lives that no longer included her. She would still see them, of course, and she might even, as Felix had suggested, return to the school occasionally as a supply teacher, but she would never be a part of their lives as she was now. Instead, she would have to become involved in a different community, with people she scarcely knew, and even more so because she would be the vicar's wife, and almost as much at their beck and call as Felix himself.

But Stella had learned in her short life that nothing stayed the same for ever. Things changed, life evolved, and when old ways altered, new ones came to take their place. There were always losses, but there were gains as well. She would be going into a new, happy and fulfilling life with Felix, and she wasn't losing any of her friends, nor even moving far away from them. She would have the best of both worlds.

Cheered by her thoughts, she came to the gates of the Barton and walked up the drive, wondering once more why neither Hilary nor Stephen had put in an appearance that morning, and hoping again that nothing was wrong.

Chapter Six

'*Married?*'

Hilary stared at Travis, hearing the blankness in her voice. She put her hand to her temple, feeling as if she had a whole hive of bees buzzing inside her head. I ought to have known this was going to happen, she thought. I ought to have seen it coming last night, when they came into the marquee together. I think I did know, really, but I pushed it aside, and then this morning ... Marianne and Robert ... It all seemed to be too much.

Her father found his voice first. 'You and Jennifer Tucker?' he said. 'Getting married?' And after only the slightest pause: 'Well, congratulations. She's a fine young woman, from what I've seen of her. A good choice.'

Travis smiled. 'I don't think I actually *chose* her, sir. We just got to know each other and ... well, there it is. We get along well, we're happy and comfortable together, and we've decided to get married. And we don't want to wait too long; we're neither of us in the first flush of youth.'

Gilbert turned to his daughter. 'I think this calls for a celebration, don't you? It's not too early for a sherry. You'll have one, won't you, Kellaway?'

'Thank you, sir. I'm glad you approve.'

'Approve? Why on earth shouldn't I approve?' Her father was in an expansive mood this morning, Hilary thought as she went to fetch the sherry and some glasses, and why not? Baden's son turning up out of the blue, his estate manager settling down to marriage, and all on the heels of the new Queen's Coronation, not to mention the glory of the British conquest of Everest. It was turning into one of the best weeks of his life. 'It's good to see you settling down,' she heard him continue, as if to confirm her own thoughts. 'I take it you'll not be thinking of moving away? Miss Tucker's almost a Burracombe woman anyway, from all I hear.'

'She certainly is, and she's been wanting to live here permanently for some time.' Travis accepted a glass of sherry from Hilary, and their eyes met briefly before she turned away. 'Not that that's why we're getting married,' he added with a smile. 'At least, I hope not.'

The Colonel cleared his throat. 'I should hope not, indeed.' He raised his glass. 'Well, here's to your very good health. You must bring Miss Tucker in soon so that we can give her our good wishes. Tomorrow evening, perhaps, Hilary?'

She looked at him. 'We do have visitors, Father.'

'Good heavens, so we do!' He turned to Travis, and she feared for a moment that he was about to tell him who the visitors were. 'Well, no matter, they'll understand. Although it would probably be good for the boy to start meeting people ... oh, very well, Hilary, I can see what you want to say, and maybe you're right. A little too soon, perhaps. Plenty of time later. All the same, we mustn't delay our proper duty to Miss Tucker. Bring her in tomorrow evening about six, Kellaway. And we'll need to be thinking about your accommodation, too. You can't set up home with a new wife in the Crockers' front room!'

'There's no rush,' Travis said with another glance at Hilary. 'We won't be getting married until the autumn at the earliest.'

'It's June now. Time goes before you know it. Luckily, Arnold Cherriman's already told me he's intending to move back to Plymouth soon. All working out very well.' Gilbert drained his glass and nodded with satisfaction. 'Yes, all working out very well indeed.'

'But Father,' Hilary protested, 'nothing's been decided yet about that house.'

'What's there to decide? It's the estate manager's house, always was, and now it can be again. Nothing simpler.'

Hilary bit her lip. She didn't want to start an argument about the so-called estate manager's house in front of Travis, but she had promised it to Val and Luke before Travis had ever appeared on the scene, and now that Val was pregnant, she was even more anxious that they should have it. Val had told her they could manage very well in Jed's Cottage, but it was quite small, with only two bedrooms, and this baby surely wouldn't be their only child. All the same, she knew that it was the estate's obligation to provide its manager with a home, and she had to admit that there was no other suitable house. With a small sigh, she acknowledged that there really wasn't any point in arguing about it.

'Aren't you going to congratulate him, Hilary?' her father asked sharply, and she flushed and lifted her glass.

'Of course I am. Congratulations, Travis. I hope you'll both be very happy.'

'Thank you,' he said. 'I believe we will. Especially with such a good place to live, and with such good friends around us.'

Good friends, she thought, and sipped her own sherry. Well, it was better than nothing, even if she had begun to hope that for herself and Travis there might be something more. It seemed that this was her fate; ever since losing her fiancé Henry in the war, every man she had felt an interest in, and who she thought felt an interest in her, had found someone else he liked better. Perhaps she just wasn't cut out to be a wife.

'Are you all right, Hilary?' her father asked, and she felt her cheeks colour again. She set down her glass.

'Yes, of course. Just a bit tired after yesterday, and I've got things to do ...' She glanced at Travis. 'Will you excuse me? Our visitors were rather unexpected. Unless there was anything else you wanted to talk about?'

He gave her a thoughtful look, and she wondered if she had sounded churlish. 'No, that's all the news I have this morning. And I mustn't be long, either – there's plenty to see to on the estate. Quite a lot of things were put aside in all the preparations.' He put down his own glass and looked at the Colonel. 'I won't keep you from your visitors.'

'Not at all. Glad you came.' Gilbert got to his feet and held out his hand. 'It's good news. Miss Tucker will make you a good wife. Most suitable.'

Travis shook his hand, and he and Hilary went out of the room together. She walked to the front door with him, and as they stood looking out towards the moor, he said, 'Is everything all right, Hilary? You seem a bit distracted. You're not upset about Jennifer and me, are you?'

'Good gracious, no!' she exclaimed. 'Why ever should I be? Father's right – she'll make you a good wife, and I hope you'll both be very happy.'

'I believe we will.' He paused. 'You know I value your friendship, Hilary. I hope it won't make any difference to that.'

'Of course it won't!' She heard her voice sounding over-emphatic, and coloured again. 'We're colleagues as well, after all.'

'Employer and employee, to be strictly accurate,' he said, his eyes on her face. 'Look, tell me to mind my own business, but there's nothing wrong, is there? These visitors ... it's not bad news, I hope.'

'Oh, no,' she said quickly. 'It's just something ... unexpected, that's all. And not very easy.' He would have to know sometime, of course, but it was too soon for the news to be broken outside the family. She wasn't even sure that it ever would be. Marianne's claim might yet be shown to be false, after all, despite Gilbert's yearning to accept Robert as his grandson. 'Look, I'm sorry, I'll have to go.' She held out her hand, just as her father had done. 'I'm really pleased about you and Jennifer. And we'll see you both tomorrow evening.'

He took her hand. 'I'm not sure. Jennifer's gone back to Plymouth this morning. She won't be here again until the weekend. Perhaps we'd better put it off for a few days. Your visitors may have gone by then, too.'

'Yes.' She had a feeling they'd be staying longer, but it would give the family a chance to decide on their course of action before introducing Marianne and her son to anyone else. 'Yes, that'll probably be best. Saturday or Sunday, perhaps.'

'I'm sure Jennifer would like that.' He let go of her hand. 'I'm glad you're pleased for us, Hilary. I value your opinion.'

He turned and strode away. Hilary watched him, feeling oddly blank, then went slowly back indoors.

She didn't know quite what to do next. Marianne was still in her room, and Stephen and Robert were probably somewhere up on the moors by now. She didn't feel like returning to the argument with her father and she couldn't settle to any estate work. She might have gone to find Travis if he had not come first with his own news, but now their relationship appeared to have altered course. In fact, her whole world seemed to have shifted on its axis; and the new era, which had begun yesterday with the Coronation of the young Queen, had taken a different and totally unexpected direction; one in which Hilary felt shaken and uncertain.

I'll go for a ride, she thought. I'll saddle Beau and we'll go up on the moor. Maybe that will clear my head.

Stephen was beginning to regret his offer to take Robert for a walk.

There was something slightly uncomfortable about this unknown nephew. He told himself that it wasn't Robert's fault – he was still only a child – but the situation itself was so strange, and had come so suddenly, that he found himself at a loss. And he wasn't quite sure how much the boy really understood.

The main problem was that he was so quiet. He didn't appear to feel the need for conversation. He walked at Stephen's side, lithe and silent as a cat, his eyes taking in everything, yet without comment. He seemed totally incurious. Surely, Stephen thought, if he knew anything at all about his father and the place where he had grown up, the place he would have owned, he must feel some interest. Yet how much *did* he know? How much had Marianne herself known, during that whirlwind courtship and hasty marriage?

Stephen himself had been younger than Robert when his brother had been killed. There had been too many years between them for them to have been real companions. Baden had been the godlike older brother, already a legend at their prep school by the time Stephen had arrived there, and a name on the memorial board by the time he reached public school. He had spent most of his schooldays feeling second-best, and convinced that he would always be a disappointment to his father, simply because he wasn't Baden. And because he believed he could never run the estate to his father's satisfaction, he had turned his back on it and made up his mind to seek a new and different life.

Now there was this boy, this French boy, who had arrived as if from nowhere, claiming to be Baden's son. Baden's *heir*. Claiming Baden's place in the family and looking likely, if Stephen had read his father correctly, to be given it on a plate.

'How much do you know about Burracombe?' he asked at last as they walked across the fields that spread across the broad valley and up towards the moorland.

'A little. What my mother has told me, and what I have read.' His English, like his mother's, was meticulously correct. Hadn't Hilary said that his grandfather was an English teacher? Had he or Marianne taught the boy for the simple love of the language, or because it was intended that one day he should come to claim his inheritance?

Come on, he told himself, you don't even know if that's why they've come. Does he even have an inheritance to claim? Surely there'll be all sorts of legal issues?

He glanced down at the dark head beside him. His nephew, he thought. He had been an uncle all these years and never known it. It was going to take some getting used to.

'Have you been to England before?'

'No. This is my first time.'

'And do you like it?' What a ridiculously banal conversation this was. 'I suppose you haven't seen much of it yet,' he added lamely.

'No, not very much. Just the train journey to London and then to Tavistock, and the road here across the . . .' He searched for the word, which for some reason pleased Stephen. 'The moor,' he finished with a half-glance upwards.

'The moor, that's right. It's Dartmoor really, because the River Dart rises up in the hills, but you can call it either moor or moorland.'

'Moor-land,' Robert said thoughtfully, and Stephen could almost see him filing the term away in his brain. 'Can we walk on the moor-land?'

'Yes, we can. Pretty well anywhere, except where the Army uses it for manoeuvres.'

'Manoeuvres?'

'Exercises. Shooting practice and that sort of thing.'

'Not exercises like this?' The French boy stretched out his arms, then pulled his fists into his shoulders and out again. Stephen laughed, and Robert's face relaxed. They grinned at each other, and some of the tension between them eased.

'Let's go up there now,' Stephen suggested. 'I'll show you the tors and the Standing Stones.'

At this, Robert's face lit up. 'Standing Stones! I've heard of these. They're very ancient, *n'est-ce pas?*'

'Yes, they are. D'you have them in France, too?'

'*Mais oui.*' His careful English was lost in his sudden

interest, but he brought it back with determination. 'My grandfather took me to see the Ménec alignments near Carnac in Brittany. There are hundreds of stones nearly four metres tall, stretching in a great avenue for almost a thousand metres. There are many others in the area, but I have not seen them all.'

'Well, you won't find our Standing Stones quite so impressive,' Stephen said. 'But we like them. And you must try to go to Stonehenge while you're here.' He realised he was beginning to talk to the boy as if he were an ordinary visitor, and added a little doubtfully, 'That's if you have time. Do you know how long your mother wants to stay?'

Robert shrugged. 'Not really. She doesn't speak to me of these things, you understand. I know that this is where my father grew up, that is all.' The blue gaze drifted over the landscape, then returned to Stephen's face. 'And you are his brother. His younger brother.'

'That's right.' There was something in Robert's tone, perhaps the minutest emphasis on 'younger', that made Stephen feel a little uneasy. He decided he had imagined it, and said, 'We'll go through this gate and along the lane a little way, and I'll show you the Standing Stones.'

Almost as soon as they were on the lane, he realised his mistake. Jacob Prout was walking slowly along, his dog Scruff at his heels, sweeping up litter and dumping it in his wheelbarrow. He stopped when he saw Stephen, and jerked his head at the pile of empty crisp packets, lemonade bottles and cigarette packets.

'You'd think folk'd have a bit of respect at a Coronation, wouldn't you? If you can carry it out full, you can carry it back empty, that's what I always say. But there, everything's different since the war.' His bright eyes took in Robert's appearance. 'This one of your visitors? I heard a taxi'd been seen turning in the Barton gates.'

I might have known it wouldn't be a secret for long, Stephen thought ruefully. He rested his hand on Robert's shoulder and said, 'Yes, this is Robert. He and his mother have come over from France for a short visit.'

'France, eh? I was there in the first war. Picked up a bit of the language, too. *Parlez-vous anglais?*' he asked Robert in a passable accent.

'Yes, I do,' the boy replied with the ghost of a smile on his lips. 'But why should I, when your French is so good?'

Jacob stared at him, then roared with laughter, and Stephen grinned. 'He's got you there, Jacob. This is Mr Prout,' he told Robert. 'He does almost everything around the village. Burracombe would be a poorer place without him.'

'Poorer? Not so rich, you mean?' Robert looked doubtfully at the barrow full of rubbish. 'How do you make your money from this, Mr Prout?'

'I don't mean that sort of poorer,' Stephen answered. 'I mean ... well, not so nice. In a lot of ways. He keeps everything looking tidy – the roads, the hedges, the churchyard and quite a few gardens. Jacob's always busy.'

'Ah, and I'm busy now, too,' Jacob said, lifting the handles of his wheelbarrow. 'Been down the fields all morning, clearing up after the do last night, and now I'm going home for a bite to eat. Thought you might be down there, too,' he added to Stephen.

'I would have been, but Robert and his mother arrived unexpectedly. Unexpectedly early,' he added hastily. Jacob wasn't a gossip but he was an important part of the Burracombe grapevine, and if you didn't want news passed on, it was best not to mention it. For some obscure reason, Stephen felt it better not to let the village know too much about Marianne and her son's sudden arrival. Not just yet, anyway. 'I'm just taking him up to see the Standing Stones,' he went on, as if Robert were any other visitor. 'Apparently they have them in France, too.'

'Did you see any when you were there?' Robert inquired, but Jacob shook his head.

'Us didn't have much time for gawping, and I were down in the trenches most of the time. Well, that be a long time in the past and best left there. Us got a future now, and it's youngsters like you that'll be part of it.' He nodded, touched his cap to Stephen, gave Robert a grin that had several teeth missing but was no less cheerful for that, and went on his way.

'He's a nice man,' Robert remarked, as Stephen led him in the other direction towards another gate. 'I couldn't understand much of what he said, though.'

Stephen chuckled. 'Jacob talks with a broad Devon accent – "broad" means "strong".' He saw Robert's baffled expression, and laughed again. 'Well, don't worry about it. What I mean is that people in different parts of England all speak English, but they may pronounce the words differently, and sometimes they even have different words. Don't you have that sort of thing in French? We call it a dialect.'

Robert's face cleared and he nodded vigorously. '*Le dialecte – oui*. My father took me to Marseilles once, to see some cousins, and I could not understand anything of their speech at first. And then I got used to it, and when we went home my mother was angry because she said I spoke like a little *Marseillaise!*'

'You'll have to take care you don't start to talk like a Devonian then,' Stephen grinned as he opened the gate into the wood. Then he bit his lip, wondering again how long the boy would be here and what his mother really had in mind. 'But perhaps you won't be here long enough for that to happen.'

They walked in silence up the narrow, twisting little path between the trees. They were in full leaf now but there was little birdsong; at this time of year, the dawn chorus gave way by six o'clock to a busy day of feeding either sitting parents or hungry fledglings. A jay screeched, and darted with a flash of chestnut and blue across their path, a green woodpecker hammered rapidly on a tree-trunk, and a red squirrel shot up a broad old oak and chattered crossly from one of the lower branches.

'*Un écureuil*,' Robert observed. 'We have those in France, too. *Mais q'est-ce que c'est?*'

They had come through the trees to the small clearing where the charcoal-burner's hut stood. The door stood open and Luke Ferris came out, wiping his long, thin hands on a paint-stained rag. His dark eyebrows rose a little, and then he smiled.

'Hullo, Stephen. Didn't expect to see anyone up here this morning. Out for a stroll?' He glanced incuriously at Robert, and Stephen realised he probably took him for either a relative or a local boy. Jacob Prout, who had lived in the village all his life, knew everyone within a ten-mile radius, but Luke was a relative newcomer and still often met people he didn't know.

'This is Robert,' Stephen explained, and saw Luke's eyebrows twitch again at the French pronunciation. 'He and his mother are staying with us for a few days. He hasn't been here before so I'm showing him the lie of the land.'

'Are you an artist?' Robert asked, eyeing the rag with its mixture of colours smeared across it.

'Of a sort,' Luke said, but Stephen said, 'Don't you take any notice of him. He's a very good artist. He might show you his paintings sometime, if you ask him nicely.'

'Please may I see your paintings?' Robert asked politely, taking Stephen literally.

'Be delighted, but I'm supposed to be down at the field helping to clear up; I've only nipped up for a few minutes.'

Stephen put his hand on Robert's shoulder. 'Luke's obviously busy now. We'll come another time. Sorry I can't get down to give a hand, Luke. See you soon.' Feeling uncomfortably that Luke must be thinking he was shirking, he steered the boy towards the trees, and they walked on up the track towards the moor.

'I would have liked to see his work,' Robert said after a moment. 'I think he would have shown it to me now.'

'Maybe, but until we know just how to explain your visit, it's best not to meet too many people,' Stephen said bluntly. He had come to the conclusion that Robert was no fool and understood more of the reasons for their arrival than he had admitted.

There was a short silence, then Robert said, 'Is it that you are ashamed of us?'

They had just stepped out of the trees and were standing by the stone wall that divided the wood from the moor itself. Stephen had begun to unlatch the wooden gate. He turned slowly and looked down at the boy's face, sharply reminded yet again of Baden. He might not clearly remember his brother at the age Robert was now, but he had seen enough photographs to know that they were almost identical.

'No,' he said quietly, 'of course we're not ashamed. But it's come as rather a shock, you see. We didn't know anything about you or your mother. Baden never even mentioned that there was a girl, and all those who might have told us were killed. We need time to understand it all, and to get to know you. You look very much like him,' he added.

'My mother says that, too. But I have never seen a picture of him, so I cannot know.' There was a touch of desolation in the boy's voice, and Stephen felt a sudden pang of compassion for him. All we've been doing is thinking of ourselves here, he thought, what it will mean to us and to the estate. None of us has given a thought to what it means to this child.

'Let's walk on up to the Stones,' he said gently. 'It's a good place to talk. And I'll tell you whatever you want to know about your father.'

Chapter Seven

'I won't come in, if it's not convenient,' Stella said. 'I've been over to see Felix, and thought I'd call in and say hello on the way back. But if you're busy ...'

'No. At least ...' Hilary glanced over her shoulder. 'It's just that we've got unexpected visitors ...' She hesitated, and Stella took her cue.

'It doesn't matter. I didn't mean to stop, anyway; I've got heaps to do. I only wanted to say what a lovely time we had yesterday.' She was already turning away, and Hilary put out a hand.

'I'm sorry, I'm being very rude. Do come in for a few minutes. We're just having coffee.'

But Stella shook her head. 'No, if I come in and start chatting I'll be here all afternoon. Honestly, it was only because I was passing. I'll see you again soon.'

'Yes. And thanks for dropping in.' Hilary watched her walk away, her fair hair bright in a sudden burst of sunshine, her summer skirt swinging round her slim legs, and sighed. Whatever Stella said, she did feel she had been inhospitable. And people were going to know soon enough that there were visitors at the Barton. Perhaps it would have been sensible to have invited Stella in and introduced her to them. Behaving as if they had something to hide was only going to create gossip.

We just need a little time, that's all, she thought, making her way back to the dining room where the others were still at the table. A little time to find out what Marianne wants and how long she means to stay. Time for us to get used to it all, and time for Father to come down to earth and make sensible plans.

For plans would have to be made, that was certain. You couldn't suddenly discover a new member of the family – and such an important member, too – and carry on as if nothing had happened. She sighed again, and opened the dining-room door.

Stephen and Marianne were still at the table, but Gilbert was on his feet, standing with his hand on Robert's shoulder before the portrait of Baden that had been painted at the beginning of the war. Baden was in his captain's uniform, proud and upright, his blue eyes steady, his chiselled lips firm, and his dark hair smooth against his well-shaped head. Once again, Hilary felt that small shock of recognition as she saw the likeness between him and the son he had never seen, never even known about. She glanced quickly at Marianne, wondering what it was like for her to see this picture of the young husband torn so brutally from her side, so soon after their marriage.

The Frenchwoman's eyes were veiled behind lowered lids and her expression was inscrutable. Hilary felt a twinge of compassion for her: so young when all this had happened; married and widowed within a few days, then discovering that she was pregnant. And all in a time of war and Occupation. No wonder she had married again so quickly; if she had been discovered by the Germans to be the wife of a British soldier, there was no knowing what might have happened to her. And now she had been widowed again, with three children to bring up, and an ailing mother and mother-in-law to care for as well.

We must help her, she thought. Father's right: Robert is Baden's son, and it's only right that he should be welcomed into the family.

'He was a fine man,' Napier was saying, still gazing at the

portrait. 'A son for me to be proud of. And a father for you to be proud of.'

Hilary shot a swift glance at Stephen. 'You can be proud of both your sons,' she said quietly.

Gilbert swung round. 'Did I say I wasn't? There's no need to be so touchy, Hilary. I suppose you want me to say I'm proud of you, too.'

'That's up to you, Father,' she said coolly.

Their eyes met, then Gilbert's face softened and he smiled at her.

'As a matter of fact, I am,' he said, and Hilary's eyes prickled with sudden tears. She moved quickly to the table and sat down. Her father was right; she was being too touchy, and Stephen certainly didn't need to be defended by his sister.

'I would like to have known him,' Robert was saying, still regarding the portrait. 'But I am proud of my French father as well. He was a very brave man.'

'Of course. In the Resistance, you said?' Gilbert looked at Marianne. 'You must all have been in danger at times.'

'All the time,' she said. 'When I lived in the "safe house", we had to be very careful. There were eyes watching everywhere. Noticing if you bought more bread than usual, if there were faces at the windows or unusual sounds from indoors – the lavatories flushing more than should be expected or when nobody was at home. Movement at night. In the end, we were betrayed, and that was when my husband and his father were both taken to Buchenwald.'

'Very sorry to hear you had such a difficult time,' Gilbert said gruffly. 'And your husband was a brave man, as Robert here says.'

'You must miss him very much,' Hilary said gently, and the Frenchwoman sent her a look of gratitude. Robert came to stand beside her, and she put out a hand and laid it on his arm. Hilary glanced at her father.

'Perhaps we could all talk about this later. Didn't Travis

say he would come in again this afternoon?' There was that to consider too, she remembered – the question of Travis's wedding and accommodation. Not for the first time, she wondered why problems all had to come along at once instead of being nicely spaced out.

'Yes, and he should be here soon.' Gilbert looked at the clock. 'Have to leave you, I'm afraid. Hilary will look after you, I dare say.'

'I need to be at the meeting, too,' Hilary reminded him. 'And Stephen has to go back this evening.'

'It is of no matter,' Marianne said. 'Robert and I can amuse ourselves. I will help prepare the meal.'

Hilary opened her mouth to say that Mrs Ellis would do this, then closed it again. It would certainly solve the problem of what to do with the Frenchwoman for a few hours, but she ought to make sure that the housekeeper would welcome the assistance. Hilary herself often helped with the cooking, but Mrs Ellis might not be at all pleased to find a strange and, moreover, foreign woman in her kitchen.

'I'd better go and see what Mrs Ellis is planning to give us,' she said, and escaped again.

To her relief, Mrs Ellis proved cooperative. 'I don't mind her doing a pudding or something,' she said. 'She runs a sort of cake-shop over in France, didn't you say? She can make something for your tea. I was just going to knock up a few scones.'

'If you're sure you don't mind,' Hilary said. 'Not everyone likes sharing a kitchen.'

'That's all right,' Mrs Ellis said. 'I can see she've made things a bit tricky for you, arriving all unexpected. I'll keep her busy, don't you fret.'

Hilary looked at her, wondering how much she had deduced from the visitors' sudden appearance.

'You don't have to tell me nothing,' the housekeeper said firmly, interpreting Hilary's look. ''Tis family business and nothing to do with me, and outside this house I won't say a word.'

'Thank you, Mrs Ellis,' Hilary said gratefully. 'I'm sure we'll get it all sorted out soon. It's good news really, after all.' But she couldn't keep the doubt from her voice, and she left the kitchen hurriedly, before she could say more. Good news it might be – or not, depending on how it turned out – but a lot of thinking and talking would have to be done before it became general village information.

Half an hour later, having seen Marianne ensconced in the kitchen with Mrs Ellis, who was being extremely forbearing, and taking various ingredients from the cupboards, she was making her way to the estate office at the back of the house. It occurred to her as she went that, despite the housekeeper's reassurances, leaving her and Marianne alone together for an afternoon might not be the best way of keeping the story quiet, but it was too late now. And Stephen had said that both Jacob Prout and Luke Ferris had already seen Robert, not to mention others who might have been strolling in the area as they walked up to the Stones. Really, it was impossible to keep anything secret for long in a place like Burracombe.

Travis was already in the office with Gilbert, poring over some documents. They looked up as Hilary came in.

'Isaac Endacott wants to put up a Dutch barn in Top Field,' her father said. 'Neither Travis nor I can see any objection. I assume you'll be agreeable?'

'Oh ... yes.' Hilary sat down. 'Father, I've been thinking.'

'If it's about the estate manager's house, there's nothing to be said. Arnold Cherriman's planning to move out during the summer, and we'll do any work it needs before Travis and Miss Tucker move in. Not that I expect there to be much,' he added. 'Arnold and his wife have been careful tenants, and she's done a considerable amount to improve the garden.'

'It's not that,' Hilary said, recognising this as a battle she had already lost. 'It's about Marianne and Robert.'

'Ah.' Gilbert looked quickly at Travis. 'I'm not sure this is the time—'

'I think it has to be. Several people have already seen Robert, and Mrs Ellis and Marianne are spending the whole afternoon together. There are bound to be conclusions to be drawn, things said. I wouldn't be surprised if the Bell Inn isn't buzzing with the news this very evening.'

'But there's no news for them to talk about!' Gilbert said, outraged. 'Even if a few people have seen the boy, what can they say? They're just ordinary visitors. There's no reason at all for gossip.'

'Burracombe doesn't need a reason,' Hilary said. 'And if they don't know the true story, they'll make one up. You know what it's like, Father. The only way to stop gossip is to tell the truth in the first place, and even then, it won't stop some of them,' she ended, a trifle grimly.

'Look,' Travis said, starting to get to his feet, 'would it be a good idea to leave this meeting for another time? You've obviously got more important things on your minds at the moment.'

'No.' Hilary put out a hand to prevent him. 'That's just the point. We've got to let the village know what's happening, and you're the best person to help us. You can go into the pub tonight and put a stop to the gossip.'

'That's right,' Gilbert agreed. 'Tell 'em to keep their noses out of what doesn't concern them.'

'*No!*' Hilary exclaimed again. 'Tell them what's really happening. They deserve that, Father. And it *does* concern them. A lot of them depend on the estate for their homes and their livings. They've a right to know.'

Gilbert scowled. 'A right? That's putting it a bit strongly. They're tenants.'

'That doesn't give us the right to treat them like serfs. Those days are gone, Father. They're good, hardworking people who deserve respect, and leaving them in the dark about something like this is *not* respectful. And isn't it better that they know the truth – which is nothing to be ashamed of, after all – rather than cook up some garbled version from bits and pieces picked up here and there?'

'But that's just the point,' he argued. 'They have no right to do that. Aren't we entitled to some respect as well? Some privacy?'

'Yes, of course we are,' she said with a sigh, 'but you know that's what will happen. And it's not just us; we have to think about Marianne and Robert as well. Especially Robert.'

They looked at each other, then he heaved a deep sigh and spread his hands. 'Very well. You win. So what do you want to do about it?'

Once more, Travis shifted uneasily. 'I really do think I shouldn't be here. You've obviously got a lot to discuss.'

'Yes, we have,' Hilary said. 'Unfortunately, we don't have time to do it before the grapevine starts buzzing. Or whatever it is grapevines do. Look, Father, I think we should tell Travis what's happened, and then he can go to the pub tonight and see what's being said. He'll know enough to be able to set them right, at least.'

'And if I wasn't planning to go to the pub tonight?' he enquired gently.

Hilary flushed. 'I'm sorry. I'm treating *you* like a serf now! Well, I still think we ought to tell you. This isn't going to go away, after all.' She smiled at him. 'And maybe you'll help, if we ask nicely!'

'I agree,' Gilbert said unexpectedly. 'It's not as if there's anything to be ashamed of, God knows. It's good news. Extremely good news.' His face flushed with warmth and he turned to the estate manager. 'The fact is, Kellaway, I've got myself a grandson!' At the expression on Travis's face, he chuckled. 'No need to look so astounded. The youngster that's here now – you wouldn't know it, but a lot of the village people will, the minute they set eyes on him – is my son Baden's boy.

68

No doubt about it. Spitting image. You only have to look at Baden's pictures – school photographs, the family album, that portrait in the dining room – to know it's the truth. And we had no idea he existed. No notion whatsoever! No wonder the village will be agog.'

'Good lord,' Travis said slowly. 'I see what you mean. It's incredible.' He glanced at Hilary. 'I'll do whatever I can, of course.'

'Thank you,' she said simply. 'But we need to tell you as much of the story as we know. Though there's not much to tell, at the moment. The facts seem to be that Baden and Marianne – Robert's mother, who brought him here – got married only a day or two before the retreat to Dunkirk. Baden was killed, as you know, and so were all his friends and officers who would have known about the marriage. Marianne found herself pregnant and widowed in more or less the same moment, and it would have been very hard for her, but fortunately her previous sweetheart was still willing to marry her and—'

'But how could he do that?' Travis broke in. 'If they were married, and she had no proof that Baden had been killed—'

Hilary explained about the civil marriage. 'It didn't exist in the eyes of the Church, you see, and there must have been a lot of turmoil with the Germans arriving at any moment. Apart from that, the town hall was gutted and all the records were lost. Anyway, that's what happened, and it seems that Marianne and her husband settled down. He accepted Robert as his own, and they had two more children.'

'So why has she come here now?' he asked. 'Why wait so long?'

Again, Hilary explained, telling him the story of the Frenchman's courage in harbouring Allied airmen and soldiers, his incarceration in Buchenwald and his subsequent frailty. 'He never really recovered. Marianne and her sister run a *pâtisserie* in the town to support the family, but when he died, Marianne felt it was time to bring Robert here and introduce him to his father's family.'

'And it's a crying shame she didn't do so a lot sooner,' Gilbert growled. 'The boy could have been having a proper education all this time. Getting to know his background. As he would have if Baden had lived.'

'Yes,' Hilary said quietly. 'There's no doubt that he would have lived here if Baden had not been killed.'

There was a long silence. Travis sat gazing thoughtfully at the floor. At last he said, 'It's a difficult situation. What does she want? Not that I want to pry,' he added hastily. 'Obviously you don't need to tell me any more.'

Hilary shrugged. 'There's no more to tell, really. We don't actually know what she wants, or if she wants anything at all, apart from some support for Robert. We haven't had time to talk about it. She was exhausted this morning – they'd been travelling for days, first through Normandy, then on the ferry to Dover and then here, and, of course, the Coronation has held them up as well – and she went straight to bed. Stephen took Robert out for a walk, but I'm not sure how much the boy told him. Luckily they both speak good English. Marianne's father was an English teacher in the local school and often brought the family to England before the war, and they spoke English to Robert at home. But we haven't had a chance to find out anything more, and we had no warning – they just appeared on the doorstep this morning.'

'I can't think why she never even wrote to us!' Gilbert expostulated suddenly, thumping the arm of his chair with his fist. 'All this time, and she never even sent a letter. Why not, for God's sake? And why not write to let us know she was coming? Did she think we'd close up the house and go away somewhere? Did she think we'd refuse to see her?' He shook his great silver head. 'Baden's son. My grandson.' His voice dropped to a murmur, as if he were talking only to himself. 'All these years ...'

70

Hilary glanced at him, realising again what a blow this had been for him. Robert's sudden appearance had been a shocking reminder of his dead son, but it had been more than that. It had brought home to him what he had missed all these years. Not just his son, who had been snatched away by war, but the years of Robert's own childhood, years when Gilbert should have been able to watch him grow, to teach him about his heritage. Years that had slipped away and could never be given back.

'I'm sure Marianne will tell us all that, Father,' she said, reaching out a hand to him. 'She's here now, and that's what matters most. We can find out about the past, but it's the present we have to live in.'

'And the future we have to think about,' he replied. 'There's a lot to be considered, Hilary.'

Travis moved again. 'So what would you like me to do?'

Hilary turned back to him quickly. 'Well, more or less what we said. Go to the pub, if you wouldn't mind, and just see what people are saying. There might not be any talk at all yet,' she added a little doubtfully. 'It's only Jacob and Luke who have seen Robert, as far as we know, and neither of them are gossips. But if people do begin to talk, well, just say that they're relatives from France. And if anyone remarks on the resemblance ...' She hesitated, looking at her father. 'I don't know, what *do* we want Travis to say?'

'We can't ask him to lie,' Gilbert said firmly. 'And for the umpteenth time, as you said yourself, we've nothing to be ashamed of. Nothing at all.'

'I know, but ... I just feel we ought to be more sure of ourselves before—'

'Look,' Travis said, 'suppose I just remain non-committal about the whole thing. I'm quite happy to say they're relatives from France, because that's true, and I'm happy to agree that there's a family resemblance, and if anyone asks any more than that, I shall simply say that it's family business and that's all.

I'm sorry, but I'm afraid there's bound to be some speculation and gossip if Robert really does look as like Baden as you say, and if some villagers are likely to notice that—'

'They'll *all* notice it,' Hilary said gloomily. 'It really is quite startling. Everyone knew Baden. They'll see it straight away.'

'Then it seems to me,' Travis said, getting to his feet and staying there this time, 'that you've got more important matters than estate business to discuss this afternoon. And I've got plenty to do outside, so I'll be getting on with it. If there's going to be the amount of speculation you expect, then you need to have some answers. And perhaps it would be better if I don't bring Jennifer to see you until things are a bit more settled.'

'Yes, perhaps it would,' Hilary said reluctantly. 'Tell her we're sorry, will you? We'll make it as soon as possible. You're right, we really can't leave this any longer. We need to talk to Marianne at once.'

'And what about Robert?' Gilbert demanded. 'What's he going to be doing while we're having this discussion? Where is he now?'

'He went up to his room. I think he was going to read for a while.'

'Boy can't be expected to coop himself up reading all afternoon,' Gilbert stated. 'Get Stephen to take him out again. He can go in that sports car of his.'

'Stephen ought to be with us. He has a right to know what's going on, too.'

'I'll take him,' Travis offered. 'He can come round the estate with me. I'll have a look at this Dutch barn Isaac Endacott wants to put up, and I've got to go to a couple of the other farms as well. It might not be very interesting for him, but it'll keep him out of the way for a few hours.'

'Interesting? Of course it'll be interesting!' Gilbert exclaimed. 'It's a good idea for him to see what estate business is about. After all ...' He caught Hilary's eye and stopped abruptly. 'Well, that's one of the things we've got to decide. Very well, Travis, you take the boy with you. It's good of you to offer. I appreciate it. And I'll appreciate your tact over what the village has to say, as well. Beyond the call of duty, I know.'

Travis shrugged slightly and followed Hilary from the room. In the corridor, she turned to him and said, 'I appreciate it, too, Travis, and I'm sorry all this should happen the day you've told us your good news. I'm afraid we haven't given it the attention it deserves. But I promise we will, once the dust has settled. And I hope – no, I *believe* – that you'll be very happy with Jennifer. She's the right person for you.'

There was a brief moment of silence, then he nodded and said, 'Thank you, Hilary.'

He turned to walk along the passageway, and Hilary followed him. She had the sensation of folding something away into a corner of her heart, where it would stay for ever but never be opened again. She sighed, and let it go. As Travis had said, there were other matters to think about now.

Chapter Eight

'And Jacob Prout told me he saw the boy and that he've got a real Napier look about him,' Dottie said as she took a Victoria sponge from the oven and tested it gently with the tip of her finger. The little dent bounced back, and she nodded with satisfaction and set the tin on a wire rack on the kitchen table beside its other half. 'So who can he be, d'you reckon? You didn't catch no glimpse of them when you called in, did you?'

'No, I didn't.' Stella felt uncomfortable. 'It's not our business, anyway.'

'To be sure, it isn't,' Dottie agreed. 'Not that I ever heard tell of any connections in France,' she added thoughtfully, 'but then us don't know all the ins and outs of the family.'

'No, probably not,' Stella said, hiding a smile as she reflected that the village grapevine must have broken down if it hadn't uncovered every last member of the Napier family. 'Anyway, if they want us to know, I expect we'll find out soon enough. They'll probably bring them to church on Sunday, if they stay until then.'

Dottie's face cleared. 'Of course they will. Now, I'm going to put some of my new strawberry jam in this sponge when it cools down, and it'll be ready for you to take to Felix next time you goes over there. He'll be glad of a bit of cake, I know.'

'I think he's been given quite a lot already,' Stella said, thinking of the three cakes she had seen in Felix's larder only an hour or two previously. 'His new parishioners don't intend to let him starve.'

Dottie sniffed. 'Maybe not, but I've never thought much of the baking over in Little Burracombe. It won't do him no harm to have a decent Victoria in the cupboard. You take it to him, with my compliments.'

'I will, but I really don't think you should keep using your sugar ration in this way,' Stella said firmly. 'Felix has got to get used to his new parishioners, *and* their baking, and they've got to get used to him. And we'll have a new curate here ourselves, soon. Mr Harvey told me yesterday they've almost decided on one, and he'll probably start in September.'

'I shan't be baking for his teas, though,' Dottie pointed out. 'You won't be bringing him back here the way you've been bringing Felix. Anyway, it's not just my sugar ration I'm using, it's yours too!'

'Yes, I suppose it is. And I'm never really sure how you manage to stretch it so far. Listen, Dottie, I honestly don't think you need worry about Felix starving. Just give him something to look forward to when he comes here.'

Dottie sniffed again but said no more. Stella went up to her room for an hour or so, preparing for the next day's lessons, and by the time she came down with some posters to take along to the school, the sponge was filled with jam and in a tin, ready to take across to Felix. She smiled to herself but made no comment, knowing that Dottie just wanted the last word, and in any case had made this cake specially for Felix and intended him to have it.

Marianne had also been baking cakes when Hilary came into the kitchen to ask if she would come to the drawing room.

'We ought to have some time together before Stephen goes back this evening,' she said, conscious of Mrs Ellis chopping meat and vegetables at the kitchen table. 'It may be a while before he can come home again.'

Marianne looked at the mixture in her bowl. 'I must finish

this first. It needs to go into the oven as soon as I have mixed it. Perhaps I can ask Mrs Ellis to take it out for me.'

'Course I will, m'dear. You go on now. Would you like me to bring some tea in?' the housekeeper asked Hilary.

'That would be nice. About three o'clock or so, perhaps.' Hilary looked at Marianne, who was busy beating eggs into the mixture. 'Can you find your way back to the drawing room, or shall I wait?'

'I'll see she gets there all right,' Mrs Ellis promised, and Hilary went back to where her father and brother were waiting.

'She's just putting something in the oven. She won't be more than a few minutes. Have you thought what you want to say, Dad?'

'I should have thought it was obvious what I want to say,' he growled. 'You're the one who's been insisting we need more facts, so I'll ask her about this marriage – just how legal it was – and what's been going on since. But what I really want to know is why she hasn't come before, or at least got in touch. I've said it before and I'll say it again: that boy's my grandson, and I had a right to know about him.'

Hilary's heart sank. 'There's no point in being belligerent—'

'*Belligerent*? I'm just asking for my rights, that's all!'

'But she has rights, too, and she's had a very difficult life. We all want to know the answers to those questions, and I'm sure she'll tell us, but we can't treat her like a criminal. She's the girl Baden married. He loved her, so she deserves our care and consideration.'

'And the boy has rights, too,' Stephen put in. 'He was telling me this morning how—'

Gilbert rounded on him. 'Rights! Yes, the boy *does* have rights, and that's another thing I want to ask that mother of his. Why didn't she bring him here before so that he could get to know about his family and his inheritance?'

There was a brief, stunned silence. Before anyone could speak again, the door opened and Marianne came in to the room. She glanced quickly from one to another and hesitated, her hand on the doorknob.

'Perhaps I should come back later.'

'No.' Hilary went towards her, her hand held out. 'Come in and sit down, Marianne. That's a comfortable chair, there. We felt we ought to have a chat before Stephen goes back, so that we have some idea of what you want to do.'

The Frenchwoman sat down in the chair Hilary had indicated. It was one of the big armchairs, and her petite figure looked almost lost in it. She turned her dark eyes on each of them in turn, her full lower lip very slightly trembling, and then she glanced up and saw the photograph of Baden in his Army uniform, standing on the mantelpiece.

'I have no photographs of Baden,' she said wistfully. 'My father took one at the wedding, but it was lost when the Germans came. Perhaps you can spare one for me to take back to France?'

'Of course!' Hilary exclaimed. 'We'll sort some out for you. You shall have as many as you like.'

'Thank you.' She inclined her dark head and waited, looking at Gilbert.

Hilary spoke again, afraid that her father would bulldoze in with his usual forthrightness. 'There are quite a few things we'd like you to tell us, Marianne. About yourself and Baden, of course, and about your life since then, but also, why did you decide to come now? And what do you want to do next?'

'You are anxious, I know,' she said. Her voice was low but composed, and she met Hilary's gaze steadily. 'It has taken me some time to deal with my husband's affairs and to look to the future, and my sister and I also had our work in the *pâtisserie* ... There has been very little time, you understand.'

'All the same,' Gilbert said, his voice rather more restrained

77

now, 'a letter, once the war was over, to let us know about Robert, and about you and Baden ...'

'We could perhaps have helped,' Hilary said gently, but Marianne shook her head.

'My husband brought Robert up as his own. He knew, of course, that he was Baden's child, but we were married before he was born, and he always considered him his son. I could not ...' she seemed to search for the right word, and eventually found it, '... *humiliate* him by asking help for Robert and not my other children. Or even for asking for help at all. He was a proud man, you see, and he had suffered much.'

'Yes, I do see,' Hilary said quietly. 'But now?'

'Now, I think it is right that Robert should know where his father came from. It is right that he should know something of his history.'

'He thinks so, too,' Stephen said. He had been sitting in the window, slightly apart, watching the others. 'He talked to me this morning, while we were out. He had no idea Baden's home was going to be like this; he thought it would be just a farmhouse.'

Hilary glanced in surprise at Marianne. 'Didn't you ever tell him?'

'I did not know, either,' Marianne said. 'Baden told me only that his family had a large house and some land. I did not know until this morning that it was so big, or that you had more than one farm.'

The Napiers stared at each other, and Stephen gave a low whistle. 'A large house and some land! Well, I guess that more or less sums us up!'

'Don't be facetious, Stephen!' his father said sharply, and turned back to Marianne. 'Do you mean you had no suspicion that Baden came from a family like ours, a family that goes back many generations, with responsibilities as well as privilege?'

'We did not have much time for talking about such things,' Marianne said softly.

There was another brief silence, then Gilbert cleared his throat.

'Well, it seems we all have a great deal of talking to do now. But I'd still like to know just *why* you came at this particular time. To let Robert see where his father came from – yes. To ask for help – yes. But what sort of help, Madame Aucoin? What are you expecting of us?'

Stephen threw his sister a now-we're-coming-to-it look, and Hilary frowned at him, though she silently agreed. It was a question that had to be asked, although she would have liked it to be asked less bluntly. But perhaps her father was right. Marianne seemed to be a direct kind of person, and might prefer directness in return.

Marianne, however, seemed less willing to give a complete answer. She shrugged a little and said, 'That is for you to decide. As you say, Robert is your grandson – your only grandson, I think? – and you must have certain wishes. I expect you need some time to consider. I cannot ask you to make any provision without thinking it all over very carefully.'

Gilbert nodded. 'Quite right. There's a great deal more to be discussed and I shall need to see my lawyer as well at some stage. We'll go into as much as possible while you're here and then, when I've consulted further and made whatever arrangements seem suitable, you can return. No doubt there will be documents to sign and so forth. Meanwhile, I suggest you leave young Robert here with us.'

Hilary gasped and glanced quickly at Marianne. She caught a flicker of expression in the Frenchwoman's dark eyes, but it was gone before she could identify it. She turned her head towards Stephen, and found her brother looking as bemused as she felt.

'Leave Robert here?' Marianne said.

'He is my grandson,' Gilbert stated. 'He needs to know about the estate, about Burracombe itself. He needs to see more of his father's heritage than he can understand in only a few days. And there is his education to consider as well.'

'Then he can't possibly stay,' Hilary said. 'He has to go back to school. He must be missing it now, isn't he, Marianne?'

'A little,' she said dismissively. 'But he is a clever boy, he will soon catch up. However, our holidays begin soon, and are longer than yours. There is no reason why he should not stay for a while.'

'But would he *want* to? Without you? Who would look after him?'

'He does not need a nursemaid,' Marianne said.

'For heaven's sake!' Gilbert exclaimed. 'Aren't you capable of keeping an eye on a boy of thirteen, Hilary? He doesn't need spoon-feeding, for God's sake. Anyway, I shall be spending quite a lot of time with him myself, and you and Travis can take him about with you, too. As his mother says, a few weeks off school won't do any harm, and we need to think about where he should go in September.'

'Where he should . . . Father, aren't you rushing things? He lives in France, with his family, and that's where he goes to school. You're not going to disrupt all that, are you?'

'Madame Aucoin has come to us for help,' he said unequivocally. 'The boy's my grandson, and obviously I wish to do for him whatever Baden would have done. That includes his education.'

'But Baden is *dead*!' Hilary cried. 'Things are different. He hasn't grown up here; he grew up in France as another man's son. You can't pretend that hasn't happened.'

'I don't have any intention of doing that. But I *will* do for him what's right.' Gilbert glared at her. 'I'm not making any instant decisions, but some things are perfectly clear to me, and I cannot for the life of me see what your objections are. And you don't have to remind me that Baden is dead,' he growled.

Hilary gave Stephen another quick look, and he pursed his lips and shrugged, as if to say there was no more to be done.

'Maybe we should ask Robert himself what he wants,' he said. 'We're all talking about him as if he were a horse, or a dog. You say he has rights, but nobody seems to be considering what rights *he* thinks he has.'

'You said yourself he wants to know more about his heritage,' Gilbert snapped.

'I didn't say he wanted to stay here for the rest of his life!' Stephen retorted, and they glared at each other.

Hilary sighed and sank back in her chair. 'Are you really happy for Robert to stay here for a few weeks?' she asked Marianne.

'But yes. It will be good for him, and he is quite old enough to be away from his mother. You need have no fear; he is not a troublesome boy.' She turned back to Gilbert. 'If you are happy with this arrangement, I will stay for a week. I would like to see the places Baden has told me about: the village green with the great oak tree; the church and the little school; and the bridge with its ... what do you call it? A fjord?'

'A ford,' Stephen said. 'I'll see if I can wangle another weekend pass and come back on Friday to take you about a bit. There'll be a fortnight's leave during the summer as well. If you let us know when you'll be back, I'll see if I can fit in with that, too.'

'Thank you,' she said, and gave him a smile that made him blink. She really is a very attractive woman, Hilary thought, and must have been very pretty when Baden had married her. It was easy to see why he had fallen for her in those chaotic weeks.

She wondered what would have happened if Robert had turned out to resemble Marianne instead of his father. It would have been much more difficult for her to prove, and more difficult for Gilbert to accept.

Her father was speaking again.

'I'll get John Wolstencroft down to go into the legal side. We'd better have a few in for dinner one evening, too, Hilary

– the Latimers and the Harveys, for a start. And Constance Bellamy, of course. Ask Arnold Cherriman and his wife, too. By the way, didn't we invite Kellaway and Miss Tucker in for drinks tomorrow evening?'

'We postponed it, Father.'

'Well, lay it on again. No reason why they shouldn't come now. Be a good idea for Madame Aucoin to meet as many people as possible before she goes back to France, especially those who have an interest in the place. Organise the dinner party for Saturday, Stephen will be here again then.' His voice was brisk, as if issuing orders to his junior officers. 'Church on Sunday, of course, and—'

'Excuse me.' Marianne's voice broke in, and he stopped, startled. 'Robert and I are Roman Catholics. We shall need to attend our own church, if there is one near enough.'

Gilbert stared at her. '*Roman Catholics*? But—'

'That is why our marriage wasn't recognised by the Church,' she said. 'My family is Roman Catholic, and so was my husband. Naturally, we brought Robert up in our faith.'

'But ... but ...' For the first time, Napier looked completely nonplussed. He spluttered a little and then said, 'But *Baden* wasn't RC.'

'If we had married in the Church,' she said, 'and we would have done, *certainement*, if there had been time, he would have had to agree to Robert being brought up as a Catholic. It would have been no different.'

Gilbert drew in a deep breath, and Hilary, seeing his colour rise, tried to interpose. 'Father, don't get upset.'

'Upset? Of course I'm upset! We've always been Church of England, always. We're strongly attached to the village church. The vicar's living here is in our gift. I can't accept that Baden would have agreed to such a thing.'

'He wouldn't have had a choice,' Hilary began, and Stephen said, 'He could hardly be brought up Church of *England* anyway, Father – not when he lived in France!'

82

Gilbert glowered at his son. 'I've already told you, this is no time to be funny!'

'I'm not being funny. It's true. In any case, there's enough to think about without bringing religion into it. I don't suppose Marianne will object to meeting Basil Harvey at dinner.'

'Of course not,' Marianne agreed. 'And please, Colonel Napier, don't call me Madame Aucoin. I am your daughter-in-law – you must call me Marianne, as Hilary and Stephen do.' She turned to Hilary. 'Is there a church nearby that we can attend?'

'Well, yes. There's a Roman Catholic church in Tavistock. I'll take you there in the car. Or Stephen can. I ought to be at our own service.' Hilary was beginning to realise that this visit might have even more complications than she had thought. Roman Catholics were, she knew, punctilious about attending mass every Sunday, and on quite a few other days, too. If Robert were to stay for any length of time, that would have to be taken into account.

'Why not come out for a walk round the village now?' she suggested. 'I can show you the things Baden told you about – the bridge and the ford and so on – and we're bound to meet a few people. I'd like to introduce you to some of my friends, too; Val and Luke, if they're around, and Stella. That's all right, isn't it, Father? We don't need to talk about anything else now, do we?'

'I suppose not,' he grunted. 'Plenty to be going on with, and the boy's out with Travis. Yes, it might be a good thing for Madame ... er, Marianne to see the village. As long as you don't mind people being curious about you,' he added to the Frenchwoman. 'Don't often see foreigners in Burracombe.'

'It is the same at home,' Marianne said. 'Our village is small, and I am sure that when you come to visit us there, people will be just as curious.'

Hilary thought it was unlikely that her father would ever visit Marianne's village, but she said nothing, and at that moment Mrs Ellis knocked on the door and came in with a tray of tea. 'I've taken your cake out of the oven,' she said to Marianne. 'And very nice it looks, too. I'll pop out to the kitchen garden and pick some of they strawberries to go with it, if you like.'

'Oh no, I will do that myself,' Marianne said, accepting a cup of tea. 'We are giving you enough trouble, I think. But first, Hilary is going to show me your pretty village.'

'And I'll get on with my packing,' Stephen said, taking a slice of fruit cake. 'I'll have to leave straight after dinner.' He grinned. 'It's been quite an eventful forty-eight hours. A Coronation, and a new sister-in-law and nephew. Who says life is dull in a Devon village?'

Chapter Nine

'I hope you're happy about this,' Hilary said, as they walked down the drive together. 'You don't have to go into the village if you don't want to. After all, you only arrived this morning.'

'It is the reason I came,' Marianne replied. 'To see Baden's home and meet some of the people who knew him. And I do not feel – what is the word? – *conspicuous*.'

Hilary glanced sideways at her. She was dressed in the red costume she had arrived in that morning, and would attract immediate attention in the village.

'I think people will notice you, all the same,' she said dryly.

They came out through the big gates and on to the road leading into the village. Ted Tozer was standing at the field gate opposite, calling his cows in for afternoon milking. He held the gate closed for a few minutes to allow the two women to walk by.

'Hello, Ted,' Hilary greeted him. 'Has everyone recovered from the celebrations yesterday?'

'Our Tom had a bit of a thick head this morning,' he said with a grin. 'And not the only one, I dare say. Those barrels Bernie sent down from the pub were a deal lighter when us took 'em back this morning. You all surviving up at the Barton?'

'Yes, thanks, Ted.' Hilary glanced at her companion. 'Marianne, this is our nearest neighbour, Mr Tozer. He farms next door to us, and you'll probably meet some more of his family, too. In fact, we might call in at the house sometime, and say hello to old Mrs Tozer as well. Ted, this is Madame Aucoin, a relative from France. She and her son Robert arrived this morning to stay for a few days.'

'How do you do?' Marianne said, holding out her hand.

Ted looked at it and then at his own. 'I don't reckon I'd better shake hands, seeing as mine are covered in cow-muck. But I'm pleased to meet you, all the same. France, you say? Quite a journey, that be.'

'It was not so bad. I used to come to England every year with my father, before the war, so I am used to it.'

The cows were ambling across the field and pressing against the gate now, so Hilary said, 'We'd better get out of your way, Ted. Come on, Marianne.'

'There are not many cows where I live,' Marianne remarked. 'It is mostly crops and orchards.' She glanced down at her feet in their black patent leather shoes.

'Your roads are probably cleaner, then,' Hilary said with a smile. 'I hope your shoes don't get spoiled. I could have lent you a pair of my boots, but I think they'd be too big for you.'

They came to the centre of the village and paused by the green in the shade of the great oak tree. After the bustle of the day before, the village was quiet, and there was nobody to be seen. On the far side of the green, the Bell Inn was still a riot of colour, with a huge Union flag stretched across its front and Dottie Friend's barrels outside, planted with red, white and blue flowers. Several other gardens had followed her lead, and it looked as if another giant flag had been dropped over them. The church lychgate stood welcomingly open but Hilary, who would normally have taken any visitor to see the old church as a matter of course, hesitated.

'Do you want to see inside? I'm not sure whether Roman Catholics—'

'But of course. It is where Baden used to go. Besides,'

Marianne added, with the first touch of humour Hilary had seen in her, 'it would have been a Roman Catholic church once, would it not?'

'Yes, I suppose it would,' Hilary agreed, surprised. 'I've never really thought about it that way. But you're right. All the old churches would have been.'

They walked up the path between the gravestones, and Marianne paused beside the war memorial and read the names carved into its plinth after the Second World War. Baden's was amongst them, and she bowed her head for a moment. Hilary cursed herself for not having thought of this, and laid her hand gently on the Frenchwoman's arm.

'I'm sorry. I should have mentioned it.'

'It is no matter. I am glad he is remembered here.'

'Of course he is. He'll always be remembered. All the village knew Baden.'

They went on up the path and into the porch. There was a stone bench on each wall, and noticeboards fixed above, with information such as flower rotas and the vicar's and wardens' addresses. The door was framed by a rounded archway, thickly carved with sinuous, twining branches and leaves; if you looked closely you could even discover a bird or two peeping out, and there was one, almost impossible to see, that was sitting on a nest. It was a game amongst the children of the village to find it when they first started to come to church, and it was seldom revealed to visitors.

Hilary pushed open the ancient oak door, and they stepped down inside. It was dim and cool, the only light coming through the stained-glass window over the altar and the plain ones along the sides. As they stood there, the sun came out and shone through the windows along the south wall, casting a pearly glow on the round pillars.

Marianne moved along the nave, pausing now and then to study the flagstones at her feet, many of them carved with the names of those who lay in the vaults beneath. On the walls were stone memorials and even a few brasses of long-dead Napiers and other people of importance in the village, but mostly the walls were of plain stone, quarried long ago from nearby hillsides.

'It's so bare,' she said at last. 'Our churches are full of colour.'

'So would these have been once,' Hilary said thoughtfully. 'I believe some old churches have murals on their walls, under the plaster that was put on later. Probably we did, too, but they've all been scraped away. All that sort of thing was destroyed or hidden in the Dissolution, when Cromwell – Thomas Cromwell, that was, not Oliver – dissolved the monasteries and tore out anything that was Catholic.'

Marianne glanced at her, and Hilary realised that English history meant nothing to her. Nor would it to Robert, she thought, even though it was part of his heritage.

'The window is beautiful,' Marianne said, looking up at the colourful panes above the altar. 'Why were they not destroyed as well?'

'The original ones were. These are later. But we do have a small piece of pre-Reformation glass.' Hilary led her along the south transept and pointed to a tiny window, the sunlight illuminating the rich crimson and purple robes of two figures and the deep blue of the sky behind them. 'Somehow, that survived. In some churches you can see windows of higgledy-piggledy old glass because someone salvaged the smashed pieces and tried to put them together, like a jigsaw.'

'Higgledy ... piggledy?' Marianne repeated. 'What is this?'

Hilary laughed. 'Sorry. It means mixed up. Or all at different levels, like roofs when you see them from above, from a church tower or a city wall, for instance.'

Marianne turned to look back down the nave. 'Is that the tower? Can we go up to the top and look at Burracombe from there?'

'I'm afraid not. Ted Tozer keeps the key. The bells are up

there, you see, and it's dangerous for people to go up if they don't know what they're doing. I'll ask Ted if he'll take us one day, though.'

'There are many bells?'

'Six. You'll hear them ringing on Sunday. On Friday evening, too, come to think of it; that's when they practise.'

'Robert would like to see that,' Marianne said in a definite tone.

'Well, it's quite interesting, and two or three village boys of Robert's age are learning to ring. We might be able to persuade Ted to take us up before the practice starts.'

The door opened, and Basil Harvey appeared, peering into the muted light. He caught sight of them and hurried forward.

'Hilary, my dear. People were a little worried that you weren't around this morning. I trust everyone is well?'

'Yes, perfectly well, thank you, Basil. It's just that we had unexpected visitors. This is Marianne Aucoin. She and her son Robert have come to stay for a few days.'

Basil greeted the Frenchwoman warmly, taking one of her hands in both his. 'How nice to meet you. And which part of France do you come from?'

Marianne explained and added, 'It's a small village. Not many people know of it.'

'Well, it's very good to see you here. I wish you a pleasant stay. And perhaps we'll see you in church on Sunday? You'll be very welcome.'

'Marianne is a Roman Catholic,' Hilary said.

The vicar nodded. 'Of course. You'll be wanting to go to Tavistock to worship.'

'One of us will take her,' Hilary said. 'Probably Stephen – he's hoping to get home again this weekend. By the way, we're having a little dinner party for Marianne on Saturday evening – I hope you and Mrs Harvey will be able to come.'

'I'm sure we'll be delighted to. I'll ask Grace; she keeps

my diary tidy, otherwise I'd be trying to be in three places at once.' He rubbed his forehead ruefully. 'Sometimes I find it quite difficult enough, being in only one place at once!'

Hilary laughed and shepherded Marianne towards the door. 'We'll see you at about seven-thirty, then.'

They walked out of the church, blinking in the sudden flush of sunlight. Along the churchyard wall were several azalea bushes, their luxuriant blooms like wide-open yellow, pink and orange mouths. Jacob Prout was moving amongst them, tidying up fallen blossom, and he lifted his hand in acknowledgement, as the two women strolled towards the lychgate. Hilary paused to introduce him.

'I thought that must be your tacker I saw this morning, with Master Stephen,' he said to Marianne. 'Handsome, well set-up youngster, and good manners, too, not like some of the young ones these days. So you'm seeing a bit of the village, Mrs ... ?'

'Madame,' Hilary said. 'Madame Aucoin. But she might not mind Mrs, if you find that difficult to say.'

'Oh, 'tain't difficult,' Jacob said, 'I was telling your boy this morning, I picked up a bit of *français* when I was over there in the first lot. The First World War,' he added, seeing her blank look. 'And how do you like Burracombe, then?'

'I 'ave not seen much of it so far. But it looks very pretty. The cottages with their ... their ...' She glanced enquiringly at Hilary. 'Roofs?'

'Thatched,' Hilary said.

'Yes, thatched roofs. And all the flowers in the gardens, and the hills all around. It is very different where I live.'

'Normandy, would that be?' Jacob asked. 'Ah, terrible flat round there, I remember. All those long straight roads with nothing but poplar trees to be seen for miles. I was glad to get home, I can tell you – not that it were the scenery that was bothering me so much,' he added thoughtfully. 'More like the trenches and the bullets and such. All over now, thank the Lord, and hopefully 'twon't ever happen again.'

'We all hope for that,' Marianne said gravely, and they walked on through the lychgate and across the green. The shops were open again after their day of closure for the Coronation, and a small knot of people was standing outside the general store.

'I won't try to introduce you to everyone,' Hilary said quietly, aware of the heads turning in their direction. 'We'll just walk on down to the bridge. Which other places did Baden tell you about?'

'The school,' Marianne said. 'He said he went to the village school until he was nine.'

'That's right. We all did, and then we went on to our prep schools. You must meet the headmistress, Miss Kemp; she was the infant teacher then. I'm not sure if she'll be there today, though. The school had an extra day off because the children would probably be tired after all the parties. It really is a shame you weren't here yesterday.'

Both Miss Kemp and Stella were in the school, pinning up new posters and preparing sheets of paper for the children to use next day. 'We're going to ask them to make little books about the Coronation,' Stella explained. 'Stories, drawings and poems about how the village celebrated it. We want them to be able to look back at in years to come and remember what Burracombe did on the second of June nineteen fifty-three.'

'That's a lovely idea,' Hilary said. 'I didn't expect to find either of you here now, though.'

'Oh, we can't keep away!' Miss Kemp said. 'And I'm making the most of Stella while I've got her. I'm not looking forward at all to losing her at Christmas.'

'Losing her?' Marianne enquired.

'I'm getting married,' Stella said. 'I'll have to leave then because I'll be living in Little Burracombe.'

The two schoolteachers looked at the stranger with interest, and Hilary hastened to introduce them.

'This is Marianne Aucoin.' Hilary hesitated, realising that this time she would have to give fuller details. 'She was Baden's wife. I told her you'd remember him.'

'*Baden's* wife?' Miss Kemp stared at her. 'But ... I had no idea he was married ...'

'Nor had we. Look, we're not really telling people about it yet – we don't know all that much ourselves ...' She glanced at Marianne, uncertain how much to say.

Stella moved away, feeling like an intruder, but Hilary put out a hand to stop her. 'Don't go, Stella. I know you won't spread anything about.'

'It's all right,' Stella said quickly. She smiled at Marianne. 'It's nice to meet you, but I have to go now. I only popped down with these posters for tomorrow. I'll see you in the morning, Miss Kemp.'

'She seems a nice person,' Marianne said, watching her go. 'Why does she have to go to another part of Burracombe, and why can't she continue to teach?'

'Little Burracombe is another village,' Miss Kemp explained. 'It's over the river. And Stella is marrying the vicar there, so she'll be kept quite busy enough, although we hope she'll be able to come and help us out occasionally. Now, I'm sure you want to know about Baden as a little boy. Why don't you come into the school house, where I live, for a cup of tea?'

Stephen was not to be allowed to escape as easily as he had hoped. He stood up as the two women left the drawing room, and moved towards the door, ready to slip up to his bedroom to start packing, but his father put out a hand to stop him.

'Sit down again, Stephen. We need to discuss this man to man.'

Reluctantly, Stephen did as he was told. He had very little

faith in his father taking notice of anything he had to say. If it hadn't been for Hilary, he thought ruefully, he would have been left out of the discussions altogether. But Gilbert had received a sharp reminder that his younger son still had an interest in the estate and family, and he had obviously decided that he must at least pay lip service to it. Or perhaps he just wanted to win Stephen over to his way of thinking.

'What d'you make of all this, Stephen?' Gilbert asked abruptly. 'No beating about the bush, mind.'

Stephen met his eyes. 'I've never beaten about the bush with you, Father. And I've already told you what I think. You need to move very carefully.'

His father's thick eyebrows came together in a heavy frown. 'What d'you mean by that?'

'Get legal advice. Get *proof*. I know the boy looks like Baden—'

'He doesn't just *look* like him,' Gilbert interrupted. 'He's Baden all over again. He moves like him. There are certain gestures, mannerisms – a turn of the head, a way of standing. You're too young to remember, but Hilary isn't and she agrees with me. That boy is Baden's son, and nobody will convince me otherwise.'

Because you don't want to be convinced, Stephen thought, but aloud he said, 'All right, but he may not be Baden's *legitimate* son. We still need proof of the marriage. And it seems to me that the only document in existence is the certificate Marianne showed us. There's nothing else. There was no church ceremony, and the town hall, where the civil documents were kept, was conveniently destroyed almost immediately afterwards. I just don't see how it *can* be proved.'

There was a short silence. Gilbert sat forward in his armchair, staring at the floor. Stephen fidgeted uneasily, and eventually his father raised his big head and looked him directly in the eye.

'And suppose I don't require such proof?' he said.

It took Stephen a moment or two to understand what he meant. Then he said, 'You mean you'll accept him whether he's legitimate or not?'

'Of course I will! The boy's my grandson – *Baden's* son. There's no disputing that. Everyone who sees him will know it at once. If Baden had lived, he would have brought him here and—'

'You don't know that.'

'What do you mean, I don't know that?' Gilbert's voice rose, filling the room. 'Of course he would.'

'I'm sorry, Father, but there's no "of course" about it.' Stephen raised his hand to stem his father's rising anger. 'Look, you said you wanted us to talk about this man to man. You asked me not to beat about the bush. Well, I'm not going to. Just let's suppose for a minute that this certificate isn't authentic, that it's something Marianne has had knocked up by a local printer, for instance. Let's suppose there was no marriage, civil or otherwise. Let's suppose that Baden did what a lot of other young soldiers do and had a flirtation with this girl—'

'A bit more than a flirtation,' Gilbert interrupted.

Stephen inclined his head and went on. 'Let's suppose he would never have gone back – how could he? By the time the war was over, he'd have forgotten all about the French girl he met just before Dunkirk. He'd have met quite a few others in those years, he'd quite probably have fallen in love with one, he might even have married and had other children. Other sons. *Legitimate* sons.'

'And if I supposed anything of the sort, just what difference would it make?'

'It would mean that Robert was not the heir. If Marianne had contacted him after the war, Baden would probably have sent her some money, and that would have been that.'

There was another silence. Then Gilbert, his face tight with anger, said, 'You suppose a great many things, Stephen, but you forget a great many more. For one thing, Baden was a man of honour. He would never have behaved like that – taking advantage of a young girl, leaving her expecting his child. He *married* her. I don't have any doubt about that, any doubt at all.'

'He was a young soldier at war in a foreign country. He did what almost every other young man would do.' Stephen stirred restlessly, frustrated by his father's determination to believe what he wanted to believe. 'Don't you realise what it is for a young man to realise that he might be killed at any moment, never knowing what it is to love a woman? Weren't you ever in that position yourself?'

'That's enough!' Gilbert thumped his fist on the small table beside him and it tipped over, sending his empty coffee cup sliding to the carpet. 'Leave it,' he commanded impatiently as Stephen moved to rescue it. 'You're going too far. I won't listen to such impertinence. I've told you, Baden was a man of honour – unlike, it seems, his younger brother. I hope we're not going to get a stream of young women through the front door carrying *your* by-blows.'

Stephen flushed with anger. 'No, we're not. But I still think—'

'That's the trouble with you, Stephen. You either don't think at all, or you think too much. And none of it matters anyway. Whatever Baden did or didn't do, I believe he married this young woman – and it's the civil ceremony that counts in law – and the boy is Baden's legitimate son. If Baden had lived, he would have sought the girl out at the end of the war, and brought her and the child here to Burracombe. There is no doubt in my mind that that is what he would have done. And that being the case, my course of action is clear.'

'You mean to make him your heir,' Stephen said quietly. 'You mean to keep him here, and leave the estate and everything in it to him. Without knowing any more than that. Without even *considering* Hilary and me.'

'You'll have your inheritance: your mother's money and a sizeable share from me,' Gilbert said brusquely. 'You've made it clear you've no interest in the estate, even though you could have had it handed to you on a plate.'

'Just as well I didn't accept it, then,' Stephen said with a short, humourless laugh. 'It would have been snatched away again now, just as it's being snatched away from Hilary.' He stood up and looked down at his father. 'Don't you care about her at all?' he demanded. 'Doesn't it matter to you that she's giving her life to this place, and now you're going to take it away and leave it to a boy we know nothing about? What do you imagine he's going to do? Turn into an English gentleman, striding the moors with his gun and his dogs, farming the land, looking after the tenants? He's *French*, Father, he's been brought up to be a Frenchman. He'll be just as likely to sell the whole lot the minute he inherits, and take the money back to France. Is that really what you want to happen?'

'It won't,' Gilbert said with confidence. 'He's young enough to be taught. He can go to a decent school and learn to be English. For God's sake, don't you think that's what his mother wants? Why else would she bring him here?'

'I can think of several reasons,' Stephen said, turning away. 'But it would be useless to try to explain them to you. All right, Father. You do what you think is best. But please, if you won't think of me – and I quite agree that there's no reason why you should, because I've already decided to make my own way in the world, thank God – then think of Hilary. She deserves better than this.' He moved to the door and stood with his hand on the knob, then turned back. 'And get John Wolstencroft down here for some proper legal advice before you do anything at all.'

He opened the door and went through it, closing it behind him with a restraint that spoke more about his simmering anger than any violent slam would have done, and Gilbert sat very still, breathing heavily, his face darkened by his own temper.

He began to get up, and then sank again heavily into the big armchair. He laid one hand upon his chest, leaned back his head and closed his eyes.

Chapter Ten

'So you'm the French lady, then,' Alice Tozer said, showing Hilary and Marianne into the kitchen. 'Us heard you was about.'

Marianne looked at Hilary, who smiled. 'Burracombe has a very efficient grapevine. Everyone knows your business before you know it yourself.'

'I'm sorry,' Alice said quickly, her hand to her mouth. 'I didn't mean to speak out of turn.'

'I don't understand,' Marianne said. 'I have seen no grape-vines. And what do they have to do—'

'It's another of those English expressions,' Hilary said. 'It means news gets passed along very quickly. I'm sure you have the same kind of thing in French villages.'

Marianne laughed. '*Mais certainement*. We call it "*le télé-phone arabe*".'

'Madame Aucoin and her son are staying with us for a few days,' Hilary told Alice. 'I'm just showing her round the vil-lage. It's their first visit since the war, but Madame Aucoin came here regularly during the thirties, with her father.'

'To Burracombe?' Alice asked in surprise. 'I don't remem-ber seeing you then, Madame.' She stumbled a little over the French pronunciation, and Hilary guessed that she wouldn't even attempt 'Aucoin'.

'No, not to Burracombe, not even to Devon. We used to visit Canterbury and Oxford, mostly. I'm sorry we didn't come here then; it is so beautiful.'

'Well, let's hope you'll come again,' Alice said. 'Now, I dare say you'd like a cup of tea if you've been walking all afternoon. It's turned warm now. And Mother will be pleased to see you; she has a rest most afternoons now, but she'll be downstairs any minute.'

'Well, we had some tea with Miss Kemp and Stella,' Hilary said, 'but we've walked down to the ford since then, and I'm sure we're ready for another cup, aren't we, Marianne?'

Before the Frenchwoman could answer, the door at the foot of the stairs opened, and Minnie Tozer came through. As always, her tiny figure was neatly dressed in a black skirt with a pink blouse, both protected by a snow-white apron, and her grey hair was rolled into a bun. She gave the newcomers a sharp look.

'Afternoon, Miss Hilary. And who be this, then?'

Hilary gave once again the brief explanation that she had settled on for most of the villagers, and introduced Marianne. 'Mrs Tozer is one of the oldest inhabitants of Burracombe, and we're all very fond of her. She was quite ill in the winter, and had us all worried, but she's better now, aren't you, Mrs Tozer?'

'I be that. 'Twill take more than a touch of bronchitis to see me off.' She held out her hand to Marianne. 'Pleased to meet you, my dear.'

Marianne took the small, wrinkled hand and held it for a moment. 'It is a great pleasure to meet you, Mrs Tozer,' she said prettily, and glanced round the big room. 'It is the first time I 'ave ever been into an English farmhouse.'

'I should be taking you into the parlour, by rights,' Alice apologised. 'But Miss Hilary always says she'd rather be in the kitchen and I never thought—'

'It's perfectly all right, Alice,' Hilary said firmly. 'We'll sit down here with you.' She turned back to Marianne. 'Is this very different from a French farmhouse?'

'In some ways. In others, it is just the same.' She watched

99

as Alice took a tin from the larder and began to set flapjacks on a plate. 'What are those biscuits?'

'They'm flapjacks, maid. I make them with porridge oats and golden syrup. Full of goodness, they be. Try one.'

Marianne took one and bit it cautiously. 'Just oats and – what did you say?'

'Golden syrup. It's like treacle, only treacle's black.' Alice took the familiar green tin from the larder and showed it to her. 'It's sweet as sugar but it was never put on ration, so we could use as much as we could get hold of during the war.'

Marianne examined the tin, with its picture of a dead lion surrounded by buzzing bees. 'What does this mean – "Out of the strong came forth sweetness"?'

'Well, it's from the Bible, iddin it, my dear? That old story about Samson and the honey-bees nesting in the lion's body. That's where Samson got his strength from, you see, and it means it's good for you.'

'But this is not honey.'

'No, and I can't say I believe it's as good as proper honey, neither, but a good flapjack will get you through the day better than any other sort of biscuit,' Alice said firmly. 'And there's farmhouse butter from our own dairy in it, too, so you eat that up, my dear, and here's your tea to go with it.'

Marianne nibbled the flapjack a little doubtfully, then nodded. 'It's good. But I cannot eat all of it. Perhaps half …'

'I'll eat the other half,' Hilary said. They had been given ginger biscuits with their tea at the schoolmistress's house, and still had dinner to come, which Mrs Ellis was sure to make a hearty one, since it was Stephen's last evening. She turned back to Alice. 'Has Jackie gone back to Plymouth?'

'She have,' Alice said with a grim note in her voice, and Hilary took the hint and looked for another subject. At that moment the kitchen door opened and Joanna came in, carrying the baby, with Robin close behind her. She paused at the sight of the visitors, but Robin marched confidently over to stand beside Hilary.

'Hello, Robin. Did you enjoy the party yesterday?'

He nodded. 'Daddy fell in the river.'

Hilary laughed. 'He was going over the greasy pole, wasn't he? I think there were quite a few people who fell in the water trying to do that.'

Robin turned his large brown eyes on Marianne, who returned his gaze gravely. Joanna took a step forward.

'This is Marianne Aucoin,' Hilary said. 'She and her son are staying with us for a few days. Marianne, this is Joanna Tozer; she's married to Alice's son Tom.'

Marianne stood up and held out her hand. 'How do you, do, Mrs Tozer? I'm pleased to meet you.'

'You'd better call me Joanna – three Mrs Tozers are too much for anybody to cope with!'

'Joanna,' Marianne said carefully, making sure of the pronunciation. 'And these are your children?' She came closer to peep at Heather, cradled in Joanna's arms. 'Oh, so beautiful. *Two* such beautiful children, and do you have any others?'

Joanna gave her a quick look, then glanced at Hilary, who pulled herself together and took charge. 'Robin's Joanna's eldest. He'll be starting school in September. He does a lot of work on the farm already, don't you, Robin? He helps collect eggs and feed the hens, and he even helps milk the cows. A real little farmer, aren't you, Robin?' She heard her voice babbling, apparently without any effort from herself, and wondered if she could stop it. Fortunately, Alice, who had been in the larder again, came out with a plate of rock buns.

'I made these specially for you,' she told her grandson. 'Sit up to the table and I'll get you a glass of milk.'

'May I hold the baby, please?' Marianne asked Joanna, holding out her arms.

The other woman hesitated. 'I'm not sure … she doesn't always go to people she doesn't know …'

'Oh, all babies love me.' Marianne kept her arms held out, and Joanna, with another glance at Hilary, reluctantly laid the baby in them. The Frenchwoman cradled Heather against her, crooning softly, and Hilary watched with a mixture of emotions. This woman had borne Baden's child, and others as well, and now – if her father really acknowledged Robert as his heir – would have the right to make Burracombe Barton her home, if she so desired. While Hilary, who had lived here all her life and helped make the estate what it was now, would have scarcely any rights at all. I'll be like the spinster daughters, sisters and aunts of a hundred years ago, she thought, eking out my existence in my own room, at everybody's beck and call to do the tasks they don't want to do.

She glanced at Joanna, and the moment of self-pity passed as she remembered what Joanna had lost. It was hard for her to hand her precious baby over to a complete stranger, and to take up the reins of normal life again. That was reality. What Hilary had been thinking was, as yet, nothing more than speculation.

'We ought to be going,' she said. 'Marianne's been travelling for several days to come here and she's still tired. I expect you'll want to rest before dinner,' she added to the Frenchwoman.

'Perhaps.' Marianne handed the baby back to Joanna. 'But I will come again, if I may. Such a beautiful baby ... And thank you for the tea and the ...' She glanced at Hilary, who supplied the word. 'The flapjack. It was delicious.'

She bade Minnie goodbye, bending over the old woman in her chair by the range, and shook Alice's hand. She held out her hand to Joanna as well, then smiled, shaking her head at herself. 'You have your hands full with the baby! And goodbye, Robin. I will see you again, I am sure.'

'Goodbye, Mrs Tozer,' Hilary said, shepherding her visitor out into the farmyard. 'Thank you for the tea, Alice. I'll pop in again soon. 'Bye, Joanna; bye-bye, Robin.' She closed the door behind her. The three Mrs Tozers looked at each other.

'Well!' Alice said. 'What do you make of that?'

'What is there to make of it?' Joanna said indifferently. 'It's a bit queer, Hilary taking her to see Miss Kemp and then bringing her here, that's all – she don't usually bring her smart visitors round the village. But I don't see there's anything else to make of it.'

'Smart?' Alice said thoughtfully. 'I don't know so much about that, Joanna my dear. That costume of hers was smart once, I'll grant you, and it's been looked after, but it's seen better days. I doubt she's got money. And I'll tell you something else. Jacob Prout said he saw the boy this morning – well set-up young chap, about twelve or thirteen years old, he reckoned – and he said ... well, I dunno as I ought to repeat it. 'Tis just gossip after all and nobody knows the truth, but since it's just between the three of us and won't go no further ...'

'Oh, come on, Mother!' Joanna exclaimed impatiently. 'What did he say?'

'He said the boy's the image of Baden Napier when he were that age,' Alice said impressively. 'The spitting image. Now, what do you make of *that*?'

Nobody in Burracombe would have said that they were gossiping about the visitors at the Barton, and they were certainly not discussed in the village street, yet somehow, in the mysterious way that grapevines work, the news passed around the village until almost everyone knew. People who had heard it in another cottage, while drinking tea with a friend, went home and told their families; someone taking cuttings round to a garden a few houses away mentioned it in the shed; mothers who had been looking after someone else's children for the afternoon were given the news when the children were collected. It was as if news passed between four walls didn't count as gossip, and, since it was usually mentioned in confidence – 'between you, me and the gatepost' – everyone who passed it on genuinely believed that it was going no further.

Val heard it from Joanna when she came round later that afternoon to collect the maternity clothes Joanna had offered her. They went up to the bedroom, and Joanna got the clothes out of the cupboard and spread them on the bed.

'There's these two smocks, and a frock I wore for best, but I'm not sure they'll be much good to you. It was winter when I was expecting, so they might be a bit too warm.'

'Well, it's not exactly tropical now,' Val said, inspecting the clothes. 'And the baby's not due until October so I'll be glad of them then. I like this green one, it's just my colour, and the dark-red will be nice and cheerful. Thanks, Joanna.'

'You're not really big enough to need them yet,' Joanna said, looking at Val's figure, which had only just begun to bloom. 'I thought that was the worst time really, when your own clothes were getting too tight and maternity things were too big.'

'I know,' Val grinned. 'Skirts done up with a safety-pin and one of Luke's shirts worn over the top! But it doesn't seem worthwhile to be making things that will fit for just a month or two. Well, I'll take these, Jo, and thanks very much. Maybe when we go to Tavistock we can find some material to make me a couple of lighter smocks, and perhaps Mum will help me make a frock that won't look too much like a tent.'

'Yes, that's a good idea,' Joanna agreed, but her voice sounded pensive, and Val gave her a quick look.

'You still feel all right about going to Tavi, don't you? I don't want to rush you into anything.'

Joanna smiled at her. 'No, you're not. It's just ... well, other than the Coronation party, I haven't left Heather, even with Mother, since ... you know – and I know Tavistock's only a few miles away but it seems so far, somehow. I mean, going on the bus and everything ... I just like to feel I can get to her quickly if anything ... if anything ...' Her voice wobbled, and Val moved quickly to put an arm around her shoulders.

'Jo, I can understand that perfectly, and I don't want to make you do anything you don't want to do. We'll leave it for now, shall we? Tavistock's not going to go away, and I'll still go almost every day anyway, until I stop work. I can always pop into the fabric shop and have a look on my own.'

Joanna put up a hand and wiped her cheek with the back of her wrist. She gave Val a shaky smile and said, 'Thanks. I know I'm being silly, but—'

'You're not being silly at all. I'd feel exactly the same. Maybe I could bring a few samples back and we could look at them together. I'd really like your help in choosing something.'

'Yes,' Joanna said. 'You could do that. But ... oh look, let's do it! I need only be away a couple of hours, and I could ring home from a phone box if I wanted to. I've got to start going out without Heather sometime.'

'I don't see why you can't bring her with you,' Val remarked. 'We could make some sort of sling to carry her in, and take turns. I've seen women in Egypt carrying their babies like that, and I always thought what a good idea it was. The babies love it – they feel they're being cuddled all the time.'

Joanna stared at her. 'That's a really good idea. I could use it around the farm, too. There are plenty of paths I can't take the big pram on, and anyway ...' She stopped abruptly, and Val thought of the big twin pram, donated by Constance Bellamy, which Joanna hadn't used since Suzanne had died in it. She would never use it again, but nothing had been done about getting a new pram.

'I'll tell you what,' she said. 'I'll get some strong fabric – calico or something, like we use for arm slings – and we'll make a baby sling. Then we can go to Tavistock and take Heather with us. How will that be?'

'It'll be lovely,' Joanna said, almost in tears again. 'Thanks, Val.'

'Nothing to thank me for,' Val said briskly, gathering up the smocks. 'Oh, by the way, Luke told me he met Stephen Napier this morning, with a boy. They were going up past the old hut, towards the Standing Stones. Have you heard anything about visitors at the Barton? They weren't there yesterday.'

'Yes, didn't you know? They're French. They arrived this morning, and Hilary brought the mother here this afternoon. Jacob Prout saw the boy, and *he* says he's the image of Baden when he was that age. Luke wouldn't have known, of course, but Jacob's got a good memory and he says there's a real resemblance.'

'Like Baden?' Val said, staring at her. 'And *French*?' They looked at each other for a moment, the same idea in both their heads, then Val turned towards the door. 'Well, I dare say we'll find out soon enough, if there's anything to find out. They're probably Mrs Napier's relatives. It's surprising how likenesses pop up in different parts of a family. I expect Hilary will tell me next time I see her, anyway.'

She went home to Luke, her mind turning over this piece of news as she walked down the track to the village street. Had Isobel Napier had relatives in France? She'd never heard of any, but then there was no reason why she should; she and Hilary had really only become friends when they'd served together in Egypt during the war. It was none of her business, she told herself, but she couldn't help thinking how strange it all seemed.

Chapter Eleven

On Friday evening Travis brought Jennifer to the Barton to receive Gilbert's congratulations. Marianne and Robert joined them all in the drawing room.

'Mr Kellaway and Miss Tucker have just got engaged,' Hilary explained as she handed round glasses of sherry or gin and tonic, with lemonade for Robert. She lifted her glass to Jennifer, and smiled. 'I hope you'll be very happy. When is the wedding going to be?'

'We thought sometime in the autumn,' Jennifer said a little shyly. 'September's a lovely month, with all the colour on the trees. It depends on you, though.'

'On me?' Hilary said, startled.

'On the estate,' Travis said. 'We need to look at when I can be spared, to go on honeymoon.'

'Oh, of course. Well, almost any time. You can leave things in my hands for a couple of weeks. You choose whichever date you like.'

'And there's Val, too,' Jennifer said, sounding anxious. 'Her baby's due then, and I do want her and Luke to be at the wedding; they've been good friends to us.'

'You've been a good friend to them,' Gilbert said. 'Letting them have your cottage.'

'Yes ...' Jennifer still sounded a little worried. 'And that's another thing: I really don't want to turn them out, especially with a new baby.'

'But you won't have to,' Hilary said in surprise. 'Hasn't

Travis mentioned it? You'll have the estate manager's house, where the Cherrimans live. Surely you've told her that?' she asked, turning to Travis.

'I wasn't sure it had been agreed. I know you wanted it for Val and Luke.'

'That was in the past,' she said uncomfortably. 'Father and I have talked about it, and obviously you must have it. And Val says she's happy to stay in Jed's Cottage – if that's all right with you, Jennifer – and Luke will use the old charcoal-burner's hut as a studio.' She remembered their guests then, and turned to Marianne. 'Luke is an artist and the charcoal-burner's hut is a little shack – a small wooden house, not much more than a shed, really – in the woods. He used to live there.'

'I've seen it,' Robert said. 'When Stephen took me to the Standing Stones, Luke was there. I wanted to see his pictures but he was going somewhere.'

'You'll have plenty of time to see them,' Gilbert said gruffly. 'Robert's mother is going back to France next week,' he explained to Travis and Jennifer, 'but Robert is going to stay on.'

'For the summer holidays,' Hilary said swiftly, and caught Travis's quick glance. He knew who Robert was, of course, but she saw no reason to let him know any more than that, not that there was any more to know, at this stage. She could feel her father's gaze on her, too, and hoped he wouldn't take the subject any further, but to her relief he returned to the topic of the estate manager's house.

'Arnold and Evelyn Cherriman have kept it in good order,' he observed. 'But their taste in decorations and such might not be yours, and it's quite a while since anything was done in that respect – paint and decent wallpaper haven't been easy to come by since the war. But now things are looking up, it would be a good time to go through the whole place. Bring it up to scratch. Have a look at the bathroom and kitchen, too, while we're at it, and do a few improvements there.'

'We wouldn't want you to go to too much expense,' Jennifer began. 'Honestly, we could easily live in my cottage if you want the house for someone else.'

Gilbert gave her a fatherly smile. 'It's in our interests to keep the place properly maintained,' he pointed out. 'And it's part of the estate; it's meant for the estate manager. Don't worry about the cost. I'm not talking about doing up Buckingham Palace!'

They all laughed, and Hilary thought with surprise that it was the first joke she'd heard her father make for quite a long time. Clearly, he was in an exceptionally good mood this evening, and it didn't take much to guess why.

She glanced at Marianne, who was listening thoughtfully, and wondered what was going through the Frenchwoman's mind. With a flicker of unease, she remembered that they still didn't know exactly what Marianne had been hoping for when she brought Robert to meet his English family. She hadn't, it seemed, expected to find anything quite like Burracombe Barton, and she might well be revising her ideas about this family, who lived in a large house rather than a farmhouse, and who apparently had other houses to give away to their staff.

The grandfather clock in the hall struck seven, and Jennifer put down her sherry glass.

'We ought to be going now. Thank you so much, Colonel Napier and Hilary. It's been lovely to see you and tell you our plans, and we're very grateful for all you're doing. And it's been nice to meet you, too,' she added, turning to Marianne. 'I hope you enjoy the rest of your stay.' She shook all their hands, including Robert's, and after a few more minutes' conversation, she and Travis took their leave.

'A very pleasant young woman,' Gilbert commented when Hilary returned after seeing them off. 'Sensible, too. She'll make Kellaway a good wife.'

'Yes, she will. Burracombe's been lucky for her.'

'Why has it been lucky?' Marianne asked, as Hilary sat down again. 'I don't quite understand about her. She has her own house here, *n'est-ce pas*? But she lives in Plymouth. It seems strange.'

'Yes, I expect it does,' Hilary said with a smile. 'It's rather complicated, but in a nutshell – to cut the story short, I mean – Jennifer grew up in Plymouth and only came here a year or two ago. She was looking for her ... for a relative.' She stopped, unwilling to reveal Jennifer's family situation to a stranger, but Marianne gave a matter-of-fact nod.

'For her father? Is that what you mean?'

'Well, yes,' Hilary admitted. 'It was quite a long story – it goes back to before the First World War.'

'And did she find him?'

'She did, although he died not long after. But she also found the man who was her mother's real sweetheart all those years ago, and he's been like a father to her. She stays with him when she comes to Burracombe.'

'*Que romantique*,' Marianne said, clasping her hands. 'And how does it happen that she has her own house?'

'Her father left it to her,' Hilary said briefly, not liking so many questions. 'Val and Luke Ferris hadn't anywhere to live when they got married, so she let it to them.' She got up. 'I'll just go and let Mrs Ellis know we're ready for dinner.'

We ought to be careful about discussing family business in front of her, she thought as she walked along the passage. Stephen's right; we don't know nearly enough about her. And this dinner party tomorrow is too soon. In fact, it's all happened too quickly.

Far too quickly.

By the time of the dinner party, other problems had arisen. One of them was what to do with Robert that evening.

'He won't want to spend the evening with a lot of people he's never met before,' Hilary argued. 'Besides, he's too young to be at a dinner party, and he needs to know a bit more about ... well, etiquette and that sort of thing.'

'So what do we do with him?' Gilbert enquired. 'Give him some cheese on toast in the kitchen and send him to bed early with a Rupert book? He may be only thirteen but he seems as self-possessed as an English boy of sixteen or seventeen. And by "etiquette", I suppose you mean table manners.'

'If you like, yes.' Hilary thought of Robert dipping his toast into his coffee. 'I'm not saying they're bad – just different. He needs guidance, that's all. It's not fair to let him make mistakes before he's ready.'

'Well, you've got time to see to that before this evening,' her father told her. 'And if we don't have soup, there shouldn't be much he can go wrong with. Anyway, I want him there. I want people to see him. I want to introduce him as my grandson.'

Stephen, who had arrived home just after lunch, came into the room at that moment and heard his last words. He gave Hilary a quick look and said, 'Do you mean what I think you mean? You're going to tell everyone at this dinner party just who Robert and Marianne are, or who they claim to be?'

'I certainly am. I see no reason to delay.'

'But I thought you were going to get Mr Wolstencroft's advice first.'

'John's coming this afternoon and staying the night,' Gilbert said testily. 'He should be here any minute. We'll have all afternoon to chew this over.'

'And will you take his advice? Even if it goes against what you want?'

'I doubt very much if it will do that. I dare say he'll want to hear the young woman's story and have a look at the boy, but I don't think there'll be any problem. And once we've got that out of the way—'

'Father, you *can't* expect it to be that easy!' Stephen expostulated. 'He can't make a judgement just like that – nobody could. He'll surely want to carry out some kind of investigation.'

'Investigation? What sort of investigation?'

'Well, into her family in France, for a start. He'll want to know that her story is true. She could have told you anything, Father, and you'd have believed it, just on the strength of a resemblance—'

'A resemblance that goes further, as I've already told you, than simply a facial one!' Gilbert bellowed. 'The boy could be Baden all over again. There is not the slightest doubt that he's Baden's son, and in that case—'

'But is he legitimate?' Stephen was as angry as his father. 'And is he the only one? For all we know, Baden played about with any amount of young girls, French and English—'

'*That's enough*!' Gilbert was on his feet, scarlet in the face and breathing hard. 'I won't have you casting such slurs on your brother's name. Get out! *Get out*!'

'Father!' Hilary leaped to her feet, too. 'Father, you mustn't get into such a state. And Stephen, you know Dad shouldn't get so upset; what you said then was completely unnecessary. You should be ashamed of yourself. You should apologise at once.'

Stephen, flushing to the roots of his fair hair, looked abashed. 'All right, I'm sorry about that,' he muttered. 'I don't really believe it. Baden wasn't that sort, I know. But I still think Dad needs to get legal advice before going any further.'

'And that's just what he's doing,' Hilary told him. She turned back to her father. 'Can we hear what Mr Wolstencroft says as well?'

Gilbert sat down again heavily. He had begun to recover himself. His face had lost its lurid colour, although his breathing was still more rapid than Hilary liked.

'No, you can't. Not at first, anyway. I want to have a talk with him alone, without any objections. Tomorrow morning, when we've all had a chance to sleep on it, we'll have a family meeting with him, but until then I'd like to remind you that this is *my* business. You needn't concern yourself about your inheritances,' he added with a flash of bitterness. 'You'll both be looked after, whatever I decide. But if he agrees – as I believe he will – that it is up to me whether I acknowledge the boy as Baden's son, then that's what I shall do.' He glowered up at them from under his heavy brows.

Hilary sighed, and looked at her brother. 'That's the best we're going to get, Steve. And that sounds like a car now. It's probably Mr Wolstencroft.' She glanced down at her father again. 'Are you sure you're fit for this meeting?'

'Of course I am. Ask Mrs Ellis to show him in. And then perhaps the two of you will get out of the house for a few hours. Take Marianne and the boy for a drive somewhere. Show 'em a bit more of the countryside. Leave John and me to have our discussion in peace.'

'That's all very well,' Hilary said tightly. 'But I can't go out for the afternoon. I'll need to see to things here, unless you want to polish glasses and get out the best china and set the table yourself. We can't expect Mrs Ellis to do all that as well as cook a meal for eleven people.'

'Stephen can take them, then,' Gilbert said inexorably. He met their eyes. 'And let's have a bit of family accord at this dinner tonight. No sulking or backbiting, you understand?'

'Yes, Father,' they said in unison, and left the room together. Outside the door, they stopped and gave each other a rueful look.

'I feel like a naughty little boy,' Stephen said.

Hilary nodded. 'The aggravating thing is, he's right. It's going to cause enough talk in the village as it is, without people getting the idea that we're all at each other's throats over it.' The doorbell rang, and she moved forward to answer it as the housekeeper came hurrying from the kitchen. 'It's all right, Mrs Ellis, I'll see to it. It'll be Mr Wolstencroft to see Father. Perhaps you could take them some tea in later? Hello, Mr Wolstencroft,' she said to the lawyer, a tall, thin man with a round, almost hairless head, and sharp blue eyes. 'It's very good of you to come at such short notice, and on a Saturday, too. Father's expecting you in his study, and Stephen and I will see you later.'

'Well, that's that,' Stephen remarked, as the study door closed. 'Nothing more we can do.'

'There never was anything we could do,' Hilary said soberly. 'He made up his mind the moment he first saw Robert, and I don't think anything is going to change it. We shall just have to cope as best we can – and we may as well start now.'

'By doing as we're told, in fact,' Stephen said, and she nodded wryly.

'By doing exactly as we're told.'

'We'll go in my car,' Stephen said, as he led Marianne and Robert out of the house. 'It's more fun than Hilary's or the Land Rover.'

Robert's eyes gleamed at the sight of the sports car which Stephen had driven down from the RAF station in Hampshire, and Marianne's eyebrows rose a little.

'It looks expensive. You must be a very important man in your Air Force.'

'Well, no, not particularly. I'm a pilot and a squadron leader, but that wouldn't pay for this little beauty.' He stopped, the thought occurring to him that it wouldn't be wise to be too forthcoming, and ushered her into the front seat. 'You can sit in the back, Robert; we call it the dicky seat. It's pretty comfortable. Now, where would you like to go?'

'To some of your villages,' Marianne said, and Robert chimed in, 'Over the moor.'

'That's easy enough. We'll do a tour, and I can show you some of the sights.'

This afternoon, Marianne was dressed more suitably for country sightseeing, in a grey skirt that allowed more freedom for walking and the closely-fitting red jacket from her costume of the day before, with a white blouse underneath it.

She was wearing sturdy, low heeled shoes, and barely reached Stephen's shoulder. As he handed her into the car, she glanced up at him, and their eyes met.

'Thank you, Stephen,' she said in a soft voice, touching his hand lightly.

Stephen got in the other side and started the car, his heart skipping a little, aware of Marianne sitting close beside him. He set off down the drive, glad that Robert was with them, and chided himself for feeling disturbed. She's French, he told himself. The French are naturally a bit flirtatious, she didn't mean a thing by it. And she'd been married to Baden, for heaven's sake; she's hardly likely to be interested in you. And you're certainly not interested in her, or in any woman, while Maddy Forsyth walks this earth.

At the thought of Maddy, he sighed. It was only three days since he'd seen her at the Coronation party, yet it seemed like weeks. And although they'd parted on the warmest terms since Sammy's death, she'd made it very clear that there could be nothing but friendship between them. Well, we'll see about that, he thought, changing gear on the hill out of the village. Of course she feels that way now, only a few months after he died, but she won't feel it for ever. And there's something very special between us. I've always known it, and she'll realise it, too, eventually.

'You seem sad,' Marianne remarked, and he jumped slightly. With some determination, he pushed Maddy out of his mind and grinned at the Frenchwoman.

'Just concentrating on my driving. You never know what you're going to meet in these narrow lanes. But we'll be out on the open moor soon, and you'll be able to see the views.'

'Oh, a lake!' Marianne said a few minutes later.

'That's the reservoir. It's not a natural lake; it was flooded years ago. There's a village down there somewhere; you can see it sometimes, when we get a really dry summer. There's not much left of it, of course – they demolished the houses and took away most of the stone – but you can still see the outline of the village street and the foundations and garden walls.'

Marianne shivered. 'I don't think I would like to see that. It would make me think of the ghosts of people who lived there.'

'I would,' Robert said. 'It would be very interesting. Are there any more Standing Stones or circles to see?'

Stephen had to think. 'There are some at Merrivale, I believe. I've never taken all that much notice, to be honest. We'll come back that way, if you like. But you might be interested in some of the old clapper bridges; they're very ancient.'

'Clapper bridges? Bridges that clap?'

Stephen laughed. 'No, I think the people clap when they've crossed them safely!' He glanced sideways at Marianne to see if she realised he was joking, and caught a flash of provocation in her smile. Colouring a little, he turned his eyes back to the road just in time to slow down for a lamb, which was crossing in a leisurely fashion after its mother. 'They're bridges made of huge slabs of granite, with no walls at their sides.'

'Why didn't they have walls?' Robert asked.

'I think it was because they were used by packhorses, and the big panniers they carried needed more space at the sides.' Stephen wondered if Robert understood all these words, but the boy seemed satisfied, although Marianne was looking less impressed. 'I know they sound boring but they really are rather picturesque,' he added, half apologetically.

They drove on over the moor. The hills swelled around them, and Stephen pointed out the rocky tors that stood on their tops. 'You don't see them in many places. Just Dartmoor and Exmoor, and I think there may be a few in the Peak District and Yorkshire, but I'm not sure. Really, they're typical of Devon. Hay Tor is the most impressive; I'll take you there. It's near the road so it's easy to climb up.'

'I shall not wish to climb up,' Marianne said, but Robert was enthusiastic, so Stephen took the turning to Hexworthy, and after a while they arrived at the smooth grey rock of Hay Tor. Stephen drew the car to a halt at the side of the road, and they gazed at it.

'I shall go and climb it,' Robert announced, and, leaping over the side of the car, he set off up the grassy slope. Stephen glanced at Marianne but she made no move. He hesitated, then said, 'Do you want me to go with him?'

'*Mais non*,' she said, and glinted a look at him through her dark lashes. 'He is a boy, and boys climb. I expect you did yourself at his age.'

'Yes, I did. I just wondered if you would prefer him not to go alone.'

'Robert is a good climber,' she said. 'Like his father, I think.'

'Baden? I suppose he was. He was good at most things. Quite hard to live up to.'

'To ... live up to?'

'I always felt I had to try to be as good as him, but never could be. Father always seemed just a bit disappointed in me. Quite a lot, at times,' he added with a small, rueful laugh.

'But that is terrible,' Marianne said, laying her hand on his arm. 'You poor child.'

Stephen looked at her in surprise, very aware of her hand. He glanced down at it, at the delicate shape and the small fingers. It was her right hand, and he noticed for the first time the gold ring she wore.

'Yes,' she said quietly, following his gaze, 'it is Baden's ring. It was all we could find; we were married so quickly. But I have worn it always.'

'But you married again. Didn't your husband mind?'

'I told you, Jacques knew about Baden. He was a kind man and I loved him, though not perhaps in quite the same way. He understood that I wished to wear the ring, so I moved it to my right hand and there it has stayed.'

Stephen gazed at her, listening to her voice, so soft, yet so candid. He was convinced that she was speaking the truth, that she and Baden had been married and that Robert was his legitimate nephew. And yet ... there was something still, lurking in the depths of her brown eyes, a faint timbre in her voice, that fed the worm of unease he had been feeling ever since he had first seen her. What do you want of us, Marianne? he asked silently. And what is it going to do to us if we give it to you?

Marianne's fingers moved slowly, gently, on his arm. He could feel their warmth through the sleeve of his shirt, and a heat began to spread slowly through his body. He moved sharply, and her hand fell away.

'He's almost at the top,' he said abruptly, shading his eyes to stare up at the tor. As they watched, Robert climbed the last few feet and stood silhouetted against the sky, slim and straight as an arrow. He looked down and waved, and Marianne waved back.

'It's tragic that Baden died,' she said. 'Not just for me and for Robert, but for your father. Nobody should lose a son, and Baden was very precious to him.' She turned back swiftly and laid her hand once again on Stephen's arm. 'But you are precious to him, too. Even more so now. I can see that myself. It's in his eyes, in his voice. You're the only son he has left.'

'I know, and it doesn't make it any easier.'

'But why not?'

'Because he wants me to *be* Baden!' Stephen burst out. 'He wanted me to do everything Baden would have done – to excel at school, at university, at sport. As it happens, I *was* good at school and university, but not at the things he wanted me to be good at. I liked maths and went into the RAF, whereas Baden did languages and joined the Army. I took up rowing instead of rugby and cricket. It never mattered that I was *good* at those things; he never praised me for them. He simply asked why I hadn't followed in my brother's footsteps. He never stopped, and he never will. I'll always be second-best.'

He ended on a bitter note that he hadn't intended, and once again he stopped, biting his lip. What was it about this woman that made him blurt out things he'd never told anyone before, not even Maddy or his sister? And what ammunition might he be putting into her hands?

'So this, perhaps, is why he is so ready to accept Robert,' she said thoughtfully. 'He has never stopped wanting Baden back, and now it seems his wish has come true.'

'Perhaps,' Stephen said, reining in his own feelings. 'But there's a long way to go before he can really accept him, Marianne.'

She turned her dark gaze upon him, and he felt again that quickening of his blood. Her fingers moved so gently he could barely feel them, yet they seemed to be burning a brand upon his forearm.

'I know,' she said softly. 'There is a long way to go for all of us. But we can help each other on the journey, can we not? You and I, especially ... we can help each other.'

From Hay Tor, Stephen drove them back to Dartmeet, where they stopped for tea at the Badger's Holt tea rooms. Here was the clapper bridge he had promised Robert, and they paused there while the boy clambered about on the huge granite slabs and then stood on the rocks beneath, his feet almost in the water and his hands splayed against the underside of the bridge, as if he were holding it up with his own strength.

'It's a pity we don't have a camera with us,' Stephen said with a grin. 'It would be some photo to take back and show your friends.'

'To my *grandmères,* and Philippe and Ginette, too,' Robert said, and Stephen thought there was a touch of wistfulness in his tone. 'They would like to see this place.'

'Well, perhaps they will, one day,' Stephen said, and immediately wondered if that had been a wise thing to say, or whether Marianne would construe it as an invitation. He added quickly, 'The bridge has been here for hundreds of years – I don't expect it's going to go away just yet.'

They went into the restaurant and ordered tea, with scones made to the restaurant's own special recipe, together with strawberry jam and clotted cream. 'A real Devon cream tea,' Stephen said. 'Tuck in, Robert.'

'Why is it called Dartmeet?' the boy asked. He seemed to have an insatiable thirst for information and had been asking questions all afternoon, but Stephen thought them intelligent questions. 'What does it mean?'

'Well, you see, there are two rivers called Dart – the East Dart and the West Dart. They both rise up on the moor above here, and this is where they come together and flow as one river down to the sea at Dartmouth – the mouth of the Dart. The mouth of a river is where it meets the sea,' Stephen explained, thinking as he did so that it was probably unnecessary. Robert was quick at picking up new words – a talent he had probably inherited from his father, Stephen thought, recalling Baden's prowess with languages. And his French grandfather had been a linguist, too. 'That's a place I'd like to take you,' he added. 'Dartmouth is a nice little town with a harbour, and it's where the Naval College is as well. It's quite different from the moor.'

'Perhaps you could take us tomorrow,' Marianne suggested, and Robert looked hopeful.

'Well, perhaps. It depends what Father wants to do, and I have to be back at the RAF station quite early tomorrow evening. I've had enough leave this week as it is. It's quite a long drive, you see.'

'Next time you come, then,' she said, smiling at him. 'You'll come again soon, won't you? They don't keep you prisoner at your station?'

'No, they don't,' he said, laughing, 'but I'm not a free agent to come and go as I please. You aren't, when you're in the Services.'

'Well, whenever you do come,' she said comfortably.

Stephen looked at her. 'But you'll probably have gone by then. You did say you could only stay a week.'

'*Oui*. I have to go back to the *pâtisserie* and to help with my mother. But Robert is staying longer and of course I shall come back while he is here. And if I let you know when that is to be, then perhaps you can arrange your next *vacances* for that time. Or you can write and tell me when you will have your *vacances*, and I shall arrange my visit. It doesn't matter which it is.'

'No,' he said doubtfully, 'I suppose it doesn't.'

'So we will write to each other, *n'est-ce pas?*' she enquired with that coquettish lift of her eyes beneath the long, dark lashes. 'We will write often?'

'If you like,' Stephen said, a little startled. 'Yes, of course we'll write to each other, if you like.'

'I do like,' she murmured. 'I like very much. And I like you, Stephen. I think we are going to be great friends.'

Chapter Twelve

Hilary and Mrs Ellis had spent the afternoon preparing for the dinner party. Hilary had been to Tavistock that morning and headed straight for Palmer's the butcher for a leg of lamb, and then to Creber's, where she bought freshly-ground coffee, three different cheeses and some savoury crackers to go with them. Cream came from the dairy behind Good's, and strawberries, salad and vegetables from Roland Bailey's. To begin the meal, she bought prawns from the fish shop, and, in case anyone didn't like shellfish, added a couple of grapefruit.

The big dining table was set with the best crockery, cutlery and glasses, and sherry, gin and orange juice were ready in the drawing room by the time the first guests arrived. Thankfully, they were Basil Harvey and his wife Grace, who could always be relied upon to set visitors at their ease, and Basil greeted Marianne like an old friend, enfolding her small hands in his and beaming all over his round, rosy face.

'I'm very pleased to meet you again,' he said. 'Let me introduce my wife. Grace, this is Madame Aucoin – I told you I'd met her with Hilary when they came to see the church. And so this is your son?'

'Yes, this is Robert,' Marianne said. 'As you see, he is very like his father.'

Hilary caught her breath. There had not been time to ask her father the outcome of his discussion with John Wolstencroft, but she was sure that he would have wanted to make any introduction himself and would never have expected Marianne to forestall him by breaking the news so casually. She threw him a quick glance but, to her relief, he was at the other end of the room, talking to the lawyer, and didn't seem to have heard.

Constance Bellamy, who had come with the Harveys, saw her expression and gave Marianne a sharp look. She moved forward and, after Hilary had introduced them, spoke quickly.

'You must come and see my garden while you're here. It's looking its best at the moment. Bring your boy as well; he can help me pick apples.'

'That's a good idea,' Basil Harvey said, picking up on the change of subject. 'We don't want any more accidents, do we?' He turned back to Marianne. 'Miss Bellamy gives us all a lot of trouble, you know. She fell out of one of her apple trees only a few months ago, and almost broke her ankle. She was lucky it was no worse.' He gave Constance a glance of mock severity, and she bobbed her head in equally artificial contrition. 'If Robert can climb a ladder, he'll be a great help.'

'But do you not have *un jardenier*, a gardener?' Marianne asked. 'Is your garden a large one?'

'A decent size,' Constance said. 'But I like to do it myself. Keeps me fit. A couple of the village boys come in once or twice a week to help with the heavier work, and Jacob Prout keeps 'em in order and does the pruning.'

'Is that young Micky Coker and his friend Henry?' Grace asked. 'They're learning to ring the church bells as well, I understand.'

'So they tell me,' Constance nodded. 'Young rascals, the pair of them, but no malice, and they're willing enough to work for a bit of pocket-money.'

The door opened, and Arnold Cherriman and his wife Evelyn were shown in. Again, Hilary made the introductions, but she was relieved to see that Stephen had taken Robert aside to show him some of the gramophone records he was intending to play later. Arnold, she thought, wasn't the sort of man to want to be introduced to a young boy, and Evelyn was too quiet and timid to do much other than listen to her husband's pronouncements.

Constance, however, knew a way to draw her out and immediately began to ask about the garden. Shyly at first, but with increasing enthusiasm, Evelyn described the azaleas and rhododendrons she had planted, now past their best for the year but still with some colour.

'The heathers are over, too, but the hydrangeas will be out soon. The soil here is so good for all those plants. And I love the little woodland at the end of the garden – it's been full of bluebells. A real picture.'

'You'll be sorry to leave it,' Grace Harvey commented. 'How long is it before you move back to Plymouth?'

'Only a month. Yes, I'll be sad to leave the garden and Burracombe, but it will be lovely to get back to our own home. It's had to be completely redecorated and refurbished since the Government gave it back to us. It was requisitioned during the war,' she explained to Marianne, who was standing at the fringe of the little group. 'It's taken them all this time to hand it back. We never dreamed it would be so long. But now it's ours again and almost ready. I'm really looking forward to being there again. I'm not really a country person,' she added apologetically.

'Well, I think you've managed very well,' Constance said robustly. 'And what about your garden there? Will you have much work to do to get it up to scratch?'

'Quite a lot, but I shall enjoy it. I'm planning a complete change, and Arnold says I can have as much help as I need.'

'It'll keep her occupied,' Arnold said, breaking off from his conversation with Gilbert and John Wolstencroft, and moving nearer, as if to monitor what his wife was saying. 'Keep her out of those new shops, too!' he added with a short bark of laughter.

Evelyn blushed and gave him a quick, pleading glance, and

Hilary, noticing that her glass was almost empty, offered her more sherry.

'Don't think she wants any more, do you, Evie?' Arnold butted in. 'One's enough, especially if there's wine with dinner, which I imagine there will be, knowing how Gilbert keeps his cellar. I'll have a drop more, though.' He held out his glass, and Hilary half-filled it. 'Oh, come on, girl, that's hardly enough to wet a sparrow's beak.' He drifted back to the men.

Hilary moved round the room, topping up glasses as required, and came to Stephen, who had now taken out the whole collection of gramophone records and spread them on the floor.

'Mind where you're stepping, Hil. We don't want any broken. We're just making up a programme for after dinner, if people want music. What do you fancy?'

'Something loud enough to drown Arnold Cherriman's voice, for a start,' Hilary said. 'I shall be glad when he moves back to Plymouth, though I suppose we'll still have to have him to dinner. I feel sorry for his wife, though, poor woman. She seems really under his thumb.'

'Under his thumb?' Robert asked, and she realised rather guiltily that she shouldn't be discussing their guests in this manner. She smiled at him.

'It's just an expression. I'll explain another time. I think dinner's nearly ready now. Steve, would you take the sherry? I'll go and see how Mrs Ellis is getting on.'

As they sat down at the table, Hilary noticed Arnold Cherriman's eyebrows shoot up as he realised that Robert was to join them. It was all the more noticeable because they didn't have an even number, but she hadn't been able to think of another person to complete the dozen. Until last week they might have invited Travis, but now that he and Jennifer were engaged he couldn't be invited alone, and the Latimers, who they would usually have asked, had gone on holiday immediately after the Coronation celebrations. In any case, it was one of Gilbert's few superstitions that there must never be thirteen at a table.

She had arranged it so that Robert sat between herself and Grace Harvey, with Evelyn opposite. Arnold was on Grace's other side, and leaned across her to speak to the French boy.

'Rather tedious for you, having to eat with us,' he boomed. 'Don't suppose you understand much English, do you?'

'He speaks English very well,' Marianne said. She was at Arnold's other side, and he turned in surprise. She met his gaze coolly, yet with a hint of a challenge in her glance. 'My father taught your language in our school. He attended Oxford University – a long time ago, *naturellement* – and he had many friends in this country.'

'I see,' Arnold said blankly, and Hilary hid her smile at seeing him, for once, nonplussed.

The meal was nearing its end when Gilbert tapped his glass for attention. Everyone stopped speaking and turned their faces towards him, and Hilary's heart sank. Here it comes, she thought.

'Just wanted to thank you all for coming,' he began in his deep, commanding voice. 'Now, I want to enlighten you as to why you were all invited at such short notice, and to let you into a secret. Not that I expect it to remain a secret for long. Nothing to be ashamed of, and everything to be proud of.' He cast an approving look down the table towards Robert, who had behaved perfectly throughout the meal, and was now sitting quietly with his hands folded on his lap. 'Thing is, this young woman' – he indicated Marianne – 'turned up on my doorstep only two days ago, completely unexpectedly, and gave me some news I'd have liked to have had thirteen years ago. It seems, to put it plainly, that she's my daughter-in-law – my son Baden's wife.'

He paused, and Hilary glanced covertly at the faces, noting which looked surprised (Grace Harvey and Evelyn Cherriman) and which shocked (Arnold Cherriman). Basil and Constance, she noted, looked merely satisfied, as if they'd already suspected the truth, which they must have done when Marianne had made her earlier remark about the resemblance.

'Yes, it seems that Baden and Marianne here married only just before Dunkirk. As you all know, he and his entire unit were killed before they could reach the harbour, and nobody was left who knew of the marriage. Marianne was, of course, not able to communicate during the war, and circumstances changed afterwards. This is the first opportunity she has had to come to England and introduce me to my grandson. Robert, come here, please.'

Robert got up and walked round the table until he stood at his grandfather's side. Gilbert stood up and laid his hand on the boy's shoulder, and Hilary, catching the look of complete joy and pride on his face, felt her eyes grow hot with tears.

'It is my very great pleasure,' Gilbert said, with a slight catch in his own voice, 'to present to you my grandson Robert. The heir to Burracombe.'

After the silence that followed Gilbert's announcement, it seemed almost impossible to go back to the discussions of local matters and talk of the Coronation which had occupied the party until then. Yet nobody – not even Arnold Cherriman, Hilary noted – felt sufficiently assured to ask questions, and Gilbert himself did not seem inclined to explain any further. Perhaps he would tell the gentlemen more, she thought as she led the ladies back to the drawing room. He had John Wolstencroft with him, after all, and it seemed that the lawyer had, if not actually given his blessing, not advised against the announcement. But even he, she thought, had looked startled at the suggestion that Robert would inherit the Burracombe estate.

All in all, she thought that it had not been a good idea. The guests were simply embarrassed and lost for conversation, and everyone seemed relieved when she rose to take the ladies out. Once in the drawing room, Grace Harvey tried valiantly, turning to Marianne and asking her about her home in France and showing interest in the *pâtisserie*, and Evelyn joined in.

'I like baking. Perhaps you'll give me some recipes.'

'Per'aps. But I think your flour may be different from ours. They may not work as well.'

'That's a pity,' Grace said. 'I love French pastries and cakes. Basil and I have been to France several times, and I'm afraid I always come back a little fatter!'

Marianne smiled. 'We like people to enjoy our food. And it is good now to be able to make more of the food we love. For too long, it was difficult in France.'

'In England, too,' Grace said ruefully. 'Not that we suffered too much here, but there were a lot of shortages and restrictions. We haven't quite finished with rationing even now.'

'Sugar,' Evelyn said. 'That's still on ration.'

Hilary glanced at her, wondering if the words really had sounded a little slurred, or if it had been her imagination. She had noticed that Evelyn, removed from her husband's eye, had drunk several glasses of wine at dinner, and remembered his intervention to stop her taking a second glass of sherry. She poured some more coffee into Evelyn's cup and then, so that it didn't seem too pointed, into her own.

'How long are you planning to stay?' Constance asked Marianne.

'I 'ave to go home next week. I have my business to attend to, and my other children to look after. But Robert is staying longer. I want him to learn about the place where his father grew up, and to be part of his family.'

There was a slight silence. Everyone, Hilary thought, must be wondering just what Gilbert had in mind, not only for Robert but for herself and Stephen. And there was the wider issue of Burracombe itself: the estate, the Barton, the village. It was a subject they could hardly discuss with herself present, but she was sure that once the news was known in the village it would be discussed endlessly. Travis's efforts in the Bell had been scarcely necessary after all.

The door opened, and everyone turned in relief to welcome the men back. Stephen made straight for the gramophone and beckoned Robert over to help him. They put on a recording of the *William Tell* overture, and the energetic music filled the room, removing the necessity to make conversation. Basil leaned back in his chair and closed his eyes, and Constance began to beat lightly on the arm of her chair in time to the music. Arnold Cherriman looked impatient and glanced at his wife, who was also leaning back with her eyes closed, but not, Hilary thought, because she was enjoying the music. She looked as if she were asleep.

'Time we were going,' Arnold said abruptly. 'Evelyn's had a busy day. Works far too hard in that garden of hers.' He rose to his feet and shook his wife's shoulder. 'Come along, dear. Time you were in your bed.'

Evelyn Cherriman's eyes flew open, and for a moment she looked almost frightened. Then she laughed a little and got to her feet, leaning heavily on her husband's arm. She waved a hand at the others.

'I'm so sorry. Must have dropped off. So rude of me. Thank you so much, Hilary, for a lovely evening. Thank you, Gilbert. It's been lovely to meet you, Madame Au- Au—' She stumbled over the name and then, with an apologetic smile, gave up and turned to Robert. 'And Robert, of course. He is *very* like his father. Such a nice young man. I remember ... yes, Arnold, I'm coming,' as he jerked none too gently at her arm. 'Well, goodbye again, everyone.'

They went out, Hilary accompanying them to the front door, and when she came back, the other guests were also beginning to take their leave. In a flurry of goodbyes and gathering of coats, they all departed, leaving the family looking at each other, somewhat at a loss. John Wolstencroft had gone up to his room for a book he'd brought to show Gilbert.

'Damn the woman,' Gilbert said explosively. 'She broke up the party. What in heaven's name's the matter with her?'

'You heard what Arnold said,' Hilary answered. 'She'd been working hard all day in the garden. She really did look tired.'

'Looked a bit tipsy, if you ask me,' Gilbert said bluntly. 'Wouldn't be surprised if there's something odd going on there. I pity Arnold, saddled with a wife like that. Always been a mouse and now it looks as if she's turning into—'

'Father!' Hilary interrupted sharply. 'You've no reason to say that. Evelyn Cherriman's a nice woman; she's just rather quiet, that's all.' And Arnold's a bully, she added silently, and I think I'd turn to drink as well if I had to live with him. 'Anyway, I'm not sorry they all went early. I'm rather tired myself, and I'm sure Marianne and Robert must be.'

Stephen went over to the gramophone and began to put away the records. 'It looks as if the evening's over, then. Unless anyone wants any more music.'

Gilbert grunted dismissively and then, as the lawyer returned, said, 'John and I'll have a brandy in my study. We've still got a few things to talk over. I dare say young Robert's ready for bed, though.'

Hilary glanced at the boy, who took his cue and wished them all goodnight, shaking hands with each person before going quietly out of the room. She said, 'I'll go and help clear up in the kitchen. Are you going to bed now, Marianne?'

'*Mais non*. I am a night-bird, *moi*.' The Frenchwoman smiled, showing small white teeth, and moved to stand close to Stephen. 'Perhaps we two can enjoy some music together. There will be no need for anything else,' she added to Hilary. 'I will see myself to bed when I am ready to go.'

Hilary opened her mouth then closed it again. Marianne didn't, she was sure, mean to dismiss her as if she were a servant. She smiled her goodnight, and, feeling that there was nothing else to do, left them.

Alone in the large room, Marianne moved even closer to Stephen and laid her hand on his arm, as she had done earlier that day in the car. She smiled up at him, and once again he was troublingly aware of the darkness of her gaze and the faint spark that gleamed somewhere deep within it.

'Let us have some music,' she said softly. 'Just the two of us. Something ... romantic. *N'est-ce pas?*'

Chapter Thirteen

Saturday had turned out quite differently for some other inhabitants of Burracombe.

'Is that the one you like best?' Travis asked in the jeweller's shop. 'The solitaire?'

Jennifer looked at the diamond sparkling on her finger. 'Yes, it is. What about you?'

'I want you to have whatever you like; you're going to be the one wearing it! But I do like that one. It suits your hand.' He looked at the salesman behind the glass-topped counter. 'We'll have it.'

The ring was taken away and put into a little velvet box, which Travis slipped into his pocket. They went out of the shop, and stood by the door, smiling at each other.

'What shall we do now?' she asked. 'It seems a bit of an anticlimax just to go home again. Shall we have a walk through the Meadows, by the river?'

'No,' Travis said, taking her hand and leading her firmly back to where he had parked the Land Rover. 'We're going up to the Pimple, and then we're having lunch at the Bedford Hotel, to celebrate. And maybe after that we'll have a walk by the river before we go back to Burracombe. And this evening, I thought we could go round to see Val and Luke. We'll buy a bottle of sherry to take with us.'

'That sounds lovely,' she said. 'But we must see Jacob first. I can't let him find out from anyone else. Perhaps he'll come to

Val's with us. And we don't need to drive to the Pimple. We can walk from here.'

They set off through the town and across the bridge that spanned the river Tavy, pausing to look down at the weir. The river tumbled cheerfully over the two falls and past the trees that grew below the little railway station, while on the other side people strolled along the path that led to the local recreation ground, known to everyone as the Meadows. Sometimes you could see fish below the bridge, and at spawning time salmon would leap up the weir to travel upstream.

There was a short cut a little further along, leading to the wide road up to Whitchurch Down. Large houses stood on either side, with equally large gardens around them, and Jennifer remarked that she had been told this was 'the best address in Tavistock'.

'I expect it is,' Travis said. 'The houses certainly must be the most expensive. Their gardens are big enough to build another house in.'

'I wish we could see them better,' Jennifer said wistfully. 'But they've all got these high hedges round them. Not that I blame them for wanting their privacy, but I do like looking at gardens.'

'You'll have your own to look at soon, and look after as well. D'you think you'll like that?'

'Oh, yes. I've always wanted a garden. I've only got that little bit of backyard at home, and you can't do much with it. And Mrs Cherriman has made a beautiful garden at the estate house. I still can't believe I'm going to live in such a lovely place, Travis. I'd have been quite happy moving to the cottage, you know. I know Hilary wanted Val and Luke to have the house.'

'I know, but Colonel Napier's insistent that we have it. I think Hilary's happy about it now, especially as Val and Luke are quite content to stay at Jed's.'

'Well, they can stay there as long as they like,' Jennifer said cheerfully. 'Until you retire, anyway, and we have to move. And by then, I'm sure they'll have found somewhere else anyway.'

They came to the top of the road, by the golf club, and paused to look at the wide panorama of rolling hills and tors. The sky arched overhead, mostly blue with small white clouds scudding along very high up, and a group of wild ponies grazed peacefully, some with foals only a few weeks old. There were a few golfers on the green, and further towards Whitchurch and Middlemoor, a flock of sheep was scattered amongst the gorse bushes. A man walked his dog in the distance, but there was nobody else to be seen.

'There'll be more people around in the afternoon,' Travis remarked. 'But just now, we've got it almost to ourselves.'

It was only a few minutes' walk to the Pimple, a small, triangular building standing on a knoll, built of local stone, with broad slatted seats on each side. One side faced across the town of Tavistock towards the hills of Cornwall: Kit Hill, with the tall tower a reminder of the mining that had taken place there; and Caradon Hill even further away. The jagged outlines of Bodmin Moor were just visible as shadows against the horizon. The second seat looked towards the stark moors surrounding Princetown with its infamous prison; and the third looked into the softer, wooded landscape beyond Whitchurch and the rolling hills above Crowndale, where Sir Francis Drake had been born in a humble farm cottage.

'It's a beautiful view,' Jennifer said, settling down on one of the seats. 'Sometime, I'd like to walk up to every tor we can see from here: Cox Tor, Great Staple Tor, Pew Tor, Sheepstor ... all of them!'

'That'll probably take us years,' Travis declared. 'But just now, there's something much more important.' He took the little velvet box from his pocket and opened it. Then he held Jennifer's left hand in his, and looked seriously into her eyes.

'This is the place where I asked you to marry me,' he said.

'Now I'm asking you again, and I hope the answer will be the same as it was then. Will you marry me, Jennifer, my love? Will you?'

Jennifer gazed at him through a sudden mist of tears. 'Of course I will,' she whispered. 'Oh, Travis, of *course* I will.'

He slid the ring on to her finger, and they both looked down at it. Then he leaned forward, slipped his arm around her shoulders and kissed her.

'Well, that's a relief,' he said lightly. 'I don't know what I'd have done with that ring if you'd said no!'

Jennifer burst out laughing and slapped his arm. 'And there was I thinking you were going all romantic on me!'

'Well, so I was,' he said. 'Just can't keep it up for long, that's all.' Then, more seriously, 'I do love you, Jennifer. You know that, don't you.'

'Yes,' she said. 'I do. And I love you, too. And it was a very romantic idea to bring me here to give me my ring.'

They sat in silence for a few minutes, Jennifer within the circle of Travis's arm, her head on his shoulder. It was very quiet, and both were thinking of the evening when they had come here after seeing the film *From Here To Eternity*, and Jennifer had told Travis the story of her first marriage. She had known in her heart that he was about to propose and that she had to tell him the truth first, even if he then decided against it. But Travis had not decided against it. He had listened, asked a few questions, and then held her close, told her that it made no difference to his love, and asked her to be his wife.

'I can't believe I'm so lucky,' she said now. 'Imagine, if I'd never come to Burracombe to look for my father, we would never have met.'

'Nor if I'd stayed in Dorset. Or if a hundred and one other things had or hadn't happened. But we did meet, and we fell in love, and now we've got a wedding to plan. But not today,' he added, drawing her to her feet. 'Today is for celebrating our engagement. And the next part is lunch at the Bedford Hotel, the best place in town. And then we'll spend the evening with good friends.'

'I can't think of a better day,' Jennifer said, her hand in his as they walked down the slope to the far corner of the Down, where another short cut led through to the road leading back to Tavistock. 'I think we ought to get engaged every Saturday!'

'I'm willing,' he grinned, 'but you'll have to pay for all those rings!'

'I've got a bit of news,' Ivy Sweet said, bustling into the little general store. 'You'll never guess what it is.'

Edie Pettifer, busy weighing out two ounces of sherbet dabs for Betty Culliford, glanced over her spectacles at the baker's wife.

'You'd better tell us, then. I hope 'tis something exciting. I feel a bit flat after all the to-do over the Coronation.'

Ivy waited until Betty had run out of the shop, then leaned across the counter, lowering her voice.

'I went into Tavi this morning to get a few bits and bobs, and who do you think I saw coming out of the jeweller's shop by Pillar's?' She waited expectantly, as Edie put the sweet jar back on the shelf.

'Since you've told me I'll never guess, it's not much use me trying. But if I was held over a cauldron of boiling oil and told I *had* to guess, I'd say it might have been Jennifer Tucker and that Mr Kellaway. I've noticed them together a bit just lately, and they seemed pretty thick at the party the other night.'

Ivy straightened up, looking aggravated. 'As it happens, you'm right, but I think you could've given me the satisfaction. It was me who went all the way to Tavistock, after all.'

Edie smiled. 'Never mind. At least you were the one that saw them. You don't reckon he was just getting his watch mended, then?'

Ivy looked disconcerted for a moment, then shook her head. 'Not from the look on their faces, no. They looked as if they were floating three feet above the ground. I'd lay a week's wages they'd just bought an engagement ring. It'll be all round the village by tea-time, you mark my words.' She glanced over her shoulder, through the open doorway. 'Oh, there goes Mabel Purdy, I want a word with her. I'll see you later, Edie.'

She marched out of the door, and Edie laughed to herself. All round the village by tea-time! It certainly would if Ivy Sweet had anything to do with it.

A moment or two later, Eileen Coker came in. Edie glanced at her face and, seeing no excitement there, asked casually, 'Heard the news, have you?'

'What news?' The blacksmith's wife dumped her shopping basket on the counter. 'I'll have half a pound of margarine, please, Edie, and two pounds of plain flour and some dried fruit. I need some sugar, too – I've got my coupons here. I want to make a fruit cake for my Alf's birthday next month. What news is this, then?'

'Jennifer Tucker and Travis Kellaway,' Edie said. 'They've got engaged! Been into Tavi this morning to buy the ring. So we'll be having a wedding in Burracombe pretty soon, I reckon.'

'Is that right? Well, who'd have thought it? I always reckoned he was sweet on Miss Hilary.'

'No, there was never anything in that,' Edie said with all the confidence of one who was making it up as she went along. 'How could there be? He's just an employee, for all he's called an "estate manager", and the Colonel wouldn't never countenance him coming in to the family.'

She bagged up the sugar and started to weigh out the dried fruit. Maggie Culliford, Betty's mother, came in just then, with Mrs Dawe, the school cleaner, just behind her. They stood waiting to be served, and Eileen Coker turned to them eagerly.

'You'll never guess the latest! Jennifer Tucker and

Mr Kellaway are getting married. Got the ring this morning. When did you say the wedding's going to be?' she asked, turning back to Edie, who was looking annoyed at having been forestalled.

'I don't know as they've settled on a date yet,' Edie said, slightly mollified. 'September'd be a good time, though, I reckon. Maybe the second Saturday. Give them time to get it all organised, that will, and settled in before the winter.'

'Where d'you think they'll live?' Hilda Dawe asked. 'That cottage young Val Tozer-as-was and her hubby live in belongs to Miss Tucker, don't it? And Val's expecting around then, too. It'll be a bit hard to force her out just when she've got a babby coming.'

'They'd never do that!' Edie exclaimed, shocked. 'No, it's for the Squire to find them somewhere to live, what with Mr Kellaway being his manager. Wasn't that house in the woods, where that optician from Plymouth lives, meant for someone like him?'

'Yes, it were, and I've heard they'm moving back to Plymouth in the summer, too,' Maggie Culliford chimed in. 'My Arthur had it from one of the estate workers he was talking to up in the woods. That's where they'll be living, you mark my words.'

The others turned to her.

'Oh, yes?' Hilda Dawe asked nastily. 'And what might your Arthur have been doing up in the woods, I wonder?'

'He was taking the footpath to see his mother,' Maggie retorted, flushing. 'As he's every right to do, *day or night*,' she added meaningfully.

The others were silent, as they remembered the night Arthur had been doing just that when – according to his story – he'd accidentally run into both poachers and gamekeepers, and young Betty had been hurt in the scrap that had followed. For once, it seemed that he'd been an innocent party, but everybody knew that wasn't always the case.

'Never mind that,' Edie said, anxious to return to the main subject of gossip. 'I dare say you'm right, Maggie. It makes sense, after all, for him to live on the estate. Well, it'll be good to have a wedding to look forward to.'

'Yes, but us have already got one,' Hilda Dawe reminded them. 'There's young Miss Simmons and the curate getting married just after Christmas. Though I did hear as they'll have that over the river,' she added disparagingly. 'I suppose they got to, seeing as he'm vicar there now. If you've finished your shopping,' she added to Eileen Coker, 'I hope as nobody minds if I do mine.'

'You go on,' Eileen Coker said, piling her purchases into her shopping basket. 'I got to get on anyway. My hubby wants his dinner early today; he's taking young Micky and Henry Bennetts up to Whitchurch for a cricket match.'

As she departed, Norman Tozer's wife Susan came in, and they all turned on her at once to babble out the news. They were talking so fast, each one desperate to be the first to break it, that she had some difficulty in sorting out what they were saying, but at last she got the gist.

'Well, isn't that lovely? A real lift. I was feeling a bit flat after the Coronation. I'll tell my Norman. He'll be pleased. He've got a lot of time for Mr Kellaway, and he likes Jennifer, too.'

'I wonder what sort of frock she'll wear,' Hilda mused. 'Her's a bit long in the tooth for white. I reckon a costume would be more suitable – a nice light shade, lilac perhaps.'

'What about bridesmaids, then? I never think they look right unless the bride's in white.'

'Have she got any little girls in her family? I did hear she's got sisters, so she might have. They'd want to be bridesmaids for their auntie, wouldn't they?'

'Where d'you think they'll have the reception? D'you suppose the Colonel would agree to them having it at the Barton?'

They were still chattering and speculating when Jacob Prout came in for his weekend packet of Woodbines. Hilda Dawe turned to him at once.

'I hear you're to be congratulated, Jacob.'

'Me?' He stopped and stared at her. 'What have I done to be congratulated for?'

'Your Jennifer, getting engaged to that Mr Kellaway,' Hilda said importantly. 'Edie here's just told us.'

He turned his gaze on Edie. 'And how did you come to know about it, then?'

'Well, I'm not sure now,' Edie said, discomfited by his look. 'I think it was Ivy Sweet told me. She saw them in Tavi, getting the ring.'

'The wedding's in September, I hear – second Saturday.' Hilda, who had never been overly sensitive to atmosphere, continued eagerly. 'You must be as pleased as a dog with two tails.'

'I would be if I'd knowed anything about it,' he said curtly, and went out without his cigarettes.

'Oh, dear,' Edie said, as she and the others stared at each other. 'Now you've upset him. 'Tis plain he didn't know nothing about it. That's put the cat amongst the pigeons.'

'Well, how was I to know?' Hilda asked, looking aggrieved. 'You'd have thought they'd have told Jacob first.'

'Perhaps they meant to. I don't suppose they banked on someone seeing them coming out of the jeweller's shop. 'Tis too late now, though; everyone in Burracombe will know by the time they get back.'

'I saw Jennifer Tucker this morning,' Ted Tozer reported as he came indoors for his midday meal. 'Going off along the Tavi road with Travis Kellaway, she were. There's something going on between those two, or I'm a Dutchman.'

'Yes, your Norman's Susan was up here just now, telling us about it,' Alice said, setting the kitchen table as he took off his boots at the door. 'Went to buy the ring, so it seems, and the wedding's the second Saturday in September. I'm really pleased for them. She's a nice little body and he's a well set-up man. I'm surprised neither of them's spoken for already.'

'That's as maybe,' Ted returned, 'but what I'm wondering is, where our Jackie is this weekend if Jennifer Tucker's in Burracombe. It means she's all on her own in that house in Plymouth, that's what.'

Alice paused. 'She did say she was working some of the weekend. She told me she wouldn't be home.'

'She didn't tell you she'd have the house to herself, though, did she? And Jennifer Tucker never saw fit to let us know she'd be leaving Jackie by herself, neither. I don't like it, Alice. That girl's only nineteen; she still needs supervision.'

'If you remember, Ted,' Alice said, 'I wasn't much above that age when we got married.'

'Yes, but you weren't living in Plymouth with a house to yourself. You were here, working in this very farmhouse, with my mother to keep an eye on you. That's different.'

'I don't remember it being all that different when we were out in the fields or in the old barn together,' Alice remarked, going back to the cooker where the frying-pan was sizzling. 'I reckon 'twas easier to get up to mischief round here than it is in a city like Plymouth, with all they people milling about all the time. I don't know how Jackie would ever find the time or place to get up to mischief.'

'And that's just what I'm telling you! She's got a house to herself all weekend. And we never got up to nothing we shouldn't, Alice, as well you know.'

'And maybe our Jackie won't, neither,' she retorted. 'Ted, you've got to let go of her. We've done our best to bring her up proper, and now her's out in the world, like it or not. There's nothing us can do about it. Anyway, she says she's likely to get a room in the hotel soon, so she'll be well supervised then.'

'It's this weekend I'm bothered about,' he began, but Alice cut him short.

'Ted, if you'm that bothered I reckon you'd better get on a bus and go down and spend the weekend with her! But you might as well have your dinner first, because it's just about ready. Look,' she went on in a softer tone, 'I know you'm anxious about her, and so am I to be honest, but there just isn't anything more we can do. Like I said, we've done our part, and now 'tis for her to make her own way and her own mistakes, and us must just trust she don't make bad ones. She's a good girl at heart, you know that, and I don't reckon she'll get into any sort of trouble. Sit down now, and have your dinner. It's pig's fry and bacon, with spring greens and plenty of mashed potatoes, and there's rhubarb crumble for afters.'

Ted sat down, still frowning, but as Minnie came in to join them, followed by Tom, Joanna and little Robin, he shrugged and joined in the conversation about the visitors at the Barton.

'I don't care what you say,' Alice said. 'It seems queer to me, them turning up out of the blue like that, and the boy looking so much like Master Baden. Why haven't us heard anything about them before? That's what I'd like to know.'

'It might be because they don't let us know all their family business,' Ted retorted, still more concerned with his own family business than the Napiers'. 'I don't know why you're getting so het up about it, Alice. The Colonel's wife might have had all sorts of relatives we never knew about, and I dare say some of them might have a family resemblance. I don't see nothing strange about it.'

'We don't even know that they've turned up out of the blue,' Tom put in. 'It could have been arranged for months for all we might know. Like Dad says, they don't have to tell us every time they has a tea party. If you're not going to eat that liver, Robin, I'll have it.'

'No, you won't,' Joanna said. 'It's not going to do him any

good going into your stomach, is it? Eat a bit, Robin, there's a good boy. It'll make you big and strong.'

'Liver's good for your blood,' Alice agreed. 'It's got iron in it.'

'Don't want to eat iron,' Robin said obstinately, and pressed his lips together. 'I'll go rusty.'

Joanna sighed. 'Just a little bit. Look, I'll cut it up small and mix it with your cabbage and potato, then you won't even know it's there.'

'It'll hurt my teeth,' he said.

'Hurt your teeth?' Minnie asked. 'How d'you make that out?'

'It's got iron in it,' he said. 'You can't chew iron. Did you eat lots of liver when you were little, Great-granny?'

'I don't know about lots,' Minnie said. 'I had to eat it when I was given it, though.'

Robin gave her a look, and Tom laughed.

'You can see what he's thinking! It didn't do your teeth much good, did it?'

'It didn't do them any harm, either,' she retorted. 'And I've still got plenty of my own left. You eat it up, Robin.'

'Anyway, it's got nothing to do with teeth,' Alice said, collecting up the plates but leaving Robin's where it was. 'Who wants some rhubarb crumble?'

'Rhubarb?' Tom said with a grin. 'Now that's something that does make my teeth feel funny! Come on, Rob, just one little bit, and then you can have pudding like the rest of us. Shut your eyes and pretend it's a toffee. Come on, now, chew ... that's it. All gone. Well done.'

'It didn't taste like toffee,' Robin said, and gave his plate up thankfully.

Alice, glad to have the subject diverted from Jackie and her possible doings in Plymouth, took the plate to the sink. She stood for a moment, looking out of the window.

Ted's right, she thought. I don't like the idea of her by

herself in that house any more than he does. Jennifer ought to have let us know. But it seems she's got other things on her mind just at the moment.

Chapter Fourteen

Jacob spent the afternoon working moodily in a neglected corner of the churchyard. He didn't normally work on Saturday afternoons, but he didn't want to be in his own garden, where any nosy villager might pass by and stop to give him more news he ought to have had before any of them. He put on his leather gauntlets and slashed with his billhook at nettles and brambles, ripping them out to make a huge, prickly pile, and stamping them down with his heavy boots. He was hot, red and sweating when Basil, who had come over to the church to collect last week's surplice for the wash, noticed him and trotted over.

'Whatever are you doing, Jacob? You shouldn't be working on a Saturday afternoon.'

'Didn't have nothing else to do,' the old man muttered. 'Anyway, this patch has needed doing for months.'

'I know, but all the same ...' Basil took a closer look. 'Is everything all right, Jacob? You look upset. You haven't had bad news, I hope.'

Jacob stopped, resting the blade of his billhook on the ground.

'I've had *news*,' he said surlily. 'I suppose you'd call it *good* news, too, but it's the way it come to me that sticks in my craw.'

Basil stared at him. 'Whatever are you talking about, Jacob? Don't tell me if you'd rather not,' he added hastily.

'I'm surprised you don't know already. The rest of the

village seems to. Come to that, I'm surprised they haven't bin to you to set the date.'

Basil's face creased with dismay, and he shook his head. 'Jacob, I really haven't the faintest idea what you're talking about. What date? Who?'

'Why, my Jennifer, of course, and that Travis Kellaway. Getting married. Been into Tavi to buy the engagement ring this morning. 'Tis all round the village. You mean to say they haven't been to see you yet?'

'No, they haven't. I had no idea. Well ... maybe that's not quite true. I did notice they were quite friendly, but nothing more than that. They certainly haven't said anything. When is this wedding to be?'

'Second Saturday in September, apparently,' Jacob growled. 'Not that they've said a word to me about it, mind. I don't seem to matter no more. Don't suppose I'll even be invited.'

'Jacob, don't be so foolish, of course you'll be invited. And I dare say they meant to tell you at the first opportunity. If they've only just been to buy the engagement ring—'

'Well, they had the opportunity to tell *someone*,' Jacob burst out. 'Otherwise how would it be the talk of Burracombe? You'd have thought they'd have the common decency to tell *me* first! Always looked on Jennifer as a daughter, I have – had her to stay with me every weekend, been into Plymouth a time or two to stay with her – and this is how she repays me. Letting me find out in the village shop, from a crowd of gossiping women. I know I'm upset, Vicar, but I reckon I got a *right* to be upset. And now, if you don't mind, I'll get on with clearing this patch of rubbish. It seems to relieve me feelings a bit.' He lifted the billhook again and swung it savagely, causing Basil to leap hastily out of the way.

The vicar looked at him for a moment or two more, then decided that the expression on Jacob's face meant he really wouldn't welcome more questions. He sighed and moved away, forgetting the surplice, and only remembering when he reached the vicarage door why he had gone to the church in the first place.

It was gone six by the time Jennifer and Travis arrived back in Burracombe. After finishing their celebration lunch at the Bedford Hotel, they had gone to Lydford and walked through the gorge. It was a wild and rocky scramble in many places, and, after the rain earlier in the week, the Devil's Cauldron and Whitelady Waterfall were at their dramatic best. They stopped and peered into the swirling depths of the Cauldron, and Jennifer shuddered a little and drew back.

'I wouldn't like to be here with anyone who didn't like me.'

'That's not very likely to happen,' Travis said with a grin. 'Everybody likes you.'

'Oh, not everybody. I can think of one or two people at work who might like to push me in there! There's one in particular who would go to some lengths to get my job.'

'Not as far as murder, I hope,' he said. 'Or I shall be worried about you all the time.' He paused, then said, 'Not that she'll have to wait much longer now. Or would you rather go on working after we're married?'

Jennifer turned and looked at him in surprise. 'I hadn't thought much about it, but I assumed I'd leave. It would be possible to go in every day by bus, but I'm not sure I'd want to – unless you want me to go on, of course.'

'Good heavens, no. I want to be able to keep my wife, and besides, I want to come home for dinner in the middle of the day whenever I can!' He bent and kissed her. 'But I don't want you to be bored or lonely there in the middle of the woods. You've been used to living in a city – it's going to be a big change.'

'A nice one, though. You know I love Burracombe, and it's not as if I don't know nearly everyone there. My best friends are in the village. And I'm looking forward to that garden, too – as well as seeing you every dinner-time, of course,' she added in a teasingly offhand tone.

'Well, I'm glad you think that'll be one of the good parts.' He kissed her again. 'Oh, Jenny, I can't wait to be living with you in our own home in the woods. We're not going to wait too long to be married, are we?'

'We did talk about September. That would be all right, wouldn't it? I don't think we can do it any sooner. The Cherrimans aren't moving out of the house till August, and Colonel Napier said we could have it decorated right through before we move in.'

'September it is, then. First Saturday?'

'The second,' Jennifer said decisively. 'The first Saturday is my sister's little girl's seventh birthday, and she's sure to have a party. We can't interfere with that.'

'The second Saturday in September,' he said. 'And this evening we'll start telling everyone. What a surprise that's going to be! Come on, let's go back to Tavistock. We'll have some tea first and then go to the off–licence and buy that sherry.'

'Tea? After that huge lunch? I hope you don't expect to eat like this all the time.' She followed him along the rocky path. 'And when we do get back, the first thing I must do is let Jacob know I'm in the village. I hadn't intended coming this weekend, after being here during the week, and he doesn't even know I'm planning to stay with him.'

'He won't mind, will he?' Travis asked, and she shook her head.

'No, Jacob's always pleased to see me. He's told me I can come whenever I like, and my room's always ready.' She hugged herself with delight. 'I can't wait to see his face when we tell him our news!'

'Oh, 'tis you,' Jacob growled when he opened the door at Jennifer's knock. 'I was beginning to think you weren't even going to take the trouble to say hello.'

Jennifer gazed at him open-mouthed. 'Jacob?'

'I take it you want to come in,' he continued in the same brusque tone. 'And your friend, as well, I suppose.'

Jennifer looked quickly at Travis, and then stepped forward. 'Jacob, I'm sorry I didn't let you know I was coming but—'

'Never been no need to let me know,' he interrupted. 'Always been welcome to just turn up on the doorstep, as well you know. I'd have liked to have bin told about your future plans before everyone else in the place, though.'

'Jacob, what are you talking about? What future plans?'

Jacob gave a short bark of laughter. 'What future plans could I be talking about? These plans to get wed, of course. Or have you got summat else up your sleeve?'

Jennifer stared at him. She drew in a deep breath, but before she could speak, Travis said quietly, 'Let's go indoors, Jacob. We can sort this out better there than on the doorstep.'

Jacob snorted, but moved back into the cottage so that they could follow him. He took them into the snug back room, where Flossie the cat was curled up in a tight ball in one of the armchairs, and Scruff the dog was stretched out on the rag rug before the fireplace. The three of them stood uncomfortably in the middle of the room, neither Jennifer nor Travis feeling that they could sit down uninvited with Jacob in his present mood.

'Well, sit you down, then,' he commanded crossly. 'You come to say summat to me, so you might as well say it.'

'Jacob,' Jennifer began, almost in tears. 'Tell us why you're so upset. We came to bring you good news, we thought you'd be pleased, but you seem really angry about something. What is it?'

'What d'you *think* it is?' he demanded. 'It's this wedding everyone's talking about, that's what. Sneaking off into Tavistock without even letting me know you'm in the village, buying yourselves an engagement ring, fixing up the date and everything, and all behind my back. I s'pose you even been to see the vicar by now, have you? He didn't know no more than me about it this afternoon, but it seems to me we were the only two in the place that didn't.'

'No!' Jennifer shook her head, distressed and bewildered. 'It wasn't like that at all. Honestly, we didn't go behind your back. You were going to be the first to know. And we haven't been to see Mr Harvey. We haven't fixed any date with him. We haven't talked to anyone at all. We haven't even seen anyone we knew, all day. Jacob, you must believe us.'

'Oh, is that right?' he said, fixing Jennifer with a hurt look. 'Second Saturday in September, that's what I heard. Where did that come from, then?'

Jennifer and Travis stared at him, then at each other. Helplessly, she leaned forward and touched Jacob's arm.

'I don't know where it's come from,' she said. 'Truthfully, Jacob, we haven't told a soul – except for Colonel Napier and Hilary. Travis had to tell them, out of courtesy, but that was only a day or two ago, and they wouldn't have spread it around. Where did you hear all this?'

'It's all over the village,' he said sullenly. 'I walked into the shop this morning, and all the old gossips were in there, chewing it over and wondering what sort of frock you were going to wear and how many bridesmaids there'd be and all that rubbish. They knew all the ins and outs, what the date was, and where you got the ring and everything. I felt a proper fool, not even knowing you had it in your minds.'

Jennifer and Travis looked at each other again.

'The jeweller's,' he said. 'Someone must have seen us going in. Or coming out. Whoever it was must have come straight back to the village and started spreading it about. I've heard of village grapevines, but this beats the lot.' He turned to Jacob. 'You must believe us. Apart from the Colonel, who I thought I ought to tell at once, we haven't mentioned it to a soul. We haven't even told Val and Luke.'

'We brought a bottle of sherry with us,' Jennifer said

miserably. 'We were going to ask you to come next door with us and help us celebrate. But now it's all spoilt.' The tears overflowed and ran down her cheeks.

Jacob gave her a quick look. He bit his lip and his face softened. He reached out his hand towards her, and his own eyes began to look a little watery.

'There then, don't take on. Maybe 'twas all gossip, like you say. We all understands what villages be like – knows your own business before you do yourself. But how was I to know?'

'You weren't,' Jennifer said through her tears. 'I don't blame you at all. It must have been really embarrassing for you, and really hurtful, too. I'm sorry, we ought to have come and told you before we went to Tavistock. But I never dreamed anything like this would happen, and I did want it to be a lovely surprise when I showed you my ring.'

'And so 'tis, now I knows the truth.' He took the hand she was holding out, and looked at the gleaming diamond. 'Proper handsome. I wish you happiness, my dear. And all congratulations to you, Travis. You got more sense than most, to see what a jewel you got here, and I don't mean this fancy diamond neither.'

'I know,' Travis said with a smile. 'And now we've got that settled, why don't we broach this sherry we've brought, and then all go next door and tell Val and Luke. Unless they've already heard about it, too,' he added ruefully. 'I don't want to have to go through all this again.'

'Better still,' Jacob said, 'you can go and invite them in here while I get out some of my own gooseberry champagne. That's better for celebrating good news than any old sherry bought down the off-licence. And I got some good lead crystal glasses to drink it out of, too, what my Sarah inherited from her great-aunt Maria. I'll get them out and give 'em a bit of a polish.'

He opened the door of the small sideboard, and Jennifer and Travis let themselves out. They stopped by the gate and looked at each other.

'That was a near thing,' Travis said. 'He was really upset, wasn't he? I didn't think we were going to be able to bring him round at all.'

'I'd have given anything for it not to have happened,' Jennifer said sadly. 'He's been so good to me and he's had a really miserable day. Oh, well. We can't change anything now. Let's go and see Val and Luke – and let's hope *they're* not sulking because we didn't tell them first!'

Chapter Fifteen

Jackie had waved Jennifer off that morning and gone back into the little terraced house in Devonport, feeling as if she'd been let out of a cage. She liked living with Jennifer, who gave her a good deal of freedom and didn't ask too many questions, but she was always aware that the older woman had promised to be responsible for her. It was as if her parents stood like watchful shadows, looking over Jennifer's shoulder.

Now, for two whole days, she was on her own, able to come and go as she pleased without answering to anyone. Able to ask friends back, if she wanted to. She could do all these things when Jennifer was there, of course, but it wasn't really the same. And she wasn't often there at weekends anyway, because she was expected to go home then if Jennifer had gone to Burracombe.

This weekend, she had at last persuaded Jennifer that she could be left in the house alone overnight.

'It's only one night. I can't go home myself because I'm working from eleven till four, and I've got to be at the hotel by nine tomorrow morning. I couldn't have the whole weekend off, not after having Coronation Day. Honestly, I don't see what difference it makes. I'm not going to stay out all night, after all!'

'No, I don't suppose you are,' Jennifer agreed, knowing that this was just what Ted and Alice worried about. 'And you're not going to have a party or anything, are you.' It was a statement as much as a question, but Jackie laughed.

'Who would I ask? I don't know anyone except the people at the hotel. Vic said he might come down and we could go to the pictures or something, but that's all,' she added carelessly.

Jennifer gave her a thoughtful look. Jackie had been going out with Vic Netherton on and off since before she'd moved to Plymouth. They'd grown up together in Burracombe, but hadn't really become friends until he'd returned from his National Service and found Jackie grown up and attractive. Although he worked in Plymouth himself, he hadn't liked the idea of Jackie living in the hotel, or even with Jennifer, and the romance had fizzled out. Now they seemed to be seeing each other more regularly again, although Jackie insisted they were no more than friends.

'So long as he catches the last bus back,' she said, and Jackie put on a hurt look.

'Of course he will. If he doesn't, he'll either have to walk back or doss down in the bus station. Really, Jennifer, you don't have to worry. I'll be all right. I'm nineteen, after all – a lot of people are married by that age.'

'Only if their parents give them permission!' Jennifer smiled. 'All right, Jackie, but remember that I'm trusting you, and your mother and father are trusting me. So don't let me down, will you?'

Left on her own at last, Jackie stood for a moment in the little back room. Vic was coming to call for her at six o'clock, so she would just about have time to get ready after her shift; she only had an hour before she was on duty this morning. Hardly time to get up to any mischief, she thought wryly, and decided to go into town early and have a look round the Royal Parade shops before reporting to the hotel.

By five o'clock she was home again, with a shopping bag containing a new blouse she'd bought in Littlewoods and intended wearing that evening. The house had no bathroom, but Jennifer had had a bath put into the kitchen, with a big lid over it. Jackie ran the bath and tipped in some Evening in Paris bath salts she'd also bought that morning. She had a long soak, enjoying the peace of the empty house. Before Vic's arrival, she would have time to do her nails and make-up, and try on the new blouse. It was red, with a low, frilly neckline, and would go nicely with her black taffeta skirt if they decided to go dancing instead.

She was in her bedroom, wearing the dressing-gown that her mother had made for her for Christmas out of an old winter coat, when the doorbell rang. She paused in the middle of painting her fingernails with a red varnish that her father certainly wouldn't have approved of, and hoped that whoever it was would go away. It was probably one of the neighbours wanting to borrow a cup of sugar or something. If she didn't answer, they'd try another house. But after a minute or two, the doorbell rang again. Jackie sighed and went into Jennifer's bedroom to look down at the front door.

Vic Netherton was standing on the pavement, wearing a brown jacket and cream trousers, whistling carelessly with his hands in his pockets.

Jackie bit her lip, but even as she hesitated, he glanced up and saw her at the window. He waved and beckoned her down.

'Vic!' she scolded, opening the front door. 'You're not supposed to be here till six. It's only half past five. I'm nowhere near ready.'

He grinned at her and stepped into the passageway. 'Doesn't matter, does it? I'll talk to Jennifer while you get ready. Not that you don't look very nice as you are,' he added, leaning nearer. 'Don't I get a hello kiss?'

Jackie gave him a swift peck, conscious of the loose dressing-gown gaping at the neck. 'Go into the back room, then, and sit and read the paper. Jennifer's not here.'

'Not here? Off out herself, is she?'

'No, she's gone to Burracombe,' Jackie said, and immediately wished she hadn't.

Vic's eyebrows went up, and he grinned mischievously. 'Has she, though?'

'Yes, and you needn't get any ideas,' she said sharply. 'You're going to sit here and read the paper, or listen to the wireless, and I'm going up to finish getting ready. What are we doing, anyway? Going to the pictures or going dancing?'

'Well, if we're going dancing there's no hurry, is there?' he said, taking off his jacket and loosening his tie. 'We needn't go till eight and you've got plenty of time. You can sit here and listen to the wireless with me, all cosy. You needn't even get dressed yet.' He indicated the armchair. 'I reckon we could both snuggle up together in that. Unless you've got any better ideas?'

'I haven't,' she retorted. 'And I think I'd rather go to the pictures, thanks very much. If we go soon we'll be in time for the first showing of the big picture.'

'Okay. And then we can come out early and go for a drink somewhere before I bring you home. Unless you feel like coming straight home.' He cocked an eye at her and winked.

Jackie could see danger in both these suggestions. 'Or we could stay on and see the picture round again,' she said firmly. 'I've heard it's really good. It's got Gregory Peck in it, and it's about this princess he meets in Rome.'

'Sounds a bit soppy to me,' Vic said.

'It's not soppy at all. It's romantic.'

'Oh, well,' he said, 'so long as it gets you in the mood. But we've got time for a cuddle first, haven't we?' He drew her into his arms and nuzzled her neck, then stepped back, bringing her with him, and sank into the armchair so that Jackie was on his lap. 'Mm, isn't that nicer than going to the pictures?'

Jackie relaxed against him. He was right; it was nice. She could feel the warmth of his body through his shirt, and was very conscious of her own lack of clothing. She was wearing only a light petticoat under the dressing-gown, and felt almost naked. She became aware that he could feel the softness of her breasts against his chest.

'Mmmm,' he said again, on a longer, lower note, and he slid his hand down the length of her body, lingering over her waist and then her bottom before returning to cup one breast. 'Now that really *is* nice—'

'Vic, don't!' Alarmed, Jackie tried to sit up, but his arms tightened around her and his fingers continued with a smooth caressing movement that made her breasts tingle. He was breathing quickly and her movements seemed to excite him even more. He began to kiss her, holding her head firmly with his other hand so that she couldn't turn away. She twisted her body in an effort to escape, but as his kisses grew deeper, the tingling sensation spread from her breasts to her stomach, and she began slowly to feel wrapped in a languorous, drowsy warmth. Her limbs seemed too heavy to move now, and she settled more closely against him, opening her mouth to his and whimpering softly in her throat.

'Let's go upstairs,' he said huskily. His hand had found its way into the open front of her dressing gown, and was warm against the skin of her breast.

'We can't ... We're going to the pictures ...'

'Blow the pictures! We've got much better things to do.' He began to stand up, hauling her to her feet, but Jackie pulled away. She felt dishevelled and shaken. She pushed back her tumbled hair and said in a trembling voice, 'No, Vic. We can't.'

'Of course we can. Nobody's going to disturb us. We've got the house to ourselves for the whole evening, the whole night. When are we going to get another chance like this?' He reached for her again.

'This isn't supposed to be a chance!' Jackie backed away, still shaking. Part of her longed to be swept into his arms again, to be kissed and caressed, to be taken upstairs to make love. But another part was reminding her of Jennifer's words as she'd left the house: *I'm trusting you, and your mother and father are trusting me. So don't let me down ...*

And even if she had been able to forget that, she still had the memory of her romance with Roy Pettifer and the fright she'd had when she'd thought herself pregnant. I don't ever want to take that risk again, she thought, and put up both hands to ward Vic off.

'No, Vic,' she said more strongly. 'I promised Jennifer I wouldn't take advantage of her being away. I'm going upstairs – *by myself* – to get ready, and then we'll go to the pictures.'

He stared at her. His face was red, but there were tight white patches around his mouth, and his eyes were narrowed. 'And what about when we come back?'

'You're not coming in,' she stated firmly. 'I'm sorry, Vic, but there it is. I'm not going to let everybody down.'

'As if they'd know!' he jeered, and then his voice grew angry. 'Look here, Jackie, you've been leading me on for months and now we've finally got the chance of—'

'I told you, it's *not* a chance! Not for what you want, anyway. I mean it, Vic. I thought we were friends—'

'So what? That doesn't stop us having a bit of fun as well.'

'And that's all it is to you, isn't it?' she flashed. 'A bit of fun! You're not even pretending to be serious. You're not even pretending you love me!'

'Oh, come on. You know I love you.' He moved towards her again. 'I don't have to keep on saying it all the time, do I?'

'I don't remember you ever saying it at all,' Jackie said coldly. 'You're only saying it now because you think it might help you get what you want.' She opened the door. 'I think you'd better go.'

'Go?' His brows came together. 'What the hell d'you mean, *go*? We're supposed to be going out. You wanted to see that film with Gregory Peck in it.'

'I can see that with someone else. Or by myself. I don't care all that much if I don't see it at all. But I'm not seeing it with you, and that's all there is to it. Go on, Vic, go away.'

'I came to Plymouth today specially—' he began, but she cut him short, indicating the open door with an impatient flick of her hand.

'Well, you've got plenty of time to go home. Or to find someone else to spend the evening with. I dare say you know plenty of girls who'll do what you want. But it's not going to be me.' She felt tears of anger and disappointment threaten, and her voice shook a little. 'Please, Vic, just get out!'

He stared at her for a moment or two, his eyes darkening, and for an instant she felt a tremor of fear. Then he smiled his cajoling smile and moved close again.

'You know you don't mean that, sweetheart. You're just saying it – all girls say no at first. But they never really mean it.' He slid his arms around her and held her tightly, pinning her arms to her sides so that she could barely move. His face was very close to hers; she saw his eyes harden with determination, and felt another quiver of fright. 'You don't really mean it, do you?' he said softly. 'You've been wanting this as much as I have. You planned it.'

'I didn't! I don't want it! Vic, please—'

'So why didn't you get dressed?' he demanded, and slid one hand inside her dressing gown, fastening it over her breast and squeezing painfully. 'Why did you come to the door with practically nothing on and tell me Jennifer was away? Come on, Jackie, stop playing the fool. You meant this to happen, and I'm bloody well not going to take no for an answer just because you've got cold feet!' He pushed her back towards the armchair.

'*No!*' In moving his hand to her breast, he had loosened his grip on her, and Jackie made a desperate struggle to free herself. She wriggled her arm free and swung it back, then slapped his face so hard that it jarred her wrist and stung her palm. Vic let her go and jumped back with a yelp, his hand at his cheek. He stared at her with fury.

'You little bitch! You've nearly broken my jaw!'

'Serves you right,' Jackie panted, moving swiftly so that the table was between them. 'Now get out!'

'You've deafened me, too,' he said, rubbing his ear. 'Bloody hell, that really hurts.'

'Well, I'm sorry, but you shouldn't have kept on at me. I told you no and I meant it.' She watched him warily. As a boy, Vic had been known for his temper, and he'd been a bit of a bully, too. She knew that he was much stronger than she, and if he caught her again she would be totally unable to withstand him. She lifted her chin and kept her eyes on his. 'Go away, Vic. Go on.'

He looked at her in silence for a moment or two, still rubbing his cheek, then his mouth tightened again and he shrugged. 'All right, Jackie, if that's what you want. I'm not sure I'd be interested in anything else myself, now. Spiteful little hellcat!' He moved towards the door, then turned, his lips curled in a sneer. 'And you needn't think you'll be seeing me again. I'm not going to come crawling round, saying I'm sorry and begging you to go out with me. You've had your chance. Like you say, there's plenty of other girls in the queue.'

'Good, I'm glad. I just hope they know what they're letting themselves in for.' She stood back, drawing the neck of her dressing-gown closely about her, and after another moment he turned away again and stalked along the short passageway to the front door. Jackie heard him fiddle with the lock, and then the door opened, letting in a gust of air, before slamming shut. The house was silent.

After a minute or so, she peeped round the door, cautiously, in case he hadn't gone at all and was still standing there. But there was nobody there and she went up the stairs and into Jennifer's bedroom at the front. She looked out of the window just in time to see Vic turn the corner, his back stiff with rage.

Slowly, Jackie went back to her own room. She looked at

the washstand with the little mirror, and her make-up and nail varnish standing on the marble top. Then she looked at the bed, on which lay her taffeta skirt and the new red blouse.

With a little moan of sheer misery, she threw them aside, then flung herself down on the bed and began to cry.

Chapter Sixteen

'So that', John Wolstencroft said, leaning back in his chair, 'is the position as I see it. I'll need to consult with my colleagues and look up French law before I can make a definite pronouncement, but I don't think it will be substantially different.'

Stephen and Hilary glanced at each other and then at their father, who was nodding with satisfaction.

'You mean Robert is the legitimate heir to Burracombe?' Stephen said at last. 'Even though there's no real proof?'

'As far as we can tell, there *is* real proof,' the lawyer answered. 'The marriage certificate Madame Aucoin has produced appears to be quite authentic, although I shall have to check it, of course. And it's the record of a civil marriage, which in law is the one that matters. It's unfortunate that the official documents have been lost, but in wartime ...' He shrugged. 'It's not the only case in which enemy action has forced us to accept things on good faith.'

'Not that it matters,' Gilbert said tersely. 'Fact is, French law don't really come into it one way or the other. I'm prepared to accept the boy as Baden's son, and that's all there is to it.'

'But in law, he isn't,' Hilary pointed out. 'He was born in Marianne's second marriage and her husband – Jacques, wasn't he? – acknowledged him as *his* son. How do you get round that?'

'I tell you, we don't *need* to,' her father said impatiently. 'Anyone has only to look at the boy to know the truth. You saw it yourself, the moment you laid eyes on him that first morning. You knew without any doubt that he was Baden's son, now didn't you?'

'Well, yes,' she admitted. 'But we're not talking about that, we're talking about the legal aspect—'

'Which is neither here nor there. How many times do I have to repeat it: I'm prepared to accept the boy, and John has confirmed that there's no reason why I shouldn't make him my heir. Look, both of you, I didn't call you in here to ask your opinions, nor to discuss it with you. I called you in so that I could *tell* you. There's nothing else to talk about.'

Stephen shifted abruptly in his chair, and Hilary saw his fair skin redden angrily. 'I'm sorry, Dad, I think there is. Maybe in *law* you can leave the estate to whoever you like, but isn't there a moral side to this? A family side? Don't Hilary and I count for anything? Hilary, especially.'

'Of course you do. For God's sake, Stephen, I'm not about to disown you. You'll both be well provided for. And I haven't finally—'

'*Well provided for?*' Stephen interrupted. 'And just what does that mean? Not that I want a penny from you.'

'Don't be so ridiculous!' Gilbert snapped. 'You're happy enough to accept a generous allowance now. You didn't buy that sports car out of your RAF pay!'

Stephen flushed even deeper. 'All right, but to be perfectly honest, I'd rather forget the allowance and have a settlement now so that when I leave the RAF I can set up business in Canada and be done with it. You can do what you like with the rest, provided you look after Hilary.'

'I don't need to be told to look after my own daughter,' Gilbert said coldly. 'Hilary will have a home here for as long as she wants it. That'll be part of the terms of my will.'

Hilary broke in again. 'Father, what makes you think that I'll want to stay here under those conditions? Stephen told you the other day that I've put my life into Burracombe. How can

163

I stand back and let someone else take it over, someone who hasn't grown up here, who doesn't feel for the land and love it as we do? I can't believe you're even contemplating it.'

'The boy's Baden's son—' he began, but she interrupted again.

'That doesn't make him Baden! I'm sorry, Dad, but you have to face facts. To all intents and purposes, he's French. He's had a French upbringing in a French family, and you *can't* expect him to feel the same as Baden, or even to *be* the same. His entire background is different. We don't know what he would do. We don't even know that he *wants* to be heir.'

'Oh, I think he'll want to, all right,' Stephen said grimly. 'And if he doesn't, his mother certainly will.'

Hilary shot him a quick glance. He was looking tired, as if he hadn't slept much, and there was an unaccustomed edginess about him. He'd come down late to breakfast and eaten very little, staring moodily at his plate and drinking several cups of strong coffee. She wondered what had taken place between him and Marianne after she and her father had gone to bed, and if they had argued.

Marianne herself had seemed quite composed, with a small smile playing about her lips, but she had said nothing beyond a calm 'Good morning'. There hadn't been much time for talk anyway; as soon as breakfast was over, she had asked Hilary to take herself and Robert to the Roman Catholic church in Tavistock, and when Hilary had returned, there was only just time to join her father for the village service. She'd preceded him up the aisle, conscious of the interested glances that followed them, knowing that the villagers were wondering about the visitors and why they weren't also present. Afterwards, she and Gilbert had returned quickly to the Barton for their last discussion with John Wolstencroft before he went back to Exeter.

'One of us will have to go and fetch them soon,' she said now. 'Marianne said she would like to have a walk round the town, but we can't leave them there for ever, and lunch will be ready.' She looked at the lawyer. 'So what you're saying is, unless you discover something different, there's no legal barrier to the Burracombe estate being left to Robert, if that's what Father wants to do?'

'As far as I can judge, yes,' Wolstencroft said rather unhappily. 'Obviously there's a great deal to be done before any will is drawn up – there are a number of conditions to be settled, and provision for yourself and Stephen is one of them.' He hesitated. 'I've suggested also that any sale of the estate, once it has passed to the new heir, must be approved by you both – but that also needs careful thought. It will all take time, and' – he glanced at Gilbert – 'you may change your mind before then, Colonel Napier. And, of course, any will is open to contest.'

'You mean when my father dies,' Stephen said bluntly. 'Hilary and I could contest it then.'

'If you wished to, yes. I can't say what view a court would take, though.'

Gilbert gave an impatient snort. 'What sort of nonsense is this? Naturally they won't contest it. If I'm of sound mind—'

'Well, that's one thing that might be contested,' Stephen muttered, but his father heard him. His face darkened and he leaned forward, gripping the arms of his chair so tightly Hilary feared they would break.

'You'll take that back at once, you young whippersnapper!' he thundered. 'You'll say I'm mad, is that it? I've a good mind to cut you off entirely for that!'

'Father—' Hilary began anxiously, and the lawyer started to his feet.

'Colonel Napier, please. Your blood pressure . . .' He turned to Stephen. 'I really think you should apologise.'

'All right, all right, no need to take it so seriously,' Stephen said, flapping his hands. 'It was just a remark.'

'A damned stupid one!'

'Yes, a stupid one, and I'm sorry.' Stephen stood up. 'I'll

go and fetch Marianne and Robert. I presume there's nothing else you want to *tell* us?' He turned towards the door.

Hilary followed him out to the hall. 'Don't get too upset, Steve. As Mr Wolstencroft says, it'll all take quite a while to organise anyway, and we still don't really know what Marianne and Robert want. When Dad sits her down to discuss it, we may find she just wants an allowance for Robert and will take him back to France. He could just come here for his holidays, and—'

'Don't get your hopes up, Hilary,' he advised, opening the front door. 'That might be all she wanted when she came, but she's seen enough now to make her think again. And don't run away with the idea that Dad will let him go back. He's got his heir now – whatever anyone says, he still, in his heart, believes he's got Baden back – and he's not going to let go of that idea in a hurry. In my opinion, things are going to get a lot worse before they get better.' He stopped, then added bitterly, 'But what does *my* opinion count around here?'

He ran down the steps and leaped into his sports car, which he had left standing in front of the house. The engine roared into life, and he swung the car in a circle, sweeping at high speed down the drive and halting at the road with a screech of brakes.

Hilary watched anxiously, then turned and went slowly back into the house. She wondered again just what had happened between Stephen and Marianne the night before, and what was likely to happen next.

'*Stephen's* here?' Maddy said in surprise. 'But I'd no idea he was coming today. It's only two or three days since I saw him.'

The Archdeacon's wife shook her head. 'He told me that himself. But he said he'd had to go back to Burracombe for the weekend and wanted to call in on the way back. You don't have to see him, if you don't want to.'

'Well, I was going to go to Evensong,' Maddy said doubtfully. 'But I can't just send him away. I wonder why he's come? He didn't say he was going home this weekend.'

'I expect he'll tell you. I've put him in the small sitting room. Of course, you can take him up to your own flat if you like.'

'No, it's all right. I don't suppose he's staying long.' Maddy handed over the dog's lead. She had taken Archie for a long walk along the West Lyme beach, and his black coat was still wet and shining from his many swims in the waves. 'I'm sorry, he needs hosing down with some fresh water to get the salt out of his coat.'

'I'll do that.' The Archdeacon's wife took the lead and called to the labrador, who came bounding over, his tongue lolling in a happy grin. 'He's obviously had a good time!'

She went round the corner to the back of the house, and Maddy went up the steps and through to the small sitting room. It was a snug, cosy room with pleasantly shabby furniture, and was usually scattered with the day's newspapers and whichever books the family might be reading at the time. Stephen was sitting on the sofa, leaning forward, his chin in his hands, gazing at the floor.

'Hello,' Maddy said, coming in and closing the door behind her. 'I didn't expect to see you today. Is everything all right at home? Nobody's ill, are they?'

He turned his head and stood up. 'No, nobody's ill. I just felt I had to see you.' He came over and gave her a kiss, holding her loosely for a moment. 'Oh, Maddy ... it's been the most incredible few days.'

'Why? What's happened?' The way he was holding her was almost as if he were resting against her, as if he wanted comfort. 'Stephen, whatever is the matter?'

'It's a long story. I hardly know where to start.' He moved away slightly and looked at her. 'D'you mind, Maddy? It's not your worry, but we're friends, aren't we? We can talk to each other about things.'

'Of course we can.' Until now, Stephen had been the one offering comfort and friendship, even love if she wanted it, and it had never occurred to Maddy that he might one day ask comfort from her. She took his hand and led him to the sofa. 'Sit down and tell me what's wrong.'

'How much time have you got?' he asked ruefully. 'Were you planning to go to church?'

'I was, but it doesn't matter. But look, before you start, I'll just let them know in the kitchen that you'll be staying to supper. It's always late on Sunday because of the service, so we've got plenty of time.'

'No, I can't stay. I've got to get back to the station. And Mrs Copley is sending in some tea – here it is now,' he added, as the door opened and a maid came in bearing a tray of tea, buttered scones and cakes. 'Goodness, look at all that! I shan't want any supper anyway.'

Maddy waited until the maid had departed, and then poured tea for them both. 'Now, tell me all about it.'

'Well, it's all very strange,' Stephen said, taking a scone and putting it on his plate. 'It started the morning after the Coronation. Hilary and I were just finishing our breakfast and thinking about going down to the fields to help clear up, when …' He went on to describe Marianne's arrival and Robert's startling resemblance to Baden. 'Father took it all in straight away, hook, line and sinker. He's already started to tell people Robert is his grandson, and he's even hinted that he's going to leave Burracombe to him. More than hinted, to be perfectly honest.'

Maddy stared at him. 'Stephen, that's amazing. Surely he can't do that, just on a family resemblance.'

'She does have a marriage certificate, but I don't know if it's really legal. There doesn't seem to be any way of proving it. He got the family lawyer down from Exeter – he came yesterday and stayed overnight – and according to him, Father can leave the estate to whoever he chooses. But it's not just that, Maddy. I don't want the estate myself, you know that, but

Hilary does. She's put her heart and soul into the place. And if Father does go ahead and change his will, and Robert inherits, what's going to happen to her? He could turn her out!'

'I can't believe it. No wonder you're upset. Your whole life's been turned upside down, and all in a few days. And nobody ever suspected that Baden had married?'

'Didn't have a clue. He never had a chance to tell us, you see. It was so chaotic during those last few days, and then when everyone in his unit got killed . . .'

'Yes, I see,' she said thoughtfully. 'What are they like – Robert and his mother?'

'He's just a kid – thirteen years old, quite bright but rather quiet. It's hard to know what he's thinking, but I feel a bit sorry for him. He's too young to have any say in what happens to him, yet he must have feelings about it all, but nobody seems to be very concerned about what they might be. I've taken him out a bit – and Marianne as well – and he seems interested in the area. They both speak good English, fortunately.' He fell silent.

'And his mother?' Maddy prompted after a moment.

Stephen looked away and then at the floor. 'I don't know, Maddy,' he said at last. 'I don't know what to make of her. She . . . well, she's French, I suppose.'

'Yes, I imagine she is,' Maddy said with a smile, although something in Stephen's manner gave her a flicker of unease. 'But that doesn't tell me much. What does she look like?'

'Oh, quite small, with dark hair and eyes, quite fashionably dressed, although her clothes have obviously seen better days. Make do and mend, you know, but very well done. She runs a *pâtisserie*.' He was silent again, his gaze fixed unseeingly on the scone still on his plate. 'I'm not sure what she's got in mind. I don't think she expected us to be as we are. It was a shock for her. Baden had told her the family owned a farm, but not much more, from what I gather, and she probably expected a family like the Tozers.'

'Does she want money?' Maddy asked.

'I think that's one of the things she came for, yes. She more or less admitted she wanted help. She's got other children, too, and her husband died about six months ago – I told you she was widowed, didn't I? – and she says it seemed the right time to bring Robert to meet his English family. But what she's thinking now, I just don't know. Except . . .' He stopped suddenly, a wash of colour creeping up from his neck, and bowed his head to look at the floor.

'Except what?' Maddy asked.

'Oh, nothing. It doesn't matter.' He sat up straight again. 'I ought to be going soon anyway. I'm sorry, I shouldn't have come, pouring out all my troubles on you like this when you've got enough on your own plate.'

'I don't mind,' Maddy said. 'You said yourself, we're friends, we can talk to each other. I'm glad you came, and it's good for me to listen to someone else for a change instead of thinking about myself all the time. But you can't go yet; you've hardly touched your tea.'

'I'm not really hungry. There'll be a meal in the mess, anyway.' He drained his cup and stood up. 'Say thank you to Mrs Copley for me, will you?' He moved towards the door.

Maddy followed him. 'You will come again, won't you? And do let me know how things go. I care about all of you, you know that. I can't bear to think how upset Hilary must be.'

Stephen paused and looked down at her. 'Well, she's not all that upset, not at the moment. The whole thing's just bowled us all over. But there's going to be a lot of talking to do and decisions to make, and I don't mean to let Hilary be done out of what ought to be hers. And yet, as Dad says, if Baden hadn't been killed, he'd have brought Marianne and Robert home and they'd have been living with us for years, and nobody would have questioned his right to be heir. It's hard to argue with that.'

'Yes, I can see that,' she said, and saw him to his car,

reminding him again to come and talk to her whenever he needed. 'We're friends, Stephen,' she said firmly again. 'Whatever else happens, we'll always be friends.'

He nodded, gave her another quick kiss, and then drove away. Maddy stood on the gravel drive, watching as the car disappeared through the big gates, and then she turned and went slowly back into the house.

The story Stephen had told her was astonishing enough. Yet there was something else in his manner that troubled her. A strange evasiveness when she'd asked about Marianne.

Maddy could not make out whether he liked the French-woman or loathed her.

Chapter Seventeen

'Hullo,' Jennifer said when she let herself into the little house in Devonport later that evening. 'Whatever's the matter with you?'

Jackie was sprawling in one of the two armchairs in the back room, looking moody and half listening to Variety Bandbox on the wireless. Her eyes were slightly swollen.

'Nothing,' she said sullenly, in answer to Jennifer's question, and then, without much interest, 'Have a nice weekend?'

'Yes, thank you, very nice.' Jennifer came over and sat on an upright dining chair beside her. 'Jackie, you look really upset. What's happened?'

Jackie scowled and pressed her lips together, then gave up the pretence and turned to Jennifer, her face crumpling like a child's. 'It's Vic,' she wailed. 'He's been horrible!'

Jennifer felt a quick tremor of alarm. 'Why, what's he done?'

Jackie started to cry in earnest, and Jennifer's alarm grew. I shouldn't have left her here on her own, she thought, putting her arm round the heaving shoulders. Now the worst has happened, and whatever are Alice and Ted going to say if . . . ? She dared not complete the thought. All her joy and happiness over her engagement seemed to drain away, and instead she felt beset by a sick anxiety. She switched off the wireless.

'Jackie. Try to stop crying. Here, have my hanky . . . now, take a deep breath. And another, that's right. Deep down into your tummy. Come on. It can't be that bad, surely?' She was afraid, all the same, that it could. 'Now, tell me exactly what happened.'

Jackie drew in a great, shuddering lungful of air. 'It was yesterday. I got home from work and I had a bath. I thought I had lots of time to get ready, but he came early and I was still in my dressing-gown and ... and ...' Her sobs overtook her again, and Jennifer's anxiety turned to dread.

'And what, Jackie?' she asked quietly. 'What did Vic do? What actually happened?'

'He ... he kissed me and he ... he touched me ... here.' Jackie touched her breasts. 'And then he said let's go upstairs and not bother about going out, and ... and ...'

'And did you go upstairs?'

'No!' Jackie drew away, staring at her with wide eyes. 'No, I didn't. I told him I couldn't, that I didn't want to. And I told him to go. I *made* him go.'

Jennifer felt a surge of relief. 'And that's all that happened? He didn't do anything else? He didn't try to force you?'

'Not force me, exactly,' Jackie said, sniffing and blowing her nose. 'But he tried to persuade me. And ... and the thing was ...' She gazed at Jennifer with wide, tear-drenched eyes. 'The thing was, I *wanted* to. I really wanted to.'

'Then you did very well,' Jennifer said briskly. 'Look, Jackie, I do know what it's like. It's a very strong feeling, to want to make love with a man you're fond of.' She stopped, feeling the colour creep up her neck as she thought of Travis's kisses the night before, as they'd parted at Jacob's cottage gate. It was not going to be easy to wait for four months. 'You are fond of Vic, aren't you?'

'I like him,' Jackie said doubtfully. 'At least, I did. I don't know what I feel about him now.'

'Then it's just as well you didn't let things go any further. You know what they say: save yourself for the right man, and you'll never regret it.'

'And how do you know who that is?' Jackie asked wistfully.

Again, Jennifer thought of Travis. He was the right man for her, she was convinced of that, but she was going to him as a virgin only because her first husband had refused to make love to her. She'd thought he was the right man, but she'd been wrong. How *did* you know?

'We just have to hope we get it right,' she said. 'Vic's a nice boy but maybe he's not the right one for you, and it's a good job you've found that out now. This sort of thing happens to all of us, Jackie, and when you do meet the right one you'll be glad you waited.'

Jackie said nothing for a moment or two. Then she raised her eyes to Jennifer's and said quietly, 'But I haven't waited, Jennifer. There was Roy Pettifer.'

Jennifer stared at her. 'Roy Pettifer? The young man who's in Korea? But he's been away for over a year, surely.'

'Yes, but before he went, for a long time really, we were friends. We really loved each other – well, we thought we did, anyway. I don't know now … Anyway, we … we got a bit carried away one day, and I thought I'd fallen for a baby. I hadn't, but it was awful at the time. It never happened again,' she added swiftly. 'I didn't want another fright like that … Val knows, but nobody else does.'

'I see,' Jennifer said slowly. Her mind was in turmoil. Jackie was more experienced than she had realised, but was she any more capable of taking care of herself? I shan't leave her alone here again, Jennifer decided. It's too risky.

'You won't tell anyone, will you?' Jackie begged anxiously.

Jennifer shook her head. 'No, I won't. Especially as you say Val knows. But what happened between you and Roy? Did you split up after that?'

'Yes. Mainly because I was so scared, I'd hardly even let him kiss me. And then he went away. But I still write to him. They think the war will be over soon, and then he'll come home. He said so in his last letter.'

Jennifer looked at her thoughtfully. There was a touch of

animation in her voice as she talked of Roy. Was Jackie still carrying a torch for him?

'Well, it seems to me that what happened with Vic is over now and wasn't nearly as bad as you think,' she said, getting up. 'It's the sort of thing that happens to most of us at some time. And now I'm going to make a cup of tea. Do you want one?'

'Yes, please.' Jackie sank back into her chair, then sat up straight again. 'Oh, Jennifer! I am awful – I haven't asked you about your weekend? Did you and Travis get engaged? Have you got a ring? Let me see it!'

Smiling, Jennifer held out her hand, and Jackie bent over it rapturously, her troubles apparently forgotten. She examined the diamond closely, turning Jennifer's hand this way and that so that it flashed with colour in the light.

'It's lovely. And when's the wedding going to be? You are going to let me be bridesmaid, aren't you? I know you'll want Pammy and Jean as well, but they're tiny, and you'll need a big one to look after your flowers and your train and everything. Oh, I can't wait! I hope it's not going to be too long.'

'It's going to be in September,' Jennifer said. 'And it'll be in the church. We were going to have it quietly in the Tavistock register office, but the village apparently thinks otherwise. Look, you wait while I make the tea, and then I'll tell you all about it.'

She went out to the kitchen and Jackie lay back again, feeling better. Maybe Jennifer was right and it hadn't been so terrible after all. It was the end of her friendship with Vic, of course, but she hadn't been that keen on him for a long time. There were plenty of other fish in the sea.

Jennifer came back with the tea and a plate of ginger biscuits, and sat down in the other armchair. She switched on the wireless again.

'Let's have some music while we talk. I want to know what you think I should wear. Not a long white dress, but I'm not keen on a suit, either – I think it needs to be something a bit more special than that. What ideas do you have?'

They settled down happily, drinking tea and munching ginger biscuits, and – for the time being, at least – Jackie forgot her misery.

The drive back from West Lyme to the RAF station at White Cheriton took Stephen across the steep green hills of Dorset and into the wooded valleys of Hampshire, but although the evening sky was a soft, tender blue, with high, streaming banners of salmon-pink and apricot clouds far above, his mind was not on the beauty of his surroundings. Indeed, he barely noticed them; the road was so familiar to him now that he knew every twist and turn, and scarcely had to think where to slow down and when to change gear. If he had been stopped and asked which village he had passed through last, he would have been hard put to answer.

There was almost too much to think about. The events of the past week had left him feeling stunned and bewildered, with a mixture of anger and anxiety jostling for place. He was angry with his father, whom he considered had been much too impetuous – and that makes a change, he thought wryly, since Dad always accuses me of that! – and he was anxious about Hilary. His own prospects came further down the list. He wasn't especially concerned about his inheritance, although he certainly wouldn't sniff at some extra money to add to what his mother had left him; but his streak of independence and desire to make a new life for himself far away from Burracombe meant that it was less important. He was confident of his ability to set up the air freight business he planned, and he'd met enough Canadians in the RAF to believe that their country was the one for him.

But for Hilary, it was a different matter. She cared passionately about the estate, and, although he didn't believe she had always wanted to give her life to it, that was what she was doing now, and it angered him to see it snatched away from her. Their father had never really appreciated what Hilary was doing, he thought. He'd been against her taking over from the start, even when his heart attack had forced him to give way. He'd been insistent that she find herself a husband, and when she'd refused to consider any of the chinless wonders he'd suggested from amongst his friends' sons, he'd treated her like a nineteenth-century spinster daughter and expected her to look after the house, handing the management of the estate to Travis Kellaway. But Hilary had rejected this and almost rejected Travis; it was fortunate that the two of them got on well together. For a time, Stephen, like a lot of other people, had wondered whether their friendship might go further and solve all their problems. Clearly, though, this wasn't to be, and now, with Robert's arrival, Hilary was again being relegated to a second-class position. And it wasn't even as if they knew what the boy was like or what his mother wanted of them.

At the thought of Marianne, Stephen felt his blood grow hot. He'd been aware of her attraction from the start; small yet curvaceous, with full, pouting lips and black curls that had tumbled around her shoulders when she had unpinned it last night, she had an earthy sensuality that seemed to call out to his most basic instincts. At their first meeting, when she had fixed those dark, sultry eyes on his face, he had had to struggle to pay attention to what was being said. He'd wanted nothing more than to gaze at her, drinking in every detail of her oval face, her olive skin, her long, thick lashes.

Yet at the same time he was repelled, almost afraid. This woman is going to bring me trouble, he thought; and even when he heard who she was and why she had come, it still seemed to mean trouble for himself in particular, and not just for the family.

It added up to a kind of fascination. He longed to be near her, to experience those heady sensations, yet when they were together he wanted to get away, and, more than anything else, to be with Maddy.

You could not, he thought, have two more opposite women. Marianne was the elder by some years, but if you stood them side by side, her striking dark looks might overpower Maddy's fair, delicate beauty. And with Maddy, you knew where you were; her honesty shone from her sky-blue eyes. Marianne was elusive; you would never quite know what was in her mind.

He had driven away from Burracombe that afternoon with his mind and emotions churning, scarcely knowing what he thought or felt. His one desire was to see Maddy. She would help him find his place in the world again. He needed desperately to look into those clear blue eyes, to hear her soft voice, to touch her small, cool hand. He needed to get this Frenchwoman out of his mind, to forget her glances, her tumbling hair, her seductive murmur. He needed to talk to someone who could stand back a little, who could help him regain his perspective. Most of all, he needed to talk to someone he loved and who he believed still harboured at least an affection for him. He needed to be with Maddy; and he had turned off the road at West Lyme and driven straight to the Archdeacon's house where Maddy worked as the Archdeacon's secretary.

By the time he left her, an hour or two later, he was feeling calmer, although he still couldn't get the matter out of his mind. Until now, his feelings about Burracombe and his family had been casual. He had taken them for granted, knowing from the cradle that he was never going to inherit, and turning his attention in other directions. Burracombe Barton was his home, but it was just a house, somewhere he knew he would be welcomed. His father's attitude was irritating, but Stephen had looked forward to the time when he could shake the dust of the place from his feet and leave it behind him as he made his own life.

He'd looked up to his brother Baden but never known him on equal terms, and he had decided long ago not to try to follow in his footsteps. His main concern had been for his sister, but she had appeared happy enough, settled into her management of the estate and leaving him free to live his own life. Although he'd known vaguely that he would miss her, apart from offering her a home with him in Canada, he'd not thought much more about her situation.

Now, he was indignant – even furious – on her behalf, and he knew that he could not simply walk away. Hilary needed him.

Burracombe needed him.

Chapter Eighteen

'You'll write as soon as you get home, won't you?' Gilbert said, as Marianne got into the front seat of Hilary's car on Wednesday morning. 'And take care on the journey. It's a pity one of us can't go with you.'

'I will be quite all right. I'm used to managing alone.' She smiled at him, then turned to her son. 'Behave yourself well, Robert, and don't be a trouble to Hilary or your grandfather. I'll see you again soon. Write to me every week and tell me all you're doing.'

'*Oui*, Maman. And give my love to *mes grandmères* and Tante Helene, and Philippe and Ginette.' He bent through the window to kiss his mother's cheeks.

Hilary finished stowing Marianne's suitcase in the back of the car, and came round to the driver's side.

'Take care of her, now,' Gilbert ordered. 'All very well to say she can manage, but it's a long journey to Dover on the train, and she has to cross from Paddington to Charing Cross. You ought to have gone with her that far at least.'

'I did offer,' Hilary said mildly. 'But you've given her plenty of money for a taxi. I'm sure she'll be all right. And once she's at Dover and catches the night ferry, she'll be almost home again.'

He grunted, and Hilary got in and started the engine. She drove off towards the big gates, and Gilbert and Robert stood watching the car, waving as it turned out on to the road.

'Well, that's that,' Gilbert said to the boy, who was still

gazing down the drive. 'She'll be back in a few weeks, and meanwhile we've got to occupy you. What d'you want to do now?'

'I'd like to know more about my father,' Robert said, turning back at last and looking up at him. 'Will you show me some more photographs? And tell me some more of the stories you told me on Sunday evening, after Stephen had gone? Do you have time to do this, or are you too busy?'

'Too busy?' Gilbert said gruffly. 'Too busy to tell you about Baden? Isn't that why you've stayed here now, so that you can find out more about him and about the place where he grew up – the place that would have been his? Of course I'm not too busy! Come indoors. We'll ask Mrs Ellis to send in some lemonade, and I'll get out all his school photos. And there are boxes full of bits and pieces in the old playroom.' He marched back towards the house. At the top of the steps, he paused and laid his hand on Robert's shoulder, turning him so that they looked out at the view of the Burra valley, with its scatter of cottages and farms, and the fields and woods rising beyond to the purple heather of the moor.

'This is the view he saw every day while he was here,' he said quietly. 'A lot of that land belongs to the estate, to the Napier family. Every one of us who inherits it, inherits a responsibility as well as land. It's our job to take care of it, and pass it on to the next generation in good heart. Do you understand what I'm saying?'

Robert nodded, as he took in the panorama laid out before them. Gilbert spoke again.

'My grandfather passed it to my father, who passed it to me in his turn. If Baden had lived, I would have passed it to him, and he to you. But it isn't passed on by right. It's our duty to see that the next generation understands their responsibility and will fulfil it, as the Napiers always have done. Are you sure you understand? I want it to be quite clear.'

'I think I understand,' Robert said carefully. 'Some of the

words I do not know, but I think you mean that if I am suitable, you may pass Burracombe to me, when you die.'

Gilbert looked at him for a moment. 'Well, that's putting it bluntly, but yes. That's what I mean. I don't *have* to do it, you see. I can leave the estate to whomever I wish.'

'So you are testing me, *n'est-ce pas?*' Robert asked, his blue eyes meeting Gilbert's. 'I am on trial?'

Gilbert hesitated, then shook his head. 'No, Robert, you're not on trial. You're just my grandson, whom I'm very glad to have here. I want you to enjoy yourself. Anything else will come later. Now, let's go and find those photographs.'

They walked into the house, together. But Gilbert left the front door open, so that the morning light could stream in, and Robert paused for a moment and looked back at the view.

His eyes moved slowly over the range of fields, woods and hills, and he folded his lips together. Then he followed his grandfather into the house.

'It's been a proper week of it, and no mistake,' Dottie declared when Felix came over to tea that afternoon. She was making Stella a new summer frock, and the material was draped over an armchair, bristling with pins. Her Singer sewing machine, which always stood in a corner, was still set up for work with a cat's cradle of Sylko threaded through its various hooks and eyes.

With the Coronation over, the village was settling back to normal, with most of the flags and bunting removed, and only the red, white and blue flowers still growing in the gardens and Dottie's tubs to lend a patriotic air to the surroundings. The parties and processions that had taken so many months to prepare seemed apparently to be in the distant past, as Christmas does by the time the New Year comes along, and the main topics of conversation now were Jennifer Tucker's engagement to Travis Kellaway, and the mysterious goings-on up at the Barton.

'I don't suppose you've heard anything about all that?' Dottie enquired, tidying away the remnants of paper pattern on the table, and putting the kettle on. 'I've heard a lot round the village, but you never know what's true and what isn't. There's one or two folk in Burracombe not above making it up if they don't know the truth. I don't gossip myself, of course, but I reckon anything you might have to tell us would be right.'

'Unfortunately, I don't,' Felix said, smiling a little. 'I did call in on Mr Harvey on my way over, but I don't think he knows much more than anyone else. The Colonel seems quite happy for people to know that the boy is his grandson, and that Baden had married just before he was killed on the way to Dunkirk. But apart from that, I don't think there's much more for anyone to know.'

Dottie paused in what she was doing. 'It's right, then? Young Robert *is* Baden's boy?' She turned to Stella, who had been upstairs. 'It's true, what Jacob told me. Master Baden got wed over in France without anyone knowing, and that boy's his. Well, when you look at him, there's no doubting it. I wonder what they'll do about it? Will they come here to live, d'you reckon?'

'I shouldn't think so,' Felix said. 'She's going back to France this week – she's got other family there.' He stopped, guiltily aware that Dottie had lured him dangerously close to gossiping. 'Anyway, I dare say we'll know whatever the family want us to know, when they decide to tell us. *If* they decide to tell us. It's not really our business, after all.'

'It's the village's business,' Dottie declared, refusing to be put off. 'There's a lot of farmland and houses around here that are part of the estate, and people who depend on it for their living. It's only natural they'll take an interest in what's going on.'

'And as I say, I'm sure they'll be told about anything that might affect them,' Felix smiled. 'Now, what's the latest news about Travis and Jennifer? Have they actually set the date?'

'The village set it for them,' Stella said with a laugh. 'Jennifer told me they'd intended to have a quiet wedding, and they thought perhaps it might be in September. They weren't going to make any announcement, just tell a few friends and put it in next week's *Tavistock Times*, but when they got back to Burracombe after buying the ring, everyone knew about it and had decided it was going to be on the second Saturday in September – and had very nearly made up their minds about the colour of the bridesmaids' dresses! Jennifer told me she hadn't intended to have any bridesmaids at all, but now she feels she's got to. I'm not even sure they intended to get married in the church,' she added with a doubtful glance at Felix.

'Not get married in church?' Dottie exclaimed in a scandalised tone. 'Why ever not? They've neither of them been married before, have they? I mean ... they're not *divorced* or anything?' She spoke the word in a hushed voice, almost glancing over her shoulder as if she were overheard.

'I don't think so. But we wouldn't really know, would we? We don't really know either of them very well. Anyway, it really isn't our business. And from what Val told me yesterday, they've changed their minds about that and been to see Mr Harvey to fix the date.'

'Good luck to them,' Felix said wistfully. 'I wish it was us fixing a September wedding.' He glanced at Stella. 'You don't think ...?'

'No, I don't. Honestly, Felix, there's barely time as it is. I've started to make lists – you've no idea how much there is to do.'

'I do have quite a lot of experience of weddings,' he said with dignity, and the two women laughed.

'Experience of other people's weddings, you mean,' Dottie told him. 'I don't suppose you've got the first idea how much planning and work goes into that moment when the bride comes up the aisle and the two of them stand in front of you to make their vows. If you think it's just a matter of Stella putting on a pretty white frock and promising to obey you for the rest of her life, you've got another think coming.'

'I should say he has!' Stella exclaimed. 'I've no intention of promising any such thing. Can you imagine, Dottie, obeying Felix for the next sixty years or so? Goodness knows what sort of trouble we'd get into.'

'But you have to,' Dottie said in dismay. 'It's part of the service: "Love, honour and obey." Isn't it, Felix?'

'I'm afraid it is. But look on the bright side, darling. I've got to promise to endow you with all my worldly goods, and apparently that includes Mirabelle *and* my oar with all the Cambridge rowing eight's signatures on it.'

'I wouldn't mind Mirabelle,' Stella said thoughtfully. 'But you can keep the oar, in exchange for me not promising to obey you.'

'I don't think you're taking this seriously,' he accused her, and Dottie, still looking horrified, agreed with him.

'I've never heard of anyone not saying it. I think you've got to.'

'Oh, no, I won't!' Stella said, with a wicked grin.

'Oh, yes, you will!' Felix retorted, and they laughed at each other. 'Oh, what does it matter anyway? So long as you promise to be my wife, and love me till death us do part, and worship me with your body and ...' He stopped, casting an embarrassed glance at Dottie, and Stella giggled.

'Oh, you needn't mind me,' Dottie said smartly, making the tea. 'I might be a spinster of this parish but that don't mean I'm not aware of the facts of life. You couldn't work in the theatre, like I did, and not know summat about all the goings-on. Not that Miss Forsyth went in for that sort of thing,' she added quickly. 'A proper lady she was. Never put a foot wrong, all the time I knew her, and brought young Maddy up the same way. Now, tea's ready but it's not much today – only bread and butter and fish paste, and this pot of fresh raspberry jam, and a bit of cake left over from the weekend and a few jam tarts I made this afternoon. I've been busy sewing, and haven't had time to do anything else.'

'Anything else!' Felix said. 'It's a veritable feast. I don't know how Stella keeps so slim with you feeding her like this every day.'

'She doesn't,' Stella said solemnly. 'I only get fed when you come to tea. I'm starved the rest of the time.'

'What are these lists you're making?' he asked, spreading his bread with salmon and shrimp paste. 'A guest list, I suppose. I'll have to get on and finish mine, or we'll be too late to send out the invitations.'

'We don't need to do that until six weeks beforehand. The end of November will do. But we do need to get the invitations printed. I suppose we ought to start thinking about that in the middle of September, but we'd better have the list ready in good time.'

'So what else is there?'

'Any amount of things! My dress, the bridesmaids – we still haven't finally decided who to ask, so we need to think about that. And then there are the flowers for church and my bouquet, and the bridesmaids' posies. And food and drink at the reception, and cars, and photographs. And if we're having the reception at the vicarage, we'll need a thorough spring-clean, and we'll have to move furniture and make sure there's enough room for everyone to sit.' She stopped and looked at him. 'Honestly, Felix, it really isn't big enough for all the guests to sit down for a meal, and you haven't got anywhere near enough chairs.'

'You're right,' Felix said glumly. 'Back to the drawing-board, then. What about a buffet meal? You don't need tables, then.'

Stella shook her head. 'That would be all right in summer, and we could even have it out in the garden – there's room on the lawn for that marquee we used for the dance last week. But not in winter. And people need something hot inside them, soup at the very least. You can't ask them to sit around in their best clothes with bowls of soup on their laps. Some of your relatives are bishops!' She sighed. 'It would be so much easier in summer, and nicer in every way. Felix ...'

'*No*,' he said firmly. 'We've set the date for just after Christmas and I'm not budging an inch. It's not just the wedding day that's important, darling, it's every day of our lives together afterwards, and I don't want to wait another six months for those to start. Look, I know there are problems but they can all be solved, and it will be a wonderful day that we'll remember for the rest of our lives. And if having the reception is going to be such a problem, why not have it in Tavistock, at the Bedford Hotel? That's good enough for any bishop. Not that they'll care that much about whether it's "good enough" or not,' he added, 'but at least there'll be plenty of room, and they won't drop soup down their robes.'

Stella gazed at him doubtfully. 'But won't that be terribly expensive?'

'Don't worry about that. I told you, my parents will foot the bill and they'll be quite happy to do so. It's their wedding present to us.'

'It might be the answer,' she said slowly. 'I did want to have it in the village, but ...'

'What about the village hall?' Dottie asked. 'We can seat getting on for a hundred in ours, and me and Alice Tozer and some of the others could do the food.'

'But what will Felix's parishioners think, if we get married over here and stay here for the reception as well? They'll be really hurt. And their hall is definitely too small. I think he's right, Dottie, it might be better to have it somewhere neutral. Besides, we want you and Alice there as guests, not working.'

'We wouldn't mind helping,' Dottie said. 'But I can see what you mean. You certainly don't want it in that poky old shed they've got over there, begging the vicar's pardon,' she added to Felix, who bowed his head graciously. 'And with all those high-up relatives he's got, it do seem a bit more fitting.'

'That's settled, then,' Stella said, and glanced at Felix. 'And just what are you looking so smug about?'

'Nothing,' he said innocently. 'Only that I'm pleased to see you've started as you mean to go on.'

'What on earth do you mean by that?'

'Why, by obeying me, of course. I knew you'd see reason sooner or later.'

'Oh, *you* . . .' Stella said, and threw the tea-cosy at him.

Chapter Nineteen

'You'd better go and have a look at that house,' Gilbert said to Hilary. 'Arnold tells me they're moving back to Plymouth sooner than they thought. The quicker we can get on with any work that needs doing, the better.'

'Shouldn't we wait until they've moved out? It's still their home, after all. I don't like the idea of poking round it while they're still there.'

'Don't see why.' As usual, Gilbert found it hard to see another person's point of view. 'They know we'll be wanting to make some improvements. It's not as if they haven't had the use of it for a lot longer than any of us expected.'

'Yes, but it might seem like a criticism. As if we're saying they haven't looked after it properly.'

'Nonsense! Not saying that at all. The place needs a bit of modernisation, needed it for years if truth be told, but you know as well as I do that the materials weren't available after the war. And Arnold knows it, too – God knows he's had problems enough getting his Plymouth house up to scratch. Now things are getting easier, it's the right time to do the same with our own. We want Kellaway and Miss Tucker to start off on the right foot, don't we? And I'm sure Evelyn Cherriman won't mind showing you round. Be glad of the company, I dare say. Never seemed cut out for living in the middle of the woods, for all she's done wonders with the garden. She'll be too pleased to get back to the city to worry about what you're thinking of the house!'

Hilary couldn't help agreeing with this, but was still feeling uncomfortable when she arrived at the door of the estate manager's house. We really ought to give this place a name, she thought. Perhaps Travis and Jennifer would like to do that. She lifted the shining brass knocker and let it fall, then stood looking around at the garden Evelyn Cherriman had created from what had never been much more than a patch of fenced-off woodland.

'Hilary ...' The door had opened and Evelyn stood there, wearing a limp cotton frock and a drooping cardigan, and looking dazed. She pushed back her greying hair, and blinked. 'I'm sorry, I'd forgotten you were coming.'

'It's all right,' Hilary said, taking in her slightly dishevelled appearance. 'I should have made sure you expected me. My father said he'd arranged it with your husband but—'

'Oh, yes, he told me. I just ...' She blinked again, nervously. 'I forget a lot of things these days.'

'Are you all right?' Hilary asked a little anxiously. 'Would it be better if I came back some other time? It's not urgent, after all.'

'Oh, no. You must come in. Arnold did tell me, and he'd be annoyed if I said you'd come and gone away again. You want to look round the house, don't you?' She sounded as if she hadn't yet woken up properly, and Hilary's concern grew.

'Yes, if it's convenient, but you mustn't feel you've got to show me today. Another time would be perfectly suitable.'

But Evelyn was already moving back into the house. Hilary followed uneasily. The feeling she'd had at the dinner-party, that all wasn't well with the Cherrimans and especially with Evelyn, increased.

'What would you like to see first?' Evelyn asked, standing awkwardly in the passageway that led to the kitchen. On either side were doors leading to the sitting room and dining room, with the stairs leading up to the bedrooms. There were three, Hilary remembered, and a small box room that had been converted to a bathroom just before the war. She hesitated, and Evelyn said, 'Perhaps we'd better look at the kitchen. Would you like a cup of coffee?'

'That would be very nice.' It might help ease the strained atmosphere, Hilary thought, wondering if Evelyn was offended by her visit. 'This must seem a terrible intrusion,' she went on quickly. 'Having me come and look round your home. Really, I'd rather have waited till you move out.'

'Oh, no, it's quite all right.' Evelyn moved unsteadily towards the kitchen. 'I realise you need to make sure it's all ready for Mr Kellaway. We've stayed here too long as it is. I kept saying to Arnold ...' Her voice faded, and she put her hand up to her head. 'I'm sorry, I've got rather a headache this morning ...' And to Hilary's horror, she swayed and almost fell against the wall.

Hilary sprang forward and caught her. 'Evelyn! Whatever's the matter? Here, hold on to me for a moment ... let's get you somewhere you can sit down ...'

She pushed open the door and supported the shaking woman to a chair by the kitchen table. Lowering her onto it, she pressed gently between her shoulder blades until Evelyn's head was between her knees.

'Will you be all right while I fetch you some water? You won't fall?'

Taking Evelyn's mumble for reassurance, she went to the sink and ran some water into a glass. She supported Evelyn's head while the woman drank, and was relieved to see a faint tinge of colour return to her cheeks.

'Thank you,' Evelyn whispered. 'I'm sorry ... I don't know what came over me.'

'Do you get many of these headaches?' Hilary asked. 'Is it a migraine? Can I fetch you an aspirin or something?'

'Oh, no,' she said with a quick, almost frightened glance. 'It's not as bad as that. I'm all right now.' She made as if to get up, but sank back again with a little moan.

Hilary put her hand on her shoulder. 'You stay there. When you feel better, I'll help you into the sitting room. You can lie on the sofa, or maybe you'd better go to bed. D'you think you'll be able to manage the stairs?'

'Oh, no, I can't go to bed. Really, I'll be all right in a few minutes. You mustn't worry. It's just one of my turns; I have them now and then. They pass quite quickly. I'll make some coffee.' She put her hand to her forehead again.

'You will not,' Hilary said firmly. 'I'll make it, and you'll sit there and drink it. Or maybe tea would be better. Would you prefer that?'

Evelyn nodded. She still looked terribly weak, Hilary thought, filling the kettle. And what was all this about 'turns'? Was Evelyn ill in some way?

By the time she had got out cups, milk and sugar, and found a tin of biscuits, the kettle was boiling. She made the tea, put everything on the kitchen table, and sat down to pour.

'How much sugar do you take?' she asked, and put in twice as much as Evelyn asked for. 'It's good for shock. Drink it up, and have a biscuit. You know, you're looking terribly thin,' she added, as Evelyn's sleeve fell back, exposing a white wrist. 'Have you seen a doctor about these "turns"?'

'Oh no,' Evelyn almost recoiled at the suggestion. 'No, I wouldn't like to go to the doctor. Anyway, we'll be moving back to Plymouth soon, so there's no point in going to someone in Tavistock now.' Her speech was slower than usual and her words slightly slurred. Obviously she hadn't yet recovered.

'But surely your husband's noticed you're not well? Doesn't he want you to see your doctor?' Hilary asked.

'Arnold wouldn't like that,' Evelyn said obscurely. 'He thinks I make a fuss about nothing.'

'Well, *I* don't think it's nothing,' Hilary declared. 'You almost fainted just now. It could be dangerous. You could fall downstairs and really hurt yourself, and you're all alone. You could be lying here for hours.'

She glanced around the kitchen. The last time she had been in the house, everything was clean and shining, with nothing out of place, but this morning it looked as untidy and neglected as Evelyn herself. Unwashed dishes were piled on the wooden draining board, from last night's meal as well as breakfast by the look of them, and a half-empty sherry bottle stood on top of a cupboard. The remains of breakfast littered the table, too: a plate with scraps of bacon and fried bread congealing in their fat, a toast rack with two pieces of cold toast in it, an opened jar of marmalade, a jug of milk. All this, Hilary was sure, would normally have been cleared away as soon as breakfast was over, yet it was now ten-thirty and Evelyn looked exhausted.

'You know, I really don't think you're very well,' she said gently. 'You ought to see a doctor. Why don't you let me take you to the village to see Charles Latimer?'

Again, Evelyn drew back. 'I couldn't do that! Arnold would ...' She faltered into silence.

'Arnold would what?'

'He'd be cross,' Evelyn muttered. 'I told you, he thinks I make a fuss about nothing, and he's right. I've always been rather feeble, and—'

'You can't have been all that feeble,' Hilary said firmly. 'Not if you managed to do all that work in the garden. You did do most of it yourself, didn't you?'

'Well, I had some help. Mr Prout came and did some of the heavy digging and planting. But it's starting to look neglected. I haven't had time lately ...'

'It looks lovely,' Hilary said, although she'd noticed a few weeds and unpruned shrubs. 'And you did all the rest, and all the planning. You *made* that garden, Evelyn. It was nothing before you came here. You've got a real talent for design, an eye for it. And it's not just the garden, either,' she continued warmly. 'It's the house. Every time I come here, I think how beautifully furnished and decorated it is, how *tasteful* everything looks. You know, you could set up in business advising people on how to arrange their homes. There's going to be a real call for that, now that things are beginning to get easier and people are thinking about their homes more.'

'Oh, I could never do anything like that,' Evelyn demurred. 'Arnold would never allow it.'

Hilary gazed at her helplessly. It was such a shame, she thought, how a woman like Evelyn, with obvious talents, should be so browbeaten by her husband, doomed to a wasted and frustrating life. No wonder she looked so wan and sad, no wonder she left the washing-up, no wonder ... Her eyes went to the sherry bottle and she looked away hastily. It meant nothing, nothing at all. Plenty of people drank sherry before their evening meal, and plenty of people used it in their cooking. She did both herself.

But was her own situation any different? Look at the battle she had had to convince her father that she had the ability to run the estate. And she'd never really succeeded, or he wouldn't have brought in Travis as manager. As for the changes that Robert's arrival might bring about, she hardly dared think about them.

'I'm not saying you *should* do that,' she said to Evelyn. 'Just that you've got the talent. And it seems to me it's a shame to waste talent. A wicked shame.' She added the last words more forcefully than she'd intended, and bit her lip, wishing she hadn't spoken them at all. But Evelyn didn't seem to have noticed. Instead, she was looking round the kitchen as if she'd only just noticed the state it was in.

'Hilary, I'm so sorry! Look at the mess. You must think I'm a terrible housekeeper.' She stood up, waving down Hilary's protestations. Her voice was a little feeble still but determined, as if she'd made a sudden decision to pull herself together. 'You've come to look over the house, and all I've done is keep you here, complaining about myself. Well, you've been very kind, but I'm quite all right now. Let's start with the sitting room, shall we? And then we'll look at the dining room and then go upstairs. It's all quite tidy up there; it's only the kitchen that's not been attended to yet.' She led the way to the door, and Hilary, bemused by her sudden change of attitude, followed.

'We haven't done any redecorating,' Evelyn went on, fluttering her hand vaguely. 'I did suggest it, but Arnold said we'd got to concentrate on our own house now, and you'd want to do it differently for the new people. But we've looked after it.'

'It looks very nice,' Hilary said, gazing round the elegant room. 'I don't think it needs any redecoration, unless Travis and Jennifer want it altered. I suppose it may not be to their taste.'

'I don't expect it is,' Evelyn agreed, going on to the dining room. 'Young people have their own ideas these days, don't they? And there's so much more choice now. Arnold and I found that when we went to choose wallpapers and curtains for the Plymouth house. It was quite bewildering.'

Hilary was quite bewildered, too. Now that she'd started to talk, Evelyn seemed unable to stop. She chattered on, fiddling all the time with the dining table, already set for dinner with gleaming cutlery and shining wine glasses. The table was highly polished, and on the sideboard Hilary noticed an array of bottles: Plymouth gin, whisky, brandy, and both cream and dry sherry. Evelyn was on her way upstairs, still talking. She seemed to have recovered from her unsteadiness, Hilary noticed thankfully, but her manner was forced and unnatural. She led Hilary into the two spare bedrooms: one pleasantly furnished with the beds made up as if guests were expected imminently, and the other clearly intended as a dressing room for Arnold, with a single bed, wardrobe and washstand bearing his shaving equipment. A cut-throat razor lay on the marble top, with a leather strop hanging on the wall beside it. Hilary shivered a little.

The master bedroom was clearly furnished to Evelyn's taste,

with a deep rose-pink eiderdown covering the wide bed, and a dressing table with a frilly lace skirt and three mirrors. There was an array of jars and bottles on top, and a silver-backed hairbrush and hand mirror. The wallpaper was sprinkled with a rose-petal pattern, and the curtains matched the eiderdown. Hilary looked around, trying – and failing – to imagine Travis in this bedroom. It wasn't much easier to think of Arnold Cherriman here, either, and there weren't many signs of his presence.

'Arnold uses the dressing room, mostly,' Evelyn confided. 'He snores rather, you see, and ...' She broke off, returning to her previous fluttery manner. 'I do like a pretty bedroom, don't you? I often sit up here and sew or read, when I can't be in the garden.'

The last room was the converted bathroom. This was another that would need attention, Hilary thought, looking at the white tiles and the heavy iron bath with its claw feet. Nobody wanted that kind of bath these days, and the geyser looked grim and forbidding, as if daring anyone to try to get hot water from it. She made a mental note to investigate modern baths and appliances.

'We're having a new bathroom in the Plymouth house,' Evelyn said. 'Arnold insisted on it. He says we've slummed it far too long – oh, I'm sorry!' Her hand flew to her mouth. 'I shouldn't have said that!'

'It's quite all right,' Hilary reassured her, feeling guilty herself. 'I wish you'd said something before. We'd have done something about it. I'd no idea it was this bad.'

'Oh, it's not *bad*,' Evelyn said hastily. She moved over and closed the door of a small medicine cupboard that had been ajar. 'I mean, I don't mind it at all. It's just Arnold's way of speaking; he doesn't really mean it.'

Hilary thought he did, and in this case she thought he was justified. She turned to go downstairs again, and then realised that Evelyn hadn't followed her. Looking back, she saw the other woman leaning with one arm against the door-jamb, trembling, her face white.

'Evelyn!' Hilary went back quickly, putting her hands out in support. 'Evelyn, you really aren't well. Now look, I'm going to help you into bed and then I'm calling Dr Latimer. No, it's no good arguing' – as Evelyn made a feeble attempt at denial – 'I can't possibly go away leaving you like this. Anything might happen. Come along now.'

She supported the sick woman into the bedroom, and pulled back the eiderdown and sheet. Evelyn sank on to the bed with a sigh of relief and Hilary looked at her doubtfully. 'Can you manage to undress yourself, or shall I help you? And would you like me to call your husband as well?'

'Arnold? Oh, no! No, please. And I don't want the doctor, I really don't.' But her voice was fading even as she spoke, and she lay back on the pillows. Her eyes closed.

Thoroughly alarmed, Hilary slipped off Evelyn's shoes and pulled the bedclothes over her. She ran downstairs to the hall and picked up the telephone. Within minutes, she was speaking to the doctor, who was just about to start out on his rounds.

'Charles, it's Hilary Napier. I'm at the Cherrimans' house. I think you ought to come and look at Evelyn; she seems really poorly. She's been odd ever since I got here and now she's collapsed ... Yes, she's in bed but I don't think she's properly conscious ... No, she doesn't want her husband called, but I really am worried about her ... Oh, thank you so much. I'll leave the front door open for you, and go back to her now.'

Evelyn's pallor was touched with green when Hilary returned. Her eyes were barely open and she was breathing heavily. Hilary picked up her hand, noticing again how thin it was, and tried to warm it between hers. I wish Val were here, she thought, she'd know what to do. Oh, when will Charles get here?

The sound of the doctor's car outside brought a wave of

relief. She ran downstairs, and caught Charles by the arm.

'She's up in the bedroom. I really am worried, Charles. I wondered if ... well, if she'd been drinking, but now I'm afraid she may have taken something as well. There's a huge aspirin bottle in the bathroom and it's half-empty. And she seems very upset.'

'All right, Hilary. Let me go and have a look at her. You'd better come, too.' They went up the stairs, and Hilary showed him into the bedroom. Evelyn was still in bed, her face still that frightening greenish pallor, her breathing stertorous. Charles pulled back the bedclothes and examined her briefly, then straightened up.

'We'd better get her to the hospital. Go downstairs and ring for an ambulance, and then call Arnold.'

Hilary opened her mouth to ask what was wrong, then closed it again, and ran back to the telephone in the hallway. There would be time for talk later, but Charles clearly considered it too urgent now. She made sure the ambulance-driver would know where to come, and then found the number of Arnold Cherriman's optician's practice in Plymouth.

'Arnold, it's Hilary Napier. I'm ringing from your house. Evelyn's been taken ill, and Charles Latimer is here. We've called an ambulance and—'

'You've done what?' Arnold Cherriman's voice cut in. 'Called an ambulance? And Latimer's there? Who told you to call him?'

'Nobody told me,' Hilary said, taken aback. 'Evelyn—'

'*She* asked you to call him? Why? What the devil is she playing at now?'

'Arnold,' Hilary said, struggling to keep her voice calm, 'I told you, nobody asked me to call the doctor. I did it because I could see Evelyn was ill. She collapsed and—'

'Oh, my God,' he said, sounding exasperated. 'And how did you come to be there?'

'I came to see what needs doing to the house. Don't you

remember? My father arranged it with you. Anyway, the important thing is that she's ill, and Charles wants her to go to hospital—'

'She's not to go.'

Hilary stopped abruptly. She looked at the telephone as if expecting to see Arnold Cherriman's face looking back at her.

'I'm sorry, Arnold, I don't understand.'

'It's plain enough, isn't it? She's not to go to hospital. Tell that old woman of a doctor to cancel the ambulance and go home.'

'But he can't! She's ill, seriously ill. She's almost unconscious. She needs treatment.'

'Listen to me,' he said brusquely, '*I'll* be the one to decide whether she needs treatment or not. And as her husband, I think I have some say in whether she's taken to hospital or not. Now, get off the phone and let me talk to Latimer.'

Hilary put the receiver on the hall table, feeling sick and shaky. She heard footsteps on the stairs and turned to see the doctor coming down. He looked at her white face and said, 'What's wrong?'

'It's Mr Cherriman,' she said gesturing at the receiver. 'He says ... he says she's not to go to hospital.'

'Not to go to hospital?' He stared at her, then snatched up the telephone. 'Cherriman? Is that you? What's all this about your wife not going to hospital?'

Hilary ran back upstairs. Evelyn was propped up on pillows, conscious again and looking a little less pale. She gave Hilary a wan smile, and spoke in a whisper, 'I'm sorry to be such a nuisance.'

'You're not a nuisance at all. I'm just glad to see you looking a bit better. Did Charles say what might be wrong?'

'I don't think so. He gave me something ... I'm not sure what.' She gave Hilary a nervous glance. 'Have you been talking to Arnold?'

'Yes, I rang him after I'd called for the ambulance.' Hilary hesitated, not wanting to upset Evelyn further by telling her what her husband had said.

'Was he very angry?'

'Well, he was a bit surprised. I expect he was worried, really. Some people do sound angry when they're worried.'

'Arnold doesn't worry,' Evelyn said, and turned her head away from Hilary. She seemed completely exhausted, Hilary thought, but she summoned up enough strength to ask, in the same faint whisper, 'Is he coming home?'

'I don't know. I expect Charles will tell him to go to the hospital.' Hilary turned, as Charles Latimer came back in to the room, his face like thunder. 'Charles?'

'Come outside for a moment, will you, Hilary? Excuse us,' he said to Evelyn. 'Just stay here and rest. Everything's going to be all right.' To Hilary, on the landing with the bedroom door firmly closed, he said in a low voice, 'That man is beyond belief. Tells me I'm not to send his wife to hospital, and that if I do, he'll sue me. And I'm not to give her any treatment until he gets here, either. He's cancelling his appointments today and coming straight home, and if he thinks it necessary – if *he* thinks it necessary, mark you – he'll take her into Plymouth to their own doctor.'

Hilary stared at him. 'But can he do that?'

The doctor shrugged. 'I can't stop him. I've no right to treat her unless he asks.'

'What about if *she* asks? Doesn't she have any say in the matter?'

Charles gave her an ironic glance. 'Can you see Evelyn Cherriman going against her husband's wishes? Even if she's at death's door?'

'She's not—' Hilary began in alarm, but he cut her off with a gesture of reassurance.

'No, no, that was a poor analogy. But she's definitely ill, and needs treatment.' He glanced at his watch. 'I really ought to talk to Cherriman. He seems to have completely the wrong idea about his wife's condition. But I've got other people to see, too. I can't wait for him to come from Plymouth. It'll take him at least an hour, by the time he's able to leave his consulting rooms and drive back. Can you stay with her, Hilary?'

'Of course I'll stay. She can't possibly be left on her own. Will you come back?'

'I think I must. He's not going to be best pleased to find me here – more or less told me to shake the dust of the house from my feet. But he's got to understand the situation, and if I'm not here to tell him ...' The doctor looked at Hilary. 'Will you be all right?'

'Yes, of course. Why shouldn't I be?'

'I don't know,' he said slowly. 'But he's a temperamental man. I've often wondered about his own health, whether he's had his blood pressure checked ... Is there any chance of anyone else coming out, to be with you?'

'For goodness' sake, Charles,' she exclaimed. 'You don't think he's going to attack me, do you? It's nothing but bluster, and he'll have calmed down by the time he gets here. He must be anxious about her really. Look, if you go now and come back in about an hour, you can talk to him sensibly. He'll probably agree to her going into hospital, then. And he'll be able to tell you a bit more about her symptoms.'

The doctor grunted sceptically, but picked up his bag and turned to go. At the door, he stopped and gave Hilary a direct look.

'Very well. I'll be back inside an hour. He probably won't be here that quickly anyway. But if he does arrive first, be careful. I've met men like Arnold Cherriman before, and they're not always what they seem to be. And you must have realised, Hilary, that there's something very wrong here. Very wrong indeed.'

Chapter Twenty

Arnold Cherriman arrived within the hour, red-faced and furious. Hilary, who was in the kitchen, tidying up as a way of passing the time, heard his car approaching too fast along the track through the woods, and hurried out to the front door, drying her hands on a tea-towel. She quailed a little as he stormed towards her, but held her ground and looked him in the eye.

'What the devil is all this about?' he demanded. 'I've had to cancel three appointments because of this nonsense.'

'It isn't nonsense,' Hilary retorted. 'Evelyn's really ill, and Charles Latimer wanted her to go to hospital. He wouldn't have—'

'Charles Latimer is an old fusspot,' he interrupted impatiently. 'Evelyn doesn't need to go to any hospital. I know exactly what's wrong with her.'

'But you haven't even seen her!' Hilary exclaimed. 'Really, Arnold, she was on the verge of collapse. I only just caught her before she fell down the stairs. And she hadn't seemed well all the time I was here.'

'And do you know why?' He marched past her and into the kitchen, looked around for a minute, then snatched up the sherry bottle and brandished it under her nose. '*That's* why!'

Hilary opened her mouth, then turned away without speaking. She remembered Arnold preventing his wife from accepting more sherry at the dinner party, then her own uneasiness earlier. The dazed look, the slightly slurred words, the headache . . .

'But that doesn't explain why she collapsed,' she said doubtfully.

'It does if you put it away like she does,' he returned grimly. 'I'm sorry, Hilary, I've tried to keep it quiet long enough but this time she's gone too far. The plain truth is, my wife is an alcoholic. She may need treatment all right, but not the sort of treatment that Tavistock Hospital can provide.'

Hilary turned back and stared at him. 'Arnold, surely it can't be that bad . . .'

'Can't it? You've seen how she is. Unsteady on her feet, hardly able to string together half a dozen coherent words, breath smelling. Don't tell me you didn't notice?'

'Well, yes. That's why I was so worried. But her breath didn't smell of drink. It smelled of something else – I couldn't think what it was.'

'No, I don't suppose it did. It smelled of those damned sweets she sucks all the time to hide it. Thinks I won't know, thinks she can take me for a fool. Well, I'll tell you this,' he shouted, thrusting his face so close to Hilary's that she took a step back in alarm, 'nobody takes Arnold Cherriman for a fool – nobody!'

'They hardly need to,' said another voice from the hallway behind Hilary. 'You're making a very good job of it yourself.'

Hilary whirled round. Charles Latimer was standing just inside the front door. She heard Arnold Cherriman's sharp intake of breath and then a growl of anger as he surged past her. But Charles Latimer was not easily intimidated. He stood firmly where he was, and raised one hand as if he were a policeman directing traffic.

'Calm down, Arnold,' he said authoritatively. 'You'll burst a blood vessel if you go on like that, and then I shall have two patients to deal with.'

'You don't even have *one*!' Cherriman bellowed. 'Get out of my house! I don't remember inviting you in, and I certainly never asked you to attend to my wife.'

'No, but now I've seen her condition I'm morally bound to insist that she receives immediate medical treatment. If you won't allow me to do it, I must ask you to call another doctor, and I think you'll find he'll say the same thing. And do it now – there's been too much delay as it is.'

Arnold Cherriman spluttered with rage. Hilary, fearing that he would either attack the doctor or, as Charles had said, suffer an apoplexy, escaped past him and picked up the telephone. But the doctor, keeping his eyes on the angry face, lifted his hand again, this time to warn her to wait before doing anything else.

'Your wife is not an alcoholic,' he went on steadily, 'although it's quite possible that she is beginning to find some comfort in drink. But that isn't what's wrong with her this morning. I've already told you, she's ill and needs treatment.'

'Ill?' the other man sneered. 'What sort of illness?'

'I need a proper diagnosis to be sure, and that means tests in hospital,' Charles said. 'But it's my belief that she's suffering from diabetes. It's a dangerous disease and, left untreated, can lead to coma, and death. It shows itself in unsteadiness, weakness, slurred speech and – you may be interested in this, Mr Cherriman – the smell of pear drops on the breath. Now, if you'll allow me, I'll go up and see her, and then we'll take her to the hospital, in either your car or mine. And it will be with *her* permission, not yours. You may think you have a number of rights over your wife, but they do not include the right to allow her to become dangerously ill through neglect.' He turned to Hilary. 'Perhaps you'd be good enough to come with me. She may need help to dress.'

At this, Cherriman leaped forward. 'No! If anyone's to help Evelyn, I'll do it. She's a modest woman; I'm her husband—'

'You'll wait here,' Charles ordered him. 'Once your wife's in hospital, she'll have to accept the help of nurses. I'm sure she won't object to Hilary giving her a hand.'

They went upstairs, leaving the optician fuming in the hall. Hilary, distressed by the thought that Evelyn must have heard the argument, opened the bedroom door, and they both went inside. Charles closed it behind him, and they looked at the pale, wan face on the pillows.

After Charles had left, Evelyn had seemed to rally a little. She had even managed to take off her clothes and put on a nightdress, though refusing all Hilary's attempts to help her. Now, she seemed weaker again, and only moved her head feebly when Hilary spoke to her.

'Charles wants you to go to the hospital, Evelyn,' Hilary said gently. 'Will you let me help you get ready? You don't need to put too much on; it's quite warm outside. The frock you had on earlier will do.'

She drew back the bedclothes and supported Evelyn to a sitting position, lifting the nightdress above her head.

Then she stopped, staring in horror at the thin, white body.

'*Charles*,' she said in a whisper, and the doctor, who had been tactfully looking out of the window, turned and followed her gaze.

'Yes,' he said quietly. 'Rather as I thought, I'm afraid.' He looked at Hilary's shocked face. 'The sooner we get this poor lady out of this house, the better.'

'Bruises,' Hilary said in an appalled tone. 'Val, there were huge bruises on her body. It looked as if she'd been *punched*.'

'I know.' Val had been on duty at the hospital when Evelyn had been brought in. Charles had brought her himself, refusing to entrust his patient to her infuriated husband. She had come straight to the Barton on her return to the village, knowing that Hilary would need to talk about it. 'We were all upset. I bathed her, but I was almost afraid to touch her. It's dreadful.'

'I suppose *he* must have done it,' Hilary said miserably. 'You know, I've never really liked him. I always thought he was a bit of a bully and not very nice to Evelyn, but I never dreamed he'd do anything like that.' She looked at her friend. 'Is it all right for you to talk about it? I know you're not supposed to discuss patients.'

'No, and I shouldn't now, to be honest, but since you were there and saw what she was like ... well, you had a shock, too, and you can't be expected to keep it all bottled up inside. I don't suppose there's anyone else you want to tell.'

'I can't imagine telling my father. He thinks the sun shines out of Arnold Cherriman.' Hilary shuddered. 'Although I don't see why he shouldn't know what he's really like. I can tell you this: *I* don't want him in the house again, and I don't believe Dad would, if he knew the truth. I think I'll have to tell him, but I can't talk to him like I can to you.' Tears welled up in her eyes. 'It's really upset me, Val. To see that poor woman, so ill, and hear the horrible way he talked about her, and then to see *that*. I keep imagining what it must have been like for her, but the thought of him hitting her, even *punching* her – it just seems so impossible.'

'And do you know what the worst of it is?' Val asked. 'She can't do a thing about it. If he did that to anyone else, they could call the police and he'd be arrested and maybe even sent to prison, but she's his wife, so the police wouldn't do anything to help. They won't interfere in a domestic situation.'

'It's disgraceful,' Hilary said angrily. 'It's positively Victorian. Did women fight for the vote just so that they could still be treated as their husbands' chattels? Surely Evelyn can do *something*. The man's half killed her. He *would* have killed her if she'd stayed there much longer, either by hitting her too hard, or just letting her die of her illness. It can't be right for him to treat her like that and get away with it.'

'Well, he wouldn't if that happened. And I suppose she *could* do something about it – she could divorce him for cruelty.

But think what that would mean, Hilary. A court case, spread all over the newspapers, and she'd have to provide proof as well. How could she do that? You and I have seen the bruises, and so have Dr Latimer and half a dozen other people at the hospital, but we don't *know* that he caused them.'

'Of course he caused them!' Hilary exclaimed. 'The man's a thug.'

'Yes, I know, but there's no proof, is there? It's her word against his. Nobody's ever seen him hitting her.'

'We've seen him being very unpleasant to her,' Hilary said bitterly. 'But I see what you mean. And it would cost her a lot of money to divorce him. I don't suppose she's got much money of her own, if any at all.'

'And she'd have to think about what she would live on afterwards. If she won the case, she'd be awarded maintenance, but you can bet that Arnold Cherriman would fight that, too. He'd hire the best lawyers, people she could never afford. And she's ill. She doesn't even have the strength to go through it.'

'So she's trapped,' Hilary said despondently. 'Poor, poor woman.'

'Yes,' Val said. 'Poor woman.'

Val left the Barton and walked down the drive, deep in thought. It seemed so wrong that a nice little woman like Evelyn Cherriman should be condemned to live with a bullying husband, with no help from the law. But perhaps he would mend his ways now that so many people – including both Hilary and Charles Latimer, who were part of his own social circle – knew about it. She hoped that he would realise his wife was really sick and needed care. It seemed that there was nobody else in the family to look after her; no grown-up children, no brothers or sisters, not even a cousin. Poor Evelyn was totally dependent on her husband.

Val turned to walk up the track to her father's farm. This was the afternoon she and Joanna had arranged to go to Tavistock together. They'd finished making the sling for Heather, and Joanna had been practising using it around the house. She met Val at the door with Heather already tucked into it.

'It works a treat. I'm really pleased with it, and Heather loves it. It's as if she's being cuddled against me all the time.'

'You could even feed her in it and nobody'd notice,' Val said, peeping at the little face and touching a cheek like a delicately ripened peach with one fingertip.

'Oh, I don't think I could do that! Not in public. I'd have to open my frock, after all. I'd probably be arrested!'

'You could wrap a shawl around yourself,' Val suggested, but her tone was abstract, as she thought of the difference between Joanna, unable to feed her baby in public, however discreetly, and Arnold Cherriman, able to beat his wife and get away with it. Life really was extraordinarily unfair at times.

'Are you all right, Val? D'you want a cup of tea before we go?'

'Oh, no. Let's have one in Good's or Perraton's. That's part of the treat. Come on, or we'll miss the bus.'

'How are you feeling?' Joanna asked, glancing at Val's rounded figure as they walked to the village. 'You're showing nicely now.'

'I know. I'll be as big as a house before I'm finished. And I feel wonderful, as if I could do anything!'

'That won't last, once you get really big,' Joanna said rue-fully. 'It's like a short course of old age. You can't bend over properly, you can't find a chair that's comfortable to sit in, you can't kneel on the floor because you'll never get up again, and you can't even turn over in bed. And you get so tired, lugging that great bump around all the time. Mind you, I was specially big – carrying two. Even though I didn't know it until they were born.'

'What a night that was,' Val said, and they were both quiet for a moment, remembering the shock of two babies being born when only one was expected, and then the later, terrible shock, when one of them died in her pram.

'Well, we didn't come out to be miserable,' Joanna said, making a visibly determined effort to be cheerful. 'This is Heather's first visit to Tavistock, so we've got to make it special!'

'It's her first time on a bus, too,' Val said, as they walked down to the village green and stood under the spreading branches of the great oak tree. There were only two buses from the village each day, one in the morning and one in the afternoon; if you wanted to go to Plymouth, Okehampton or Tavistock at any other time, you had to walk the mile to the main road and catch the hourly one there. But the two village buses each gave you a couple of hours in Tavistock, which was enough for most people to do their shopping, browse round the pannier market or go to the library.

There were a few other people waiting, and they all wanted to see the baby, crowding round as Joanna parted the soft shawl that Minnie had knitted from wool so fine you could barely see it, and giving little cries of admiration.

'She'm a lovely little girl,' Mabel Purdy said, fishing in her purse and taking out a sixpence. 'Here's summat to put in her money-box, for luck.'

Several of the others did the same thing, and Joanna thanked them, knowing that it was traditional to give a baby a silver coin the first time you saw it. 'She'll have enough to pay all our fares soon,' she said, laughing, as the bus arrived and they all clambered aboard. The driver wanted a look, too, and when everyone was settled he set off. They bowled through the lanes, calling at two other villages, before reaching the main road.

The bus was almost full by now, and alive with chatter. For some of the women, it was their main social event of the week and a chance to catch up with gossip from the other villages. They sat with their shopping bags on their knees, exchanging news about their families and telling each other about the latest scandals, lowering their voices to a whisper if they were imparting anything particularly shocking, even though everyone else on the bus could have heard them. It wasn't long before the talk turned to the recent events at Burracombe Barton.

'Foreigners, so I heard,' a woman from one of the outlying farms commented. 'Young woman with a tacker about twelve or thirteen, saying he was Master Baden's by-blow. Wanted money, I dare say.'

'Never!' Her friend, from an even more remote farm, had obviously not heard anything about this. 'Well, I don't suppose her got much change out of Squire. Sent her off with a flea in her ear, I don't doubt.'

'No, what I heard was he took them both in and treated 'em like royalty,' a third woman joined in. 'Making everything over to the boy, he is: the estate, the big house, all the farms and everything, lock, stock and barrel.'

'My stars! You don't mean it! How did you get to hear that, then?'

'I had it from the postman – not the regular one, he's on his holidays in Clacton, at Butlin's holiday camp – and he says—'

'Clacton? That's a long way to go.'

'Gone by coach, they have. It was in the *Tavistock Gazette* back in the winter, you could book then. Me and Joe thought about it but we decided—'

'Never mind that,' someone else interrupted. 'What about this business up at the Barton?'

'Oh, yes. Well, that young chap from Sourton's doing the round while he'm away, and he got it from his cousin over to Lydford. She works at the Dartmoor Inn, and one of the other barmaids knows Mrs Ellis that's housekeeper at the Barton, and she says—'

'Maud Ellis won't never have said nothing. Close as an oyster, she be, and never gives away a word about the Napiers.'

'No, but when this woman from the Dartmoor Inn asked her if it was money they wanted, she wouldn't say yes and she wouldn't say no, and she wouldn't say yes or no when she was asked if the Colonel meant to make it all over to the boy, neither, so if you ask me, that proves it!' She sat back, pursing her lips and nodding her head with satisfaction.

The others digested this in silence, unsure whether they were convinced or not. Val and Joanna glanced at each other and grinned.

'Never say you don't know how rumours start!' Val murmured. 'It was just the same the other day about Travis and Jennifer. They really thought they'd kept it all quiet, but by the time they got back to the village after buying the ring, the entire wedding had been settled for them.'

'I can't believe the Napiers would be very pleased if they knew about all this tittle-tattle, though,' Joanna replied. 'Nor would Mrs Ellis. She's being made to sound a real gossip.'

'And by not saying a word,' Val agreed. 'Well, I don't think we'd better get sucked into this. Thank goodness we're nearly there.'

The bus drew into the bus station, and everyone got off and made for the town. It was only a short walk to the shops, and Val and Joanna headed for the fabric shop first, to look at patterns and to choose material for Val's maternity outfits. She had decided to have one for the rest of the summer, with a warmer one for the last two or three months.

'I can wear those smocks you gave me for round the house,' she said as they pored over the pattern books. 'Oh, look, I like this dress. It's got a nice collar, and if I have a cotton one for summer and a wool one for winter, I can use them as dressing-gowns afterwards.'

'Don't you think you'll want them again as maternity wear?' Joanna asked. 'You're not going to have just one child, are you, Val?'

'No, of course not. You're right, I'll need to keep them. But

I'll have this pattern. I like it, and it looks as if it'll be easy to make. I can borrow Mum's sewing-machine. Now, what about materials?'

They chose a pretty cotton with a pattern of yellow flowers, and a lightweight wool in plain dark blue. By the time they'd picked out matching Sylko and buttons, it was time to go for a cup of tea in Perraton's, the big café overlooking the square. Joanna found a table, with Heather still cuddled against her breast, and Val collected the tea and scones.

'It's nice to sit down,' she said, sinking on to the chair. 'You're right, Jo: being pregnant is like being old. I think I'm even developing varicose veins.'

'Don't talk about varicose veins,' Joanna said ruefully. 'I had my first with Robin, and now I've got them in both legs. And then there's the stretch marks …!'

'I'm using olive oil,' Val said. 'I rub it in after a bath. But those little bottles from the chemist are so expensive, I wonder if it's worth it.'

'None of it really matters,' Joanna said quietly, looking down at Heather, who was awake now and gazing up at her mother's face. 'Not when you've got your little one in your arms.' And a small tear dropped on to the baby's cheek.

'Oh, Joanna, I'm sorry. I didn't mean to upset you.'

'You didn't. Almost anything upsets me these days. I think I'm all right, and then somebody says something – or I say something myself – that reminds me, and off I go again.' Joanna brushed the tears away with the back of her hand. 'I'm the one who should be sorry.'

'No, you're not. You don't have to be in the least bit sorry. It's only been three months, almost no time at all. I think you've been tremendously brave to come and help me choose maternity things this afternoon.'

'I've enjoyed it,' Joanna said, smiling a little through her tears. 'Honestly, I have! It's been nice to get away from the farm and the village, and just be myself, out for the afternoon with you. But I couldn't have done it if I hadn't been able to bring Heather with me. I know Mum and Gran would look after her, but I just can't bring myself to leave her.'

'You don't have to. We'll do it again. And Heather's been as good as gold in her sling.'

'It's a marvellous idea,' Joanna said. 'I don't know why more people don't think of it. I shall use it all the time, until she gets too big.'

They finished their tea and wandered around the town for a while before going to catch the bus. Val glanced up the road leading to the hospital and wondered how Evelyn Cherriman was getting on. She remembered the thin, bruised body and Dr Latimer's fears for Evelyn's health, and shivered as she thought of the woman having to go back to her bullying husband. Worse still, they would be returning to Plymouth soon, and although they had friends there, it wasn't like being in a village where people would soon notice if anything was wrong, and do something to help.

Not that it had happened in Evelyn's case, she thought ruefully. Stuck in the middle of the woods and rarely coming into the village, she had had nobody to call on for help, nobody to notice that she was in trouble.

What might have happened to her if Hilary hadn't called that morning?

Chapter Twenty-One

Jackie was more shaken than she had first thought after her experience with Vic. But after a few days, she began to wonder if she had led him on without realising it. Ought I to have known? she asked herself. He made it pretty obvious what he wanted, and I went through it all with Roy, two years ago. Only that time, I wanted it, too.

Jackie and Roy Pettifer had been sweethearts since Jackie was fifteen. They'd been inseparable then, but their romance had foundered when Jackie had feared she was pregnant. Thankfully, it had been a false alarm, but Jackie had been so frightened that she'd lost all feeling for Roy and, on his first leave after he'd joined the Army, she'd told him she didn't want to see him any more.

All the same, she'd written to him when he was sent to Korea, and, after a shaky start, they'd corresponded regularly, though neither had ever mentioned what had happened before he left. She'd found herself looking forward to his homecoming, but now that it was almost due she felt nervous and shy. What would he expect of her? Did he think they would pick up where they'd left off, before she'd told him it was over between them? And what did she herself want?

I just want to be friends, she told herself firmly. I've had enough of boys who think they're God's gift to women and expect you to let them do what they like. I've got a nice job in a nice place, where I could get on. I could be housekeeper one day, like Miss Millington, and be in charge and wear nice suits. I might even go to London and work in one of the really posh hotels there. I don't need people like Vic Netherton and Roy Pettifer thinking they own me and getting in my way.

'I don't think your parents were too pleased that I'd left you here by yourself,' Jennifer had told her. 'You'd probably better come back with me at weekends until you're living in. It's not that I don't trust you,' she added quickly as Jackie opened her mouth, 'but I must admit I'd feel easier in my own mind. I don't like to think of you here on your own if Vic gets ideas again.'

'He won't. I've told him where he gets off.' Jackie sighed. 'Well, it's not your fault, I suppose. It's not fair of Mum and Dad to hold you responsible, but there's nothing I can do about that. I'm only going home until I get a room, mind. I'm nearly twenty now; they've got to let me have my independence soon.'

'Parents are always like that,' Jennifer said with a smile. 'And once you are independent, it'll last the rest of your life. It's not a long time to wait, when you think of all the years ahead of you.'

'Yes, but I'll be old then. It won't be any use to me. I want to be free *now*.' She stretched her arms as if they were wings. 'I want to *enjoy* my life.'

Jennifer smiled. She might be 'old' by Jackie's reckoning, but she was enjoying life, more than she ever had when she was nineteen. She thought of the bitter pain of her first, disastrous marriage. Ronald had been charm itself when they first met and as he courted her. Tall, handsome and attentive, he had swept her off her feet, and they had been married within three months. She only discovered on their wedding night that what she had taken for sensitivity and chivalry was really a complete lack of interest in making love to a woman. Worse still, he was clearly revolted by the whole idea.

For years, the memory of that night had made her burn with humiliation. The realisation that he had only married her to save his career in the Royal Navy, and the misery of having the marriage annulled, had driven her back to her home in Devonport, where she'd lived ever since, giving up all hopes of marriage – until the day she had met Travis. Even then, she had never dared to hope that he would take the slightest interest in her.

There was no danger, she thought now, that Travis wouldn't want to make love to her. He'd shown that very clearly.

'I'm quite willing to prove it before the wedding, if you like,' he offered one day, straight-faced but with a twinkle in his eye. 'I quite understand that you don't want to risk a repetition.'

Jennifer looked at him, and thought what a long way she had come in the past few weeks. There was a time – and not so long ago, either – when such a remark would have reduced her to tears of mortification.

'You don't have to go to those lengths,' she told Travis, matching his solemn tone. 'And, actually, I would quite like to go to the altar as a virgin. Now that we've decided to get married in the church, I want to do it all properly.'

'Then that's how it shall be,' he said. 'You didn't mind me saying that, did you? Only I do want it to be all open and easy between us.'

'No, I don't mind,' she said thoughtfully. 'You know, I've never been able to laugh about it before. Maybe it means that I've managed to put Ronald into the past at last. It's where he belongs, after all. He's got nothing to do with us now.'

'Nothing at all,' Travis said, and kissed her. It was a gentle kiss to begin with, a mere stroking of her lips with his, and then it deepened until she felt that her whole being was being swept up into his, and the entire world was contained in the whirl of emotion between them. He ended it at last, and she rested her head against his chest, feeling the beating of his heart beneath her cheek.

'I'm glad we don't have to wait too long,' he murmured

huskily at last. 'At this moment, three months seems like a lifetime.'

Evelyn Cherriman was, as Charles had expected, diagnosed with diabetes. It meant a long stay in hospital while her condition was assessed, with frequent blood tests and medication and changes to her diet, until the doctors were satisfied that she was stable. Even then, she was told, she would have to take great care for the rest of her life, and would probably have to have further stays in hospital as her body changed.

'They say I've probably been ill for years,' she told Hilary one afternoon as they sat in the big, sunny ward overlooking the Tamar valley. 'It explains why I get so tired, and why I was always drinking water. It was much worse in the past few months, of course.'

'Well, I'm glad they've found out what it is and can help you,' Hilary said. 'And I'm very glad I happened to come along that morning. I was really worried about you.'

'Yes,' Evelyn said. 'So was Arnold.'

There was a slight pause. Then Hilary said carefully, 'He does realise now that you really are ill, doesn't he?'

'Oh, yes. He's very upset about it. I can't blame him for not seeing it, you know. I mean, there were no real signs, just that tiredness and feeling weak all the time. He used to tell me to buck myself up. It's quite understandable,' Evelyn went on earnestly. 'He's such a strong person, and so full of life, he just couldn't see how I could be so exhausted when all I had to do was stay at home and look after the house and garden. And he did his best to help me. He insisted I have a sherry every evening, and it really did seem to help, so sometimes I would have one before he came home, too. And then another one later on,' she added with a swift glance at Hilary's face. 'The evening of your dinner party, I'd had two before we left home, because I was feeling so worn out. That was why

Arnold wouldn't let me have more than one. And then I was so thirsty during dinner ...'

Hilary remembered that. Evelyn had drunk three glasses of water as well as her wine. Why hadn't it occurred to her that it was due to illness?

Because I'm not a nurse or a doctor, she reminded herself firmly. And to Evelyn, she said, 'But he does realise now that it's not good for you, doesn't he? And when you go home, he will look after you?'

'Of course he will!' Evelyn blushed, perhaps not expecting her voice to sound so vehement. 'I know what you're thinking, Hilary. You saw my bruises, didn't you? The nurses and doctors here saw them, too. Even Val Ferris. I know what you're all thinking.'

'Well, what else are we to think?' Hilary asked. 'You don't get bruises like that from walking into the corner of the table. Evelyn, we're not being nosy; we care about you.'

'I bruise easily,' Evelyn said. 'And my illness makes it worse. Arnold only has to touch me and I bruise. He loves me. That's all it is.' She looked Hilary in the eye. 'Perhaps you don't know what I mean, not being married yourself.'

Hilary felt her colour rise, and didn't know whether to feel contrite or angry. She was quite certain that Evelyn's bruises had not resulted from Arnold's lovemaking, but she knew that if Evelyn was determined to say it was, there was nothing anyone could do about it.

'All right, Evelyn,' she said. 'I really don't want to pry, but if ever you need help, of any sort at all, you know you can come to me, don't you? I mean that.'

'Yes,' Evelyn said more quietly. 'Thank you, Hilary. But I'm sure I'll be all right, once they've got me stabilised. And we'll be back in Plymouth soon. Arnold's fixed a date and organised the removers. I'll probably go back there straight from hospital, and never have to go to the house in the woods again.'

Hilary looked at her, feeling slightly shocked. Had Evelyn really been so unhappy there? 'But won't you want to see your garden again?' she asked. 'You did so much work there, and made it so lovely.'

'That was just while we lived there. My real garden's in Plymouth. Arnold says I can have a gardener two days a week, maybe even three, and I can make it even better than it was before. You'll have to come and see it when it's done.'

'I'd like to come before that,' Hilary said. 'To see *you.*'

She left the ward feeling slightly bemused. Evelyn, who had seemed so vulnerable before, appeared to have constructed a shell around herself, a shell she was determined Hilary would not penetrate. She had seemed almost hostile, as if somehow blaming Hilary for knowing too much about her. Hilary remembered how she had refused help to take off her clothes and put on her nightdress on the morning of her collapse. She hadn't wanted anyone to see her bruises, and she felt humiliated and angry because they had.

On her way out, Hilary met Arnold Cherriman coming in. It was the first time they had met since that dreadful morning, and they both stopped and looked warily at each other.

'You've been to see my wife, I take it,' he said at last.

'Yes,' Hilary returned in a cool tone. 'She seems a lot better now.'

'She'll be all right once the medics have got her sorted out.' His small, pale eyes seemed to bore into her. 'Hope she's told you that. Told you we're moving back to Plymouth, too, I dare say.'

'Yes, she did. She seems very pleased.'

'So she should be. Better all round. I'll be able to take better care of her there.'

'I hope you will, Mr Cherriman,' Hilary said, meeting his eye, and walked past him to the door.

Outside, she got into her car and sat there for a few minutes, trying to control her shaking. She didn't know whether she was more upset about Evelyn's rejection of her, or Arnold Cherriman's obvious, though unspoken, denial that he had ever neglected or mistreated his wife. He knows I know the truth, Hilary thought bitterly, and he also knows there's not a damned thing I can do about it. He's a horrible man, a bully through and through, and Evelyn's a fool to stay with him.

Yet ... what else could she do? Ill, in her forties, unfit for any sort of life outside her home, totally dependent on her husband – what other course was open to her?

I just pray he'll treat her better from now on, Hilary thought, starting the car. And at least she'll be under medical supervision. Someone will keep an eye on her. It just won't be me.

She set off back to Burracombe, saddened by the whole story but feeling that, for her, it was at an end. She would visit Evelyn in Plymouth, but she was pretty sure that it would be no more than an 'afternoon tea and a look round the new garden' visit, with no reference made to her illness (apart from the usual enquiries) or of what had happened in Burracombe. And she hoped fervently that she would never see Arnold Cherriman again in her life.

Chapter Twenty-Two

The last week in July brought changes both to the world and to Burracombe.

'It's over!' Jackie cried, coming into the kitchen where Jennifer was preparing their supper. 'I've just heard it on the News. The Korean War's over!'

Jennifer laid down her vegetable knife and gave Jackie a hug.

'Thank goodness for that. Now perhaps we really *can* have peace. There'll be a lot of mothers and sweethearts giving thanks tonight that their boys will be coming home.'

'Yes,' Jackie said in a different voice, and turned away.

Jennifer glanced at her. 'Here, have my hanky. It's all right, Jackie. Don't be ashamed of a few tears at such good news. And you must be thinking of your friend Roy, too.'

'Yes,' Jackie said, sniffing. 'I didn't realise I'd been so worried about him. It's not as if he really means anything to me now, but, you know, we grew up together out at Burracombe and he was my first boy, and ... well, I suppose I do still care about him a bit. I mean, I wouldn't want anything to happen to him.'

'Of course you wouldn't. I'd feel just the same.' Jennifer hesitated. 'Look, you're on afternoon shift, aren't you? Why don't you pop home for the night? You could go and see Roy's mother. She must be just as happy, and I'm sure she'd be pleased to see you.'

Jackie looked at her. 'Well, I could, I suppose ... But you're getting supper ready.'

Jennifer laughed. 'That doesn't matter! I'm only making a salad to go with this ham. Tell you what, I'll put yours into a sandwich and you can eat it on the bus.'

'All right, I will.' Jackie ran upstairs and came down a few minutes later, changed and with the bag she used to carry her things in when she went home at weekends. She took the sandwich Jennifer had popped into a paper bag, and dashed out to catch the bus.

Jennifer smiled and finished making her own salad. She took it through to the back room and sat down at the table to listen to *The Archers* while she ate it.

Still cares about him 'a bit'? she thought. Hmm. It'll be interesting to see how she reacts when he actually comes home ...

The second big event was Marianne's return to Burracombe.

By now, Robert had become a familiar figure in the village. There had been some debate as to how they should pronounce his name, with some insisting on the French 'Rob-air' while others favoured the English form. In the end, Jacob Prout had settled it by referring to him as 'young Master Rob', and it had caught on. Even Hilary found herself using the abbreviation, since Robert seemed to have no objection.

'It seems more friendly,' she had said to her father. 'It makes him seem more like part of the family and the village.'

'So you're dropping your opposition to him,' Gilbert said.

'I was never opposed to him. He's just a child, and he's obviously Baden's son. What I didn't like was the way you simply decided overnight that he was to be your heir, before you really knew the truth.'

'Well, we know the truth now. As far as anyone can possibly tell, Marianne's story is accurate in every detail. Robert' – he still used the French pronunciation himself – 'is Baden's legitimate son and as such would have been the next heir, after his father. And that being the case—'

'Yes, I know,' Hilary interrupted tiredly. 'That being the case, he still should be the heir. It follows as night follows day. But it doesn't help Stephen and me.'

'Are you telling me that if we'd known about the boy, if he'd been here when his father died, if there had been no question about his inheritance, you wouldn't have helped to take care of the estate until he was old enough to take over? For Baden's sake, if not his own?'

Hilary sighed. 'Father, that's unfair. How can anyone say what they would have done? And if that had happened, I would at least have had a choice at the time. I might even have been allowed to live my own life. Come to that, would you have even *wanted* me to take over? I've had enough struggle getting you to accept my working on the estate as it is.' She paused. 'And what about Travis? What's his position now?'

'What do you mean, what's his position? It hasn't altered.'

'Maybe not now. But in ten years' time? Is Rob going to keep him on if he inherits and has the final say in everything? Do we even know he wants to inherit, anyway? Has anyone asked him? Have *you* asked him?'

'I've talked to him about it, of course I have. And naturally he wants to inherit. Nobody would be fool enough to turn that down, and his mother would never allow it anyway.'

'No, I don't imagine she would,' Hilary agreed wryly, and then, not wanting to get further into such a discussion, turned back to her former question. 'But have you really thought about Travis? Is he going to have to look for another job when he's in his late forties?'

Gilbert snorted. 'Now you're the one asking the impossible. Look, Hilary, nobody can ever be sure of what the future holds. I'd have thought you of all people would know that.'

Hilary bit her lip. Her father was quite right. If she cast her mind back ten or twelve years ago, she would never have expected to be still at Burracombe, unmarried and doing what most people still thought of as a man's job. She would have seen herself, in her early thirties, married with her own home – probably one not unlike Burracombe Barton – and with a family. Living, in fact, the kind of life her mother had lived.

'Times have changed,' she said shortly. 'And we have to change with them. Things are different now, Father, and I don't think it's unreasonable to wonder what is going to happen when you die.'

'I've told you before, you'll be well looked after, and I intend to stipulate that there is always a home for you here.'

And what if I don't want it? she thought. What if I can't live with Rob and his ways, or with his wife, for he's sure to marry. Or am I to be the spinster aunt, looking after their children in return for my board?

'Anyway,' Gilbert went on, apparently oblivious to her chaotic thoughts, 'it's virtually settled. I'm seeing John Wolstencroft tomorrow to finalise my new will, and Marianne will be here next week to discuss Robert's future. If she's wise, she'll agree to his staying on and going to school here. Fortunately, there's a place at Kelly College, and he can start there in September.'

Hilary stared at him. 'Well, you *have* been busy. I'm surprised they could take him at such short notice.'

'Always a good thing to keep up with old friends. The Head and I have known each other for years. You know that.'

Hilary shrugged. 'I don't keep tabs on all your friends. I suppose that means he'll come home at weekends, since it's so near.'

'That remains to be seen. Meanwhile, there'll be all his kit to buy – the school will send a list soon. That's something you and Marianne can attend to together.'

'Father! I've got a job to do.'

'And Travis to help you do it,' he said, waving a dismissive hand. 'How are the alterations to the estate manager's house getting on, by the way?'

'They've only just started,' Hilary said. 'We didn't know

the Cherrimans were going to move out quite so soon – they said August – and I had a job to find a plumber who could do the bathroom so quickly. And until he's finished, and the kitchen has been refurbished, there's not much point in doing any redecorating.'

'Shouldn't have thought it would need much. Arnold kept it up to scratch and Evelyn seems to have been a good house-keeper, until she started having those problems, anyway.'

'She's *ill*, Father.'

'Yes, yes, I know that,' he said testily. 'But Arnold hasn't had an easy time with her.'

Hilary felt her anger rise. She had respected Evelyn's confidence and not told anyone but Val of the bruises, but she had given her father enough hints to make him realise that there was more to Evelyn's collapse than her illness.

'He's a bully,' she said coldly. 'He's been horrible to her.'

'And that's enough of that kind of talk,' Gilbert snapped. 'Arnold Cherriman's an old friend of mine, as well you know, and he's been a guest in my house. I won't have you making slanderous remarks about him.'

'They're only slanderous if they're not true.'

'If he's that bad, why hasn't the woman complained? She's got a tongue in her head, hasn't she?'

'Evelyn will never tell anyone the truth, and she'll never ask for help because she's afraid to. And because she has nowhere else to go. It's a tragic situation, and she's got nobody to help her. And the worst of it is, she's really ill.'

Gilbert looked at her and seemed to see something in her expression that told him further argument would be unwise. Instead, he observed, 'It's none of our business, anyway. And you're not likely to see much of them now they're back in Plymouth.'

'I hope I won't see anything of *him*,' Hilary said. 'I'll visit Evelyn, but only when he's not there, and if you invite him here, Father, I warn you I shall make arrangements to be out.

Now, if you don't mind, I'll go and get on with some of the jobs that are waiting to be done. Including getting Marianne's room ready and, apparently, making time to go and buy the hundreds of items required by Kelly College.'

Marianne arrived later that week, looking smart and fashionable in new clothes, which Hilary was sure had been paid for by Gilbert. She greeted Gilbert prettily and Hilary with a warm kiss on both cheeks. When Robert came into the room, she threw her arms about him and exclaimed in rapid French how much she had missed him, how the whole family had missed him, and how he had grown while she'd been away. 'Your brother and sister miss you, too,' she said, holding him at arm's length to study him. 'They keep asking me when you will come home again.'

'I miss them, too,' he said. 'When *can* I go, Maman?'

'No reason why you shouldn't visit before school starts,' Gilbert said. 'You could have brought them with you, come to that, Marianne. Make sure you do, next time.'

'Thank you,' Marianne said with a smile. She glanced around the room. 'And Stephen? Is he here, or is he flying his aeroplanes?'

'Stephen's coming at the weekend,' Hilary said. 'He'll have two weeks' summer leave then, but I don't know whether he plans to spend it all here. He doesn't always.'

'Oh? He stays with friends, perhaps?'

'Yes, sometimes, and of course he'll want to go and see Maddy.'

'Maddy? I have not heard of this person – or is it a place?'

'No, she's a person, a young woman. She's Stella Simmons' sister – you remember Stella? We met her at the school.'

'Ah yes, the little teacher,' Marianne said dismissively. 'And so she has a sister, and Stephen goes to visit her. She is not his fiancée, though? I think he would have mentioned this.'

'No, they're not engaged,' Hilary said, a little shortly. She felt annoyed, both by the Frenchwoman's inquisitiveness about her brother, and by her casual dismissal of Stella Simmons. As if a schoolteacher was less worthy than a woman who baked cakes! 'I think Stephen would like them to be,' she went on, driven by a sudden desire to take the complacency from Marianne's expression, 'but unfortunately Maddy's fiancé was killed in an accident a few months ago and she hasn't got over it yet.'

Marianne nodded as if she'd lost interest, and moved over to the big window. She gazed out across the terrace to the broad lawns, the trees at the bottom of the drive and the purple heather of the moorland rising beyond. 'It's very beautiful here,' she murmured, and beckoned her son to her side. 'Robert, you will have to show me all the places you have discovered during the past few weeks. And I'm sure you have much to tell me, too.'

'*Oui*, Maman,' he answered dutifully.

As they stood side by side, gazing out of the window, their backs to the room, Hilary felt suddenly excluded, and was gripped by an urge to remind them of where and who they were.

'I think Rob has enjoyed staying with us,' she said, a little loudly. 'We've certainly enjoyed having him.'

Marianne turned sharply. 'Rob? You have shortened his name?'

'I'm sorry, I didn't mean to call him that to you,' Hilary said. 'It's only that some of the villagers weren't sure how to pronounce it, so we thought perhaps the short form would be better. Naturally, while you're here—'

'Rob-*air*,' Marianne said, with some emphasis. 'It is not so very difficult to say. I think they can learn, *n'est-ce pas*? It's important, I think, that such people know their place.'

Hilary stared at her. 'Our villagers know their place very well, Marianne. We think they are as good as we are, don't we, Father?' She turned to him, praying that he would back her up.

Gilbert Napier harrumphed a little, shrugged and then said, 'Fine people, the Burracombers. Salt of the earth. Do anything for anybody.'

He hadn't exactly given Hilary the affirmative she wanted, but it would have to do. She gave Marianne a challenging look, and then, to her relief, Robert himself stepped into the breech.

'I've met many of the people of the village,' he said. 'I don't mind if they call me Rob. It makes me feel English, like my father.'

Hilary saw Marianne's expression change almost with her thoughts. She opened her mouth as if to remind him of Jacques, the man who had been a father to him, then raised her eyes swiftly towards Baden's portrait and closed it again. She threw a swift glance at the window, then took a step towards Gilbert and said sweetly, 'You see, Papa? Already he feels himself a part of this place.'

Papa! Hilary thought. She'd never called him that before. It was as if, while she had been away, Marianne had decided to take their relationship a step further – several steps further, in fact. She knew, of course, that Gilbert had arranged for Robert to go to the local public school, and had agreed to this, knowing that it meant he would be spending a good deal of time at Burracombe. He had been accepted – by Gilbert, at any rate – as part of the family. But did she have to be part of it as well, Hilary thought resentfully. After all, she'd married again, and had plenty of relatives in France. What more did she need from the Napiers?

Hilary had an uncomfortable feeling that the answer was all too plain, but even more uncomfortable was the sensation that she herself was being selfish and mean-minded. What, after all, did she really know of Marianne's life? It had been a difficult and often unhappy one, a life lived in danger and deprivation. And a life lived in grief, too, for a young husband who had been taken from her only days after their wedding.

You're a selfish pig, Hilary told herself, and determined to make a fresh start with her sister-in-law. Nothing would be achieved by upsetting her, and even less by upsetting her father.

Once again, she felt as if she had been led into a trap.

Chapter Twenty-Three

'I *am* feeling better,' Maddy said. 'Sometimes, I feel almost happy. And then I remember, and I feel as if I'm betraying him by forgetting. Whatever I do, you see, he's still dead, and nothing is ever going to change that.'

Stephen put his hand on her knee. They were sitting on the wooden seat at the top of the cliff overlooking Lyme Bay, and Archie was lying stretched out in the shade of a nearby hawthorn tree. The bay swept round before them in a huge blue crescent, speckled with white horses. A few boats made their way across the glimmering waters, and the only sound was that of seabirds, crying like lost souls as they dipped and soared in the cloudless sky.

'We can't really change anything that happens,' he said quietly. 'We can only make the best of it and struggle on. And it is a struggle, sometimes. But – it does get easier, after a while. It really does.'

Maddy turned her head and looked at him. 'Are you thinking of the girl you knew, the one who died?'

'Yes, I am, partly. You never really forget someone like that. I don't even know for sure whether there would have been anything lasting between us, or whether it was just a boy–girl romance. But I felt – we both felt – very strongly at the time, and we believed it would last. And she died while we still believed that, so it was never over for me.'

There was a short silence. Then Maddy said, 'Would you like to tell me about her?'

Stephen didn't answer at once. When he did speak there was a different tone in his voice, a tone Maddy had only heard once or twice before. It seemed to come from a deeper part of him, a part he rarely revealed.

'She was seventeen,' he said. 'I wasn't much older myself. I was in my last year at school and she was my housemaster's daughter. We weren't supposed to see each other at all – we boys were hardly supposed to know she existed. But we did, of course, and I think half the Sixth Form was in love with her. Probably more than half.'

'Was she very pretty?'

'Oh, yes, but there was more to her than that. She was bright and clever, and she ... well, the only way I can describe her is to say that she *sparkled*. And so did everything around her. It was almost as if she scattered fairy dust.' He stopped, his fair skin colouring a little. 'It sounds very silly, doesn't it?'

'It doesn't sound like you,' she said, 'but it doesn't sound silly. She must have been lovely.'

'Yes,' he said, 'she was.'

They were quiet for a few moments, then Maddy asked, 'What happened to her?'

'She caught meningitis and it turned to septicaemia. They thought she was going to recover, and even got as far as bringing her home from hospital. Then she had a relapse and – just died.'

'Stephen! That's terrible! Were you able to see her?'

'No,' he said bleakly. 'We weren't even supposed to know each other, you see. We used to meet in a quiet spot in the school grounds – a little woodland dell a long way from anywhere – and just talk. We kissed a few times, but that was all. We were both very innocent, I suppose, and it probably wouldn't have lasted. But we were both head over heels in love, and as I said, it never properly ended. I knew she was ill, but I didn't know how serious it was until the Head announced in Assembly that she'd died.'

'Oh, *Stephen*. And you were there with all those other boys. You had nobody to talk to?'

'I did have one friend who knew about it – Justin Thornhill, who had been my best friend ever since our first day. He knew we were meeting but he never told anyone else. But when she died, he didn't really know what to say. It was just too big, I suppose.'

'At least he knew, though,' Maddy said. 'You weren't entirely alone.'

'No, I wasn't. He used to come with me for walks – we were allowed to go out of the school grounds one afternoon a week – and we'd walk for miles on the hills, hardly saying a word. But it was good to have him with me.'

There was another silence, then Maddy asked, 'What was her name?'

'Rosalie,' he said. 'Rosalie Dunnett.'

'Rosalie,' Maddy said softly. 'It's a pretty name.'

'Yes. A very pretty name.'

The silence this time was so long that Archie opened one eye to see if they were still there, then came over and laid a heavy black paw on Maddy's knee. She and Stephen laughed.

'He wants to go down to the beach. Shall we?'

Stephen got up and pulled her to her feet, keeping hold of both her hands. 'Thank you, Maddy. I've never told anyone about it until now. Not the whole story, anyway.'

'I'm glad you told me,' she said quietly, and their eyes met.

'Oh, Maddy,' Stephen said after a moment. 'If only things were different ...'

Maddy said nothing for a full half-minute. Then, in a tone so low he had to bend his head to hear her words, she whispered, 'Perhaps they will be, one day. I don't know. I can't promise anything, and you might not want to wait so long. But ... *perhaps*.'

He drew her gently towards him, and she laid her face

against his chest. He cupped one hand around the back of her head, and bent to rest his cheek on her hair. In a moment or two, he felt a warm dampness on his shirt and knew that there were tears trickling from his own eyes, and that he and Maddy were mourning together, each for a love that had never been fulfilled.

Then they drew apart, smiled a little shakily, and began to descend the steep path to the beach.

Marianne was at the door of the Barton when Stephen's car drew up. She waved vigorously, then ran down the steps and flung her arms around him.

'Stephen! I am so pleased to see you. I was *verrry* disappointed to find you not here when I arrived.' She rolled her r's and peeped up at him from under her long, dark lashes, and Stephen felt the now familiar and disconcerting lurch of his insides.

'My leave didn't start till today,' he said, feeling inadequate. He turned away to heft his suitcase from the back of the car. Marianne stayed close and hooked her arm through his as they walked towards the house.

'No matter. You came as soon as you could. But Hilary said you might go to see your little friend – Maggie, is it? – on the way here.'

'Maddy,' Stephen said. 'Yes, I did. I had lunch there and spent the afternoon with her.'

'Oh!' She pouted a little. 'So you left your station early this morning? And you didn't hurry straight home?'

'No, I didn't,' he said firmly. 'I wanted to see Maddy first. And I may be going again, while I'm here, to collect her for a week or so in Burracombe. That's if Felix and Stella can't pick her up.'

'She's coming here?'

'Of course. Her sister lives in the village.'

'Ah, so she will stay with her sister. Not at the Barton.'

233

'No,' he said, 'but until Stella came to Burracombe, Maddy always used to stay here. Her mother was a friend of my mother's. We've known each other a long time.'

Marianne pouted again, but before she could say anything else Hilary appeared at the door, and they went inside. Hilary immediately began to ask about Maddy, while Marianne followed behind, a little sulkily.

'She's not too bad at all,' Stephen answered his sister. 'Her arm seems OK now, and I think she's a bit brighter. Got some colour in her cheeks, too, but she says she spends a lot of time outdoors, walking with Archie.'

'She ought to bring Archie with her when she comes,' Hilary said. 'He'd get on well with Bart and Selsey, especially as they're all black Labradors.'

'But she won't be staying with us,' Marianne put in swiftly. 'Stephen says she stays with her sister.'

'Yes, she does usually, but I think it would be nice to invite her here this time. I'm sure Stella wouldn't mind, and Aggie Madge usually has visitors in the cottage in the summer. She's got several families who come regularly now. She'd be company for you, too, Marianne, while I'm busy and Stephen's off on his own exploits.'

Marianne's face darkened but she said nothing.

Stephen said, 'I'm not sure, Hil. I don't think she's ready for very much socialising yet. I think she just wants to be with Stella, and she says it's all fixed with Aggie Madge. There are no holiday visitors booked in for the last few days of my leave, and Dottie's going to sleep there so that Maddy can stay at the cottage.'

'Oh well, that's all right, then,' said Hilary, who hadn't missed Marianne's phrase 'staying with *us*'. 'I hope we'll see something of her, all the same. We'll invite them both here for dinner one evening. And Felix, too, of course.'

'Felix?' Marianne asked.

'Stella's fiancé. He used to be the curate here but now he's vicar of Little Burracombe. Didn't you meet him when you were here before?'

Marianne shook her head. 'I met the vicar – a little fat man – but I don't think his name was Felix.'

'No, that was Basil Harvey, our vicar,' Hilary said, smiling. 'Felix is quite different!'

Stephen took his suitcase up to his bedroom, and Hilary and Marianne went out to the terrace, where Gilbert was sitting in the shade of an old sun umbrella, enjoying a gin and tonic before dinner. Robert was there, too, drinking lemonade and poring over a book of Dartmoor history.

'Oh, Crossing's *One Hundred Years on Dartmoor*,' Hilary said, looking at the cover. 'You'll learn a lot from that. He really gives you the flavour of the moor.'

'I don't understand all the words,' Robert said. 'They seem to be in a different language.'

'That's Devon dialect. You've heard people talking like that around here.' Hilary poured drinks for herself and Marianne. 'Which bits are you trying to read now?'

'This bit.' He read aloud, his French accent lending a different twist to the literal rendering of old Devonshire words.

I've spaint my live 'pon Dartymoor, an' most of mun I knaw;
I've zeed'n in the zinshine, an' I've zeed'n in the snaw,
An' in the summer an' the winter aich hev got their work, you see,
Like the joys and sorrows of our lives that make us what uis be.

Hilary took the old book from him and translated it.

I've spent my life on Dartmoor, and most of it I know;
I've seen it in the sunshine and I've seen it in the snow,
And in the summer and the winter, each have got their work, you see,
Like the joys and sorrows of our lives that make us what us be.

235

'If we were speaking normal English, we would say "make us what we are" ,' she added.

'Mr Prout speaks like that,' he said. 'I don't always understand him. But the man isn't really talking about the weather, is he? He's saying that if you have bad things, like snow in winter, it helps to make you a stronger person.'

'Yes,' Hilary said, looking at him with surprise and respect, 'that is more or less what he's saying. That everything comes with a purpose – snow in winter isn't really a bad thing, because it does the land good – and as the snow and the sun do their work, so the things that happen in our lives make us the people we are.'

'Snow's not a bad thing at all,' Stephen declared, joining them and accepting a drink from Hilary. 'You couldn't go sledging if there was never any snow! Or make snowmen, or have snowball fights, or skate on the lakes. Or ski.'

Robert turned to him at once. 'Have you been skiing, Uncle Stephen?'

'A few times, yes, in the past couple of years. It's great fun. You should go, next winter.'

'I will be at school,' he said. 'And in the Christmas holidays I expect I will go home.'

'Go home at Christmas?' Gilbert said suddenly. 'But you can't miss Christmas at Burracombe. Your first year here.'

Hilary glanced swiftly at Marianne. Surely she would want her son at home for Christmas. He would have seen little enough of his family by then. But she was smiling the dark, secretive smile that Hilary had already noticed several times.

'*Naturellement*, Robert would want to enjoy your English Christmas,' she said. 'And I would, too. To be here where Baden grew up, spending Christmas as he did …'

'But your other children—' Hilary began, and Marianne turned the smile upon her.

'There is no reason why they should not come, too – if you would welcome them.'

'Of course we'd welcome them,' Hilary said. 'And Rob must see his brother and sister. I just thought he'd like to go home in the holidays.'

'He will have time for that, too. And perhaps Stephen would take us skiing as well.' The smile was directed at Stephen now. 'There are mountains in France where it is possible.'

There was a short silence. Stephen's eyes met Marianne's briefly, then flickered away.

Gilbert gave his usual harrumph and said gruffly, 'We've plenty of time to be thinking about that. It's summer at the moment, and we need to make plans to entertain Marianne now she's here. Stephen, you'll take her out and about a bit, show her the sights. Go down to the coast – Newton Ferrers, Salcombe and Dartmouth. Robert can have a look at the Naval College. Exeter and Plymouth, of course, and maybe a trip down to Cornwall. Plenty for you to see.'

'Yes, of course I'll take them both about, some of the time,' Stephen said. 'There are a few other things I want to do, though – friends to see, that sort of thing.'

'And perhaps Robert will not always want to come with us,' Marianne put in softly, her dark eyes fixed on Stephen's face. 'We can have a few days out by ourselves, *n'est-ce pas?*'

He flicked her another quick glance, then looked at Hilary. She said, 'I think we should take each day as it comes. Not make too many plans. You know what happens to the best-laid schemes of mice and men – they all go aggley!' This had been a joke between herself and her brothers after a Scots friend of Gilbert's had visited them years ago and read Burns' poems to them in a broad Scottish dialect.

Marianne looked bewildered, and Stephen hastened to the rescue. 'It's too complicated to explain. It just means that if you make too many plans, something's bound to go wrong. Hilary's right – we'll just take things easily and decide from day to day. But you must tell me if there's anything you really want to do while I'm here,' he added, turning to Robert. 'There are plenty of Standing Stones and circles and things you haven't seen yet. Crossing talks about them in that book you've got there. Things like Childe's Tomb and Grimspound. We could have a few good long tramps across the moor to see them.'

Hilary saw Marianne frown at this. She stood up. 'I'll go and help Mrs Ellis with the dinner. It should be nearly ready now. Would you mind giving me a hand, Marianne?'

The Frenchwoman opened her mouth as if to protest, then shrugged prettily and got up, touching Stephen's shoulder as she passed behind his chair. He felt the tingle but didn't turn his head, and continued to talk to Robert.

Gilbert Napier sat without speaking, watching his son and grandson together. His gaze drifted past and around them, taking in the wider expanse of the house and gardens, the fields and moors beyond, and he let his mind drift back to earlier times, between the wars, when it had seemed as if the Great War of 1914–18, 'the war to end all wars', which would make Britain a land fit for heroes, had really lived up to its promise. He thought of the early days of his marriage to Isobel, and the birth of their first child, Baden, the son he had longed for to carry on the line. His own father had still been alive then, a grey-bearded patriarch, who seemed to have grown out of the soil of Burracombe and was soon to return to it, but was deeply thankful to have lived to see the next heir born.

It should have been a golden age, almost a return to the idyllic days of the Edwardian years of his youth. But there had been dark shadows in the skies: first, the devastating influenza pandemic which had killed so many; then the General Strike of the 1920s, the Depression of the 1930s, and the gathering storm-clouds of Nazism and the rise of Hitler. And then – suddenly, if you had not been aware of the dangers – the eruption of a second world war and the realisation that the land made fit for heroes was going to call on those heroes to fight and die, just as their fathers had done before them.

Baden had been one of those to die, and for the past thirteen years Gilbert had lived with the sorrow, not only of losing his elder son, his firstborn, but of losing his heir. He had watched Stephen grow up, and away from the life he longed for him to live. He had seen his daughter, unmarried at thirty, taking over the reins of what he still considered a man's job, and he had thought there might never be a true heir for the land that had been bred in his bones.

And then Robert had come along.

Gilbert had begun to make plans for Robert as soon he had realised fully who the boy was, and what his coming meant. But it wasn't just for Robert that he was planning, and that was what he felt Hilary and Stephen had failed to understand. The plans he was making were for Burracombe. It was his duty to look after the estate and all that it entailed; it was his duty to entrust it to the person who would best continue its tradition. It was his duty to ensure that Robert, the natural heir, would also be the fittest.

It might be his last chance to continue the tradition of care that had been part of the Napier family ever since they had first been granted the lands generations before, and he meant to do his utmost to fulfil that duty – whatever Hilary and Stephen might say.

Chapter Twenty-Four

'It's going to be lovely,' Jennifer said. 'I can't believe that in just a few weeks I'm going to be living here, in this beautiful place, with you. Pinch me, will you, so I know I'm not dreaming?'

Travis obliged, and she squeaked. 'Well, not that hard!'

'You did ask.' He slipped his arm round her waist, and they stood gazing at the house. 'You don't think you'll be lonely here, after living in Plymouth?'

'Not a bit! I'll have the birds for company, and I know so many people in Burracombe already. I'll be able to see more of Jacob, and Val and Luke and the others. And I'll have my bike, so I can easily cycle to the village. I've been longing to live here.'

'I'm beginning to suspect that's all you're marrying me for,' he said slyly.

She punched him on the arm. 'Of course it is! Didn't you realise? Let's go inside and see what's been done.'

Jennifer and Hilary had been busy since the Cherrimans had moved out, going from room to room and deciding where redecoration might be done – as Hilary had said, it was all in good order and was often just a matter of taste – and where real alterations were needed. The bathroom was Jennifer's pride and joy, and she showed it off to Travis as if she had done all the plumbing herself.

'Isn't it gorgeous? A real modern bath and a washbasin. And the lavatory is next door. I did wonder about having them both in one room, but Hilary said we'd need to knock down the wall for that, and it's more convenient to have them separate. We do have the outside one as well, of course.'

'It's very smart.' Travis said, admiring the white bath and basin. 'I like the linoleum you've chosen, too, and the way it matches the wall tiles and paintwork. You've got a very good eye for colour.'

'It comes from working in Dingle's. I didn't get to be senior buyer in the clothes department for nothing.'

'Won't you miss it?' he asked, suddenly anxious. 'You've had a busy life, and you've got a really good job. It's a lot to give up.'

'Yes, I will miss it a bit,' Jennifer said. 'A big department store is like a world of its own – there's always something going on. But it can be difficult, too, and I've been there so long, I'm more than ready for a change. I want a different sort of life now. I want to be a wife and, maybe, a mother.' She glanced at him. 'You want that, too, don't you? A family?'

'Yes,' he said. 'Yes, I do. As long as you're happy about it.'

'I know I'm not a young woman any more,' she said seriously. 'But women older than me have had first babies. I don't see why I shouldn't, too.'

'Neither do I.' Travis went into the main bedroom, which had been redecorated with a white and blue patterned wallpaper, and pale-blue paintwork. 'And you certainly won't be lonely, with half a dozen youngsters to look after.'

'Well, I didn't say anything about half a dozen!' she protested. 'Two or three, perhaps. And while we're waiting, I was just wondering ...'

'Yes?'

'I think we ought to have a cat or two about the place. And maybe a dog. I know you've got Meg and Barley, but they're with you all day and they'll live in their outdoor kennel. I'd quite like a dog of my own, to stay at home with me.'

'Hmm,' he said. 'That's not a bad idea. It would be company for you, here in the woods. What sort would you like?'

'I don't know. Nothing too big. A terrier, perhaps, one of those white ones.'

'Or a Jack Russell,' Travis said. 'They're good, tough little dogs. Good ratters, too. It would work well with the spaniels.'

'It's staying with me,' Jennifer said firmly. 'Not going out working with you.'

Travis laughed. 'Well, we'll see. I'll keep my ears open for anyone with a bitch in whelp. Let's get back to what we're here for – sorting out our ideas for the house. We need to think about furniture.'

'I've got quite a lot of what we'd need,' Jennifer said doubtfully. 'It's all quite old now, mind you, and it was never the best quality – we couldn't afford it. I dare say some of it would be all right, and I could sell the rest. I'll put a card in the corner shop. You'd better come down to Plymouth next weekend to have a look at it. Once we know what we're keeping, we'll know what we need to buy.'

They went outside again and wandered round the garden. It had been neglected during Evelyn's illness, and Jennifer bent to pull out some weeds. 'I suppose there's no reason why I couldn't start coming over for an hour or two at weekends to tidy up,' she said. 'Colonel Napier wouldn't mind, would he?'

'I should think he'll be delighted. You can get Jacob to give you a hand; he can tell you which ones are the weeds.'

'I know which are weeds,' she retorted haughtily. 'I'm not completely ignorant.'

'That's all right, then,' Travis said with a grin. 'It's just that what you've pulled up are Chinese lanterns. They don't look much now, but in a few weeks they'd be covered in papery orange globes. They're rather pretty.'

'Oh.' Jennifer looked at the bunch of stalks in her hand. 'Oh, dear.'

Travis chuckled. 'I shouldn't worry. They'll recover. And how could you know, anyway? You've never had a proper garden, have you?'

'No, I haven't. Jacob's shown me quite a lot when I've helped him, but he doesn't really trust me to weed by myself.' She looked rather helplessly around the garden. 'There's such a lot to learn.'

'You'll learn it,' he said comfortingly. 'You'll have plenty of time, after all, in between the cooking and the cleaning and the washing ... You really are sure you want to go through with this?'

'I'm quite sure,' Jennifer said, and reached up to kiss him. 'I'm going to love every minute of it. Almost as much as I love you.'

'There you are, maid,' Alice said, as Val came through the back door. 'I'd almost given you up. Thought maybe you weren't feeling too good.' She started to fold up her ironing board.

'I'm all right.' Val sank into Minnie's armchair. 'Just a bit tired, that's all. I don't like this sudden heat we're getting.'

'That's unusual, coming from you,' Alice observed, putting the two flat-irons by the sink to cool down. 'Can't get enough of it as a rule.'

'I'm not pregnant as a rule,' Val said with a wry grin. 'Not that I'm complaining about that! But I must say, I'll be glad when it's over.'

'Of course you will. Some folk enjoys expecting – I reckon Maggie Culliford must be one of they! But most of us just goes through it with a smile because us knows it'll be worth it in the end. And you forget it all the minute you hold your babby in your arms, you know. You forget all the bad bits.'

'There haven't been too many of them.' Val accepted a glass of water, and drank gratefully. 'Apart from a bit of morning sickness, some heartburn and one or two varicose veins I'm going to have for the rest of my life, and the backache and the swollen ankles and not being able to get comfortable in bed, I can't say it's been any trouble at all! A lot of people have much worse.'

'That they do.' Alice opened the door of the warm cupboard beside the range, and put her ironing on one of the shelves. 'I knew one poor soul was sick the whole way through, from six weeks to the day the baby was born. Couldn't hardly keep a morsel of food down, and had gone down two dress sizes by the time her was out and about again, but the baby was a real bouncer; nearly nine pound, he were!'

'I think the baby takes all it can, and the mother just gets what's left over,' Val said, putting her hand on her stomach. 'You know, this one is going to be either a footballer or a boxer; it never stops kicking and punching.'

Alice laughed. 'I used to like that feeling. Reminds you the little one's still alive. And how are you getting on with the bedroom?'

'Oh, it's finished. Luke did the last bit of painting last night, and I put the curtains up. It looks really nice. You'll have to come down and see it.'

'I will. Your gran can come with me. She was saying yesterday we haven't seen much of you lately.'

'I don't know how she can say that! There's more of me than there's ever been.'

'You know what I mean. Anyway, she'll be down in a few minutes. She still has her rest in the afternoons, has done ever since she was poorly at the back end of winter. Strikes me she gets more tired than she wants to let on.'

'I expect she does. She's getting on for ninety, after all.' They looked up, as the door at the bottom of the stairs opened and Minnie came into the kitchen. Val looked at her carefully and thought she appeared tinier than ever, her face as creased as a scrap of old parchment and her bones no thicker than a bird's. Yet she seemed still as wiry and tough as always, and her eyes were just as bright.

'Our Val! And how be you, my pretty? Looking blooming, I see.'

'Blooming big, you mean!' Val smiled, and reached out to kiss the crumpled cheek. 'I'm in your chair, Gran. You sit here, and I'll sit at the table.'

'Bless you, no, you stay there. I'm not the one that's expecting.'

'That's a relief,' Alice remarked, pouring boiling water into the fat brown teapot. 'I don't know how we could bear the shame of it, if you were.'

'Mum!' Val protested, laughing, and Minnie gave her daughter-in-law a withering look.

'You'm getting as bad as our Tom with your jokes. She gets 'em off the wireless,' she told Val. 'Listens to that Frankie Howerd and Derek Roy on Sunday evenings, and Charlie Chester, and that one with Jimmy Edwards and Dick Bentley – *Take It From Here* – and *Ray's a Laugh*. Even *The Goon Show*. I don't think there's one she doesn't listen to.'

'Well, I like a good laugh,' Alice said. 'And I don't listen to *The Goon Show* – it's our Tom who likes that. I can't make head or tail of what it's all about, although Harry Secombe's got a lovely voice when he sings.'

'I've seen you laughing when it's on,' Minnie said, but Alice tossed her head and went outside for the milk. By the time she brought it back in, Val and Minnie had passed on to other topics.

'I don't suppose you know how poor Mrs Cherriman's getting on, now you've stopped work? I hear they've gone back to Plymouth.'

'So I believe,' Val said. 'I don't suppose we'll hear much more of them. They never did mix much with the village, and if they come back at all it'll be to go to the Barton to see the Napiers.' She didn't repeat what Hilary had told her, that if Arnold Cherriman ever came to the Barton again she would be out, nor that Evelyn had refused even to acknowledge that he bullied her. 'I hope she manages to stay well,' she added. 'Diabetes is horrible. People can go blind from it, and lose their legs – all sorts of things.'

'It's a shame,' Alice said. 'She always seemed to be a nice little body, just a bit quiet and mousy. And I never did like him. He was a nasty, loud sort of man. I'm not a bit surprised to hear he knocked her about.'

'Mum! Wherever did you get that from?'

'Never you mind where I got it from. Someone told me, that's all. It's true, isn't it? You ought to know, having seen her in the hospital.'

Val lifted both hands and let them fall into her lap. 'This place is terrible for gossip! I'm not saying whether it's true or not.'

'It is, then,' Alice said. 'Or you'd have said no.' She poured out the tea and pushed a cup across the table. 'Drink that while it's hot.'

'I'd just as soon have a cold drink,' Val said, taking a sip. 'It's too hot for tea.'

Alice gave her another glass of cold water, and she held it against her forehead for a moment before drinking.

'Are you all right, my pretty?' Minnie asked. 'You'm looking a bit leer.'

'I'm just tired and got a bit of a headache, that's all. Actually, I feel a bit funny all of a sudden. I think I might go home, Mum, instead of staying to tea.'

Alice was at her side at once, her face full of concern. 'How d'you mean, funny?'

'I don't really know. I haven't been feeling right all day, but it's nothing I can put my finger on. I don't suppose it's anything serious, just the hot sun. I'll be all right, and Luke'll be home soon.'

'You're not walking home by yourself,' Alice declared, untying the strings of her pinafore. 'I'll come with you, and stop till Luke arrives. And I think you'd better go straight to bed.'

'I don't need to do that. I'll just put my feet up on the settee for a bit. Honestly, Mum, I'll be fine.'

'Well, I'm not taking any chances.' Alice threw a light cardigan around her shoulders. 'Are you all right to walk? Should I get Tom to bring the truck? Or maybe you'd better stop here. You can lay on Joanna's bed and we could get Dr Latimer to pop in.'

'No! I wish I hadn't said anything. All this fuss ...' Val stood up and swayed a little, but Alice had turned away and didn't notice. After a moment, she walked to the door, then turned and gave Minnie a smile. 'I'll come over again tomorrow, Gran. I'll be all right, then. It's probably just because I woke up early and didn't go back to sleep.'

'And why was that, then?' Alice demanded. 'You ought to be getting all the sleep you can. I'm still not at all sure you didn't ought to be stopping here and calling the doctor.'

'I'd rather be home. It's only a step.' She swayed again and put out her hand, then sat down rather suddenly on the nearest chair. 'Well ... if Tom is around, maybe it would be a good idea to go in the truck. I do feel rather queer ...' She bent forward as far as she could, and put her face in her hands.

Alice clucked and snatched up the glass of water. 'Here, drink this. And I don't care what you say, I'm ringing for the doctor. I'll ask him to come as soon as he can.' She watched anxiously as Val sipped from the glass held in front of her face. 'Now, d'you reckon you can get up the stairs?'

'I ... yes, I'm sure I can ...' Val stood up, resting her hand on the table. 'I ... I'm not sure. I feel ...'

Alice caught her just as she began to slip, and eased her back on to the chair. 'Good job she was falling that way anyway, or we'd have been in a real mess,' she panted to Minnie as she propped Val against the table and helped her bend forwards again. 'Mother, will you telephone the doctor, please? I daren't let go ...' She tried to give Val some more water, but Val shook her head weakly and rested her forehead on the table. Alice stood beside her, keeping her arm across Val's shoulders, while Minnie picked up the telephone with trembling hands and gasped out a message to Mrs Latimer.

'She says she'll let the doctor know as soon as possible,' she reported, putting down the phone. 'He'm out on his rounds at the minute, but she reckons he'll be calling in at the Barton so she's going to telephone there and ask him to come straight round. She says he shouldn't be more than twenty minutes, unless something else has happened.'

'Let's hope it hasn't, then.' Alice bent towards her daughter. 'Val? How are you feeling now? Any better?'

'Not really. My head's worse and I've got a tummy-ache. And I feel sick – oh!' She began to retch, and Minnie grabbed the enamel bowl from the kitchen sink and handed it to Alice. Val heaved and spluttered for a minute or two, but could bring nothing up apart from some yellow bile, then she leaned back against her mother, breathing heavily, her forehead sheened with sweat.

'I don't like this,' Alice murmured to her mother-in-law. 'I hope she'm not going to lose this baby.'

At this, Val seemed to go into a panic. Her eyes flew open and she clutched her mother's hands. 'No! No, don't say that! I can't lose it, I can't! Not again. Please God, not again ...' The moment of frenzy passed, leaving her weak and limp, while Alice and Minnie stared at each other.

'Whatever—' Alice began, but she was interrupted by the sound of a car pulling into the yard. Minnie went quickly to the door and opened it just in time for the doctor to hasten in. He came straight over to the sick woman and took her hand in his, tilting back her head with the other hand so that he could look into her eyes.

'Val? Val, can you hear me?'

'Yes,' she murmured in a slurred whisper.

'You know who I am? Now, tell me what's been happening.'

But Val shook her head feebly and didn't answer. He looked at Alice, who said quickly, 'She seemed all right when she got here, Doctor. Complained about the heat and said she'd got a bit of a headache and felt tired – and that she'd got varicose veins and heartburn and her ankles were a bit swollen – but she didn't seem what you might call poorly. Talking and laughing same as always, she was. And then, all of a sudden, she came over faint. Wanted to go home, but when her stood up, her nearly fell straight down again, and her's just got worse all the time since then. I tell you, I'm really worried.'

'Yes,' he said, taking Val's pulse and frowning. 'Yes, that's a bit fast. I'd like to take her blood pressure but she'll need to come to the surgery. Would you mind coming with me if I take her now, in my car?'

'No, of course not.' Alice ran her hand anxiously across her hair. 'You'll be all right here, won't you, Mother? Joanna should be back soon; she just went down to the village to see her friend. If Luke comes—'

'I'll tell him, don't you fret,' Minnie said. 'You go off now and look after our Val. Might be as well to take her straight home after.'

'Yes, we probably will.' Between them, Charles Latimer and Alice supported Val out of the kitchen and across the yard to his car. They got her into the back seat, with Alice beside her, and set off.

Minnie watched them drive out of sight, then turned back into the kitchen. Joanna would be home soon, and then Luke, and Tom and Ted would be in as soon as they'd finished milking. She filled the kettle again and put it on the range. Tea was what everyone wanted at a time like this.

Then she sat down in her rocking chair, folded her hands across her lap and began to think.

Just what had Val meant when she said, 'Not again'?

Chapter Twenty-Five

'I don't know what it is, but I reckon it's something serious,' Alice said later, as the family gathered round the supper-table. 'The doctor seemed really worried.'

Joanna pursed her lips. 'Is it to do with high blood pressure? A lot of people get that when they're expecting.'

'Well, the first thing Dr Latimer did was take her blood pressure. And he wanted a sample of her water, too. He was going to take it to the hospital straight away to have it tested. He drove me and Val back to the cottage first, and said she'd got to go straight to bed. He says she might have to stay in bed until the baby's born.'

'My stars,' Tom said. 'That's another two months. Val will go mad.'

'I know. She do hate not being able to do things. He didn't say this, mind, but I reckon he thinks she could lose the baby.' Her eyes met Minnie's, and she knew they were both thinking of Val's wild cries at the thought of miscarrying. 'But it probably won't be that bad,' she added hastily. 'As long as she does as she's told.'

'If that's what she has to do, she'll do it,' Ted said. 'She's a nurse, after all, so she knows what's what. She wants this baby. She won't take risks.'

'Is Luke home yet?' Joanna asked. 'He was supposed to be coming here for supper, wasn't he?'

'Yes, but we caught him just as he was coming up the drive on his bike. He went straight back to the cottage. I told him one of us would slip down in the morning before he goes to work, to see how she is.'

'We'd better make sure there's someone there all the time,' Joanna said. 'If you go first thing, Mum, I'll pop down later on when I've settled Heather. I expect Dottie will look in as well, and Jacob's right next door if Luke needs to get in touch with us during the night.'

'It's a worry,' Alice said. 'She and Luke were afraid they weren't going to be able to have a family. I don't know why.' Her eyes met Minnie's again. 'She's a strong, healthy young woman. Ought to sail through. But you can never tell.'

They finished their supper and cleared up, and Joanna and Tom went through to their own small sitting room to listen to the wireless. Ted sat down with a new copy of *Farmer's Weekly*, and Alice and Minnie went out into the garden to enjoy the last of the sunshine.

'I hope that girl's going to be all right,' Minnie said. 'Us have had enough trouble in this family just lately. Joanna's not anywhere near got over losing little Suzanne, for all that she manages to put a brave face on it.'

'I know. It's going to take her a long time, and I don't suppose she'll ever really get over it. I've always thought there's nothing worse that can happen to a woman than to lose a child.' Alice was silent for a moment, then she added quietly, 'You've been thinking the same as me, haven't you, Mother? I could see it in your eyes more than once this evening.'

'About what Val said? Well, she was upset, of course she was – any young woman would be. But ...'

'But there was more to it than that. "Not again," she said. "Please God, not again." There's only one thing she could have meant by that.'

'I don't know,' Minnie said. 'Us mustn't jump to conclusions. The poor maid was ill and frightened; her probably didn't even know what her was saying.'

'She wouldn't have said it at all if she'd been in her right

mind. But that's it, isn't it, Mother? It's when we're not properly in control that the truth slips out.' She stared at a weed
growing in the vegetable bed, and pressed her lips together
tightly. Then she burst out, 'I tell you what, I think our Val's
been in the family way before, and none of us knew anything
about it. If you ask me, something happened to her during the
war, when she was away from home – out in Egypt, maybe
– and she's kept it quiet all these years.'

She paused briefly, then added, 'And I wouldn't be at all
surprised if it's why she's got this trouble now.'

'Pre-eclampsia,' Dr Latimer said to Luke, as they stood in the
little back room of Jed's Cottage after he had returned from
the hospital. 'I'll know for certain when we have the results of
the urine test, but that's what I suspect it is. All her symptoms
suggest it.'

'Pre *what*? I've never heard of it.'

'No, it's not very common. It's not really known what causes
it, but it raises the blood pressure and leaks protein from the
kidneys into the urine – that's why I need that test to be quite
sure. It can cause a lot of other problems, too. It might affect
the liver, the kidneys, or the lungs or even cause a stroke.
Now, I don't want you to worry about any of these things,' he
added quickly, putting his hand on Luke's arm as the young
man made an involuntary movement towards the stairs. 'I just
want you to understand what might happen if Val doesn't take
great care. At the moment, her condition isn't severe, and with
rest and some medication to bring her blood pressure down,
there's every hope she won't get any worse.'

'But will that be enough? Would she be better in hospital?'

'Not if everyone is sensible about it. I'll call in regularly
to keep an eye on her, of course, and I'm sure her family will
rally round. The other thing we have to consider is the baby.'

'The *baby*? You mean it could affect him, too?'

Charles Latimer smiled a little, but didn't remind Luke

that the baby could well be a girl. 'I'm afraid it could. You see, it seems that in these cases the blood supply from the placenta isn't so good, so the baby might not get all the nutrients or oxygen it needs. Babies born to mothers with pre-eclampsia are often smaller, and sometimes it's best to deliver them early, by Caesarean. But that's something we can think about later. It would be too early at this stage.'

Luke digested this, then asked, 'You call it *pre*-eclampsia. Is there an eclampsia itself, then?'

'Yes, there is, and I'm afraid that's a much more serious condition. It causes severe convulsions, and it can be fatal if not treated very quickly. That's why it is so important for Val to observe complete rest and not take any chances at all.' He paused. 'I'm telling you all this, Luke, because you're an intelligent man and you won't panic, and because Val herself will have a fair idea of what it all means. But I don't want you to worry too much. If we look after her, she'll probably go to full term and deliver a lovely healthy baby.'

'I hope so.' Luke thought for a moment, then said, 'One last question. You said eclampsia could be fatal if it's not treated quickly. What *is* the treatment? Can't you give it before it gets that bad?'

The doctor looked at him gravely. 'There isn't any actual treatment, Luke. The only possible thing to do in that case would be to deliver the baby – whether it's ready or not. But as I said, we've every hope that it won't come to that.' He put his hand on the young man's shoulder. 'I'm sure you'll do all you can for your wife. I'm happy to leave her in your hands, and I know you'll have every support from the family and your friends in Burracombe. Val couldn't be in a better place.'

Luke nodded, and Dr Latimer turned to leave. They went to the front door together and stood for a moment at the gate, then the doctor shook Luke's hand and walked away to his car.

Luke stayed there for a while longer, looking at the long

shadows cast by the evening sunshine. The cottage gardens were filled with flowers, and the scent of Jacob's roses drifted in the still air. Several windows were open, allowing the faint sound of music from the wireless to mingle with the last muted twitterings of the birds settling for the night. One or two people were working in their gardens, and they saw Luke and lifted their hands in greeting. He raised his own hand briefly in reply, then went quickly back indoors.

He stood at the bottom of the stairs, thinking of Val and all that she had suffered before he had come back into her life, then he dashed the back of his hand across his eyes and went up to be with her.

Travis and Jennifer were walking back through the village when they saw Luke at his gate. As he lifted his hand in answer to someone's wave, they quickened their steps, but he turned away without seeing them, and went swiftly up his short garden path and indoors, closing the door behind him.

Jennifer gave Travis a quick look. 'He seemed upset. D'you think something's wrong?'

'I hope not. I thought I saw the doctor's car a minute or two ago. Should we knock and see if there's anything we can do?'

Jennifer thought for a moment, then shook her head. 'I don't think so. They've got all the Tozer family around them if they need help. And Jacob's right next door, as well as Dottie just along the road. Jacob might know what's going on, anyway.'

They turned in through the gate next door to Jed's Cottage, and went round the side to the back garden. Scruff and Flossie were stretched out side by side in the warmth of the sun, and Jacob was picking raspberries. He straightened up when he saw Travis and Jennifer, and came towards them.

'Is anything wrong next door?' Jennifer asked in a low voice, glancing up at the open bedroom windows. 'We saw Luke, and he looked a bit upset.'

'Ah, there is.' He tilted his head to beckon them inside, and they followed him into the tiny kitchen. 'Val was took poorly up at the farm this afternoon, and they got the doctor in. He took her straight round to his house, to the surgery, and then brought her back here in his car. Sent young Tom Tozer off to the hospital with a sample of her water and they'm waiting for the results, but I heard him tell Luke that she've got to stop in bed till the babby's born, not put a foot to the floor.'

'Oh, poor Val,' Jennifer said at once. 'Did he say what it was?'

'I never heard him say. I wasn't *listening*, mind,' Jacob added, as if afraid they would accuse him of spying. 'I just had the window open. I couldn't help hearing. Anyway, I dare say it'll be all round the village by morning.'

'I dare say it will,' Travis agreed gravely, and Jennifer's lips twitched as she remembered how their own plans had been decided by the village, even before they'd begun to think about them. 'Well, I hope it's nothing too serious and that Val will be all right. I'd better be going now – I've got an early start in the morning. I'll come along at about eight and take you out to the main road,' he said to Jennifer, as she went to the door with him to say goodnight.

'I'm really sorry to hear about Val,' she said, when she came to the kitchen. 'It must be quite serious, if she's got to stay in bed all that time. It'll break her heart if anything goes wrong.'

'Ah, it will. Her and Luke've put their hearts and souls into doing up that bedroom ready for the little un. And the Tozers have had enough trouble for one family, they don't deserve no more.' He came into the back room, carrying a wooden tray with two mugs and a plate of biscuits. 'Well, they know we're here if they need any help in the night, so there's not much us can do now. Here's your cocoa, maid, and Dottie Friend gave me these biscuits this afternoon, said they were a new recipe – oats and ginger – and she wanted an opinion on them. I tried one out, and they're not bad at all. Enough ginger in them to take the roof of your mouth off, though.'

'There is, isn't there?' Jennifer said, nibbling carefully. And then she began to tell Jacob about the new house, and they almost forgot about Val Ferris.

Almost, but not quite. As Jennifer got ready for bed later, in the bedroom that Jacob now considered her own, her thoughts went back to the couple next door, and she wondered how they were settling down for their own night's sleep. Were they frightened about the future, afraid they would lose their baby, even afraid perhaps that they might lose each other?

Jennifer shivered, feeling as if a cold shadow had passed across the room. We're so happy, Travis and I, she thought. I can't bear to think of any more tragedy in the village.

In the next cottage, Luke was lying on the bed beside Val, his arm beneath her shoulders. She had one arm across his chest and her face was turned into his shoulder, but she wasn't crying. She'd already cried all her tears for tonight.

'Why don't you get into bed?' she murmured after a long silence. 'I can't get close enough to you like this.'

'I will in a minute. I want to get you a cup of Ovaltine first, and make sure you've got everything you need.' He hesitated. 'You wouldn't rather have the bed to yourself, would you? You'd be more comfortable.'

Her arm tightened over his chest. 'No! I want you with me. I can't bear the thought of being on my own. Don't leave me, Luke.'

'It's all right, darling. I won't ever leave you. You know that.'

'I feel so frightened,' she whispered. 'I'm so afraid I'm going to lose this baby. I don't know what I'll do if that happens, Luke.'

'It won't. We won't let it.'

'We might not be able to stop it,' she said dismally. 'I know what Dr Latimer thinks this is, Luke, and if it gets worse they'll have to do a Caesarean. They'll have to take the baby out, and it's not ready to be born yet. It's too soon.'

Luke couldn't answer. The doctor had already told him this, but he hadn't been sure Val had realised it. He stroked her hair, trying to imagine how she must be feeling, with her baby in mortal danger and knowing that she might be as well. I could lose them both, he thought with a sudden piercing agony. All this – our marriage, our happiness, our love – could be taken away from me, and there'd be nothing left.

'I keep wondering if it's my fault,' she murmured. 'There's something I've done that I shouldn't have. Perhaps I worked too long or didn't rest enough. Luke, I keep thinking about Johnny. What if I can't ever keep a baby? What if I'm *always* going to lose them?'

'Val, you mustn't talk like that! It's *not* your fault. Dr Latimer told me nobody knows why this happens. It's something to do with the placenta – it just doesn't work properly. There's nothing you could have done to cause it.'

'How can you say that, if nobody knows why it happens? And I *have* already lost one.'

'Not in the same way,' he pointed out. 'You weren't ill then, were you? And it was much earlier on, too. It's not the same at all.'

'You don't know that. You weren't there.' She moved restlessly, turning her bulk away from him, and he sat up, leaning over her and keeping his arm across her body.

'Val, stop it! You're working yourself up and if anything's bad for the baby, that is. You've got to stay calm. *Rest.* Getting yourself in a state isn't resting, even if you're lying in bed. Now, look at me. Properly.' Reluctantly, she turned her head and met his eyes. 'I love you, Val,' he said in a low, intense voice. 'Whatever happens, I love you. Remember that. And we're going to have this baby. You're going to rest in bed and not get yourself upset or blame yourself for what's happening.

Or for what happened to Johnny. There's nothing you can do about Johnny, but there *is* something you can do about the baby that's inside you now. And I can look after you and be with you. I'm home now until the beginning of September. We can do it together. All right?'

Her eyes still on his, she nodded. A tear slid down her cheek, and he wiped it away gently with his thumb.

'You must concentrate on resting,' he told her. 'It's the only thing that will really help. And if it means our baby being born healthy and growing up into a fine, healthy son or daughter, are a couple of months in bed too much to give?'

'No,' she whispered. 'Nothing's too much.'

'That's all right, then. And now I'm going to bring you a bowl of warm water, that nice bar of soap you had for your birthday, and the best towel, so you can have a wash. And then I'll bring you a cup of Ovaltine and a biscuit, and I'll cuddle you to sleep.' He grinned. 'Would you like me to tell you a story, too?'

Val laughed a little tearfully. 'So long as it has a happy ending.'

'It will,' he said, getting up. 'It will be our story and it's going to have a very happy ending.'

Chapter Twenty-Six

The news of Val Ferris's illness travelled swiftly round Burra-combe, and reached the Barton next morning. Mrs Ellis told Hilary about it as they prepared breakfast together.

'Poor Val,' Hilary said in dismay. 'I'll go and see her this morning. It's lucky Luke's on school holidays and can look after her, but I expect she'll be pleased to have visitors.'

Stephen and Marianne were already in the breakfast room with her father, who was, as usual, deep in *The Times*. She told them the news, and Gilbert shook his head.

'Doesn't sound too good. Wouldn't she be better off in hospital?'

'Presumably Charles would have sent her there if he'd thought it necessary,' Hilary said a little coldly. She still hadn't quite forgiven him for his dismissive attitude towards Evelyn Cherriman. 'But he's keeping a close eye on her and if she gets any worse, he'll have her taken in straight away. That's what Mrs Ellis says, anyway.'

'Hmph. Better make sure of your facts before you go repeating village gossip.'

'Mrs Ellis isn't a gossip. She told me because she knows Val and I are friends, and she thought I'd want to know.'

'Who is this Val?' Marianne enquired.

'She's one of the Tozer family, but she's married now and lives in a cottage in the village. Her husband Luke is an artist. Rob met him when you first came here.'

'An artist? Is he famous?'

'He ought to be. He's very good. But when he and Val got married he decided he should have a regular job, so he teaches art at the local grammar school. He still paints in his spare time, though.'

'And they are expecting a baby, *n'est-ce pas*? Is it their first?'

'Yes,' Hilary said shortly. She was one of the few people who knew about Johnny, and added, almost to herself, 'Val must be terribly frightened she's going to lose it.'

'Then of course you must go to see her. Stephen will amuse me today, won't you, *cheri*?'

'Oh, goodness,' Hilary said. 'We were going shopping for Robert's school uniform, weren't we? Well, we still can. I'll just slip down to the village and see how Val is. I needn't stay long.'

'But she may need help. If she was only taken ill yesterday, there may be things they need from the town, shopping to do. And her husband will not want to leave her, I think.'

'You're probably right,' Hilary admitted. 'I suppose we could go tomorrow. It won't make that much difference.'

'It will make no difference at all,' Marianne smiled. 'So, it is settled. Stephen will take me out for the day, so that I am not "under your feet". I heard this expression from the nice Mrs Tozer when we went to buy eggs yesterday. You could take me to the castle you told me about,' she added, turning to Stephen. 'Where the famous King Arthur was born.'

'Tintagel,' Stephen said, adding, with a note of relief, 'Yes, Rob will like that, too.'

'But no. Robert will want to go to visit his new friends, Micky and Henry. I promised him he could on the first day he was free.'

'But we didn't know he would be free,' Hilary pointed out. 'He was going to come with us to buy his uniform.'

'And now he is not. So he can spend the day with his friends, and we can enjoy our trip *à deux* to Tintagel.' She smiled charmingly at Stephen. 'See how well it's all worked out!'

Stephen threw his sister a helpless glance, but before she could speak – if she'd even been able to think of anything else to say – Gilbert said, 'Don't know that those two are the best sort of friends for Robert. Just village boys, after all.'

'They're perfectly good friends,' Hilary said. 'They're both going to the grammar school in September, and their parents are good people. As you said yourself, the salt of the earth.'

'So they may be, but those two seem to get into a lot of scrapes. Don't want them leading young Robert into mischief.'

'Leave him alone, Dad,' Stephen said. 'He needs a few boys of his own age to knock about with. Micky and Henry are all right. They'll look after him.'

He seemed to have accepted the fact that he had been manoeuvred into taking Marianne out for the day, though Hilary wondered a little at his reluctance. He seemed, she thought as she poured more coffee, to have a somewhat ambivalent attitude towards his brother's widow. She could have sworn that when they first met he had taken an instant liking to her, yet now he seemed more and more disinclined to spend any time alone with her. Well, it wouldn't hurt him to take her out for the day, and it would certainly get Marianne from under *her* feet. A few hours without her constant presence would be a considerable relief.

'Will you excuse me?' she said, getting up from the table. 'If I'm going to see Val, there are a few things I need to do first. Will you take a picnic with you, Stephen, or will you have lunch somewhere?'

'Let us have lunch together,' Marianne said at once. 'It will make the day into a real holiday for us both, and will be less trouble for Mrs Ellis. Isn't that the best thing to do, Stephen?'

'Yes,' he muttered, giving Hilary another look, of resignation this time. 'Yes, that'll be fine. We'll do that.'

Marianne got up, too. 'So let us waste no more time,' she declared. 'Let us go at once for our day out in *rrrromantic* Tintagel!'

'She couldn't get him out of the house fast enough,' Hilary told Val a little later. She'd found her friend sitting up in bed eating the breakfast that Luke had brought her, looking rather pale but reasonably cheerful. After Hilary had heard the story of Val's collapse and the doctor's visit, Val had begged her to talk about something different.

'I'm tired of thinking about myself and tired of wondering what I'm going to do, staying in bed for two whole months. Tell me all the gossip. How are your visitors getting on?'

Hilary had told her about the plans for Robert to go to Kelly College, and about Marianne's arrival. 'I can't quite make her out,' she confessed. 'She seems like two people – all sweetness and light at one moment, then like a cat unsheathing her claws the next – and you never know which way she's going to jump.'

'You don't still think she might be an impostor?'

'I don't know that I ever did think that, really. It did sound a strange story, and that marriage certificate *could* have been forged, but there was Rob. It's not just that he looks like Baden; he has Baden's gestures and mannerisms, too. They couldn't be faked. And once Dad had accepted him as Baden's son, there was no question that he'd be acknowledged. It didn't even matter whether Baden and Marianne had been married or not. Dad wanted an heir, and Baden's son was it.' She sighed. 'I have to admit that it's what would have happened if Baden had lived, so there's not much point in worrying about the legalities of it all.'

'What does Stephen think about it?'

'It's hard to say. He's nearly as bad as she is – he seems

to change his attitude with the weather. And, in a sense, it doesn't really matter all that much to him. He intends to shake the dust of the Barton off his shoes the minute he's out of the RAF, and go to Canada.'

'And what will you do?' Val asked, watching her friend's face.

'Me? Oh, I'll just soldier on, keeping the place running until Robert's of an age to take it over, and then I shall retire to my attic and spin. What else could good old Hilary do?'

'My goodness,' Val said after a moment, 'you do sound bitter.'

Hilary looked at her, startled. 'Yes, I do, don't I? It was meant to be a joke, but it didn't come out like that. Sorry.'

'You don't have to be sorry with me,' Val said. 'I don't blame you for feeling put out. I would, too, in your place.' She leaned back against the pillows. 'Actually ... could you pass me that glass of water? I'm feeling a bit off.'

Alarmed, Hilary held the glass to her lips, and Val sipped, then put her head back again and closed her eyes. She looked paler than before.

'D'you want me to call Luke?' Hilary asked.

'No ... it's all right. This happens every so often. I've probably been talking too much.' She moved her head on the pillows. 'Did Luke tell you what the doctor said? About them having to do a Caesarean if it gets any worse?'

'Yes. But you're over seven months, now, aren't you? The baby would be all right?'

Val shrugged slightly. 'Who knows? The trouble is, the placenta's affected. The baby will probably be small even if I go to full term. And ... and there might be other things wrong. If it hasn't had enough nutrients, or enough oxygen. Organ damage ... brain damage ...' She reached out and gripped Hilary's hand. 'Hil, I'm so scared. I'm scared of what's going to happen. And I keep thinking of Johnny.'

'This one won't be the same,' Hilary whispered, wishing

desperately that she could know for certain. 'This one will be all right ... As long as you do as Charles says, and rest, everything will be all right. You have to believe that, Val, because if you give up hope, nobody will be able to do anything for you. It's your hope that will keep your baby alive now. Yours.'

Val opened her eyes to look into Hilary's face. She gave a faint nod. 'I know. I think that, too. But – oh, Hilary, it's so hard to keep hoping and believing all the time, when I feel so weak. I can't do it all by myself. I can't.'

'You don't have to,' Hilary told her. 'We'll all be here to help you. Luke and me, and Dottie and Stella, and Felix and Jennifer – all your friends. We'll be here as much as you need us, and we'll help you to hope.'

Val nodded again, a tiny nod that seemed to take all the strength she had, and then she closed her eyes again. Her grip on Hilary's wrist slackened, and, after a few minutes, Hilary realised she had drifted off to sleep. She waited a little longer, then quietly stole from the room.

Luke had taken advantage of her visit to go to the village shops. He was coming in just as she arrived downstairs, and he unloaded the shopping on the table, his eyes dark and anxious as he looked at her.

'She's asleep,' Hilary said softly. 'Oh, Luke, she looks so white and exhausted. And she's frightened, too. She told me she keeps thinking about Johnny.'

Luke nodded. 'I know. I'm trying to get her to let him go, to leave him in the past. But she doesn't seem able to.'

'He was her child,' Hilary said soberly. 'Her first baby, even though he never lived. I don't think she can ever really let him go. But she'll get through this, I'm sure. We'll all help her. Luke, if you need me at any time, day or night, promise you'll send word. I'll come straight away. Val's one of my best friends, and I'll do everything I can to help her.'

'Thanks,' he said. 'I will. Just let's hope I never need to.'

*

'This is so beautiful,' Marianne said. 'So wild and dangerous. We have nothing like this in Normandy.'

Stephen stood beside her, looking over the cliff at the waves breaking into a cloud of foam on the rocks far below. The rugged contours led to the remains of Tintagel Castle, its ruined tower seeming almost a part of the crags that surrounded it. The only way to reach it was by a steep, narrow and dizzying path, which Marianne's shoes were certainly not fit to negotiate.

'And so this is where the famous King Arthur was born and had his Round Table?' she asked, slipping her hand through Stephen's bare arm.

'It's supposed to be. But nobody knows whether he really existed. And there are quite a lot of places in the country that claim him as well.'

'Which places? Can we visit them?'

'I don't think so. One's in Yorkshire, where he and his knights are supposed to be sleeping in a cavern under the great rock there, ready to wake when England is in danger – although they seem to have slept quite peacefully through two world wars! And there's a round table in Winchester Castle which is supposed to be his.'

'But this is the place where he was born?' she insisted.

'Yes, perhaps. It's an interesting legend, anyway.'

'It's *verrry* romantic,' she sighed, and tightened her hand on his arm. 'I'm glad we came, Stephen. I'm glad we can see it together.'

Stephen did not reply. He was acutely conscious of her fingers on his skin. They were moving very slightly, very softly, like the caressing paws of a kitten. He closed his eyes, fighting the surge of emotion, and shivered a little.

'Are you cold, my Stephen?' she said at once, and he opened his eyes quickly and stepped away.

'No – it's probably just the height. A touch of vertigo, you know.'

'But you are a pilot! You fly aeroplanes.'

'It's different.' He spoke awkwardly because the truth was he had never suffered from vertigo in his life. 'Let's go and find some lunch. I'm starving.'

They found a restaurant in the village, with a table at a window overlooking the sweep of the cliffs and the ruins. Marianne sat with her chin in her hands, gazing out to sea, and sighed.

'If only Baden had been able to bring me here,' she said softly. 'I would have liked more time with him. I would have liked him to bring me to England, to Burracombe, and show me places like this. He did not have time to tell me of many, you know, but he did tell me about Tintagel and a day when you all came here together.'

'I remember that,' Stephen said, surprised. 'It wasn't long before the war. Mother wanted us to have a day out together, a picnic. We brought a huge hamper and took it down to the beach. We swam before lunch, and then we went up to the cliffs and walked to Boscastle and back. It was a day just like this – hot and sunny – and it was still light when we got home, with a huge moon coming up like a golden Chinese lantern. It was our last day out together.'

His voice had changed as he spoke, the memories sweeping in and bringing with them a sensation of loss that he had known and yet forgotten. He fell silent, staring out of the window and thinking of that final day when the family had been complete and happy together. After a moment, Marianne reached out and touched his arm.

'Baden remembered it well,' she said. 'It was one of his most precious memories. I am glad you share that memory, Stephen.'

He turned his head and looked at her, feeling ashamed that until now he had forgotten it. The sensation of her fingers on his arm was different this time, bringing him comfort, an acknowledgement of a shared grief, and without thinking, he put his own hand over hers.

'I'm sorry it ended so quickly for you and Baden,' he said. 'I'm sorry you didn't have more time together.'

She shrugged, with the small, pretty movement of her shoulders that could mean so much or so little, and said, 'Well, it was a long time ago, and I had a happy enough marriage with Jacques. But I would have liked Baden to know his son, and I would have liked to know you much sooner, Stephen. We would have been such good friends all these years.'

'Yes,' he said, because he couldn't think of anything else to say.

'Now, of course, it is not at all the same,' she went on, fixing her dark eyes on his. 'Baden has been dead for thirteen years. You were a boy when he died, but now you have become a man. Things between us are very different, *n'est-ce pas?*'

Stephen swallowed. 'Er – different?'

'But of course.' The stroking fingers had begun to burn his skin. 'Do you not feel it as well, my Stephen? Do you not feel the *attraction* between us?' She gave the word its French pronunciation and lowered her voice, so that it sounded almost like the growl of a small, predatory animal.

Stephen cast his eyes about for a waiter, and said nothing.

Marianne went on, her voice soft, 'If Baden had lived, we could never have been more than brother and sister to each other. But now ...'

To Stephen's relief, a waiter appeared and handed them a menu each. Stephen, aware of the heat in his face, asked for a jug of cold water, and opened his menu.

'What do you fancy?' he asked. 'The fish will be very good, but of course you're used to fish, aren't you? Perhaps you'd like a steak instead. Or an English roast – they're offering lamb with mint sauce and new potatoes. That looks rather good. I think I'll have it myself.' He was aware of gabbling. 'Will you have lamb, Marianne?'

'I'll have whatever you're having,' she said, her eyes amused. 'I think our tastes are very similar, don't you?'

Stephen gazed at her as if hypnotised. Did she realise that every word she said seemed to have a double meaning? When the waiter returned, he handed back the menu as if he were a drowning man returning a lifebelt to its rightful owner, and looked out of the window again. Marianne had removed her hand from his arm while choosing her meal, and he was thankful when she didn't put it back. And then, following hard on the heels of his relief, came a feeling of disappointment, and he found himself craving her touch again.

After lunch, Marianne said she would like to walk along the cliffs again. Stephen cast a doubtful glance at her footwear.

'I'm not sure you've got the right shoes on. It's very rough in places, and very steep.'

'Well, let us go a little way, then,' she said, and they set off along the path to Boscastle. The path was too narrow for them to walk side by side, so Stephen took the lead, uncomfortably aware of her eyes on his back. Her voice still rang in his ears, as if she were repeating over and over again in that low, purring voice, *the attraction between us, the attraction between us ...* and his forearm felt as if it had been branded. Why on earth did I agree to come on this jaunt? he asked himself. I knew it would mean trouble. Why did I even have to come home on leave? And why, why, *why* can't it be Maddy here with me instead?

'It's a wonderful view,' Marianne said suddenly, and he stopped, so that she collided with him. She had been closer behind him than he had realised. Automatically, he reached out and caught her round the waist, afraid she was going to fall, and felt her body against his, soft and warm through their light clothing. For a dizzying moment the world swung about them, then stood still. He looked down into her face and something in her dark eyes, in the full, slightly parted lips, drew him close. She slid her arms around his neck, and he bent his head and kissed her.

He was shaking when they drew apart. He let her go and brushed one hand over his forehead, pushing back his fair hair. His body was seething with emotion; with urgent, pulsating desire, and at the same time with dismay. He stepped away, stammering out his apologies, but Marianne only laughed.

'You have no need to be sorry. It was a kiss, that is all. A wild, romantic kiss on a wild, romantic clifftop. You are a very funny boy!'

It was those words that shook Stephen back to his senses. *A funny boy!* When he knew that he had put all the passion he was capable of into that kiss, passion he hadn't even known he felt. He flushed and turned away, feeling humiliated and angry.

'I'm glad I amuse you,' he said stiffly. 'Yes, the views are very good from here. That rocky island out there is the Sisters Rock, and the one beyond is called Lye Rock, and this bay we're coming to now is called Bossiney Haven. I think this is as far as we can go. It gets very steep after this.'

Marianne hooked her arm through his and stroked his cheek. 'Now I have hurt you, and it is I who should be sorry. Oh, my Stephen, I didn't mean to be cruel, and after such a passionate kiss, too. It *was* a passionate kiss, *n'est-ce pas?*'

He couldn't answer. Still hot with embarrassment, he pushed past her to lead the way back. Marianne said no more, but when they could walk side by side again she slipped her hand into his, and he found that he liked the feel of her small fingers clasped within his. They walked back to the car and stood for a moment without speaking, just looking at each other.

'You know what is happening to us, my Stephen, don't you?' she said at last.

He thought of Maddy and tried to deny it, but the allure in her eyes and face overrode him. He stared dumbly at her, and she went on in that soft voice, which seemed to be made of silk yet with a tiny thread of steel hidden somewhere within its core, 'We cannot leave it there. You know that, don't you?'

'Marianne, I—'

'I don't lock my door at night,' she murmured. 'At least, not while I am alone.'

Chapter Twenty-Seven

Robert watched his mother drive off with Stephen, and mooched back into the house, his hands in his pockets. Hilary was passing through the hall.

'Would you have liked to go with them, Rob?'

'There are ancient ruins there,' he said. 'I wanted to see them. And tin mines all over Cornwall. Maman knows I would be interested in them.'

Hilary regarded him with some sympathy. He had made it clear that he wanted to go, and Marianne had made it equally clear that he wasn't invited. He could spend the day with his new friends, she had said. Explore the moor. Take a picnic. There would be plenty of time for him to visit Tintagel.

'There are old mines in this area, too,' she suggested. 'Why don't you get Micky and Henry to take you to see them? Not to go inside, of course,' she added hastily. 'But you can see the tips all around. You might find something interesting. We used to go looking for marcasite, or lumps of tin or copper ore.'

'I could take my hammer,' Robert said, brightening a little. Gilbert, on learning of his interest in geology and ancient remains, had given him a geological hammer, and he was rarely without it, tapping away at any likely-looking rock. He had already amassed quite a collection of stones and rocks, which were arranged outside the kitchen door.

'I'm going to see my friend Mrs Ferris now,' Hilary said. 'You can walk down with me and see if the others want to come with you. I'll ask Mrs Ellis to make you up a picnic.'

Micky and Henry, who were also at rather a loose end, were delighted to be asked to show the French boy round the old mines. They fetched the picnic and set off for Neston, a small settlement of cottages that had grown up around the mining area a mile or two away from the village.

'There's still a few people in they old cottages,' Micky explained as they marched up the valley. 'Shirley Culliford's gran lives in one, and there's old Ebenezer Bray next door. Bad-tempered old codger, he is. Comes hobbling out shaking his stick and bellowing at the top of his voice if he sees any boys around. Us'll go through the trees when us gets near.'

They soon came upon a row of four cottages, each with a scrap of garden in front, and four or five more scattered in a rough triangle, with a scrap of green between them. A red telephone box stood against the hedge, and another rough, narrow track led downhill and past a farm towards the river. There seemed to be nobody about, and the three boys, creeping cautiously through the band of windblown trees, emerged on to the lane, passed a small chapel that stood on the very edge of the moor, and came at last to the broken ground that denoted mining activity.

'It's a good place for blackberries, come August and September,' Henry commented. 'We picks loads, and our mums make jam with them.'

Robert nodded. He was accustomed to picking blackberries in the lanes of Normandy. 'Where are the mines?' he asked.

'They'm all under our feet.' Micky waved his hand to indicate the extent of the old workings. 'Riddled with 'em, it is round here. All these lumps and bumps are the old spoil heaps – stuff they brought up and didn't have no use for. They didn't always dig tunnels, mind; some of it was so near the surface, they could just dig it up from the top. That's what these long trenches were. But a lot of the time, they'd go in deep underground. They had trolleys on little rail tracks to fetch it up, and there's huge great caves down there where they dug so much out.'

'Where are the openings?'

'Adits, they're called. They'm mostly blocked off now so people can't get in. There's still one or two, though.' Micky led the way along a winding, overgrown path, beating down nettles and brambles with a stick as he went. The other two followed, with Robert last. After a few minutes, in a hollow out of sight of the path, they stopped, and Micky indicated an opening into the bank. It was about four feet across and almost invisible behind a curtain of overhanging brambles and bracken.

'That's Wheal Betty,' he said proudly. 'The proper mine's about half a mile away – you can see the old chimney still there. But this was a sort of back door to it.'

'Can we go down?' Robert asked eagerly, pushing forward for a better look.

The boys looked at each other.

'It's a bit dangerous,' Henry said dubiously. 'The roof could fall in any time.'

Micky shook his head. 'If it hasn't fallen in until now, I don't see as it's going to today. Us ought to have brought a torch.'

'I've got one.' Robert dug in the rucksack and brought out a large flashlight. 'It was in the gun room.' He switched it on and directed the beam into the tunnel.

The three boys gathered closer and peered in. The tunnel appeared to run straight into the hillside, sloping down slightly. It was floored in places with wooden boards, but for the most part the way seemed rocky, with puddles glimmering dully in the murk. The walls and roof of the tunnel were of reddish earth, and there was a constant sound of dripping water.

Henry shivered. 'It's spooky. I bet there's dead miners down there what they could never get out.'

Micky nodded. 'They used to have explosions and flooding

and all sorts, in mines. My dad says that even if they didn't get killed down there they'd die afterwards. He says it rotted their lungs.'

'Why did they do it, then?' Robert asked. 'Why go underground when they could stay up in the fresh air?'

Micky gave him a withering look. 'Well, it was work, wasn't it? They had to eat, didn't they?'

'But was there no other work? The farms? The towns?'

'Mining was all the work there was round this way,' Henry said. 'There are farms on the moor but it weren't much of a living. You couldn't grow no corn or barley – nothing like that. Just a few scraggy old sheep and some ponies, that's all. And towns, like Tavistock and Chagford and Ashburton and such, they depended on the mines, too. Stannary towns, they were. See, it was all over the moor, the mining were.'

'Stannary towns?'

'Where they weighed and measured the tin,' Micky said with a hint of impatience. 'There's a bit of a stone on the front of Tavistock town hall tells you all about it.'

Robert nodded, losing interest in the past. 'So how far can we go?' he asked, moving forward and shining his torch in again.

'Dunno,' Micky said, moving in front of the other two so that if they went in, he would be in the lead. 'I ain't been up here since I were a little tacker. Us never went in very far then, did us, Henry?'

'My dad always said you shouldn't go in at all. He says it's real dangerous.'

'It's safe if we have a torch,' Robert asserted with all the confidence of one who knows nothing about it. 'I'll go first.'

Micky shrugged and stood aside. It made sense for the one with the light to lead, and he knew Robert well enough by now to realise that he wasn't going to give up ownership of the torch. The three boys ducked their heads and crept cautiously into the entrance to the mine.

'We'd better leave the rucksack here,' Micky said, dumping it by a bush. 'It'll only be a nuisance.'

Once inside the adit, the roof grew a little higher and they were able to straighten up. Robert moved slowly, keeping the light shining at his feet, as they sloshed through puddles and soft, smelly mud, with occasional boarded stretches that they assumed covered deeper puddles.

'Mind your head,' Micky cautioned him. 'Sometimes there's big rocks sticking out. I knew someone went in one of these and nearly knocked his head clean off his shoulders.' His voice echoed in the darkness.

'I can't shine the light at the floor and the roof at the same time,' Robert objected, but he directed the beam at the roof and just avoided hitting his own head on a protruding lump.

'There's enough light to see our feet,' Henry said. 'I wonder how deep this one goes.'

'It must go miles. I told you, it's Wheal Betty, and the shafthouse is right over the other side of the hill. I bet there's millions of tunnels leading off this one.'

Henry stopped. 'Here, us'd better not go too far, then. You can get lost in places like this and wander about for weeks. It's like a maze.'

'You couldn't wander for weeks,' the pragmatic Micky argued. 'You'd die of starvation and thirst before that. I read that you can only go three days without water.'

'Well, there's plenty of water,' Robert said. 'It's dripping down the sides and off the roof all the time. You could drink that.'

'What, lick it off the walls?' Micky jeered. 'Anyway, it'd be poisonous. They got lead here as well as tin, and that's deadly poison. I don't know if you'd die of that first, or starvation, though,' he continued in a conversational tone. 'You can go three weeks without eating.'

'Only if you stay still all the time and don't use no energy,' Henry objected. 'And that wouldn't do you much good.

Nobody would just sit still for three weeks if they were lost down a mine. And what about—'

Engrossed in their argument and following Robert, they'd stopped taking much notice of the tunnel itself, and were jerked roughly back to the present when the torch suddenly went out. At the same moment, Robert screamed in fear, and there was a clattering noise. As they felt the wooden boards at their feet tilt alarmingly, Micky and Henry reached out and grabbed each other's arms.

'What's happened to the light?' Henry's voice was high with panic. 'What are you playing at, Rob? Turn it on again.'

'Come on, Rob,' Micky yelled, his own voice only marginally less fearful. 'It ain't funny. Switch it on.'

There was a silence, and they gripped each other a little more tightly. Micky called out again, an uncertain tremor in his voice. 'Rob? Are you all right?'

The silence seemed even deeper, and the darkness was so thick they could almost touch it. It seemed to hang like a cloak about their shoulders. Micky was sure he could feel something crawling on his skin, and he had to fight his terror to repress another scream.

'Rob?' he said, when he had got his voice under control again. 'Rob, where are you? Answer us, for Pete's sake.'

'He'm dead,' Henry said, his voice shaking. 'He's fell down a shaft and he'm dead. What are we going to do? They'll say we killed him. They'll say we'm murderers. We'll have to go to prison – they might even hang us! Oh, I wish us had never come down this horrible old shaft, I wish us had just gone blackberry-picking. I wish—'

'*Shut up!*' Micky was aware that Henry's panic was affecting him as well. He gripped his friend's arm so hard that Henry yelped. 'How can we hear anything if you keeps on babbling like that? Rob!' he called again. 'Tell us where you are. Us can't do nothing to help you otherwise. And you just be quiet, Henry Bennetts. You'm worse than a babby.'

Henry gulped and swallowed his fear, although Micky could still feel him trembling. They stood very still, hardly daring to breathe; and then, to their relief, they heard a movement somewhere below their feet.

'He's still alive, anyroad,' Micky muttered, and called again. 'Rob? Are you all right? Where are you?'

The sound of Rob's shaky voice seemed at that moment to be the best sound they had ever heard, and Henry let out a choking sob.

'I think so,' the French boy said, his voice sounding hollow and coming apparently from somewhere deep below them. 'I don't know ... I think there's a big hole ... I fell through ... I lost the torch and my ankle hurts ...'

'He've gone through the boards,' Micky said. 'Don't move, Henry, or we might go through, too. How far down are you? Us might be able to pull you up.' He knelt down, feeling cautiously in front of him and found the jagged edge of the broken wood.

'He's too far down,' Henry said, recovering himself a little now that they knew Robert was alive. 'You can tell by his voice. Anyway, he could pull us down there with him.'

'We needs another torch,' Micky stated. 'Can't you find yours?' he asked, addressing the invisible Rob.

'It fell out of my hand. I heard it hit something a long way down. I'm on a sort of – of shelf. I think there's a deep hole here – a pit, did you call it? I can't move; I'll fall in ... ' The French boy's voice was sounding increasingly panic-stricken, and his fear communicated itself to the boys above.

'I wish we'd never come,' Henry said wretchedly.

'Well, us did, and now us got to get out. We'd better go and get another torch and some ropes. We won't be long,' he said down the hole. 'Don't you move. You must be on a ledge. You'll be all right so long as you don't fall off,' he added, although it seemed likely that Robert already knew this.

'*No!*' Robert's voice rose to a shriek. 'No, don't leave me here by myself! I can't see anything. There might be dead miners, and it's hundreds of feet deep, I know it is!'

'Well, one of us has got to go,' Micky said reasonably. 'Us can't stop here for ever.'

'I will,' Henry said, desperately anxious not to be left in the dark. He stood up carefully, trying to make out Micky's face in the impenetrable blackness. 'Which way did we come in?'

There was another moment's panic as they realised that they had lost all sense of direction. Then Micky's common sense reasserted itself and he said, 'We never walked over the hole, so it's got to be the other way. You'll have to feel your way by the walls, Henry, and for Pete's sake, don't bang your head on the roof. Nobody's going to come looking for us down here, and me and Rob don't want to die of starvation.' He wondered briefly if they would be reduced to licking the walls, despite the risk of lead poisoning. 'You'd better get someone to come and help. The fire brigade have got ropes and ladders and things, and good torches, too.'

'My dad will skin me if I has to call out the fire brigade,' Henry said, resisting.

'So will mine, but we can't do this by ourselves, and us can't leave Rob here or we really will be murderers. You all right?' he inquired of the hole, and added encouragingly, 'Us'll soon have you out of there.'

His only answer was a muffled sob, and he gave Henry a push between the shoulder blades. 'Go on, Hen. Our dads might skin us, but the Squire'll do a lot worse if us don't get his precious grandson out safe and sound. He'll probably hang, draw and quarter us.'

'You got to have a ship to do that,' Henry began, but Micky increased his pressure, and he gave a little sob, not unlike Robert's, then began to move slowly back along the passage-way. Micky, who didn't like the idea of being left here alone any more than his friend did, swallowed his dread and said,

278

'You'd better crawl. You won't bang your head then, and it'll be easier to feel your way.'

'*Crawl?*' Henry squeaked. 'What, through all them puddles and that stinking mud? And what if I falls through the floor as well?'

'You'll do that just the same if you were walking. Get going, will you! I wish us'd brought the rucksack in with us,' he added, as the sounds of Henry crawling miserably along the rough, wet floor of the passage began to echo around them. 'At least us could have had a sandwich or two to pass the time.'

'They're ham,' Robert said mournfully from somewhere below. 'And there are bananas. Mrs Ellis put in some fruit cake as well. And a big bottle of lemonade.'

The two boys sat in silence, thinking about sandwiches and cake, and home-made lemonade. The sound of Henry's progress was growing fainter now, and Micky felt more optimistic. It wouldn't take him long to crawl out, surely. They'd only walked in for about a quarter of an hour, as far as he could tell. And then it was only about ten minutes' walk or so back to the telephone box, where he could ring up for help. He'd be able to dial 999, Micky thought jealously. And he'd be out in the fresh air and sunshine, too, while Micky and Rob were stuck here in this pitch-dark tunnel where the roof might collapse at any minute. Rob could even fall further down the pit. He'd probably break his neck and be killed.

If he does that, me and Henry'll be had up for murder, he thought miserably. And Henry's right – our dads'll skin us alive even before the police get us.

It seemed to Henry that he had been crawling along this cold, wet, dark tunnel for his whole life, and the rest of it was just a dream. Perhaps it was me who fell down the hole, he thought, putting his hand into yet another squodge of thick, oozing mud, and I'm really dead and have gone to Hell, like Mr Harvey says we will if we're wicked. I know I've been wicked, because Mum and Dad have said so lots of times, and Shirley Culliford said it that time I put a big spider down her neck. So if I did get killed and I'm in Hell, I'll never get out, and this is what it's going to be like for ever and ever and *ever* ...

The tears were pouring down his face now like rain, and he gave great, gasping hiccups of misery, but he still kept crawling along, stretching out a hand now and then to make sure the walls were still there. There didn't seem to be anything else to do. There was still a chance that he wasn't dead and in Hell, after all – and now he came to think of it, wasn't Hell supposed to be hot, with fires burning and devils everywhere with toasting forks in their hands? – and if he kept going he might come to the opening eventually, out in the fresh air and sunlight, and able to run for help.

That's if fresh air and sunlight weren't really a dream, he thought again, giving an occasional yelp of pain as his knee or his hand pressed down on a sharp stone. Oh, I wish we'd never thought of this. I wish we'd never come here. I wish I could just lay down and go to sleep, then wake up and find all *this* is really just a dream ...

Please, God, he prayed, let me get out. Please let me get out, and let Rob not die, and let Micky and me not be hanged for murder. I'll be good for ever. I won't put spiders down girls' necks, and I won't want any Christmas presents ever again, and I'll let our Billy play with my Meccano as much as he likes, only please, *please*, let me get out ...

He banged his head on a protruding rock and realised he had started to veer sideways. He stopped to lean more heavily on one hand so that he could rub his throbbing head with the other, and a new fear struck him. Suppose he had strayed into a side passage? He might never find the way out. He'd be lost down here for ever, until he died, too weak from thirst and starvation even to lick the walls. A fresh wave of tears overtook him, and – no longer caring that he was sitting in a puddle

– he leaned against the wall, pulled his knees up to his chin, and gave way to hopeless, desolate crying.

After a while, his tears began to diminish, and he wiped his streaming eyes and nose on his sleeve. He could almost hear Micky's admonishing voice, telling him to get on with it, and he heaved a deep, sobbing sigh and prepared to crawl on. At least, he thought, he could see the walls now, very faintly, and there seemed to be a dull gleam of light somewhere far ahead, so surely he must be ...

It took a minute or two for the truth to sink in. The darkness was not thick and black any more. He could see the walls. He could see a gleam of light. *He could see ...*

I'm nearly there, he thought with a surge of relief so violent he almost collapsed on his face. I'm nearly out! Oh, thank you, God, thank you, Jesus, thank you, thank, you, thank you ...

With each creeping movement, the light grew stronger, and soon he could see well enough to stand up. He scrambled shakily to his feet and stumbled the last few yards on legs that threatened to buckle under him, almost falling several times. Bending again to crawl out of the small opening, he clung to the root of a bush before straightening painfully and blinking at the bright daylight.

His clothes were soaked, his hands and knees were scraped, bleeding and filthy, and his face was streaked with tears and grime; he wanted nothing more than to lie down on the soft grass and cry, but the thought of Micky and Rob, waiting in the inky blackness behind him – especially of Rob, who seemed to be perched at the top of a drop that might be hundreds of feet deep – drove him on, and he began to scurry towards the path, tripping over roots and boulders as he went. By the time he had run all the way back to the scatter of houses, he was out of breath, sobbing and clutching his side where he had a stitch. The telephone kiosk was like a beacon, and he felt that once he reached that, everything would be all right, the whole thing taken out of his hands; but as he made for it he was brought up short by the sudden eruption from a gateway of a lean, black-and-white collie, barking ferociously and leaping about him. He stopped, trying to ward it off with both hands, and then saw old Ebenezer Bray following it, waving a thick, gnarled walking-stick.

'Here, what be you doing to my Jack? I seen you go past an hour ago – three of you there was. What be you up to?'

'Get him off!' Henry screamed, flapping his hands at the frenzied dog. 'Get him away from me. I haven't done anything to him, and I've got to get to the phone. Let me get past.'

The old man peered suspiciously at him. 'Why, what be the matter? And what have you bin doing of? You look like you bin pulled through a hedge backwards.'

Another of the cottage doors opened, and an old woman came out. Henry recognised her as Shirley and Betty Culliford's grandmother. 'What's going on? Can't a body get a bit of peace these days? What's the matter with this boy?'

'I've got to call the fire brigade,' Henry gasped, still trying to get past the leaping dog, and shouting to be heard above its barks. 'My friends are in the old mine – one of them's fallen down a hole. I've got to get help.'

'In the mine? What be you doing of there, then?' The old man showed no signs of calling off his dog. He came closer, still waving his stick censoriously. 'You'm not supposed to have been in there. 'Tisn't allowed.'

'Well, we *were* there,' Henry snapped and, losing patience, he thrust the dog aside and marched towards the telephone kiosk. Without looking back at the two old people, he jerked the door open and stepped inside.

For a moment, he stared at the appliance as if he'd never seen such a thing before. The black receiver, on top of the large box with its buttons A and B, seemed utterly unfamiliar, and he felt another swift panic at the realisation that he had no money. Then his head cleared as he remembered that he needed no money to call 999, and he lifted the receiver and put his finger into the '9' hole of the dial.

The operator seemed reluctant to take his word for what had happened. He had to repeat three times where the mine adit was, and even then she didn't seem to believe him. 'You know you can get into trouble for making hoax calls?' she warned him. 'If the fire brigade comes out for nothing and there's a real fire somewhere, somebody could get killed. And don't think you can get away – the police will come out, too, and they'll soon catch you.'

'It's not a hoax call, it's true,' Henry sobbed into the receiver. 'Micky Coker and Rob Aucoin are down the mine at Wheal Betty, not the main part, the one that goes in near Neston, and Rob's fallen down a pit and he's hurt his ankle, and what's more he's French but he speaks English as well as anybody, and they're in there in the pitch dark, and if they get thirsty they'll have to lick the walls and die of lead poisoning, and—'

'All right, all right,' the operator interrupted, evidently concluding that nobody could make all this up just for a prank. 'I'll send the fire brigade out, and an ambulance in case anyone's injured. You'd better wait by the phone box so that you can show them where it is. Don't go away.'

'No, I won't,' Henry promised, weak with relief. 'I'll stay here. Do you think—' But the operator had hung up, and he leaned against the wall of the kiosk for a minute, shaking, before realising that there were two old faces pressed against the glass, staring at him.

Ebenezer Bray pulled open the door. 'Is that true, then? Alf Coker's boy's stuck down the mine, and that foreign tacker with him?'

'Yes, it is. I've got to stay here and wait to show them the way.'

'You'd be better off to come in with me and have a drink of

water,' old Mrs Culliford said, putting out a wrinkled hand. 'Come along, now.'

Henry pulled away. 'I told you, I've got to wait. They won't know where to go, else.' He planted himself firmly against the door of the kiosk, feeling better now that help was on its way, and thrusting aside his worries about the consequences. 'I expect I'll have to ride on the fire engine,' he added with a sudden sense of importance.

'Fire engine!' Ebenezer exclaimed, and cackled with glee. 'Us haven't had one of they out here since old Nan Bellifer set fire to her kitchen range. You remember that, Marge? It was Coronation Day.'

'But Coronation Day was only a few weeks ago,' Henry said, diverted for a moment, and the old man gave him a scornful glance.

'Not *that* Coronation! It were the old King's coronation – Edward the Seventh. Fifty-one year ago, that were, and old Nan had put the frying pan on for her man's breakfast and then run out to see Jack Bellamy's cart go by all done up in red, white and blue, and forgot all about it. Next thing we knew, there was flames …' He rambled on, Mrs Culliford joining in with her own reminiscences of local fires and disasters, and Henry leaned against the kiosk, watching anxiously for the first sign of the fire engine, and wondering if they would ring their bell.

They might even let *me* ring it, he thought. Micky's never done that!

Chapter Twenty-Eight

'Thank goodness you're back,' Hilary said, coming out to the front steps, as Stephen drew the car to a halt on the drive. 'We've had a bit of excitement here.'

'What sort of excitement?' Stephen asked, opening the passenger door for Marianne. He was thankful to be home, and not sure he wanted any more excitement. 'Dad's okay, isn't he?'

'Oh, yes, he's fine. It's Robert.' She glanced apologetically at Marianne. 'I'm afraid he's had an accident. It's not serious,' she added quickly, as Marianne started forward with an exclamation. 'He just got into rather a scrape with the other boys. He's hurt his ankle, that's all.'

'Hurt his ankle? How? Which other boys?'

'Micky Coker and Henry Bennetts. You remember, you said he should spend the day with them.' Hilary's tone was slightly acid. Marianne would have every right to be angry about what the boys had done, but it had been her decision to let Robert go out with them. 'They went out for a picnic and apparently decided to visit one of the old mines. They went inside—'

'They went down a *mine*?' Marianne exclaimed. 'But why were they permitted? Surely there are men there, working? They should not allow boys to go down.'

'It's a disused mine. There are a lot of them around here. Mostly, they're blocked off, but Micky knew of one you could get into.'

'Micky would,' Stephen said, sounding amused. 'Which one was it?'

'Wheal Betty, they think. Not the main entrance – it was a small adit near Neston. It's not a pit,' she explained to Marianne. 'It's more like a tunnel, going into the hillside. Anyway, they went in, and it seems that Robert fell through some rotten boards and down a shaft. He's not badly hurt,' she said hastily. 'He landed on a ledge. He's just a bit grazed and bruised, and the hospital doctor says the ankle's sprained but, as far as he can tell, nothing's broken.'

'*As far as he can tell?* What treatment has he had?' Marianne's cheeks reddened and her dark eyes flashed. 'You have not been taking proper care of my son!'

'Yes, we have!' Hilary retorted indignantly. 'You may recall that *you* were the one who went off and left him for the day, *and* you agreed that he should spend his time with the other boys. In fact, it was your suggestion in the first place!'

'I did not suggest that they take him into danger,' Marianne said icily. 'And if *you* recall, 'ilary, your father did not think they were suitable boys for Robert to spend time with. It was *you* who said they were suitable. I left him in *your* hands, thinking he would be safe, and *this* is what has happened. Where is he?'

Almost too angry to speak, Hilary indicated the small sitting room. The Frenchwoman hurried in, leaving Hilary and Stephen on the doorstep.

'I might have known she'd blame me,' Hilary said furiously. 'Doesn't she realise I have work to do? Doesn't anyone else ever take any responsibility around here?'

'I shouldn't worry,' Stephen said easily. 'She'll get over it once she realises he's all right. All the same, it must have been a bit of a to-do. How did they get him out?'

Hilary grimaced. 'They were quite a way in and had lost their torch – Rob had taken one of ours from the gun room, and it seems he was going first, carrying it – so they couldn't see to help him out. Just as well, probably, because it was a deep shaft and they could all have been killed. We'd never have known what happened to them.' She shuddered. 'Anyway, they seem to have behaved quite sensibly then. Henry went to the phone box and called the fire brigade, and they went in with ropes to get him up. He was pretty shaken, but it could have been a lot worse. They'd got an ambulance out there, too, and took him straight to Tavistock hospital for a check-up, but apart from the ankle and a few bruises, they decided he was okay. He hadn't bumped his head, luckily.'

'Good lord,' Stephen said. 'And all this was happening while Marianne and I were at Tintagel.'

'It might have been better if we'd gone to buy the school uniform after all,' Hilary said wryly.

'Yes, perhaps it would,' Stephen said, thinking of what else had happened while he and Marianne were at Tintagel. 'Still, I suppose all's well that ends well. It'll be something for them to talk about for the rest of their lives! What about the other two, are they all right?'

'It shook them up, too. Henry was in a real state by the time the fire engine arrived, and Micky and Rob were beginning to think nobody was ever coming. It was pitch dark in there and they were both terrified to move. I don't think any of them are likely to go exploring mine adits again.' She looked at her brother. 'How did your day go?'

'Oh, all right.' That was something he didn't want to talk to his sister about. He hadn't even begun to sort out his own mixed emotions – the wild, dark surge of desire, the passion of the kiss, the guilt and the misery when he thought of Maddy. He turned away. 'I'll go and put the car in the garage. What does Dad think about all this, by the way?'

'He was livid. Said he'd warned her about letting Rob go about with those two. I have to admit, he's right about them getting into a lot of scrapes, but they're decent boys at heart. There's not a bit of real wickedness in them.'

'There doesn't need to be, does there?' he grinned. 'They can get into enough trouble without being wicked.' He started down the steps, then turned back. 'I forgot to ask – how's Val Ferris?'

'She seems okay, as long as she stays in bed, but Dr Latimer says she's got to be really careful and call him the minute she feels bad again. It's a dangerous condition, apparently. But Luke won't let her take any risks; he's treating her like a porcelain doll.'

'Not really Val's style,' Stephen remarked.

Hilary laughed and shook her head. 'No, it's not, but I don't think she's got much choice. The world's beating a path to her doorstep. Her mother arrived just as I was leaving, Joanna was going down this afternoon, Dottie Friend said she was baking a sponge cake to take in on her way to the pub, and Stella Simmons was going to pop in as well. I think Luke will have to draw up a rota of visitors or she'll be worn out.' She sighed and turned back into the house. 'I'd better go and see how Rob and Marianne are. You won't be long, will you? It's less than an hour till dinner, and you know Dad likes us all to be there for a drink beforehand.'

Stephen nodded. 'I'll have a quick bath and come down.' He had determined to allow Marianne as few opportunities as possible to be alone with him. He got into the car and drove it round to the stable yard, then went into the house through the kitchen door and up the back stairs to his bedroom.

As he had his bath, he wondered what difference Rob's accident would make. Would Marianne be a fussy mother, wanting to stay with her son, or would she look on his restricted mobility as another opportunity to spend more time with Stephen? Well, if it's only a sprained ankle, he thought, there's no reason why we can't take him with us if we go out again. And there'll be no solitary walks in lonely, romantic places.

All in all, the boys' escapade might turn out to have been a good thing.

Gilbert Napier did not agree that it had been a good thing.

'I don't know what the young fools were thinking of,' he said for the hundredth time as they met in the small sitting room for their sherry. 'Everyone knows how dangerous these old mine adits are. To take my grandson into such a place ...' He shook his head, still unable to believe the enormity of it. 'I just hope their fathers are showing them the error of their ways.'

'I'm sure they will,' Hilary said, thinking of Alf Coker, who was known to be a stern disciplinarian, and feeling rather sorry for Micky. 'And they didn't mean harm, Father. I don't expect they'll do it again.'

'They'll not get the chance,' Gilbert growled, and directed his sharp gaze at the boy, who was propped on the sofa with his legs up. 'You'll see no more of those two, Robert, d'you understand? Keep clear of them.'

'But I like them,' Robert protested. 'They're my friends.'

'Not any more. You'll make plenty of friends when you get to Kelly College, the sort of friends you'll need. Not village louts.'

'Father!' Hilary protested. 'Micky and Henry aren't louts – they're ordinary boys with a bit of spirit and a sense of adventure. All right, it leads them into trouble now and then, and I admit this could have ended a lot less happily, but there's not an ounce of malice in them, and they're bright lads, too. I think they're very good friends for Rob.'

'You don't imagine they're the only ones to have gone exploring in the old adits, do you?' Stephen joined in. 'I should think every youngster for miles around has been in at least one.'

'Including Baden,' Hilary observed.

Gilbert's head snapped round. '*Baden?*'

'Yes. You don't imagine he was a little saint, do you? He took me into one of the adits when I was about ten years old.

He had a sort of den in there, not very far in, but he called it his cave. He had candles and a tea-chest for a table and cupboard, a stool he'd made, and an old rug. It was pretty dismal, to tell you the truth, but it was his own place and that was the important thing.'

The others listened, Stephen with amusement, Marianne with amazement, and Gilbert with disbelief. He opened his mouth but Robert spoke first.

'I think I would have liked my father.'

Hilary looked at him and smiled. For a moment, she had forgotten that Baden's son was in the room with them. She thought of the hours he had spent with Gilbert, hearing stories of Baden as a boy and a young man, and it occurred to her that this was probably the first that had presented him as a real person, a spirited boy with his own ideas and wishes.

'Of course you'd have liked him,' Gilbert said impatiently. 'He was your father.'

'Doesn't always follow, though,' Stephen murmured under his breath, and Hilary gave him a quick frown. Gilbert, however, appeared not to have heard.

'Anyway, all that's by the way,' he went on. 'We'll get a few other youngsters round for you to meet. Ought to have done it before. Hilary, you must know people with lads the same age as Robert. Get something arranged.'

'Like what?' she asked, seeing her time taken up with organising yet more social activities. 'Tea parties? Games on the lawn? And who am I supposed to invite?'

'Don't be sarcastic,' he snapped. 'It's one of your biggest faults and it's not becoming in a young woman. You know perfectly well what I mean. There are plenty of people in the area – the Foxtons, over at Meavy, for instance. They've got a young family, haven't they? And the Marrabys in Buckland Monachorum. You can think of something, surely. Tennis parties, that sort of thing.'

'Robert's a bit young for tennis parties. Apart from which,

he's got a bad ankle. And the Foxtons are away for the summer, and all the Marrabys' children are girls. Honestly, Father, Micky and Henry are perfectly suitable, and I'm sure they won't be so foolish again.'

'You might even find that Alf Coker and Stanley Bennetts aren't too keen on their sons spending their time with Robert,' Stephen remarked. 'From what he's been telling me, he was the one who was most eager to see the mine in the first place.'

'I *was* interested,' Robert confirmed. 'And when Aunt Hilary suggested it—'

'*You* suggested it?' Gilbert demanded, swinging his head towards Hilary again. 'What in God's name—'

'I didn't suggest they should go inside,' she protested. 'I just thought Robert would be interested in what's on the tips. We used to go looking when I was a child – Baden took me – and find all sorts of things.'

'And that was a pretty stupid thing to do, too,' he snapped. 'They used to mine arsenic in some of those places. You could have poisoned yourselves.'

'Well, we didn't,' she said, growing tired of the argument. 'Look, Father, what's happened has happened, nobody's very much the worse for it, and I'm sure the boys have all learned their lesson. Let's leave it there, shall we?'

'Yes, and let Robert make his own friends,' Stephen added. 'When you come to think of it, Micky and Henry are much more the sort of boys he'd be making friends with back in France than people like the Foxtons and the Marrabys, aren't they?'

Gilbert glowered, but before he could say any more, Hilary got up and said firmly, 'Dinner must be ready now. I'll help Mrs Ellis bring it in. Stephen, give Robert a hand, please. I've put a chair on the end of the table for you, Rob, so that you can keep your foot up on a stool. I hope it'll be comfortable for you.'

'He will be perfectly comfortable,' Marianne said, in a tone that reminded Hilary that Robert was her son. 'He will sit between me and Stephen. We will take care of him.' She gave Stephen a sly glance. '*N'est-ce pas?*'

The evening ended early. Everyone seemed tired after the events of the day, and after playing a few games of Ludo with Robert and then helping him up to his room, Stephen said he was going to bed. He avoided Marianne's gaze, kissed her cheek and went upstairs. He shut the door and leaned against it, his eyes closed, breathing deeply.

There had been no escape for him during the past few hours. Sitting round the small table pulled up beside the sofa, so that Robert could play comfortably, he and Marianne had been forced to sit close together on small chairs, almost touching. Hilary had perched on the sofa, careful to avoid Robert's injured leg, and had apparently not noticed Marianne touching Stephen's arm as she leaned forward to make her moves, and sliding her dark eyes sideways in a secret smile when he succeeded in getting one of his pieces home. By the time the board was folded up and the counters scooped into their little bag, he was desperate to be out of her orbit, and even the thought of Maddy wasn't enough to silence his pounding heart.

He took his washbag and towel to the bathroom and washed swiftly, frantic to be safely back in his room before Marianne came upstairs. Then he slipped into his pyjamas and stood for a while by the window, looking down at the garden. The moon was just off full, a slightly flattened pearly disc high in the sky, casting a glimmering light on the flowerbeds, and the lawns and the woods beyond. He knew there would be no sleep for him tonight, and thought of dressing again and going out for a walk, but he was almost afraid to leave his room. After a while, he turned away from the window and got into bed.

The moon rose slowly across the sky beyond his window. He heard his father come upstairs to bed, then Hilary and the lighter footsteps that were Marianne's. For a moment, he held his breath, but the sounds tapped past, and he breathed again.

He turned over and tried to sleep, but his mind now was filled with Marianne's voice, telling him in that seductive murmur that she did not lock her door at night. Was she waiting for him now? Was she lying in her bed, watching for the door handle to turn? He imagined himself getting out of bed, creeping along the landing to her door, pushing it gently open, closing it behind him, and he clenched his fists beneath the sheet. No. *No* ... He closed his eyes tightly and kept them closed.

He did not see the handle of his own door turn. He did not hear the soft sound the door itself made as it swung open under a small, careful hand. He felt the change in the air, the slightest of draughts, but he didn't register its meaning until she leaned over him, her hair brushing his cheek and the scent of her filling his nostrils.

'You're not asleep, are you, my Stephen?' the teasing whisper came. 'I've been waiting for you, but I decided to wait no longer. So you see, *mon cher*, I have come to you instead ...'

He opened his eyes, feeling as if he were drugged, and he knew that, like a drugged man, he had no strength to resist any further. He saw her leaning over him, her hair a dark cloud, her eyes pools of liquid jet, her breasts full beneath the thin, silky nightgown, and he felt his helplessness wash over him.

Almost without thinking, he pulled back the sheets and held out his arms, drawing her down against him.

Chapter Twenty-Nine

'*Leaving?*' Hilary echoed in astonishment. 'But why?'

She had just returned from an early-morning ride on Beau, to find her brother mooching about in the stable yard. She led the horse into his stable to brush him down, and Stephen followed her miserably. 'I can't tell you that. But I've got to go, Hil. I just can't stay here – not with *her* in the house.'

'Her? Marianne, do you mean? Why, what's she done? I thought you two got along quite well.'

If only that were all, he thought. But he shook his head. 'It's not just that. I promised a fellow I know that I'd try to get up to his place for a few days this leave. And there's not much I can do here, with Rob crocked up. She'll want to stay and look after him. Can't take them out and about much.' He tried a laugh but it sounded hollow, and Hilary looked at him doubtfully.

'I'm sure they'd like your company. I don't understand, Steve. When you came back from Tintagel yesterday you seemed to have had a really good time. Don't you like her? I'm sure she likes you.'

'It's not that.' He began to feel irritated, although he knew the feeling came from guilt. 'Just let it alone, please.'

'But what about Maddy?' Hilary persisted, examining Beau's hooves. 'She'll be coming soon. Weren't you going to go and fetch her, if Felix couldn't manage it? What's she going to do?'

Maddy, he thought. Maddy was one of the reasons why

he had to get away. He tried to speak casually, as if it didn't matter to him.

'Oh, I expect Felix will be able to do it. If not, there are trains – she's come that way before. Anyway, she's made it clear she isn't interested in me.'

Hilary stared at him. 'You know it's only a few months since Sammy died.'

'Yes, I know. But a chap can't hang around for ever.' He tried another small laugh. 'I've got to get my own life in order, Hil. Think about what I'm going to do when I get out of the RAF. It's not all that long now, you know.'

'And you have to do that now? This minute? Steve, we all thought you would be here for the whole fortnight. And I need you here. You know the situation – it's not easy. I've got work to do ...'

'So you thought you could rely on me to babysit.' He turned his irritation on his sister, knowing he was being unfair. 'Well, sorry, but it's my summer, too, and I've decided to spend it as I want to. I'll tell Dad at breakfast and get packed, and I'll be off by lunchtime.'

'And that's it? We won't be seeing you again before your leave finishes? You won't even pop back for a few hours to see if we're still alive?' She turned away to fill the horse's hay net.

'Oh, for goodness' sake!' he exclaimed bad-temperedly. 'I'm not going to the other end of the earth. You'll see me often enough, the same as usual. I just don't want to stay here now, that's all.'

'While Marianne's here,' she said flatly. She gave him a close look. 'There's something you're not telling me, isn't there? What's happened between you two? *Was* it while you were out yesterday? Did you have an argument?'

'Something like that. I don't want to talk about it. I just wanted to tell you what I'm going to do, that's all.' He walked out of the stable, and Hilary gave Beau a last pat and followed him. 'It's no good, Hil, I'm not saying any more. I've made up my mind, and that's it.'

Disturbed, she walked back to the house beside him. There was something very wrong here, but she couldn't imagine what it was. She cast her mind back to the previous evening. Robert's accident had taken precedence over everything, and she tried to remember if there had been any particular atmosphere between her brother and Marianne. They'd played Ludo together all evening, the four of them, and it had seemed friendly enough. Maybe a little too friendly on Marianne's part, as if she were trying to make up for some quarrel? But if so, why couldn't Stephen tell her about it? It could only have been about the inheritance, and Hilary was as deeply involved in that as Stephen – more so, in fact. She glanced sideways at her brother's face, wondering if she should try once more to get the truth from him, but his expression was hard and closed, and she knew it would be useless.

'I just hope you know what you're doing, that's all,' she said, as they reached the side door and went into the gun room, where Hilary kept her riding hat and boots. 'God knows what Father's going to say. But I suppose there's nothing any of us can do to stop you.'

'No,' Stephen said. 'Nothing at all.'

Marianne did not appear for breakfast. She had already told them that the English breakfast was much too large and heavy for her, and she preferred to stay in bed – a rare treat, for she had to be up early baking cakes for the *pâtisserie* at home – and have some coffee later. Hilary herself had taken a tray to Robert's room, making sure he'd had a comfortable night, and knew he wouldn't be making an appearance for a while. So the family were able to continue their argument unheard.

Hilary did not join in. She sat and listened while Gilbert repeated all the things she had already said, and saw the same shuttered, obstinate expression on her brother's face. Again, she wondered what could have happened to change his mind about staying the full fortnight of his leave. *Something* must have happened in Tintagel, but what?

'I can't see why you're so annoyed about it, Dad,' Stephen was saying. 'I'm old enough to decide for myself, and I don't know why I should be expected to spend all my time at home. Can't I have a holiday, too?'

'*Too?*' Gilbert exclaimed. 'Who else around here is having a holiday? Your sister hardly ever has as much as a day away from the estate, and it's not as if you lift a finger to help when you are here. You take no responsibility at all, and you don't do much more than play when you're on that air station. You spend your entire time flying aeroplanes. Your whole life is a holiday!'

'It's actually rather hard work, and I'm responsible for a squadron,' Stephen said tightly. 'Anyway, there's no point in arguing about it, Father. I'm going off for a week or so, and that's it. I'll come back for the last couple of days if that'll make you feel any better.'

Gilbert drew in a deep breath through his nose, as if he were about to say more, then thought better of it and compressed his lips. Hilary's heart sank. All these worries and disputes were no good for him, she knew, yet she could see no way out of their situation. Not for the first time, she wished heartily that Marianne and Robert had never come to Burracombe. Better still, that Baden had never met and married her.

'We might as well accept it,' she said. 'Steve's right – he's old enough to do as he pleases, and you have to admit he's been very good, coming home as often as he has. There must be other things he'd rather be doing.'

'Humph,' her father said. 'I dare say you're right. All the same, we're in an unusual situation, and in my opinion the family should stick together.'

'Oh, should we?' Stephen asked in a nettled voice. 'When you've made it quite clear that this new grandson of yours is taking precedence over the children who've been with you all your life? You'd throw us both out, if it suited you. Just why *should* we stick together? What are you going to do for us, apart from throw us a few crumbs?'

'Stephen!' Hilary protested, but Gilbert was on his feet, scarlet-faced and thumping the table.

'That's enough!' he roared. 'If all you can think about is what you can get out of me when I die – or even *before* I die – then maybe it would be better if you *did* get out! I thought better of you, Stephen. Little though you've ever done to make me proud of you, I still harboured the hope that you had some family feeling in you. Obviously I was wrong. Go, if that's what you want. Go now!'

'Dad!' Hilary cried, and jumped up, taking her father's arm and trying to press him back into his chair. 'Dad, remember your blood pressure—'

'Tell *him* to remember my blood pressure,' he snarled, resisting for a moment and then, reluctantly, sinking back. 'He's the one bringing all this trouble to the house.'

'That's not really fair, is it?' she said gently. 'But don't let's argue any more. Have some more coffee and calm down before we discuss it again. Stephen won't go rushing off straight away, will you, Steve?'

She glanced at him, hoping to see signs of capitulation, but Stephen's face still wore the same look of obstinacy that she'd seen before. Before he could speak, however, the telephone rang in the hall, and with some relief, she let go of her father's arm and went to answer it.

Stephen and his father sat silently, not looking at each other. Gilbert's breathing had slowed down. He lifted his cup of coffee, but his hand was shaking, and he put it down again. He glowered at his plate.

Stephen felt acutely uncomfortable. He had never meant the argument to go so far. Indeed, he'd never anticipated an argument at all. He'd thought that he was free to spend his leave as he chose, and, although he knew his father and sister would be disappointed, and expected much more resistance from Marianne, it had never occurred to him that it could blow up into a full-scale row. All the same, he was determined to go. To stay, after what had happened last night, was impossible.

Hilary came back into the room. She looked at her brother and said, 'It's for you.'

'For me? Who is it?' He began to get to his feet, wondering whether this was his relief. Somebody inviting him to stay, perhaps. Or even the air station, requesting his immediate return.

'It's Maddy,' Hilary said. 'She wants to come back to Burracombe as soon as she can – today, if possible. Felix has a funeral to conduct and can't do it, so she's asking if you can go instead.'

As he drove along the south coast road towards West Lyme, Stephen felt as if he were approaching his doom.

He had never wanted a journey to go so slowly, nor had he ever wished less to see Maddy Forsyth. He had no idea what he was going to say to her, or how he could look her in the eye. And it was too soon. He felt as if Marianne's scent was still on his body, in his sweat and in his breath, and the knowledge of what had happened was in his eyes, clear to anyone who wanted to look. Hilary had come close, he felt sure, and Maddy would know at once.

His misery grew, as the sports car proceeded through the towns and villages. Honiton ... Axminster ... Morecombelake ... Charmouth ... each mile taking him nearer to Maddy, each mile hammering the knowledge of his betrayal into his brain. I can't do it, he thought, I can't face her.

Twice, he stopped at the side of the road and stared over the rolling Dorset hills to the sea. He thought of turning inland, heading into Wiltshire or Somerset as he had planned, driving until he was exhausted and finding a bed in a cottage somewhere. Some small village or town where nobody knew him, where nobody would see or care what he had done. Somewhere that he could lose himself, forget the torture of simultaneously wanting and hating Marianne, the knowledge that even as he gave in to his clamouring body, he would be filled with self-loathing only a few hours later.

Twice, he dragged his tattered sensibilities together and continued along the road to West Lyme. Maddy had sounded distraught on the phone that morning. He'd had no choice but to agree to bring her back to Burracombe. But once he'd done that, he vowed, he would go away, as he had decided he must. With Maddy in the village, it would be impossible to stay; impossible to walk down the street, with Marianne hanging on his arm and the danger of meeting Maddy at every turn; impossible to remain in the house, with Marianne likely to come to his door, and his bed, at any moment during the night.

At last he could postpone the moment no longer. He was in West Lyme and at the gate to the Archdeacon's house. He was passing between the trees and shrubs that lined the drive. He was stopping at the foot of the steps, and the front door was already open and Maddy running down to greet him.

'Stephen! Oh, Stephen, I'm so glad you're here. Thank you for coming – thank you very, very much.'

He got slowly out of the car, and Maddy ran into his arms. Automatically, he put them round her, holding her close and breathing in the sweet, fresh perfume of her, so different from the dark, musky scent of Marianne's skin. He laid his cheek against her fair, soft hair and closed his eyes, and wished that they could stay like this for ever.

'It was seeing Ruth and Dan again,' Maddy told him as they sat on the bench overlooking the bay, with Archie, as usual, panting at their feet. 'I hadn't been to Bridge End for a while and I thought I should go, before having my holiday in Burracombe. Oh, Stephen, it's so sad. I don't know whether they're ever going to get over losing Sammy.'

'It's still early days, I suppose,' Stephen said, trying to shift his emotions from his own distress to someone else's.

'I know, but after the funeral they seemed to be coping quite well with it. They were terribly upset, of course, but Dan was being strong for Ruth, and Ruth was trying to comfort him. They were helping each other. But now, they seem to have lost their way somehow. They're obviously still dreadfully unhappy, but they're hiding it from each other, and it's driving them apart. And there's Linnet, too – that poor little girl. She's lost her big brother, and her mum and dad can't seem to give her what she needs. They either turn away from her or they smother her. It's so sad.'

'Perhaps it's just a stage they have to go through,' Stephen said, trying to remember his own experience of bereavement. 'When we heard that Baden had been killed, Mother spent weeks hardly coming out of her room, and when she did appear she looked like a ghost. And when *she* died, it was even worse. Dad seemed to shut himself away completely. I was away at school then, but they brought me home for the funeral, and I had to tiptoe about and pretend I wasn't there. Hilary was the only one who noticed me, and she was having to manage everything, so she didn't have much time.' He hesitated. 'And then there was Rosalie. I didn't have anyone to talk to about her. Except for Justin, and you know boys of that age don't tell each other about their feelings much. So I suppose I shut it away, too.'

'Poor Stephen,' Maddy said, and put her hand over his. He looked down at it, and felt his eyes blur. If only she knew, he thought, she wouldn't want to touch me at all ... He felt soiled and dishonest.

'Perhaps you shouldn't have gone to Bridge End,' he said gently. 'It was bound to upset you.'

'I know. But that's no reason, is it? I mean, why shouldn't I be upset? People want to shelter me all the time, but that's wrong. I have to feel my sorrow. If I don't, I think I'll be like Dan and Ruth, and never get over it. And besides that, we need to share it. We're the people who are suffering the most. If we can't give each other comfort, who can?'

'And do you think it helped?'

'I don't know,' she said sadly. 'How can we ever be sure? We were all upset – we cried together, even Dan – and I came back just needing to go home to Burracombe, to be with Stella and all the other people I love. Perhaps they felt worse after I'd gone, too. But we have to see each other; we have to share it. Maybe you're right and it's something we have to go through. I just wish ... I just wish it didn't have to hurt quite so much.'

Her voice broke and she turned to him, burying her face against his chest. He held her close in the circle of his arm, and, with his other hand, felt for a clean handkerchief. Maddy took it with a little sob of thanks, and pressed it against her streaming cheeks.

They sat for some time after that on the bench, with the sea foaming on the rocks below, and Stephen thought about what she had said. *To be with Stella and all the other people I love ...* Was he one of those people? And if he were, would she still feel any love for him if she knew what he had done?

She need never know, of course. But he knew that he would have to tell her, if they were to have any honesty, any true feeling between them. The question was, just when should he confess? Certainly not at this moment, when she was still so distressed over Sammy, and now Dan and Ruth.

Yet it couldn't be left too long. It was a living lie between them, and, like all living things, it would grow. If left too long, it would become a monster.

Chapter Thirty

'I don't know what to make of him,' Maddy said to her sister.
They were sitting together outside Dottie's back door, the
evening sun warm on their faces. 'He seemed so understanding – almost wise – when I told him about Ruth and Dan,
but on the way home he seemed to change. It was as if he'd
drawn into himself and shut me out. I keep wondering what I
could have done or said to upset him, but I really can't think
of anything.'

'Men are funny creatures,' Stella observed. 'You don't
think he could have been a bit jealous, do you?'

'What, of Ruth and Dan? Or Sammy?'

'Well, you don't make any secret of the fact that Sammy was
the most important to you,' Stella said gently. 'And there's no
reason why you should. But you know Stephen's always carried a torch for you, and I think he still does.'

'You mean I talk about Sammy too much? But Stephen's always told me he didn't mind that. I thought he understood.'

'I'm sure he does. It may not be that at all. It's more likely
to do with what's happening at the Barton. You know, I think
they're all at sixes and sevens there. Hilary told me the other
day that it looks as if Robert's going to stay there permanently.
Colonel Napier wants him to go to Kelly College. It must be
difficult, after she's done so much on the estate.'

'But will it make so much difference to her? If he's at school
during the term and goes home to France in the holidays ...'

'I'm not sure that's the plan, though. She didn't say as

much, but she hinted that her father might leave the whole place to Robert. It must be terribly worrying for her, and for Stephen as well.'

'Goodness me, yes. Stephen didn't mention that. I knew there'd been talk, of course, but he didn't say there was anything definite. No wonder he seemed a bit distracted. And I kept going on about my own problems!' Maddy sighed. 'I really am a selfish little so-and-so at times.'

'No, you're not! You've had a horrible time, and Stephen understands that.'

'But we're supposed to be friends. He ought to be able to tell me his problems as well, or it's all one-sided.'

'I don't suppose he wanted to burden you with any more just at the moment,' Stella said. 'Not when you're already upset. He'll probably talk to you later. You'll see him again while you're here, won't you?'

'I don't know. He's talking about going away for the rest of his leave. I don't understand it, Stella. He never said anything about that before. I thought perhaps he didn't want to see me any more. I thought he was trying to avoid me.'

Stella looked thoughtfully at her sister. There was a hint of tears in Maddy's voice, and Stella realised that she was feeling particularly vulnerable just now. Was she depending more than she realised on Stephen – and if so, was it really a good thing? It was hardly fair to him if she leaned on him now and then withdrew later, when her strength began to come back. Perhaps Stephen realised it, and that was why he had decided to go away.

Or was there another reason?

'I don't think it's that,' she said. 'I think maybe things at the Barton are getting more difficult, and he just doesn't want to be involved. He's still talking about emigrating, according to Hilary.'

'I know,' Maddy said in a small voice. 'To Canada.' She was silent for a moment, then she turned to Stella and said in a voice filled with woe, 'Why does everyone I love have to go and leave me?'

'Not everyone,' Stella said soothingly. 'We've found each other again, haven't we? And you know I'll never leave you. And you've got plenty of other friends as well – Dottie, and Val and Luke, and everyone else in the village. And Fenella. Why don't you go over to France and stay with her for a while? I'm sure she must miss you.'

'She's coming to England soon,' Maddy said, but her voice was still flat and despondent. 'She's coming for a month. I'll see her then.' She gave a deep sigh and seemed to pull herself together. 'I'm being selfish again! Tell me about Val – is she really going to be all right? I was worried when I heard.'

'You can see for yourself. She asked me to take you in to visit her. She hates staying in bed all the time, so she wants plenty of company. We'll go in the morning.'

Maddy nodded. 'And I want to see the Tozers as well, and Jennifer Tucker – she must be really busy now, getting ready for the wedding and the new house and everything. And talking of weddings, what about you and Felix? Have you started to make plans yet?'

'Oh, there's plenty of time for that,' Stella said serenely. 'Though I suppose once term starts it will fly past, so perhaps I ought to think about it. You can help me, while you're here. For one thing, we've got to decide what to do about your dress. And the other bridesmaids as well,' she added with a tinge of gloom in her voice. 'It looks as if we're going to have to have at least six!'

'It's a shame it's not a spring wedding,' Maddy said. 'Everything's so pretty then. Can't you put it off till Easter, Stell?'

'*I* could, but Felix couldn't. He'd get married tomorrow if it were possible. He says the important thing is to make our vows, and none of the rest really matters. He's right, really.'

'He's not!' Maddy said definitely. 'Of course it matters, or people wouldn't have gone on doing it for hundreds of years. It's like funerals – there's a pattern that we seem to need, which makes it either a celebration or … or a comfort.' Her voice wobbled, and Stella laid a hand over hers. Whatever you said, she thought, whatever you talked about, it always came back in the end to Sammy. Maddy's grief was still very near the surface, and the slightest reminder could bring the tears welling up.

Perhaps, after all, that really was why Stephen had decided to go away.

Val Ferris was pleased to see Maddy and Stella next morning. They sat by her bed and asked how she was, then Maddy told her about West Lyme and Archie's latest escapades, and Val told her the story of the three boys in the mine.

'Micky and Henry are in real trouble over it. They're not allowed to see each other for a week, and they've both got to stay at home and work. It's not so bad for Micky, because he likes working in the forge, but Henry's father works in Tavistock, so Henry is having to stay at home and do housework and gardening! He probably feels completely humiliated.'

Maddy laughed. 'Well, so long as it all ended well. It's a good thing nobody was badly hurt, though. Those old mines are terribly dangerous. Why wasn't that one blocked off?'

'I don't think anyone knew it was there – except for the boys, of course, and they weren't going to tell anyone. I dare say they'll talk about it for the rest of their lives, and when they're grown up and got children of their own, they'll make sure they never go down there!'

They chatted for a while, discussing Jennifer and Travis's wedding, and then Stella's. Val had some good ideas for the bridesmaids' dresses, and Stella decided that she and Maddy would go into Tavistock, or perhaps even Plymouth, and look at patterns and fabrics. After a while, noticing Val's pale face, she said, 'I think we ought to go now, Val, and let you have a rest. We'll pop in again tomorrow. Let us know if there's anything you want us to bring you.'

'I'm all right, thanks.' Val lay back on her pillows. 'I do feel a bit tired, to tell you the truth. I'm all right most of the time, but every now and then I get this peculiar sick, dizzy feeling.'

Stella gazed at her in concern. 'Do you want us to call anyone? Should we get Dr Latimer?'

'No, no, I'm fine really. He looks in every day anyway, and Mum said she'd pop down sometime this morning. You'll probably run into her on your way out.'

Stella and Maddy took this for dismissal. On their way out of the door, as Val had predicted, they met Alice coming up the garden path, and stopped for a moment's conversation.

'How is she?'

'She seems all right,' Stella said. 'But she gets tired easily, and she said she felt a bit sick and dizzy. I wanted to get the doctor but she said you were coming.'

Alice nodded. 'She does get those turns, but Dr Latimer says we're not to worry unless they get worse. We'll all be thankful when this is over and the baby's safely born – as if we hadn't had enough trouble in the past few months.'

'It's been a difficult year,' Stella agreed, with a swift glance at Maddy.

Alice saw the look. 'And how are you, maid? You'm looking a bit better than the last time I saw you.'

'I'm all right, thank you,' Maddy said. 'It's nice to be back in Burracombe again.'

'Well, you must come up to the farm one afternoon and have a cup of tea. Mother will be pleased to see you. Always fond of you, she were, when you were a little maid.'

She went on into the house, and unloaded a basket of eggs, milk and fresh baking on to the kitchen table, calling up the stairs to Val that she was there. Then she made a pot of tea and poured out two cups, setting them out on a tray with a plate of Minnie's biscuits, and carried it all up to the bedroom.

'And how are you this morning? I ran into Maddy and Stella on my way in. That poor maid – she's still looking very drawn. 'Tis a pity she can't stop longer in Burracombe. 'Twould do her the world of good.' She put the tray down on Val's washstand and looked at her critically. 'I hope you'm not doing too much.'

'I'm not doing anything at all. I'm just lying here in bed, wasting all this lovely weather.' Val glanced fretfully towards the open window. 'I don't know why I can't go down to the garden and sit in a deckchair.'

'Because the doctor says you got to be in bed, that's why.' Alice passed her a cup of tea. 'You don't want to take any risks with this baby, do you?'

Val looked at her uneasily, aware of something odd in the way her mother had said 'this baby'. 'No, of course I don't,' she said. 'Why d'you say that?'

Alice sat down rather heavily on the kitchen chair Luke had brought up to put beside the bed. 'Well, I didn't mean to get to this quite so quick,' she said. 'But now it's come up, there's something been worrying me ever since you were took poorly up at the farm. Something you said.' She paused, but Val remained silent, watching her with wary eyes. 'You said "not again". Mother and me both noticed it, and I'm sorry, Val, but it's been on my mind ever since and I've got to know. What did you mean by it? Is it ... is it what I think it might be?'

Val stared at her. Her face paled and she looked down, but not before Alice had seen the trembling of her lips and the sudden tears in her eyes. She drew in a deep, shuddering breath.

'Don't tell me if you don't want to,' Alice said quickly, regretting her words. 'I shouldn't have asked. 'Tis none of my business.'

'No, it's all right, Mum. I'll have to tell you now.' Val lifted her head and met her mother's anxious gaze. 'You've guessed anyway. I have lost a baby before. It was while I was in Egypt.

At least, it was on the way home that I lost it. Nobody knew, except for the girls who were with me, the other VADs. And Hilary knew. But I never told anyone else until ... well, until Luke ...' She looked away.

'He knows?' Alice said. The revelation, although she had suspected as much, still came as a shock. 'But what did he think when you told him? Another man's baby ...'

Val met her eyes again. 'No, Mum. It wasn't another man's baby. It was Luke's. He didn't know a thing about it. We'd thought it was all over before I knew I was pregnant, and I was on the ship coming home and didn't think I'd ever see him again. I'd broken it off with him, you see. I'd told him I was engaged and had to keep faith with Eddie. And then Eddie was killed, and I felt as if it was a sort of punishment. Retribution. I felt so guilty about it all. As if Eddie and the baby had both died through my wickedness.'

'Oh, *Val*!' Alice exclaimed, her heart going out to her daughter. 'Oh, you poor maid. As if God would be so cruel!'

'Well, the Bible says he could be,' Val said drearily. 'Anyway, that's what I felt. I couldn't get over it for a long time.'

'No, you couldn't,' her mother said thoughtfully, remembering how depressed Val had been after the war. Alice had tried everything to bring her out of her gloom, thinking that it had been caused solely by the loss of her fiancé. But it hadn't. She'd lost Luke and she'd lost a baby as well, and she'd been racked with guilt over the whole thing. No wonder she had been so sad.

'But Luke came back,' she said. 'He found out where you were and—'

'No, he didn't do that. It was sheer coincidence that he came to Burracombe. Truly, Mum, I was never so shocked as the first time I saw him here. I didn't want to have anything to do with him. It all seemed too much, all the explanations and everything. It was only after I'd finally realised we really loved each other that I told him. So you see, we both want this baby so much ... There's nothing I won't do to make sure it's born safe and healthy, nothing.'

Alice sat in silence for a few minutes, grappling with the new knowledge, trying to come to terms with a daughter who was a little different from how she had always seen her. A daughter who had been through experiences she had not suspected, who had suffered a loss she had never dreamed of.

'Oh, Val,' she said at last, moving forward to gather her into her arms. 'You poor maid. You poor, poor maid ...'

As Alice walked back to the farm an hour or so later, her mind moved from one daughter to another, and then to her son and his wife. Why was it they all seemed to be going through difficulties at the same time? Why did troubles never, as Minnie often said, come singly?

Alice knew that she would have been shocked and ashamed if she had known that her elder daughter was pregnant without being married. Yet she also knew that the shame was often forgotten when the baby arrived, 'bringing its love with it' as Minnie also said. Upset though she and Ted might have been, they would have stood by Val in her trouble, and she was sad to think that Val had had to go through the loss of her baby – she'd even given him a name – with none of the family even knowing about it.

Well, if this baby came safely, perhaps Val would be able to put Johnny into the past. Us must all make sure of it, Alice thought determinedly. It might even help Tom and Joanna, too, and take their minds off their own sad loss.

That left Jackie. She had moved into the hotel now, and although Ted still wasn't happy about it, Alice had finally come to terms with the fact that her younger daughter had left home. After all, she thought, I'd left home at that age to come and work as a maidservant on this very farm, and for the first time in her life it occurred to her to wonder if her own mother and father had felt so anxious and bereft. I suppose all parents do, she thought with surprise, and the children never even realise it!

Her main concern was that Jackie would meet someone unsuitable, who would take advantage of her. That could happen in the village itself, of course, but at least she knew all the young men, and could keep an eye on what was going on. Alice had never really liked Vic Netherton – too smooth and too full of himself – and had been sorry when Jackie and Roy Pettifer had drifted apart, even though she'd thought they'd been too close for a while.

She thought of Maddy Forsyth, still grieving for her lost fiancé. Alice had never met Sammy Hodges – Maddy had wanted to bring him to Burracombe at Easter, which, of course, never happened – but it was plain that the girl had thought the world of him. To most of the village, it had been a surprise that she hadn't taken up more with Stephen Napier – they'd been seen about together in that little sports car of his quite a lot last summer – but although they still appeared to be friends, it didn't seem likely to become any more than that. It would take her a long time to get over what had happened, and the word was that Stephen was thinking of going to live abroad. A pity, because it would have been a happy ending, and Alice did like happy endings.

But by that token, there were two happy endings to put a smile back on her face: Travis and Jennifer, getting married in only a few weeks' time; and then Stella and Felix right after Christmas. Nothing was going to go wrong there, Alice was sure. And by that time, Val would have had her baby and all this worry would be safely past.

There was a lot to look forward to, after all.

Chapter Thirty-One

Returning to the Barton, Stephen felt like a runaway dog creeping home for its supper, its tail between its legs.

'So you've come back,' his father said, meeting him in the hall. 'Didn't any of your friends want you?'

'I went to collect Maddy,' Stephen said, his voice tight. 'She was upset and wanted to come home to see her sister, and there was no one else to do it.'

'Couldn't have come by train, then? It had to be you?'

'I don't think she even thought of the train. And she's still grieving, Father. She wouldn't have wanted to sit amongst strangers in a railway carriage. She needed someone who ... who cared about her.'

Gilbert grunted. 'So what are you doing now? Staying the night? Off again in the morning? Treating the place like a hotel?'

Stephen took in a breath. He had made up his mind not to quarrel again with his father. Apart from the fact that it was bad for Gilbert's health, he never got anywhere. He couldn't remember the last time anyone had won an argument with the ferocious old man.

'I don't know,' he said wearily. 'I don't know what to do.'

At that moment, Marianne appeared on the landing and ran down the stairs, crying out with pleasure. She stood on tiptoe to kiss Stephen's cheek, and held both his hands in hers.

'Stephen! You 'ave come back. It's so good to see you. I was afraid you had deserted us. But now you are home and you won't go away again ... will you?' She slid her arm through his, and smiled up at him.

'Well, it looks as if someone wants you,' Gilbert said, more accurately than he knew. 'I must say it'll make things easier if you can spare a few more days of your precious time with us, what with the boy being crocked up as well.'

Stephen looked down into Marianne's face and met her dark, glowing eyes. He thought of Maddy, and resolved he would not succumb again. Trying not to make it too obvious, he withdrew his arm and turned away.

'I'll go up and get washed. The road was pretty dusty. I'll see you at dinner.'

'It will be something to look forward to,' Marianne purred, and he felt her gaze on his back as he leapt up the stairs two at a time.

In his room, he leaned against the door, breathing deeply. Marianne's touch had stirred his body and left his mind weak, and he knew that if he stayed he would have no defence against her. There wasn't even a lock on his door – the key had been lost years ago. And he couldn't go to the lengths of putting a chair against it. The resulting clatter if anyone tried to force it open would wake the whole house.

Maddy, he thought, trying to draw strength from the idea of her ... Maddy, Maddy, Maddy ...

Travis and Jennifer had spent the afternoon at the estate manager's house, trying to decide on furniture.

'We really must give the house a name,' Jennifer said, standing at the garden gate. 'I can't think why the Cherrimans never did. What happened to their post?'

'They had it addressed to the Barton, and the postman just used to separate it out and bring theirs here. I suppose Mr Cherriman thought it was a better address, and the Colonel evidently didn't mind. But I agree, we don't want that. We'll

313

want to give people our own address. What sort of name would you like?'

'Nothing too fancy. Something that describes it, like Cottage in the Wood – not that, but that sort of thing.'

'Wood Cottage?' he suggested, and Jennifer nodded.

'That's perfect. We'll call it that. Can you make a sign for it?'

'I'll do it straight away. There was an oak tree felled the other day in Long Meadow. I'll see if Jacob will cut me a slice of one of the bigger branches. Let's go inside.'

They stood together at the front door, and Travis took Jennifer's hand in his. 'Our first home together,' he said softly. 'We're going to be very happy here.'

'I know.' They went inside slowly, looking around almost as if savouring it. It was empty now of all the Cherrimans' possessions, and the redecorating had been finished a few days earlier. Although they had been inside before, this was the first time they had been able to see it alone, with nobody painting or wallpapering; empty, pristine, waiting for their occupation.

'It's really nice,' Jennifer said, going into the sitting room. 'What a good size this room is. The fireplace is in just the right place – it'll be so cosy in winter. And look at the view of the garden and the woods! I think I shall probably spend all my time here.'

'It's a good thing the kitchen's got a good view as well, then,' he said, leading her firmly out. 'I'll put up some bird-feeders to make it even more interesting. How d'you like it now that it's been painted?'

'It's lovely,' she said, looking at the yellow walls. 'Like being in sunshine all the time. Yes, I expect I'll spend quite a lot of time here as well. And it's big enough for a good-sized table. We can eat most of our meals in here. We won't want to use a proper dining room very often.'

'That's what I thought. Let's go up and look at the bed-rooms.'

They toured the rest of the house, admiring the new bathroom and deciding on furniture. Jennifer's bed, which had belonged to her parents, was old and sagging now, so they agreed to buy a new one but to use her bedroom furniture, at least until they could afford to replace it. She also had the single bed, washstand and small wardrobe from the room Jackie had been using. The third bedroom would be left empty for the time being – 'until we know we need a nursery,' Jennifer said. Downstairs, they could furnish the dining room from Jennifer's house, but would need a new three-piece suite, a small table or two, and a bookcase.

'We'll start with those things, anyway,' Travis said. 'We should have a few rugs as well. The new linoleum is good, but I like a rug to put my feet on, especially in winter.'

'A carpet square in the sitting room,' Jennifer suggested. 'And I've got a couple of rugs that will look nice in front of the fireplace, ones that Mum made in the last two or three years before she died.'

'That's all settled, then. We'd better go to that furniture shop in Tavistock for the things we need to buy. And then I've got a surprise for you.'

'A surprise?' Jennifer turned and looked at him. 'What sort of surprise?'

'Well, I can't tell you, can I? It wouldn't be a surprise, then. But sometime tomorrow I want to take you to see someone I know in Peter Tavy.' He took her in his arms and gazed around the empty room. 'Our new home,' he said quietly. 'Do you know, I didn't think I'd ever find someone I wanted to spend the rest of my life with.'

'Neither did I,' she said, turning her face up for his kiss. 'And after Ronald, I didn't even know if I wanted to!'

After Alice had left her, Val lay back on her pillows feeling exhausted. She had never expected to have to tell her mother the truth about Johnny, but to her surprise Alice had taken the news quite calmly – perhaps because she already suspected it. She had listened to Val's story, and then put her arms around her daughter and held her close.

'You'm not the first young woman that's happened to, my dear, and you won't be the last. And 'tis all over now, though it's sad that you've had to carry the sorrow all this time on your own.'

'Well, not all the time,' Val said through her tears. 'Luke knew – but not for a long time. And Hilary Napier knew as well. But things were so different then, you see – out in Egypt, it was a different world, so hot and so strange, and there was fighting going on all around; once, we were evacuated from the hospital at almost a moment's notice. There was no time to pack or even put anything away; we just had to gather ourselves and our patients, and go. You never knew what was going to happen from one day to the next, or even if you'd ever see home again. You just took what happiness you could while it was there – and Luke and I did love each other, even though it all went wrong for a time.'

'You don't have to say no more about it, unless you want to. And not just now, anyway – you're looking tired out.' Alice stood up. 'I'm going to make you another cup of tea, and then I'm leaving you in peace for a while. I'll pop down again this evening for five minutes, just to satisfy myself you're all right.'

When the front door closed behind her, Val drew in a deep breath of relief. She had never realised quite what a burden her secret had been. Coming home from Egypt, having undergone one of the most distressing experiences a woman could know, yet unable to tell her closest family about it, had been a pain she could never assuage. If it had not been for Hilary's steadfast friendship, Val thought she would have broken down completely.

Now that her mother knew what had happened, the burden seemed to have rolled away from her shoulders, and a sense of peace settled around her like a soft, comforting eiderdown. It was always there between us, like a kind of barrier, she thought. Something important about me that she didn't know and would never suspect. I never realised before how a mother must feel about her child, even when the child is grown up. How she must step back at each stage; how, slowly and gradually, she is shut out; how she must long, all through her life, to be as close as she was when the child was a baby, yet know how impossible that must be.

Deep in her abdomen, Val felt her own baby move. A flurry of limbs, a more forceful kicking of legs. She laid her hand over the movements, trying to send a message of comfort to the tiny being inside. *I am here, I am your mother, I will always look after you.* And yet she knew that there would come a time – many times – when her child would step away from her, move into its own life, its own world, where there were secrets she could not share.

But I'll always be here if you do want to share them, she thought. Whatever happens in your life, I will always be here. However old you may grow, you will always be my child, the child of my heart.

Dinner was over, and still Stephen had managed not to be alone with Marianne, even for an instant.

He had agreed to stay a few more days. He could not leave Maddy in her distress, and he could take Robert out in the sports car. Hilary and Marianne were to go shopping together for the school uniform, which would take them a whole day, and with luck he could continue to avoid the Frenchwoman – at least during the day.

He tried not to think about the nights.

The meal passed uncomfortably. The Napiers were all aware of the unresolved quarrel of the morning, and it was obvious that Marianne knew there was something wrong between them. Her behaviour, however, was charm itself, directed at each one of them. To Gilbert, she was the sweet, still grieving widow of his son; to Hilary, the loving, companionable sister-in-law; to Stephen ... well, what did she mean to be to him? he wondered. As sweet and as loving as to both the others, yet with that subtle hint of seduction in her dark eyes; a reminder of what had happened during the night – was it really only last night? – and the heady promise of what might be to come.

No, he thought, tightening his fists beneath the table. No. And yet, at the same moment, his blood stirred, and he knew despairingly that if she were to come to him again, he would have no power of resistance.

At last the evening was over. Dinner finished, they went back to the drawing room, although Hilary disappeared to finish some work in the office. Gilbert turned on the television bought specially for the Coronation, and they watched a Roy Rogers show, which, in any other circumstances, Stephen would have enjoyed. When it ended, Gilbert grunted disparagingly and turned the set off.

Marianne stood up and said prettily, 'I think I will go to bed now. Goodnight, Papa.' She kissed Gilbert on both cheeks, then turned to Stephen and held up her face for his kiss.

'Goodnight, Marianne,' he mumbled, giving her two quick pecks that barely touched her skin, and restraining himself, with an effort, from sweeping her into his arms. 'See you in the morning.'

She had already turned towards the door, but at this she turned back and gave him an unfathomable glance.

'Ah, yes,' she said. 'The morning ...' and glided from the room.

Stephen glanced at his father. Gilbert was hunched in his chair, surly and unapproachable. Stephen sighed and said, 'I'm sorry about this morning, Father.'

At first, there was no response. Then the old man looked up, and Stephen was shocked to see the drawn look on his face and how his eyes seemed suddenly to have sunk deep into their sockets. He felt a pang of guilt and added, 'I mean it. I really don't want to quarrel.'

'You don't understand at all, do you, Stephen?' Gilbert said at last. 'Probably you never will. Not until you are as old as I am anyway, and have a son who … oh, never mind. Let it go. We'll never see things in the same way: the family, the land, the Barton. We never will. And you'll never, never know how lonely that's made me, all these years.' He seemed almost to have been talking to himself, but now he looked up, his haunted eyes deep with sorrow. 'We've nothing more to say to each other. Go to bed. Go now.'

Stephen stared at him. He made a brief effort to speak, but Gilbert flapped a weary hand and turned away. Deeply appalled, he made his way to the door and went slowly up the stairs.

As he passed Marianne's door, he hesitated. He had never, since he was a small boy, felt so in need of a woman's comfort. But he fought down the longing and passed to his own room, where he undressed, washed and then slipped into bed, to lie staring wide-eyed at the pale rectangle of the window and the moon riding high in the sky.

He thought she would come to him. He lay awake for many hours, watching the moon pass out of sight, waiting in an agony of apprehension and yearning.

But Marianne did not come.

Chapter Thirty-Two

Felix was working in his study with the radio on, when Stella and Maddy walked across to visit him.

'Sssh,' he said, waving them to a chair and putting his finger to his lips 'It's just about to finish. Half the Australians were out for sixty-one within the first hour, and we had only thirty one runs to make up. We could actually win the Ashes!'

The two girls sat down obediently, hardly daring to move, as the commentator's voice gathered in excitement. The Test matches had gripped everyone this summer. After four draws, this was to be the decisive match, and had been allocated six days. But it looked as though it would be decided on the fourth, and Felix, who had been following closely, was as tense as if he were at the Oval himself.

'What—?' Maddy began, but he shushed her with an agonised expression. With a rueful glance at Stella, she subsided, and they all listened until the commentator's voice rose to a climax of jubilation and, to a thunder of cheers from the spectators, declared England to be the winners.

'Hurrah!' Felix cried, leaping from his chair and brandishing his fists in the air. 'Hurrah, hurrah, hurrah! We've won! England's won the Ashes! Do you realise, this is the first time for nineteen years? *Nineteen years* – think of it! The Australians must have thought they'd got them for good, but we showed them! Hah! This'll make them laugh on the other side of their faces. They won't be so cocky now!' He sat down again and began to explain the game to the two girls. 'You see, it all depended on the captains. Ours is Len Hutton, of course, and he's streets ahead of Lindsay Hassett, the Australian captain. Mind you, we've got a marvellous side: Alec Bedser, Tony Lock, Jim Laker, Peter May ... My word, I wish I could have been there to see it. I'd have—'

'I rather wish you could have been there, too,' Stella said when he paused for a moment to think what he would have done. 'Then Maddy and I could have gone blackberrying instead of tramping all the way over here to bring you some of Dottie's lemon puffs, and then not be allowed to open our mouths.'

Felix stopped searching for words and stared at her. 'Am I going on about it too much?'

'Just a little,' she said, smiling at him, 'but we'll forgive you. Shall I make some tea?'

'If you wouldn't mind,' he said humbly. 'I'm sorry, but it really was exciting.' He gazed pensively at the sheets of paper before him. 'I was wondering if I could work it into my sermon somehow.'

'Oh, I'm sure you'll think of a way,' she said gravely, and went out, leaving him with Maddy.

Felix pushed the papers aside and looked earnestly at Maddy. 'And how are you? Is it getting any easier?'

Maddy found her eyes filling with tears. She rubbed them with her fingers and said. 'No. Yes. Well, sometimes it is but ... I'm feeling a bit down at the moment.' She told him about Ruth and Dan. 'I *want* to go and see them, and I think they like me to, but it just seems to upset us all even more. And I feel so terribly sorry for them – I feel as if it's my fault. If Sammy and I hadn't gone to Southampton to buy the ring, if we hadn't stayed out longer than we'd meant to ... I could have made him go back earlier, you know. I knew they were waiting for us.'

'But it wasn't really to do with you and Sammy, was it?' Felix pointed out. 'It was because of what was happening to

Lizzie and Alec, and Floyd. If Floyd hadn't come back – if he and Lizzie hadn't let their feelings get the better of them – if Alec hadn't reacted as he did – it would all have ended very differently. None of that was your fault. It was just terrible luck.'

Maddy, who had begun to cry again, looked at him through tear-filled eyes. 'You really believe that? It was just luck? It wasn't meant in some way?'

Felix hesitated, aware that he must tread with care. He looked at the distressed girl and said, 'How can any of us know? I do believe that there's a great purpose behind everything that happens, so perhaps to say that it was "terrible luck" is wrong. But I realise that you can't understand what possible purpose there could be in Sammy's death. I don't understand it myself. I just have to have faith.'

'I wish I could have that sort of faith,' Maddy said drearily. 'But I don't. I've lost too many people, you see. My mother and father, my baby brother. I even lost Stella for years and years. And now Sammy. I can't see any purpose in any of it. I can't really see any purpose in anything at all.'

Her voice was flat and steady, but tears were rolling down her cheeks, and Felix looked at her carefully. His excitement over the cricket had been laid aside, and he was giving his full attention to the girl before him. He said, 'I don't think now is the time for you to be worrying about that, Maddy. You still need to grieve. You can't be looking for purpose in anything just yet. The moment will come, I promise you, when you can see clearly again, and then you can begin to think about such things. But not just yet. It's too much to expect of yourself.'

'But how will I know when the moment comes?' she asked in a small voice. 'How can I tell?'

'Oh, you will know,' he assured her. 'You won't have any doubt about it. You'll know.'

The door opened, and Stella came in with a laden tray. Felix shoved his papers over to make a space and she set it down,

322

glancing quickly from face to face as she did so. Whatever she saw seemed to satisfy her, but she made no comment. Instead, she laid her hand lightly on her sister's shoulder, and gave Felix a look full of gratitude and love. Their eyes met in a long look of complete understanding, and then she turned away to pour the tea.

The village of Peter Tavy seemed almost asleep, as Travis and Jennifer drove in and parked the Land Rover near the track leading to the church. They got out and stood for a moment by an old stone barn, and Jennifer gazed around at the cluster of cottages with the tall church tower rising above them. In the centre of the village, near the Post Office and shop, was a small stone bridge with a brook tumbling beneath it, and just along the lane, apparently used as part of the farmyard, stood the ancient Peter Tavy Inn.

'What a nice village,' she said. 'Almost as nice as Burracombe!'

Travis nodded. 'It's a good place. I come over here sometimes to join the bell-ringers. The parson, Prebendary Pratt, has a fine team here. There's a good fellowship amongst them – amongst the whole village, in fact. Anyway, the man I want you to meet lives along here in one of the cottages by the brook.'

Wonderingly, Jennifer followed him to a tiny cottage, set back from the road. Travis opened the garden gate and ushered her through to a tiny lawn surrounded by a hedge entwined with honeysuckle and rambling roses. The cottage windows were wide open, and outside a stable door a fat tabby cat lay stretched on an old wooden bench in the sunlight. The only sounds were those of a blackbird singing in a nearby tree and the babble of the stream as it tumbled over the rocks.

'What a lovely—' Jennifer began, but as soon as she began to speak, the peace was broken by a furious barking from indoors. Startled, she jumped back, and Travis laughed. A head appeared at one of the windows, then withdrew. A few seconds later the barking diminished, and an old man appeared at the stable door.

'Ah, 'tis you,' he greeted Travis. 'And this be your young lady, I take it? Come to see Meg and her little 'uns, have ee?'

'That's right,' Travis said cheerfully. 'Good to see you, Barty. Keeping well, I hope? And Mrs Yeo?'

'Mustn't grumble. Her'll be out dreckly. Her's just taking summat out of the oven. Well, you'd better come inside, both of ee.'

He stood back, and Jennifer, still wondering what this was about, followed him inside, with Travis behind her. After the bright sunshine it took a moment or two to adjust her eyesight, but gradually she saw that she was in a small, square room, which probably took up most of the downstairs of the cottage, with a little kitchen leading off it opposite the door, and stairs going up along the side wall. The wall opposite the stairs was almost entirely taken up by a large inglenook fireplace, and beside the fireplace was an alcove which had been temporarily boarded off at waist height and from which came a frenzy of excited yapping.

'Oh!' Jennifer exclaimed. 'Puppies!'

'Well, 'twould hardly be kittens, now, would it?' the old man said with a grin that showed a number of gaps in his teeth. 'Seein' as our Meg's the mother. Come you in now, Meg. 'Tis all right. Nobody's going to hurt your little 'uns.'

Turning, Jennifer saw a Jack Russell, which had evidently been taken out of the room and was now being allowed back in. A small, wiry woman with eyes like black buttons, grey hair tied back in a bun, and wearing a flowery crossover pinafore, came through the door and nodded at them.

'This is the wife,' the old man said, and Jennifer put out her hand. The old woman grasped it with surprising strength, giving her a sharp look and then another quick nod, as if Jennifer had passed some kind of test.

'So you've come to choose one of the pups, I take it?' she said. 'Well, there they be.'

Jennifer gasped and looked at Travis, who was smiling broadly. '*Have* we? Is this why you brought me here, to pick out one of these puppies? Oh, Travis – they're adorable! I want them all!' She bent over the makeshift fence and gazed in rapture at the squirming bundles on their bed of newspaper. 'Just look at them!'

'We'll restrict ourselves to one, if you don't mind,' he said with a chuckle. 'But you can choose. It's to be your dog, after all.'

'You mean 'tis to be a pet?' Barty asked. 'Not a working dog?'

'I've already got the spaniels. I hope Jennifer will let me borrow it sometimes, for a spot of ratting, but mostly it's to keep her company while I'm out.'

'Ah.' He nodded sagely. 'Well, you couldn't ask for better company than a Jack Russell. Tough little dogs, too, and Meg and the father are both good stock. You won't have no trouble with one of they.'

'Have you had a dog before?' Mrs Yeo asked, and Jennifer shook her head. 'Well, you might pick out a bitch, then. More faithful, like, and a bit quieter. There's three bitches – that one, with the black behind, and the white one and the one with the brown ear. All nice little critturs.'

'Let 'em out,' her husband commanded. 'Then the lady can see which one's got the most life in her. You want to pick one with a bit of spirit, see, not the one that hangs back in a corner. Sit over there in that old chair, and see if one of 'em runs over to you.'

Jennifer did as she was told, and Travis squatted beside her. Barty pulled up a couple of boards and the puppies ran out, to be intercepted by their mother, who gave each a thorough licking as if making them presentable first. Then they began to mill about over the floor, tumbling over each other and

325

batting each other with tiny paws, until suddenly they seemed to notice Jennifer and Travis, and stopped abruptly.

Jennifer held her breath, willing the one she most liked the look of to come over to her. After a moment, two or three began to creep across the floor, stopping to investigate her shoes, and then one reached up and pawed at her leg.

'Oh, that's the one!' she cried delightedly. 'The one with the brown ear. She's so perky. I liked you the moment I saw you,' she crooned, lifting the fat, wriggling body carefully on to her lap, and receiving a lick on her face. 'And you like me, don't you? You want to be mine!'

'Well, that was pretty easy,' Travis remarked, as the others laughed. 'So that's settled, is it? I hope all our other decisions will be made as quickly.'

'When can I have her?' Jennifer asked. 'How old are they now?'

'Near on four weeks,' Mrs Yeo said. 'Sometimes we lets 'em go at six weeks but eight's better. They'm proper independent then, see. And 'tis better for Meg, too, gets her milk properly dried up and by then she's had enough of them. Will that be all right for you? I hear the wedding's about then.'

'Second Saturday in September,' Travis said. 'And we're having a week's honeymoon in Cornwall. We could collect the puppy when we come back, if that's all right?'

The old couple nodded, and Mrs Yeo bustled out to make tea. Barty put the other puppies back into their enclosure, and they went out into the garden, Jennifer still carrying the one she had chosen. The cat was shifted without ceremony from the bench, and sat washing itself reproachfully, while Jennifer and Travis sat down and Barty dragged out a couple of kitchen chairs.

'Isn't she gorgeous?' Jennifer said. 'I love her. Thank you so much, Travis.'

'You'll have to think of a name for her,' he said.

'I've already thought of one. Tavy – the name of the river.

It's so bubbly and quick, just like she is. Don't you think it suits her?'

Travis nodded. 'It's a good name. The sort of name I wouldn't be ashamed to call out when I'm taking a dog ratting.'

'Ratting?' Jennifer said indignantly. 'Who said anything about taking her ratting? Oh, thank you,' she added, as Mrs Yeo came out with the tea. 'Tell me more about Meg. Has she had lots of puppies?'

'This is her third litter, and a good little mother her be, too. I shan't let her have no more, though. 'Tis too wearing for her. And that reminds me, you ought to see the father as well. He's up at Bellamy's farm – nice little chap, name of Sid. Call in on your way past and have a look.'

'We will,' Travis said, and turned to talk to the old man about farming matters, while Jennifer began to ask Mrs Yeo about feeding and house-training. After a while, they got up and took their leave, promising to come back to see the puppy again before they collected her, so that she could get to know Jennifer before leaving her mother.

'She'll be right as rain,' Mrs Yeo said, coming to the gate with them. 'Nice little pup, and her'll have a good home with you, I can see that.'

'I can't wait to collect her,' Jennifer said, smiling. 'But we'll see you again before that.'

They sauntered back to the Land Rover hand in hand. Jennifer was wreathed in smiles, and Travis, glancing at her, thought how lovely she looked and how she had blossomed in the time that he had known her, from a quiet, rather mousy little woman who seemed unsure of her place in the world, to this happy, confident person strolling by his side, shining with health and contentment. As they stopped by the vehicle, he took her in his arms and smiled down into her face.

'Happy?'

'Oh, yes! *So* happy.' She wound her arms around his neck.

'Thank you so much, Travis. It's the best wedding present I could have. How am I ever going to be able to find something as nice to give you?'

'You don't have to think of anything,' he said. 'You'll be giving me yourself, and that's the only present I'll ever want.'

Chapter Thirty-Three

The day's shopping for Robert's school uniform left Hilary feeling drained. They had to go to Dingle's for blazers, caps, ties, socks and sports gear, and the big store was full of other parents on the same mission. Most had their sons with them, and the boys were half excited and half bored, eyeing each other with suspicion as they were cajoled, persuaded and, in some cases, almost forced into various items of clothing. Hilary was thankful they didn't have Robert with them, but aware that it made everything much more difficult, despite their having measured him from every angle before coming out.

'I'm glad Stephen could take Robert out for the day,' Marianne said, as they ate lunch in Dingle's restaurant. 'Poor boy, he gets bored sitting at home, and it would have been difficult to bring him to the shops with his ankle so painful.'

'It's getting better quite quickly, though,' Hilary said, trying not to notice the tone of reproach in Marianne's voice. 'Dr Latimer thinks he'll be able to walk again by next week. We could have postponed the shopping until then.'

'But no. Look at all the boys here today. The shops would have nothing left.'

'Oh, I should think they always have enough. The school must let them know how many new boys there are going to be, after all, and the new class must be the biggest.'

'It is so kind of Papa to provide all this,' Marianne said, tackling her grilled trout. 'To send Robert to such a good school, and to pay for all the uniform. I didn't know he would need so much. A blazer, a cap, a winter coat, two ties, pullovers, four shirts, all his underclothes, socks, shoes, boots – the list is endless. And football boots and gym shoes and shorts, and pyjamas and a dressing-gown ... And name-tapes to be sewn into every item, even each sock. But you will help me with that, won't you, Hilary?' She put on her winsome smile.

So she's ready to forgive me when she wants something, Hilary thought cynically, and her heart sank. Sewing was not amongst her favourite occupations. 'I'm afraid I do have work to do,' she pointed out. 'Especially with Travis getting married soon. And since you don't really have much to do during the day ...'

'Ah, but Stephen has promised to show me more of Devon. However, we shall have the evenings. We can sit and sew together, then.' As if conferring a great favour, Marianne declared, 'I will do as much as I can before I go back to France.'

Hilary gazed at her, knowing this meant that the lion's share of the work would be given to her to complete. She decided to leave it for the time being. 'Will you be taking Rob back with you?' she asked instead. 'I'm sure the rest of the family will want to see him, and there won't be another chance before Christmas.'

'Ah, yes,' Marianne said. 'I too have been thinking about Christmas. Papa is right. It would be a pity for Robert to miss his first English Christmas, yet, as you say, his brother and sister will be missing him. It seems to me that it would be best for us all to come to you for the holiday. Then you and Papa can meet the rest of my family as well. And Stephen will be home again then, too, will he not?'

'Perhaps. I don't really know,' Hilary said with a sigh, her heart sinking even further at the thought of a large Christmas house party. 'Stephen seems to be a law unto himself these days.'

Marianne glanced at her curiously, as if about to ask for an explanation of this remark, then looked down at her plate with a smile curving her lips. Hilary wondered briefly what she was thinking, then took out her list and ran her finger down the items on it.

'We've still got quite a lot to get. Shall we just have coffee and then start again? I really don't want to have to spend another whole day shopping.'

'But of course. And you must allow me to pay for our lunch. You give me so much hospitality; I must repay it a little.'

It was tea-time before they arrived home, and Gilbert was on the terrace looking through several sheets of estate figures that Travis had brought in. Marianne immediately ran to kiss his cheek, then dropped on to a chair, talking animatedly, while Hilary carried the bags into the house and went to the kitchen for fresh tea and scones.

'And where are Stephen and Robert?' Marianne was asking Gilbert when Hilary returned. She took a scone, and piled strawberry jam and cream on top. 'I hope they've been 'aving a good day. Where did they go?'

'I think Stephen was planning to take the boy to Plymouth Hoe and the Barbican. He should be able to hop along the quays on that old crutch we found in the box room, and watch the fishing boats. Plenty down there for a youngster to see.'

'I should think they'll be home soon,' Hilary said. She glanced at the sheets of paper by Gilbert's elbow. 'What are those figures, Father?'

'Oh, the latest stock and feed prices and so on. Kellaway dropped them in earlier. They seem all right.'

'May I have a look?' She held out her hand.

Gilbert shrugged. 'Can if you like, but there's really no need. I'll talk them over with him in the morning.'

'In that case, I'd better see them,' she said steadily. 'So that I know what we're discussing.'

'Why, you're not planning to be there, are you? I thought you were taking a bit of time off from the estate. Got enough on your plate, helping Marianne to get the boy ready for school and showing her around and so on.'

'Of course I'm happy to do that *in my spare time*,' Hilary said, 'but I still have a job to do on the estate and I don't see any reason to neglect that. And Travis has his own concerns as well – in case you've forgotten, he's getting married in a month's time.'

'I don't expect that to have any effect on his work,' Gilbert began, and she interrupted smoothly.

'Quite. And neither should our family situation have any effect on mine. And Marianne won't want to be going out much now, will you, Marianne? You'll be wanting to spend as much time as possible with Robert before you leave again – and there are all those name-tapes to sew on,'

She smiled at them both, then stood up.

'I'll go and help Mrs Ellis with dinner now. Would you like to give me a hand with the crockery, Marianne? I think we've all finished now, haven't we?'

Loading a tray with plates and cups, she marched into the house without looking round. Her moment of elation was already passing. She had never been accustomed to this kind of skirmishing, while to Marianne it seemed to come naturally. She felt quite sure that the Frenchwoman was planning her next move to ingratiate herself with the family, and especially with Colonel Napier.

For the first time, it occurred to Hilary to wonder just what would have happened if Baden had lived. Would this hasty, youthful marriage have lasted, or would he have seen her for the scheming coquette Hilary was coming to believe she was? Marianne, as a Roman Catholic, would never have agreed to a divorce, and Robert would still have been born, but at least the family would have had the past thirteen years to come to terms with the situation. They might have had Robert with them all that time, without his mother, or he might have become simply a part of Baden's past and never come to Burracombe at all. But then, she thought, it wouldn't have been any less complicated, because Baden could never have married again or had more children ... unless the marriage could have been annulled ... But then ...

She shook herself irritably. Speculation could drive you mad. The situation was as it was now, and they had no choice but to deal with it as best they could.

Stephen and Robert had had tea in Plymouth. They had been on the Hoe, where they sat on a bench for some time looking out across the Sound at the boats going to and fro, and watching a Naval frigate steam slowly up the river into Devonport. Stephen told the French boy about Sir Francis Drake's famous game of bowls here, when the Spanish Armada had been seen approaching, and showed him Smeaton's Tower.

'It was one of the Eddystone lighthouses. You can see the present one out there on the horizon, if you look hard.' It was a clear day, and they could just pick out the thin pencil shape in the distance. They turned back to the red-and-white banded tower standing proudly on the Hoe, and Stephen went on, 'The one out there now is the fourth lighthouse to have been built. Smeaton's was the third.'

'When did they begin to build them?'

'Oh, back in the seventeenth century, I think. The first was built of wood and was destroyed in a storm, and the second burned down. This one was stronger, but the rocks it was built on kept shifting, so they took it down and built the last one nearby. I think the stump's still there. They must have saved a lot of ships from being wrecked.'

'But how do you build something like this in deep sea?' Robert asked, staring up at the tower.

'Well, I suppose it wasn't actually so very deep, if they were building on rocks. But it's amazing engineering, all the same. Not so bad when you get further up, but laying the foundations must have been incredibly difficult and dangerous, especially in those days, with none of the machinery we have now.'

They gazed together at the shadowy pencil so far out to sea, thinking of the men who had gone out there in boats and set about building a structure on jagged rocks, amidst a surging swell, or crashing waves. They must have taken materials with them, and heavy tools. How many, Stephen wondered, had died in the process?

'The man who built the first one was killed when the storm destroyed it,' he remembered. 'And it must have been terrifying when the second caught fire, knowing that there was nowhere to go for safety. And pretty lonely at the best of times.'

'I don't think', Robert said, 'that I would like to be a lighthouse keeper.' He looked at the tower again. 'I might like to be an engineer, though. To build something like this – that would be something to be proud of.'

Stephen glanced at him with interest. 'Would you? Well, when we've been down to the Barbican and looked at the fishing boats and had some lunch, I'll take you round to see Brunel's railway bridge across the Tamar. Brunel was one of our great engineers.'

'Oh, yes, I've heard of him,' Robert said. 'His father was French and he was also an engineer. He left France during the Revolution but he designed bridges in France. He was the first man to understand how to build a tunnel under water.'

'That's right!' Stephen exclaimed. 'And father and son built the first tunnel under the Thames. I learned quite a lot about it at Cambridge, when I studied mathematics and engineering. I even thought about becoming an engineer myself.'

'But you are now a pilot.'

'Yes, and I really like flying. It's the best thing in the world. When I leave the RAF I want to go to Canada and set up my own freight flying business.'

'Canada!' Robert said, his eyes glowing. 'I would like to go to Canada, too. We have relatives there, you know – relatives of my other grandfather. Perhaps when I am old enough I will visit you there. We might even work together!'

Stephen looked at him, startled. Until now, Robert had been quiet and rather enigmatic, rarely volunteering a remark and giving away little about himself. Now, it was as if a spring had been touched.

'Well, maybe,' he answered rather cautiously, imagining what his father would say if he heard this. 'Probably better to leave any plans like that for a while, though. You might change your mind – I changed mine a hundred times before I joined the RAF. I thought about going to America, but now I think Canada would be better.'

'Perhaps,' Robert agreed. 'And there is Burracombe, of course. My grandfather wants me to learn about the estate, and my mother says I must do as he wishes. But I think I will prefer to be a great engineer.'

Stephen did not reply. He was struggling with yet another shift in his thinking about the family situation. The only way either he or Hilary had been able to come to terms with it was to assume that it would have been the same if Baden had not died and Robert had been expected to inherit from him. He would have been brought up in that knowledge, of course, and that would have coloured his own thinking, but there was no reason to suppose that he would not still have been fired up by the thought of becoming 'a great engineer'. Stephen knew, however, that his father was pinning great hopes on the boy, and his disappointment would be bitter if Robert turned his back on all that was being offered.

There's no point me worrying about it now, though, he concluded. It's happened the way it has, and what will be, will be. And I rather think I'll be thankful to be out of it!

They arrived home with time to change for dinner, and Stephen went straight to his room without encountering Marianne. After her non-appearance last night, he was beginning to think that she had regretted coming to his room and that he would now be safe. And it seemed he was right, for when they met for sherry in the drawing room, she was no more than pleasant to him; even a little cool.

'Ah, Stephen,' she greeted him. 'Robert has been telling me about the so interesting day he has had with you. It was very kind of you to take so much trouble.'

'It was no trouble at all,' he said. 'Robert and I have quite a lot in common.'

'And Hilary and I too 'ave 'ad an interesting day. I think we now 'ave almost all Robert's uniform, and there are many name-tapes to sew on. We are going to be very busy, Hilary, are we not?'

'Well, someone certainly is,' Hilary agreed, determined not to get landed with this job. 'You may have to take some to France with you, and post them back!'

Stephen, who knew how his sister felt about sewing on name-tapes, this having been her job also for him when he was at school, not to mention sewing on her own, grinned.

Marianne looked startled. 'But I have been looking forward to it! You and I, sisters, enjoying peaceful afternoons together as we sewed. What could be more pleasant?'

'I'm sure it would be a delight,' Hilary said smoothly. 'Unfortunately, I have estate work to do, and it can't be neglected.'

'Estate work – pouf!' Marianne said. 'That is man's work.'

'That's what I keep telling her,' Gilbert agreed. 'Won't take any notice, though. Still, I'm sure she's only teasing you about this. She'll be glad to help, won't you, Hilary?'

'When I can,' she replied coolly. 'But as you know, Father, the estate work must come first. I need to see Travis first thing in the morning, after our meeting. I want him to show me the field where Crocker wants to put the new Dutch barn. There may be a problem with the drainage ...'

Marianne, looking put out, came to Stephen's side. She

stroked his arm and murmured in his ear. 'I 'ave missed you today, my Stephen. Hilary is a very nice person and I am glad to 'ave 'er for a sister, but it is not the same as being with you.'

Stephen glanced at her. Her dark eyes were half closed, and her fingertips were like small, hot flames licking his arm. He felt his heart lurch.

'If you think of Hilary as your sister,' he muttered hoarsely, 'then you must think of me as your brother, and so ...'

'But no, not at all. That is quite, quite different.' Her voice was low and sultry. 'We are not brother and sister. We are something much deeper than that, *n'est-ce pas?*'

'Marianne—' Stephen began desperately, but at that moment Mrs Ellis rang the bell out in the hall, and they all got up to go into the dining room.

For the rest of the evening, he managed to avoid being close to her. He helped Robert up to bed, then popped his head back into the drawing room to announce that he was going for a walk and might call in at the Bell. He was gone before Marianne, already half on her feet, could say that she would come, too, and slipped across the lawn and out through a side gate in case she pursued him down the drive. It then occurred to him that she might even go to the Bell herself, so he walked for over an hour before ducking his head through the low doorway into the bar, where Dottie was serving and the bell-ringers were sitting around their usual long table after their weekly practice.

Stephen, who had learned to ring when the bells had begun to sound again after the war, bought himself a pint of ale and joined them.

'What's the latest news in the bell-ringing world?'

'Oh, there's plenty going on,' Ted Tozer said. 'You ought to come back with us when you'm here. You had the makings of a decent ringer.'

'Maybe I will, when things have settled down a bit. Not

that I'm here much these days.' He glanced at Travis. 'Will the bells be ringing for your wedding?'

'Try and stop them!' Norman Tozer said. 'Us have been practising a special new peal for the occasion. Travis is going to join us while he'm waiting for the bride. That's unless her comes to her senses on the day!'

Travis grinned. 'And I want young Micky and Henry to be part of it. They've worked hard and they're doing well, both of them.'

'Ah, they're not so bad, for tackers,' Ted conceded. 'Got to keep an eye on 'em, mind. You never knows what tricks they two might be up to behind your back.'

Travis smiled and Stephen thought of the boys' escapade in the mine adit. He felt himself relax for the first time for days. Here in the inn, with local men around him, straightforward and plain-speaking, he realised just how much Marianne had bemused him with her soft words and caresses, her dark glances and her murmured insinuations. His heart still quickened at the thought of her visit to his room the other night, but he knew that her allure lay solely in the desire she aroused in him, and had nothing to do with love.

I'll get through this night, he thought, and then I'll go. I'll see Maddy and tell her I have to go away. Perhaps I'll never be able to tell her the truth after all, but at least I can make sure it never happens again. The first time, I was too startled and too helpless to stop her, but if it happens again it will be my fault, and that will be a real betrayal.

Feeling the strength of companionship supporting his resolve, he drained his tankard and stood up.

'Thanks for that. I'll come round to the tower next time I'm here – that's a promise. And if I don't see you again before the wedding, Travis, good luck to you, and all best wishes to you both.' He held out his hand, and the estate manager shook it firmly. Stephen sketched a salute at the others and went out.

He walked up the drive through the gathering twilight – the

'dimpsy light', as locals called it – and decided not to go and say goodnight to the others, but simply to slip unnoticed up to his room. And this time, he would definitely put a chair under the handle of the door.

The hall was unlit and he could hear the murmur of voices coming from the drawing room. Quietly, he took off his shoes, climbed the stairs and padded along the landing to his bedroom. He opened the door and slid inside, closing it softly behind him, and leaned against it, closing his eyes in relief.

From his bed, Marianne's voice murmured huskily, 'Ah, my Stephen ... You are home at last ... I was almost tired of waiting for you ...'

Chapter Thirty-Four

Hilary slept badly that night. Her mind was filled with a jumble of thoughts and emotions: resentment at the way she was being manoeuvred into looking after Marianne as well as her son; the manner in which she was being sidelined in matters of the estate; and her father's entire attitude towards her, which she knew had not changed one iota since she had first suggested taking on the management. He's never going to acknowledge what I've done here, she thought despairingly. I might as well do as Stephen suggests and abandon it all; shake the dust of Burracombe off my feet and go to Canada with him to start a new life. At least I could be independent. I could be myself.

Yet she knew that, bad as things seemed to be, they would have to be a great deal worse before she could do this. Burracombe – the estate, the Barton, the village itself – were in her bones and in her blood, as they were in her father's and had been in Baden's, but never in Stephen's. She could not go away.

I'm trapped here, she thought. And she turned over and fell asleep at last, only to dream of a mountain of grey school socks and another mountain of name-tapes waiting to be sewn on, and neither of them growing any less.

She woke at six, with a jump. Something had disturbed her, but she didn't know what. Some sound – a knock, a small clatter – that she couldn't identify. She closed her eyes again, trying to go back to sleep, even if it did mean returning to that frustrating dream; after all, with a number of people in the house, there were bound to be sounds. But then it occurred to her that she might have heard Robert trying to move about – to go to the bathroom, perhaps – and falling. She sighed and threw back the bedclothes, wrapped her dressing-gown around her and opened her door.

Marianne was just coming out of Stephen's bedroom.

Hilary froze. Unable to speak, she stared at the Frenchwoman, swathed in a gown of scarlet lace, her feet bare, her dark hair loose and tangled around her face. And Marianne looked back, a smile curving her reddened lips, a glint of triumph in her eyes. She lifted her chin a little in defiance and said, 'Good morning, Hilary. I hope you had a good night? You were not kept awake by any ... noises?'

Her smile widened and she lowered her lids for a moment, then turned and glided away.

Hilary stood gazing after her, dumbfounded. She felt dizzy and slightly sick. She looked at Stephen's door and wondered if he had heard, and if she should go in at once and confront him. But her courage failed her, and, with tears already on her cheeks, she turned and went back to her own room.

'What in God's name were you thinking of?' she demanded a few hours later. She had had time to get over the shock, had gone for a furious gallop on Beau and missed breakfast, and sat through a meeting with her father and Travis before managing to buttonhole Stephen on his way to the small barn where the cars were garaged. She'd ignored his protests that he was going on an errand to Tavistock, got into the front seat and demanded that he take her somewhere where they couldn't be overheard. Stephen, recognising that this was serious, had stopped arguing and obeyed, and they were now sitting in a small disused quarry, used by tourists as a parking spot, on the road to Princetown.

'She stayed the night with you, didn't she? You slept with her. Have you gone completely mad? Was it the first time?'

'No, it wasn't, and I haven't gone mad. Or perhaps I have,' he amended miserably. 'I'm sorry, Hil, I honestly don't know how to explain it. I don't love her – I don't even *like* her much – but I can't seem to help myself. When she looks at me ... or touches me ...' He shivered. 'You wouldn't understand.'

'No, I wouldn't,' Hilary said icily. 'I thought you were supposed to be in love with Maddy. What would she think about this?'

'God knows. She'd never want to speak to me again, and I wouldn't blame her. I tell you, she couldn't loathe me any more than I loathe myself. It's been torment, Hilary, honestly.'

'My heart bleeds for you. You didn't exactly try to prevent it, did you?'

'I did! Why do you think I wanted to go away? I would have, too, if Maddy hadn't wanted me to go and fetch her. Even then ... but I had to promise to stay for at least a few days. The first night I was back, she didn't come to my room, and I thought it was over. But last night ...That's why I went out for a walk. I went to the pub and stayed till closing-time, and when I came back I went upstairs as quietly as I could. I thought she was still in the drawing room. But she was already in bed – *my* bed.'

'So you took advantage of the fact,' Hilary said with contempt. 'Oh, come on, Steve. You and Marianne have been having an affair ever since you first came on leave—'

'No! There was only once before that!'

'Once? When?'

'The night before Maddy rang up,' he said wretchedly. 'She did more or less the same thing then. I know I shouldn't have given in, but ... I just couldn't help it. I really couldn't.'

'You sound like a sixteen-year-old virgin,' she said scornfully. 'Like that girl in the song from *Oklahoma* – "I'm Just a Girl Who Cain't Say No". Steve, you're a grown man.'

'Yes, and a very unhappy, frustrated one,' he retorted. 'How do you think I've felt these past few months, Hilary? It's Maddy I want, and always has been ever since we first met. But first I had to stand back and watch her fall for that young sprog Sammy Hodges and get herself engaged to him, and then see him die before her eyes – which means he'll always be first with her – and now I've got to be her best friend and always be there when she needs me, with no hope of ever being able even to give her a proper kiss. Have you any idea what that's like for a man? I want to *love* her – love her properly. I want to marry her. But I don't think it's ever going to happen. And then along comes Marianne, offering herself to me on a plate. What am I supposed to do? All right, don't tell me, I know what I'm *supposed* to do – turn away and say no. But it's not that easy, Hil. Not when you're desperate to make love to the girl you want, and know you never will, and then someone else gets into your bed – that's what she did, that first night and ... and does what she did. I don't know any man who could resist that. I hated myself every minute, but *I just couldn't stop*.'

Hilary stared at him. Then she turned her head away, and there was a long silence.

At last, she said, in a curiously dead, flat voice, 'Well, I hope there isn't going to be any outcome to this.'

'What do you mean?'

'What do you think I mean?' she flashed, whipping back at him. 'A baby, of course! Steve, this is your brother's wife – his widow! What's it going to do to Dad if he finds out? As he most certainly will, if there's a child. Or didn't you think of that?'

Stephen's mouth opened and closed slowly. Then he shook his head and said numbly, 'No. I didn't think of that.'

'Oh, for pity's sake!' Hilary put both hands up to her face. 'You mean you did *nothing*?'

'I didn't use anything, no. How could I? I had no idea it was going to happen. I don't keep these things in my dressing-

343

gown pocket. I ... I suppose she might have done. There are things for women, aren't there? Caps, or something?'

'I very much doubt if Marianne possesses such a thing,' Hilary said coldly. 'She's a Roman Catholic, remember? From a Roman Catholic country. Well, we shall just have to wait and hope for the best.' Her face tightened, and she thumped her fist on her knee. 'Oh, if things weren't bad enough already!'

'I'm really sorry, Hil,' he said humbly. 'But I don't think it'll happen again. Not now that you know.'

'You're damned right it won't! I'll find the key to your door and lock you in there myself!' She drew in a deep breath and let her shoulders slump. 'Well, nothing more can be done about it now. You'd better drive us back. I've got work to do, and I suggest you come and help me do it. You can spend the next few days helping on the estate. There's harvest to be got in on some of the farms, they'll all be glad of a hand. And you'd better see Maddy as well, since that's supposed to be why you're staying.'

'I don't think I can,' he said, with such despair in his voice that Hilary, angry as she was, could not help but feel sorry for him. 'I know she doesn't love me, but I still feel I've betrayed her. I don't think I can ever look her in the eye again.'

Hilary glanced at him, then put her hand on his knee. 'Oh, Steve,' she said. 'What a mess. What an awful mess this whole thing is.'

'I thought Stephen might have come round yesterday,' Maddy said, as she and Stella sat outside the back door, drinking their morning coffee. 'But I suppose he's too busy up at the Barton, with their visitors.'

'I suppose so,' Stella said. 'They must take up quite a lot of time. I shouldn't think Hilary was too pleased to have to spend a day in Exeter buying school uniform. She'll be wanting Stephen to take his turn! But I thought you said he was going away for the rest of his leave.'

'He said he'd stay and spend some time with me.' Maddy's voice was despondent. 'But obviously he's changed his mind. I hear Madame Aucoin's a very attractive woman,' she added.

Stella gave her a quick glance. 'She's very striking. I'm not sure if that means she's attractive.'

'Well, of course it does! She is older, though, in her thirties at least. Even if she was very young when she married Baden ...'

'That's just the point,' Stella said. 'She married Baden. She won't be interested in his brother.'

'Why not? It isn't illegal.'

'I know, but ... She's had another husband since then, anyway. And I don't really know why you're so worried about her, since you're not interested in Stephen yourself.'

'I'm not worried about her! And of course I'm interested in Stephen. He's my friend. I don't want to see him get hurt.'

You don't want to see yourself get hurt, Stella thought, but she didn't say it. It wasn't surprising if Maddy felt she'd been hurt enough already. She said merely, 'I don't think Madame Aucoin is any danger to Stephen. She'll be going back to France soon, anyway, and I'm sure he'll come to see you the minute he gets the chance. But, you know ...' She hesitated, and Maddy turned to her at once.

'What? What were you going to say?'

'Oh, nothing much. Just that ... well, maybe you shouldn't get too used to relying on him, even as a friend. It's not really fair, is it? I'm not sure he knows where he is with you. He's obviously still in love with you—'

'I don't know why! I've never given him any encouragement.'

'Well, whether you have or not,' said Stella, who privately thought that her sister had given him at least a little encouragement, 'he may think you have. I mean, asking him to go and fetch you the way you did—'

'I had to! I was so upset. I just wanted to be here with you. And Felix couldn't do it; he had that funeral.'

'He could have done it later,' Stella pointed out. 'Or you could have come by train. Don't look like that, Maddy – I'm not telling you off. All I'm saying is that you didn't actually have to ask Stephen to drop everything and come. You mustn't take advantage of him.'

'He didn't mind,' Maddy muttered, looking so much like the little sister Stella remembered that she couldn't find it in her heart to reproach her any further.

She patted Maddy's knee and said, 'Well, as I said, I'm sure he'll come soon, and in the meantime we can do something by ourselves. Why don't we go into Tavistock, and get the bus to Calstock and walk round the river to Cotehele? Felix and I went there a little while ago and it's lovely – a beautiful medieval house and wonderful gardens, and you can sit on the quay and watch the river. It's so peaceful, I'm sure it'll do you good.'

'I suppose we could,' Maddy said unenthusiastically.

Stella smiled and jumped up. 'That's settled, then. Come on, I'll see what's in the larder and make a picnic, although I think we can get cups of tea there, or an ice cream. We'll take Felix's old rucksack – he left it here last week after we'd been walking.'

'Won't he wonder where we've gone?' asked Maddy, evidently determined to make difficulties, and Stella laughed and shook her head.

'No, he won't, because he isn't coming over today and I'm not going over there. So he won't even know. And I'll leave a note in the kitchen for Dottie, so she won't wonder, either. Now come on, Maddy, take that miserable look off your face and enjoy yourself. You know, you're just sulking because you think Stephen's deserted you. He can't always be at your beck and call.'

'I don't want him to be!' Maddy exclaimed, then saw the

expression on her sister's face, and grinned sheepishly. 'Well, perhaps I do, a bit. All right, Stell. I'll stop being a grump. I know you're doing your best to cheer me up.'

'I am. But you're going to have to start trying to do it for yourself sometime, Maddy. You've had a hard time, but nobody would want you to spend the rest of your life being sad. Sammy wouldn't want that.'

Maddy opened her mouth to argue, then closed it again. Her eyes filled with tears, and Stella was afraid she'd gone too far. Then, to her relief, Maddy nodded and said, 'I'm feeling sorry for myself, aren't I? And I promised myself I wouldn't be. I'll try to stop it.'

'You don't have to try to stop all at once,' Stella said gently. 'We all know how awful it's been for you. So long as you can move forward a little bit each day, that's all you have to do.'

'Yes,' Maddy said with a sigh. 'It doesn't sound so very much, when you say it like that. But ... oh, Stella, it's so hard at times. And I can't do it all on my own.'

Chapter Thirty-Five

'So how do you like living in at the hotel?' Val asked, picking at the grapes Jackie had brought her.

'Oh, it's smashing. The other girls are all really nice – well, except for Doreen Curtis, she's a bit of a cat, but nobody likes her much so that doesn't matter. I've got a good-sized room that I share with two other girls, with my own chest of drawers and wardrobe, and a bathroom just across the passage. We're right at the top of the building with a gorgeous view of the Sound, and it's lovely to be able to get up in the morning and go to work without having to catch a bus or walk in the pouring rain, and be close to all the shops and the pictures and everything.'

'You're a proper city girl now, aren't you?' Val said, amused. 'Nobody would ever think you grew up on a farm.'

Jackie made a face. 'I don't tell them if I can help it. They all think country people are stupid.'

'Well, I hope you tell them different!' Val exclaimed. 'You owe us a bit of loyalty, I should think.'

Jackie looked a little abashed. 'I know that. But you don't know what it's like, Val. It only wants one girl to start picking on you, and the rest join in. It's not that they're spiteful or anything, they're really good friends, but they're just funny about country people.'

Val looked at her thoughtfully. Jackie had always been easily led, but she was old enough now to make her own judgements – and her own mistakes. And she was the one who had to live with these girls, after all. Val had had her own experience of living with a lot of other young women, although in very different circumstances, and she knew how cruel they could be if they turned on one. It was up to Jackie to strike her own balance.

'Are you looking forward to the wedding?' she asked. 'How's your dress coming along?'

Jackie's face lit up. 'Oh, it's smashing! I decided to make it myself; did Mum tell you that? She said she'd help, but I'm doing most of it when I come home on my days off. I was quite good at needlework at school, and I made this frock I'm wearing now, so it's not too hard. It's nearly finished. I tried it on before I came down here. Will Dr Latimer let you come, d'you think?'

Val shook her head dolefully. 'It doesn't look like it. I had another funny turn yesterday, and he says I've really got to stay in bed all the time or he may have to send me to the hospital. And I couldn't go to the maternity home in Tavistock, either – I'd have to go to Plymouth, to Freedom Fields. I don't want that.'

'Gosh, no! Oh, Val, that's awful if you can't go to the wedding, not when you and Jennifer have been such good friends, and with her practically living next door at Mr Prout's.'

'I know. But she's promised to come in and see me before she goes to the church, and bring you bridesmaids as well, so that I know what you all look like. And I'll be able to hear the bells ringing, so I can imagine I'm there.'

'Well, I think it's a shame,' Jackie said stoutly. 'But I'll pop in and see you afterwards, too, if you like, and bring you some cake.'

Val smiled. 'And how about you? Any new boyfriends, or have you made it up with Vic?'

'No, and I'm not going to, either. He seems to think he's God's gift to women. I don't want a boyfriend at the moment, anyway. I'm enjoying myself going round with the other girls.

We go to the dances together and have fun, and then go back together. That's good enough for me.'

'Nothing wrong with that,' Val observed. 'Oh, by the way, Mrs Pettifer popped in yesterday. She says Roy's expected home any time now.'

'Oh, yes, I think he is,' Jackie said casually. 'I had a letter about three weeks ago, and he did mention that they'd be embarking pretty soon.' She got up and started to gather her belongings. 'I'll have to be off now. I promised Joanna I'd fetch Robin home from the Bennetts. He's been to tea with little Martin – they're starting school together next month.'

She kissed her sister and departed. Val lay back on her pillows, tired from the visit but smiling to herself as she thought of Jackie's reaction to her comment about Roy. Those two should never have split up, she thought. It's obvious Jackie's still hankering after him. But I wonder how he feels about her ...

While Jackie Tozer was revelling in her new life in the city, Jennifer Tucker was looking forward to leaving it for the village. She had given in her notice at Dingle's, and was leaving at the end of the month. She had also given notice to the landlord of the house in Devonport, and was busy clearing out many of the possessions accumulated through the years. Some of the furniture was being taken to the new house – Wood Cottage, as she was getting used to calling it – while the rest was going to a second-hand shop nearby. There were clothes and bedding, too, some left by her mother, which could also go to a second-hand shop, and the rest she bundled up to give to the rag-and-bone man when he came round with his cart.

'I'd no idea I'd collected so much rubbish,' she said to Travis when he came to help. 'Look at all this! And there's this shoebox full of old photos, too – what shall I do with them?'

'Keep them,' he said promptly. 'You can spend the long

winter evenings sorting through them and putting them into an album. What's this?'

'Oh, that's my mother's necklace, the one Dad gave her on their wedding day.' She took the thin gold chain with its teardrop-shaped gold filigree pendant enclosing three tiny garnets on minute pendulums. 'It's pretty, isn't it? She said I should have it when she died.'

'I think you should wear it on the wedding day,' Travis said. 'It suits you.'

'Yes, I will. I always remember her wearing it when I was very small and she was doing something for me – putting on my shoes, that sort of thing. I'd be sitting on a chair and she'd be bending over me, so it was just at my eye-level. I loved looking at it. It can be my "something old".'

'And this,' Travis said, putting his hand into his pocket, 'can be your "something new".' He handed her a small velvet box.

Jennifer looked at it in surprise. 'Whatever is it?'

'Well, there's an easy way to find out,' he said with a grin.

She opened it slowly and then gave a cry of delight. 'Oh, Travis, it's beautiful! And it'll go with the necklace.' She took out a thin gold chain bracelet and held it up, letting it fall in a coil in her palm. 'But you shouldn't have done that. You've already given me my lovely ring.'

'That was for your engagement. This is for your wedding.' He kissed her. 'I was going to save it for the day but I couldn't wait that long, and when I saw your mother's necklace – well, it seemed like the right moment. But you can't wear it until then, mind, or it won't be new.'

'I'll save it for the day,' she promised, and put it back in its box. 'You're so good to me, Travis.'

'I know my own luck,' he said. 'And you're not too sad about leaving your home here, and your job, are you?'

'Not in the least! I've always wanted to live in the country. My mother used to tell me about it, and sometimes we'd go out on the moors for picnics. I always felt so shut in, coming back here. As for the job – well, I've enjoyed it, but I'm quite happy to look after you instead. I'd have left Dingle's eventually – I'll never leave you.'

'I'm pleased to hear it,' he said solemnly. 'And how about all the arrangements? Are all those bridesmaids getting sorted out?'

'Yes, my sisters' little girls are thrilled, and she's almost finished their dresses. Jackie knows them quite well, of course, and she'll look after them. I hope your best man will be as efficient!'

'He'd better be,' Travis said grimly. He had taken Jennifer to his home in Dorset to meet his family and his old school friend, Davey, who had struck her as being extremely likeable but worryingly scatter-brained. He was a wild-haired, lively and merry young man with a plump, placid wife and a brood of small children, who were, thankfully, being left at home on the big day. 'Don't worry, darling, he'll be all right. Sarah will make sure the ring's tied on to him!'

'I hope she also makes sure it can be untied,' Jennifer said, envisaging an unseemly grappling at the altar, ending with Basil Harvey being dispatched to the vestry for a pair of scissors. 'Well, that's your department. I've got enough to worry about without wondering if the best man's going to remember his duties! Now, about this furniture – I've got to be out of the house by the weekend, and I'll be staying with Jacob after that. So can you bring the truck in to collect it the day after tomorrow? It's all right with Colonel Napier, isn't it?'

'Haven't asked him, but Hilary says so. There's something very odd going on at the Barton,' he added, frowning. 'I thought they'd got young Rob pretty well organised with his admission to Kelly College and so on, but there's a real atmosphere around the place at present. It seems to be more to do with his mother.'

'You don't like her, do you?' Jennifer said, noting his expression.

'No, I don't much, to tell you the truth. A scheming minx, is what my mother would have called her. Not that I've any reason to think that, apart from the way she seems to have inveigled her son in to the household ... but there, it's none of my business and I shouldn't be talking about my employers' private affairs.'

'Not to anyone else, anyway,' Jennifer said. 'But I'm going to be your wife. You can tell me anything – and I promise I won't go spreading it around.'

'My wife,' he said, and drew her close again. 'My stars, as Minnie Tozer would say, that does sound good!'

Stella was also giving in her notice.

'I know I don't really have to do this until the first day of term,' she said to Miss Kemp as they surveyed the classroom. School was starting again the following week. 'But I thought I'd get it over with, and it's not as if it's coming as a surprise.'

The headmistress took the envelope from her and turned it over in her hands. 'It's your resignation, I assume?'

'I'm afraid so. I'm really sorry. I've loved being here, working with you and the children – it'll break my heart to leave. I didn't think it would be so soon, either. I thought I'd be here for years and years.'

Miss Kemp laughed. 'I didn't! It was my only reservation when we offered you the job, that you were such a nice, pretty young woman that we'd lose you almost immediately. Mind you, we all thought at first it would be Luke Ferris. You saw quite a lot of him to begin with, didn't you?'

Stella blushed. 'He was only a friend. And he was helping me to trace Maddy, that's all.' She saw the headmistress's eyebrows rise a little and laughed. 'All right, I did rather fall for him at first. But he was never really interested in me. It was Val all the time for him. And then, when Felix and I started to get to know each other – well, there was no question about it. I knew I'd never love anyone else. I was just surprised – I still am, sometimes – that he could feel the same about me.'

'You're very good for that young man. You tone him down a little. And he's been good for you, too.' Miss Kemp put the envelope into her pocket. 'I'll pass this on to the governors, and we'd better start thinking about a replacement. It would be nice if we find one before the end of term so that you can introduce her to the children yourself. I always think that helps to start everyone off on the right foot.'

'That would be good – although I'm not sure it's really wise in this case,' Stella said with a grin. 'Unless we can arrange for the Crocker twins to be absent that day!'

Chapter Thirty-Six

'There you are, my Stephen,' Marianne said, her cat-like smile curving her lips. 'I wondered where you had gone.'

'I was out with Hilary.' He looked down at her gravely. 'Come for a drive with me, Marianne. I've got to talk to you.'

'This sounds *très sérieux*,' she said, hooking her hand through his arm. 'Where are you taking me? Somewhere very quiet and very private, I hope?'

Stephen didn't reply. He led her out of the house to where his sports car stood on the drive. They got in, and he set off along the road leading through the village and across the moors. Marianne settled back in her seat, and Stephen glanced sideways at her, thinking she looked now like the cat that had got the cream. Cream, he thought, that was about to turn sour.

Since his talk with Hilary that morning, he had been doing a lot of thinking, and had come to some painful conclusions. Most of them were about himself and his own behaviour, which he had already known had been irresponsible and reckless, and he was determined not to lose control again. Even Marianne's touch on his arm, sending tiny, searing bursts of flame through his body, didn't shake his resolve, and he hoped desperately that he would be able to keep his strength of mind.

'Where are we going?' she asked after a few moments.

He shrugged. 'Nowhere special. I just want to be out of Burracombe. I want to be sure we won't be overheard.'

Marianne shivered. 'Oh, you are so mysterious, my Stephen. And so masterful. I like it.'

You won't for much longer, he thought, and turned right along a narrow track leading through a conifer wood. Marianne gave a little squeal of pretended fear, and he felt a sudden, unexpected spurt of irritation. Did she really have to behave like an attention-seeking eight-year-old all the time?

He stopped the car beside a wide, swift stream crossed by an ancient clapper bridge. There was nobody else about, and when the engine died, all that could be heard was the occasional chatter of a bird in the nearby gorse bushes, and the rustle of a squirrel somewhere amongst the branches.

Marianne snuggled up against him. 'So what are we to talk about that must be said in such privacy?' she purred. 'Is it something you want to ask me, my Stephen?'

'No,' he said. 'There's nothing at all I want to ask you. And I am not your Stephen.'

There was a moment of silence. Then she sat up, drew away and stared at him.

'Stephen?' And, when he didn't speak, 'Is it that you are a little cross with your Marianne?'

'And you are not my Marianne,' he said, slowly and deliberately. 'We do not belong to each other. In any way at all.'

A small frown appeared between her delicate brows. 'I do not understand. What do you mean?' She stroked his arm.

'I mean this has got to stop.' He removed her hand and laid it back in her lap. 'I've been very wrong to behave as I have, and you've been very wrong to encourage me. If you hadn't come to my room—'

'Ah, so the fault is mine!' she cried, her eyes flashing. 'And did you tell me to go away? Did you lock your door?'

'I don't have a key,' he began, before realising how ludicrous this sounded. 'No, I didn't tell you to go away. I couldn't. You knew I couldn't.'

'You are a child,' she spat. 'A mere boy. You do not even know *how* to love a woman – you need someone like me to teach you.'

'Thank you, but no,' Stephen said, fighting down his anger at her scorn. 'I mean it, Marianne. I don't want any more to do with you. I don't know why you've been doing this, but it's going to stop now, this minute. There's to be no more. And I think you should go back to France. As soon as you can. Tomorrow, if possible.'

'That is ridiculous! You know I cannot go so soon.'

'I don't see why not. We can arrange a ferry ticket for you.'

'What would your father say? And your interfering sister?' Her eyes narrowed. '*She* has told you to say this, hasn't she? She saw me coming out of your room this morning, and she's told you to send me away.' Suddenly she moved closer and snuggled against him again. 'Well, we needn't take any notice of her,' she murmured, putting up one hand to stroke his lips with her forefinger. 'We will be more careful, that is all. It is none of her business, anyway.'

Stephen sighed and turned his head away. 'It *is* her business, Marianne. It's affecting our family and that's very much Hilary's business. She's put all she knows into Burracombe—'

'Ah, now we have the truth! She is jealous – jealous and afraid because Robert is the rightful heir and she thinks he will take her home away. And so he may, if he chooses! When your father dies, he will be able to do just as he pleases!'

Stephen stared at her, shocked, and she laughed at him.

'You see? You are beginning to realise just what it is you are throwing away. But it does not have to be this way, my Stephen ...' Once again, she drew close, her hand now moving on his thigh, slowly, sensuously. 'We could be so happy together. Those things I said just now, I didn't mean them. You know that, don't you? We can have it all, you and I. We could marry—'

'*Marry?*' He jerked away. 'Marianne, I wouldn't marry you if you were the last woman alive!'

'No?' she asked, raising her eyebrows in amusement. 'But think about it, my Stephen. Think of all we have done together. You may *have* to marry me, *n'est-ce pas?*'

She met his eyes, and he groaned and pushed her hand away. 'You mean ...'

'How can I know, so soon?' She shrugged. 'But you needn't worry – you will be the first to know if there is good news.'

Stephen got out of the car and walked away. He felt sick and trapped. He thought of the outrage it would cause if the worst were to happen: his father's baffled fury; Hilary's anguish; the shock-waves reverberating through the village. And, worst of all, Maddy's betrayed and bitter disappointment in him.

He turned and walked back. 'Is this why you did it? In the hope that you would become pregnant?'

Marianne eased herself out of the car, and lifted one shoulder. 'But of course. I could never be quite sure of your father, you see. He made up his mind quickly, too quickly. He might change it again just as soon. But if you and I were married, with another grandchild on the way ... Robert and I would be secure. And remember, I have other children to consider. The *pâtisserie* cannot keep us all. Not, I think, as Baden would have liked us to be kept.'

Stephen gave her a bitter look. 'My brother didn't know you at all. He was younger than I am now, and he was away from home, at war, knowing he might be killed at any moment. You swept him off his feet, and he married you without really knowing what he was doing. All those stories you told about not knowing what his home was like, thinking he just lived on a farm – they weren't true at all, were they? You knew very well what sort of home he had.' As she approached him again, he held up both hands, as if warding off an evil spirit. 'I think it was probably just as well that he died, because you would have made him very unhappy indeed.'

If he expected Marianne to react to this, he was wrong. She simply laughed, and lifted her chin. Her dark eyes were half-closed and her full lips narrowed to a thin red line. Her nostrils flared in a sneer.

'Perhaps. And perhaps he would have made me unhappy. Who knows? But that is over now, and it is just you and I. And if we marry and I come to live at the Barton, will we make each other unhappy, too? I think it would be foolish to do so – especially when we know what pleasures we can give each other.'

Stephen stood very still, his hands clenched at his side. He drew in several very deep breaths and then he said quietly, 'We'll cross that bridge when we come to it – *if* we come to it. But there are going to be no more "pleasures" as you call them. From now on, you stay well away from me. And if you are not pregnant, then you'll pack your bags and go back to France. And I just wish I could make you take your son with you – but since my father won't countenance that, I hope you'll leave him to learn to be an English gentleman, as his father was. At least he'll have a chance, then.' He strode back to the car and held open the passenger door. 'Get in. We're going back to the Barton now, and I want you to keep your distance. If you try playing any more of your little games with me, I shall go straight to my father, and I think he will believe me and Hilary before he believes your slimy little lies!'

Marianne threw him a look of hatred, but did as she was told. They drove back to Burracombe in silence. When he stopped the car at the Barton, she got out without a word and stormed up the steps. Stephen watched her, then drove round to the stable yard.

He sat still for a few minutes, trying to calm his thundering heart. Oddly enough, despite his fury and his apprehension, he felt a strange sense of exhilaration. He felt as if he had passed some kind of bizarre test.

He felt as if he had grown up.

Chapter Thirty-Seven

'Well, you do look grown up,' Alice Tozer said, regarding her grandson with admiration. 'Look at you, in your new blazer and cap, and smart new shoes. A proper schoolboy.'

Robin looked down at himself proudly. The blazer was two sizes too big and the cap almost covered his ears, but nobody bought school clothes the right size, especially for the smallest children. They were bought to 'grow into'. They didn't even have to have blazers, since there was no actual school uniform, but, as Joanna said, Robin had to have something to wear to school, so he might as well look tidy.

'Not that he'll look tidy for long,' Ted had remarked. 'Not if he's anything like his father. I remember our Tom coming home many a time with his trousers torn and his socks down round his ankles, and I reckon we lost count of the caps us had to buy him.'

'He can start off looking nice anyway,' Alice said. 'Are you looking forward to school, Robin?'

The little boy nodded. 'I'm going to learn to read and write and do sums. And I'll be able to play football with the big boys. I'll be able to play with George and Edward Crocker.'

'I'm not so sure about that,' Joanna began, but Tom grinned at her.

'You can't shield him from the villains of this world for ever, Jo. He's going out into the big wide world now.'

'If you can call the village school the big wide world,' Alice commented. 'Well, I think you look very nice, Robin. I tell you what you can do now. You can come to see Auntie Val with me and show her how grown up you look. I baked an extra pie today for her and Luke to have for their supper, seeing as they can't come up here just now.'

'Val must feel as if it's going on for ever,' Joanna said. 'She's been in bed for weeks now, and there's still over a month to go.'

'I know, and proper fed up she is, but bearing up well, considering. She don't mean for anything to go wrong.' Alice sighed a little, thinking of the secret of Val's first baby. She had told no one, not even Ted; it was water under the bridge now, and there was no point in stirring it up and making it muddy. Val and Luke had had their troubles but now they'd made a fresh start, and Alice hoped as fervently as Val herself that all would go right this time.

With Robin trotting along beside her, she set off down the farm track and made for the village. Jacob Prout was in his front garden, next door to Jed's Cottage, and straightened his back as she put her hand on the gate.

'Afternoon, Alice. How be 'ackin', then?'

'Doing well, thankee, Jacob.' She rested her basket on the wall for a moment. 'I dare say you'm looking forward to the wedding. Not long now.'

He nodded. 'Just on a fortnight. Mind you, I reckon young Travis'll be glad when it's over. Worse than getting ready for the Coronation, it is. I tell him, you stay out of it, boy, weddings is women's business. All us men got to do is turn up on the day with our best suits on and our shoes polished. I suppose you'm getting a taste of it up your place, with young Jackie being a bridesmaid and all.'

Alice laughed. 'We all seem to be involved, one way and another. Ted's mother's working out some special harmonies on the handbells; we're ringing them while the register's being signed. And Joanna's helping make a garland of autumn leaves round the lychgate and another one round the church door. It's a bit early for the best colours, mind, but she reckons they can find quite a bit, and there's plenty of dahlias and chrysanths for the church flowers. Jennifer's set on having everything from in the village – nothing from outside. But you'd know all about that, of course.'

'Oh, ah. Her's told me all about it. Talks of nothing else. Making her bouquet from my own roses, her be.' He tried unsuccessfully to conceal his pride. 'That's why I'm out here now, making sure there'll be a few blooms left by then – lucky I got a few late-flowering ones.'

Alice smiled at him and went on into the cottage. As she reached the door it opened, and Hilary Napier came out. Alice thought how tired she looked.

'Is everything all right?'

'Oh, yes,' Hilary said. 'Val's fine. She's been helping me with some sewing. I'm just on my way home.'

That wasn't what Alice had meant. 'Have you still got your visitors with you? I hear the boy's going to Kelly College.'

'That's right. He'll be off next week. That's what the sewing was – the last of his name-tapes. There seemed to be hundreds of them.'

'I dare say his mother did most of them, didn't she? French-women are handy with their needle, so I've heard.'

'I'm not sure where you heard that,' Hilary said wryly. 'It doesn't apply to Marianne, anyway! Although she's clever enough with her own clothes.'

'And will she be going back to France when he's at Kelly?' Alice asked, then caught herself. 'I'm sorry, I'm asking too many questions! I don't mean to pry, only we'm all interested, you see.'

'I know you are.' Hilary sighed. 'To be honest, Alice, I don't know what she plans to do. I thought she'd be going back before now – she's got two other children, and her mother and mother-in-law to look after – but she hasn't said a word about going back. Her sister's taking care of everything at the moment, but ...' She drifted into silence, and Alice looked at her with some anxiety. Poor soul looks proper worn out, she thought. Doing too much, that's plain to see.

'I dare say she'll go back once she's happy the boy's settled,' she said comfortingly. 'And didn't I see Master Stephen's car go through your gates a bit earlier on? It'll take a bit of weight off your shoulders to have him with you for a couple of days.'

Hilary gave her an unfathomable glance, and for a brief moment Alice feared she was about to burst into tears. But all she said was, 'Yes. I expect it will.' She turned away quickly, then said in a muffled voice, 'I'll have to go now. Val's waiting for you. Goodbye, Alice ...' And she almost ran down the garden path and out of the gate.

Alice stared after her. Well! she thought. Whatever can be the matter with her? Maybe what my Ted says about visitors is right. Like fresh fish, they go off after three days. Maybe she and Mr Baden's widow don't see eye to eye as much as us all thought.

She turned and went through the door, calling up to her daughter as she went through to the kitchen, and dumping her basket on the table.

'I've brought you and Luke a pie. And there's a blackberry and apple crumble as well. And just wait till you see the smart young man I've brought with me!'

Hilary walked back to the Barton slowly, aware that her feet were dragging, aware also that it was because, in truth, she did not want to reach home.

The atmosphere, since Stephen had come home again that morning, had been almost unbearable. Marianne had been at her most cat-like: purring with affection one moment; extending her claws – or so it seemed – the next. It had been bad enough for the past few weeks, since Hilary's discovery of their affair, but once Stephen had gone back to the airfield there had at least been the relief of knowing that it could go no further – for the time being. Not that there could be much relief in anything, while there was the possibility of Marianne being pregnant.

Now, though, it was all infinitely worse, and hiding it from her father was almost more than Hilary could manage. Only the fear of what it could do to his health prevented her from breaking down and blurting out the whole sorry, sordid tale.

Slowly though she might walk, she was bound to arrive eventually, and for the last stretch she straightened her back and held up her head, determined not to let Marianne – who might be watching from any window – see her misery. Apart from when Gilbert or Robert was with them, they had abandoned all pretence at friendship, and most of the time maintained a hostile silence.

'When are you planning to go back to France?' Hilary broke the silence to ask once. 'Your sister and other children must be missing you.'

Marianne had merely smiled. 'When I can be certain what plans I must make,' she'd answered, and Hilary, understanding that she meant when she knew if she was carrying Stephen's child, turned away, sickened.

She was convinced now that Marianne had set out deliberately to seduce Stephen with exactly this possibility in mind. It was an added guarantee of her place in Burracombe. As the mother of both Gilbert's grandchildren, by each of his sons, she could never be turned away. She had probably made up her mind as soon as she saw the house and estate that she and all her children would make their home there. She saw herself as mistress of the Barton and all it owned, and Hilary would be forced to leave. Gilbert might say there would always be a home for her there, but Hilary knew that with Marianne ensconced as Stephen's wife, her position would be untenable. And by the same token, Stephen would never be able to leave. He would be trapped.

Oh, Steve, she thought for the hundredth time, how could you be such a fool?

'So, my Stephen,' Marianne said, standing beside him at the window, 'have you missed me while you've been away?'

He didn't reply. He was watching his sister come up the drive, her head bowed and her footsteps slow. He knew exactly what she was feeling and thinking, and he recognised the irony that it had taken this Frenchwoman, Baden's widow, to bring him and his sister closer than they had ever been. As if he could read Hilary's mind, the same thoughts ran through his head: Marianne and himself married; Marianne the mistress of the house; Hilary unable to live with her sister-in-law; himself trapped, all his plans destroyed. And a child on the way.

He wondered how he would feel about that. At present, it seemed no more than another set of teeth in the trap that Marianne had sprung, yet it would be an innocent child, *his* child. If Stephen had ever thought at all about children, he would have seen them as his and Maddy's. But Maddy was lost to him now, a tiny figure in the distance.

'I asked if you had missed me,' Marianne repeated, and her fingers touched the back of his hand.

Stephen jerked away as if he had been burned. 'Don't do that! Don't touch me!' He turned on her. 'No, I haven't missed you. It's been a relief to be away – and if you want to know the truth, I didn't want to come back this weekend. It's only because Father asked me – *demanded*,' he amended bitterly. 'And as you know, Hilary and I don't want to take any risks with his health. He seems to think I should be here for Rob's last weekend before going to Kelly. And your last weekend in Burracombe.'

'*Perhaps* my last weekend in Burracombe,' she corrected him. 'I may be compelled to stay longer, my Stephen. There may be other plans to make.'

'I hope to God there aren't.' He stared restlessly into her eyes. 'When will you know for certain?'

She shrugged. 'Who can tell? It is still less than a month since those two so wonderful nights. They were wonderful, were they not, my Stephen? So passionate, so intimate.' Her fingers touched his hand again, and he felt like a rabbit, caught in headlights, unable to tear his gaze from hers. 'Why don't we start again?' she whispered, leaning closer. 'Why not forget the hasty words and remember the delight of those nights? There may, after all, be a lifetime together ahead of us, and surely we should take what pleasures we can from it? It would be foolish not to.'

Stephen dragged his gaze away, and looked out of the window. Hilary was closer now and as he watched, he saw her straighten her shoulders and lift her head, as if she had made up her mind not to be beaten. He felt a swift beat of strength touch his heart, and his own chin lifted in response. He turned back to Marianne and plucked her hand from his sleeve.

'Leave me alone, Marianne,' he said coldly, and walked out of the room.

But before he closed the door behind him, he heard her soft laugh and the murmur of her voice.

'Tonight, *mon cher* ... tonight ...'

Once again, Hilary slept badly. It was a hot night, and she opened her windows wide, threw off her blanket and lay under a cotton sheet, listening to the hooting of a pair of owls and the distant bark of a fox. She heard no other sounds. No soft opening and closing of a bedroom door; no padding of footsteps along the landing; no muffled voices or soft laughter. Yet still she couldn't quite believe that Stephen could keep his promise and resist the temptress who had come amongst them, and she had to fight her own temptation, to go to her own door and open it, hoping to catch one of them.

She must have fallen asleep at last, for suddenly the sky was light and the sun slanting in through her window. She got up, feeling worse than if she hadn't slept at all, and pulled on her dressing-gown to go to the bathroom, hoping that this time she wouldn't meet Marianne.

To her dismay, the Frenchwoman was just coming out of the bathroom. They stopped and regarded each other for a few moments, then Hilary made to brush past her.

'Excuse me. I need to go in.'

'Wait.' Marianne put out a hand. 'It is not what you think.'

'Oh? And how do you know what I think?' Hilary enquired coldly.

'Let us not play games. I need your help.'

'My *help*?' Hilary stopped and looked at her in astonishment. 'What on earth do you mean?'

Marianne shrugged. 'I 'ave the woman's problem, and nothing with me. It is early, you see.' She glanced slyly at Hilary 'In truth, I 'oped it would not come at all.'

Hilary stared at her, slowly taking in the meaning of her words. Then a feeling of enormous relief washed over her, so powerfully that her knees sagged and she had to hold on to the door-jamb to steady herself. Just in case she heard wrongly, she said in a trembling voice, 'You mean you have your period?'

'Yes,' Marianne said, and a curiously sullen look passed like a shadow across her face. 'Yes, that is what I mean. Now, can you please help me, or must I go to Mrs Ellis?'

'No, of course not,' Hilary exclaimed, wanting to leap in the air with joy. 'I mean, of course I'll give you some sanitary towels. I'll go and get them at once. Wait here.' And she half ran in to her own room, rummaged in a drawer to find what she wanted, and dashed out again.

Marianne was standing where she had left her, and took the package without comment. She said, 'Always I must stay at home for the first two days. After that, it is better and I can go about again. I think that will be the time for me to go back to France.'

'Yes,' Hilary said. 'I think you should.'

'It is for Robert to make the best he can of his new life and his new family,' Marianne said. She cast a withering glance at Stephen's door, still firmly closed. 'There is nothing more for me to do here.' She paused, then added softly, 'For the present, at least.'

She turned, and went back into the bathroom.

Stephen refused, absolutely and categorically, to take Marianne to Exeter to catch the train back to London.

'I can't get any more leave. I'm not a free agent, you know. It's a miracle I've been able to come home as much as I have, and now I want to put in some more flying hours. I'm in the Armed Forces, Dad, and you of all people ought to know what that means.'

'The RAF. Humph!' Gilbert snorted, leaving no room for doubt as to what he thought of Britain's youngest Service. 'Seem to have had plenty of time for junketing about so far.'

'Yes, well, now I haven't,' Stephen said tersely. 'I have to go back tonight and I can't come back again in a couple of days' time. In fact, I may not be back for quite a while.'

Gilbert's head came up. 'What do you mean by that? Being posted, are you?'

'No. I just mean I can't come back at all soon.' Stephen held his father's gaze. 'Sorry, Dad, that's all there is to it.'

Gilbert glared at him but said no more. He turned to Hilary. 'It'll have to be you, then. And don't say you've got too much work to do.'

'I shan't. I'll be glad to do it,' Hilary said, thinking how true this was and how impossible it would have been to ask Stephen to do it. She had seen, when she'd broken the news that there was no pregnancy, just how relieved her brother had felt, and knew that he would never take such a risk again. But Marianne was dangerous – more dangerous than Hilary had ever really appreciated. It was far better if they were never left alone together again.

'Rob can come with us,' she added, noticing a somewhat forlorn look on her nephew's face. 'He'll want as much time as possible with his mother before she goes home and he starts school, won't you, Rob?'

'I think I would like to go home, too,' the boy said, surprising them all. 'I don't have to go to this English school, do I?'

'Don't have to go?' Gilbert exclaimed before anyone else could speak. 'What in heaven's name do you mean? Don't you *want* to go to a fine school and have a proper education?'

'I want to see my family again,' Robert said, his voice shaking. 'I want to see Philippe and Ginette and Tante Helene and my *grandmères*. If I go to school now I don't know when I'll see them again.'

'Of course you'll see them again,' Gilbert said impatiently, but Marianne was already at Robert's side, kneeling close to him and taking his hands in hers, speaking in rapid French. He answered with tears in his voice, and Hilary, watching, felt sorry for him. She had thought more than once that he was being treated as if he had no say in or even feelings about his own future, and she felt that she was as guilty as the rest of them. Only Stephen had really talked to the boy, she thought.

Marianne asked her son a question and he nodded, reluctantly it seemed, but it was enough for her to turn to them with triumph in her face.

'He is feeling a little homesick, my poor lamb, but it is all settled now. He will go to this fine English school and be educated as you wish, but we have agreed he will spend half his holidays at home in France, if you will agree to his brother and sister spending Christmas here in Burracombe. So, we shall all grow to know and love one another – a big, happy family!' She stood up and spread out her hands, smiling prettily. '*N'est-ce pas?*'

Hilary glanced helplessly at her father.

But Gilbert was nodding slowly. 'Yes,' he said. 'That seems fair. I don't want to separate the boy from his other relatives. Bring them here for Christmas, and we'll show 'em just what it can be like in England!'

And Hilary knew that, although Marianne had lost the war, she had won this small battle, and would, in all likeliness, go on to fight others. She would never, ever give up.

There was a long, long journey ahead of them.

Chapter Thirty-Eight

The day of Travis and Jennifer's wedding dawned with a soft, pearly mist in the valley and a glow of sunshine promising to break through as the day warmed up. The horse-chestnut trees were beginning to colour, and the grass was soaked with glimmering dew and spread with gossamer tents, as if spiderlings had laid their blankets out to dry. In the gardens of Burracombe, roses were putting all their strength into a last, overblown flush, and chrysanthemums, dahlias and michael- mas daisies were taking the place of the summer flowers. The air was still, but full of the twitter of swallows and house martins, getting ready for their long flight to Africa.

In Jacob Prout's cottage, Jennifer was awake early. She lay gazing at her wedding dress, hanging from the picture rail. It was a simple princess style in shining cream satin, with a high collar sewn with tiny pearls in a delicate pattern repeated at the wrists, and fastened at the back with pearl buttons. It fitted Jennifer exactly, showing off her slim waist and gentle curves, and with it she was to wear a short veil of fine Honiton lace, which Jacob's own mother had worn at her wedding.

'Made in Beer, that were,' he had said when he unwrapped the yellowing tissue paper and shown it to her. 'Us had rela- tives there. All the women in Beer and Branscombe made lace – made it for Queen Victoria's wedding dress, God bless her. My mother wore this, and my Sarah wore it when her married me, and your dear mother would have worn it, too, if us had been married. You don't have to wear it if you got summat else in mind, but I'd be proud to walk down the aisle with you wearing that old veil.'

Jennifer's eyes had filled with tears as she gazed at it. Then she kissed his stubbly face and said, 'I'd love to wear it. Thank you, Jacob.'

Jacob was to give her away, of course, and had had his best Sunday suit cleaned and pressed specially. He'd worn it at his own wedding, and then at every wedding and funeral he'd been to since, and was proud of the fact that it still fitted perfectly. He'd agreed to buy a new tie and had gone to Tavistock specially, coming home with two white shirts and a new pair of black shoes as well, and getting his hair cut at the barber's to complete his wedding look.

Travis's family had arrived and were staying with various people in the village. Jennifer's sisters Audrey and Betty, with Audrey's two little girls, who were to be bridesmaids, were arriving later in the morning, and Jackie Tozer would be coming down from the farm so that they could all get dressed together. Val and Luke had suggested that Jacob should get ready in their cottage next door, and he'd agreed thankfully. 'Get me out of the way of all they women,' he'd said, and had taken his suit round the night before.

The wedding was to be at twelve – 'so we can have dinner at the proper time,' Jacob observed – and Jennifer had drawn up a timetable so that everything would run smoothly. The reception was to be in the village hall, where Alice, Dottie and a few others had been working hard to put up tables covered in white sheets, decorated with small bowls of flowers, and laid with the best cutlery. They were having ham salad, followed by summer pudding, stuffed with blackberries, apples and late raspberries, and large bowls of clotted cream.

Jennifer was just deciding that it was time to get up, when Jacob knocked on the door and came in, bearing a tray of tea, cornflakes, toast, and bacon and eggs keeping warm under an upturned pudding bowl. The teacup and plate were from his mother's best bone china tea set, and there was a tiny late rose-bud laid carefully on the snow-white embroidered tray-cloth.

'Oh, Jacob!' Jennifer exclaimed, sitting up. 'You shouldn't have done that.'

'Last chance I'll get,' he said gruffly, placing the tray care-fully across her knees. 'You won't be staying here no more, after today.'

Jennifer stared at him. In all her excitement, this aspect had never occurred to her. She put out a hand and touched his arm.

'Oh, Jacob. So I won't. But you'll see just as much of me – more, even. I'll be living in Wood Cottage and around the village all the time. And you know you'll always be welcome there.'

He shook his head. 'I'll come when invited and be glad to, but you don't have to fear I'll be popping my head round the door every five minutes. Newly-weds needs their privacy. But you don't need to wait to be asked to look in here, any time you like, and that goes for your man, too.' He grinned at her. 'Reckon I done a good day's work when I asked him round for supper backalong. Now, you eat a good breakfast, m'dear, and then take your time getting ready. I'm putting the bath down in the kitchen and there'll be cold water in it ready for you to add hot – there's kettles on the range. I'm going in next door, so you'll have the house to yourself. I'll come in again when it's time to go to the church.'

'I'll see you before that. We're coming in to say hello to Val and show her our dresses, remember?'

He nodded and went out. Jennifer ate her breakfast, know-ing that she would be hungry by the time they sat down at the reception if she didn't. I don't want to faint at the altar, she thought, and give everyone the wrong idea!

Pushing the tray away, she let her thoughts drift back over the past few years, since she had first come to Burracombe in search of her father. It had all turned out very differently from how she had expected, but she had found Jacob and a village full of friends. Most of all, she had found Travis.

I didn't think this was ever going to happen to me, she thought, gazing at her wedding dress. I thought I would stay in Devonport all my life, working at Dingle's until I retired, and then living alone, maybe with a cat for company. Instead, I have all this: friends, a man who loves me as if I really were his daughter, and a wedding to a husband I know will treasure me always. I don't know what I've done to deserve it all. I must be the luckiest woman in the world.

She heard the door downstairs open and close; Jacob was going next door. It was time to get up and have her bath before the others arrived. From now on, the day was going to be very busy indeed.

In no time at all, it seemed, the little cottage was full of women, and the masculine neatness of Jacob's home had disappeared under a froth of muslin and net dresses, flouncy petticoats and bouquets. Jennifer had had her bath and was wrapped in an old dressing-gown when Audrey and Betty arrived with the two small bridesmaids. The two husbands were immediately dispatched for a walk round the village, with instructions to be at the church by eleven-thirty to fulfil their duty as ushers, and told that they would know when this was because the bells would start ringing then. Jennifer made tea, and Betty produced a bottle of sherry.

'Goodness, I can't drink that!' Jennifer exclaimed. 'I shall be weaving down the aisle like a drunkard, and the vicar will smell it on my breath.'

'It's just for a little sip before we go to the church. It puts a bit of colour in your cheeks. Now look, the best thing to do is get the girls ready, then they can sit at the table and look at their books – no, Pammy, you can't draw, you'll get crayon all over your frock – and then Audrey and I will get ready, and we'll do you last. You don't want to be sitting around in that lovely dress and get the back all creased for everyone to see when you're standing at the altar. And have you rubbed the price off the bottom of your shoes for when you kneel down at the altar?'

Jennifer laughed and said she had. Betty, although the youngest of the sisters, had always been the bossiest, but she seemed to know what she was doing, and Jennifer was glad to relax and let her take charge. She sat back in her chair, sipped her tea and watched them get the little girls ready. As they were doing so, Jackie Tozer arrived, with her own dress in a large bag, and found a corner for herself.

At last they were all ready, and the bells had begun their peal. Their music sounded through the open windows with that particularly joyous clarity which they always seemed to have on such special occasions, and Jennifer looked around at her little entourage and said, 'Time to go next door and show Val what we look like.'

'It's safe to go out, is it?' asked Audrey, always a stickler for observing rituals and superstitions. 'You mustn't let Travis see you until you're at the altar.'

'No, he'll be there ringing the bells. He said it would help settle his nerves.' They heard a clash as two of the bells struck simultaneously, and Jennifer giggled. 'It doesn't seem to be working so far!'

She lifted her long skirt with both hands and led the way out through the front door, the two small bridesmaids holding the train at the back. Jackie followed them, and they processed out into the village street and through the gate next door. For a wonder, there was nobody about just then, and they got safely through Val's door without being seen.

Luke let them in and whistled.

'My goodness, what a bevy of beauties! Jennifer, you look amazing. If I weren't already happily married I might think of abducting you. Jacob, come and see what a gorgeous woman you'll be escorting up the aisle.'

Jacob came out of the back room and stared at her. His eyes grew suddenly wet and he brushed his hand across them, then pulled out his handkerchief and blew his nose. He said huskily, 'Your mother would have been proud of you, m'dear. And I be proud, too, to have the pleasure of giving you away.' They all laughed, and he realised what he had said and grinned waveringly. 'Well, you knows what I mean. This is a very happy day for me, and I hope it'll be the first of many happy days for you, too.' He blew his nose again.

'Thank you, Jacob,' Jennifer said, and came forward to kiss him.

'Is that you, Jen?' Val called from upstairs. 'Come on, I'm dying to see you all.'

With Jennifer once more in the lead, they trooped up the narrow stairs and crowded into the bedroom. Val was in a new nightgown, sprigged with a dainty flower pattern, with her hair curling around her face. She had a pink rose pinned to her bed jacket.

'I had to dress up, even if I can't be there. Jennifer, you look so lovely. That dress is exactly right for you. I can't remember what it's like to be that slim!' She patted her bulging stomach ruefully. 'I do wish Dr Latimer would let me come.'

'Travis and I'll come in again afterwards, on the way to the reception,' Jennifer promised. 'And don't the bridesmaids look sweet in their blue and white?'

'They look like fairies. Except for Jackie, of course – she's never looked like a fairy!' Val grinned at her sister. 'But you look very nice, Jackie. That frock really suits you.'

'It'll do for dances and things afterwards,' Jackie agreed, smoothing down the pale blue satin. 'Are you feeling all right, Val?'

'Never better. And I've got my prayer book here, see, so that I can follow the service right through. I'll even be able to sing the hymns at the right moment, and – *ohhhh!*'

'*Val!*' They all gasped, as she suddenly jerked back against

376

the pillow, flinging her arms wide so that the prayer book flew across the room. Her eyes rolled upwards, and as her back arched, her body began to twist alarmingly. Horrified, Jennifer rushed forward and caught the flailing hands, while Jackie screamed for Luke to come at once.

He came bounding up the stairs, his face ashen, and took one look at his wife's convulsing body.

'Oh, my God! She's having a fit! Jacob, quick – go and get the doctor. He'll probably be at his surgery – no, he may be on his way to the church, he said he'd try to go to the service if he could finish in time. Hurry, for God's sake ... Val ... Val, darling, can you hear me? Get those children downstairs,' he ordered, his eyes fixed on Val's white face, and there was a flurry of movement, as Audrey and Betty ushered the frightened girls out of the room. 'Val ... *Val* ...'

'What's happening?' Jennifer asked in terror, dropping her bouquet of Jacob's roses on the wide window sill. 'Is she going into labour?'

'No. I don't think so. It's probably eclampsia – the doctor warned us it might happen. She's got to be taken to the hospital as fast as possible.' Val was quietening now, and Luke held her hands firmly, watching her eyes. 'Val, sweetheart, it's me, Luke. Can you hear me, love? It's all right, you're at home and I'm here ... just try to stay quiet ... oh, where's that doctor? Jacob must have got there by now.'

Jackie Tozer was still at the door, her face pale and scared. Jennifer glanced at her and said, 'Go downstairs and make some more tea, Jackie. I'm sure he'll be here soon,' she said to Luke as Jackie departed. 'Jacob's only been gone a minute or two.'

'But it's urgent! Once this starts, they have to act very quickly. God, where *is* he?'

Val opened her eyes and turned her head, seeking frantically. '*Luke* ...'

'I'm here, love. I'm here. You're all right. The doctor's coming ... just rest quietly, there's a good girl ...'

'What happened? I feel funny.'

'Sssh,' he murmured. 'Sssh ...' There was a sound of a door opening and closing below, hurried male voices and then footsteps on the stairs. Luke and Jennifer turned in relief as the doctor appeared, already opening his bag, his eyes anxious. Quickly, in a lowered voice, Jennifer explained what had happened, and he nodded and came over to the bed to give Val a quick examination.

'I was afraid of this,' he said quietly to Luke. 'It'll have to be the hospital, I'm afraid. I'll go and ring for the ambulance. The Post Office is nearest – I'll go there.'

'But suppose it happens again? What should I do?'

'Just stay here and try to keep her quiet. There's nothing else you can do at this stage. Don't leave her!'

Luke looked at Jennifer. 'As if I would.' He seemed suddenly to notice her dress again. 'Oh, lord, and it's your wedding day, too!'

'It's all right, Luke,' she said steadily. 'I won't leave you. There's still a bit of time, and everyone will understand.'

'How long is it all going to take?' he asked agonisedly. 'Getting the ambulance here, and then into Plymouth? It could be an hour before she's at the hospital. Suppose the ambulance is already out somewhere else, suppose she has another fit – oh, *God* ...' Val was beginning to twist again, and he gripped her hands in a frenzy of terror. 'Val, Val, don't ... don't leave me now. *Val* ...'

Dr Latimer returned, calming them both. 'It's all right, Luke. The ambulance is on its way. They'll get her there in time, I'm sure.' He looked at Jennifer. 'It's almost twelve.'

'I'm not going until the ambulance is here,' she said, and moved to the door to call down the stairs. 'Jackie! Jackie, you and the others go to the church, will you, and explain. Tell Mr Harvey I'll be there as soon as possible. Oh!' She turned back to Luke and the doctor. 'All the Tozers are there – Val's mother and father and the others. Shouldn't we tell them?'

'There's nothing they can do, but yes, I think they ought to be told. Don't let them go rushing into Plymouth, though. Tell them to telephone once the service is over. She'll be going to Freedom Fields.'

Jennifer called down to Jackie. 'Tell your father first,' she added. 'He'll be in the tower; they'll ring until I get there. He can tell your mother and the rest of the family. And Travis will need to know why I'm late, but you can't go into the church and upset everyone else ...'

'I'll tell Mr Harvey,' Jackie said, and vanished. They could hear her explaining to the others, and then there was a flurry as they left the house, leaving it silent. Jacob trod heavily up the stairs and knocked on the door. 'Be there anything I can do?'

'Just wait outside for the ambulance and make sure they get the right house,' Dr Latimer said. 'And then take this beautiful bride to her wedding.'

Jennifer looked helplessly at Luke. 'I feel dreadful, going off to a wedding while Val—'

'Don't be silly,' Luke said roughly. 'It's not going to help her, is it? And she'll be furious when she finds out. Oh God, she's starting again ...'

'The ambulance is here!' Jacob shouted up the stairs. 'And half the village is outside waiting to see Jennifer go to church. I've told 'em to go away but they won't budge.'

'Never mind them,' the doctor said, as two men in dark-blue uniforms ran up the stairs. 'This woman needs urgent treatment,' he said to them. 'Go very carefully with her; she could go into labour as well. Luke, does she have a suitcase packed?'

'Yes, it's here. I told her it was too soon yet, but she would insist.'

'Just as well.' The doctor watched as the ambulance men

lifted Val carefully from her bed. They carried her downstairs and laid her on to a stretcher, then took it out through the front door.

The waiting crowd of villagers, who had come to see a bride, exclaimed in dismay.

'It's Val Tozer as was! But her babby's not due for another month or more.'

'Haven't you heard? Her's been in bed these past four weeks. Real poorly her's been, not allowed to put a foot to the floor. I reckon 'tis serious.'

'Move out of the way!' the ambulance driver commanded curtly. 'We've got to get her to hospital quick. Where's the husband? Oh, there you are – are you coming with her?'

'I most certainly am!' Luke jumped up into the ambulance and knelt beside Val, holding her hands and murmuring in her ear. Dr Latimer climbed up with him, and looked down at Jacob and Jennifer.

'Go and have a good wedding,' he said. 'And try to persuade the Tozers not to worry and definitely not to rush into Plymouth. There is nothing anyone here can do, but I am sure that Val and Luke will have a very fine baby by this evening and everything will be all right.' He closed the ambulance door, and the vehicle shot away through the village.

Jacob and Jennifer looked at each other.

'Reckon he'm right, maid,' Jacob said at last. 'Tidden no good us standing around wringing our hands. And it's well past twelve now, so if you'm ready, us might as well go.'

Jennifer nodded and took his arm. The villagers, caught up in the excitement of the ambulance's arrival, seemed to have forgotten they had actually come to see a bride on her way to church, and begun to move away. Maggie Culliford, with two or three small grubby children hanging on to her skirts, shouted after them, 'Here! What about Miss Tucker here? Isn't nobody going to wish her well?'

They turned back, half laughing and chiding each other in

spite of their anxiety, and formed two lines along the street for Jennifer and Jacob to process through. As they went along, more and more people came to join them, and the two lines stretched nearly as far as the church itself. They were just crossing the green, when Jennifer stopped and her hand flew to her mouth.

'What is it, maid?' Jacob asked in dismay. 'Whatever's gone wrong now?'

'My bouquet!' she exclaimed. 'I've left my bouquet behind on Val's window sill! I haven't got any flowers to carry to my wedding!'

The reception was well under way before any news came about Val.

The wedding itself had gone more smoothly than anyone could have hoped. Travis, who had continued to ring with the others until the vicar came in and beckoned him out, had not even realised how late Jennifer was – there was no clock in the ringing chamber, and he hadn't been able to look at his watch. He called, 'Stand', and the bells stopped.

'There's been a delay,' Basil Harvey said. 'Jennifer will probably be another ten minutes or so. You may as well continue ringing until she arrives.'

'I'll go and get into my pew,' Travis said. 'My best man seems to be on hot bricks. You're supposed to be steadying *my* nerves,' he said to the red-haired young man, who was jiggling nervously about behind the vicar. He turned to Ted, who was still holding the tenor's rope. 'Might as well give one of those boys a turn in my place.'

'But it's the wedding peal!' Ted said, outraged. 'Oughter be the best ringers, not a learner.'

'I need to speak to you as well, I'm afraid, Ted,' Basil said, and drew him through the door into the church. Ted looked exasperated but turned back and said to Norman, 'All right, you'd better let 'em both have a go. And mind you makes a good job of it,' he said sternly to Micky and Henry, who were already reaching for their ropes. 'Everyone'll be listening.'

The congregation watched curiously and began to whisper amongst themselves, as Ted listened to the vicar's murmured words, an expression of concern and then outright panic appearing on his face. Alice caught his look and stood up quickly, making her way past the others in her pew and catching him by the elbow.

'What is it? What's happening?'

'It's our Val,' he said. 'Been took worse. The doctor's sent for an ambulance; her's on the way to Plymouth.'

'Oh, no!' Her hand went to her mouth. 'Ted, we've got to go!'

'I don't think there's any need for that,' Basil said. 'The doctor was particular to say that everyone should just carry on. Luke's gone with her, and you can telephone for news in an hour's time, when they'll know more. But he's sure everything will be all right.'

'But I'm her mother! How can I sit through a wedding, knowing she'm in trouble?'

Ted looked at the vicar. 'I think us ought to go. Luke needs someone with him, anyway.'

'Yes, perhaps you're right,' Basil admitted. 'Well, we shall just have to manage as best we can without you. Shall I tell the rest of the family, or will you?'

'I'll tell them,' Alice said, taking charge. 'Ted, you go and get the truck, you can drive us there in that. I know the way to Freedom Fields. I'll just go and tell Tom and Joanna ...' She hurried to the family pew, watched by a hundred curious eyes, and whispered to them. Joanna half rose in her seat, but Alice pressed her firmly back, murmured something else to Tom, then hurried out. Everyone turned to each other, asking questions that nobody could answer, and then, as the buzz of muted conversation rose, the bells stopped ringing and the organ began to play 'Here Comes the Bride'.

Travis, sitting in his pew and facing forwards, had been aware of the whispers but had seen nothing of what was happening. Now he stood up and turned to see his bride coming down the aisle towards him.

Jennifer looked pale but composed. Her face was set, as if she were suddenly nervous, but the dress shone like an ivory beacon in the dimness of the church, and the veil of Honiton lace drifted about her head like a cloud of gossamer.

In her hands she carried a bouquet, not of roses but of dahlias, chrysanthemums and a few early michaelmas daisies, picked from the village gardens nearest to the church.

Alice and Ted found Luke sitting outside the labour ward, his hands clenched into tight fists between his knees as he sat staring into space. He started to get up as he saw them, but Ted pushed him gently back.

'Us had to come,' Alice whispered, sitting beside him. 'What's the news? What's happening?'

'They're doing a caesarean,' Luke said. 'It's the only thing that'll save either of them now. Even that's touch and go.' His voice broke, and Alice clutched his hand. 'My poor Val – she's had such a terrible time and she's never complained. If she comes through this, I swear I'll never put her through such a thing again.'

'It's not your fault. It could happen to anyone.'

'It *could* be my fault,' he went on, babbling a little now that he had someone to talk to. 'They don't know what causes it, so they can't say it's not. I let her work for too long, perhaps that's it. Or maybe I—'

'You didn't do anything,' Alice said firmly. 'Plenty of young women work till they're seven months gone, and what about women who've already got little uns? You can't say *they'm* not working, right up to the last minute. You did all you could, Luke, and got nothing to reproach yourself with.'

'But ...' he began, and then jumped up as a nurse came

through the swing doors and approached them. 'What is it? What's happening?'

'Will you come, Mr Ferris?' she asked. 'I think your wife needs you.'

Without a backward glance, Luke followed her. Alice and Ted looked at each other.

'Oh, Ted,' she said tremulously, and laid her head against his shoulder. 'Ted, why can't nothing go right for our family just lately? Whatever do you think is happening?'

He put his arm around her shoulder. 'I dunno, maid,' he said heavily. 'But it don't look good, do it? It don't look good at all.'

'... And that's why I be so very proud to stand here today and give my Jennifer to Travis Kellaway,' Jacob finished, as the guests sat at their tables in the village hall, replete with ham salad and summer pudding. 'She's a lovely young woman and he's a fine young man, and, to my mind, they make a very good couple. I'd like to propose a toast now to their very good health and lifelong happiness, so please be upstanding and raise your glasses. To Jennifer and Travis!'

'Jennifer and Travis,' they chorused obediently.

The bride and groom smiled and nodded their thanks, but, under cover of all the chatter and laughter, they were still anxious. Jennifer had murmured the news to Travis as they walked down the aisle together, and although they had smiled for the photographer, both felt their smiles were fixed and artificial. Only at the moment when they made their vows, looking deep into each other's eyes, did Jennifer feel the world and its anxieties slip away, leaving only herself and Travis in their own small space, where nobody else could intrude. In those few minutes, she felt that nothing else could touch them, nothing intrude upon their happiness and commitment to each other. But now the memory of those terrible moments in Val's bedroom came rushing back to her, and she had to blink away her tears.

'She'll be all right,' Travis murmured. 'I'm sure she'll be all right. Latimer's a good doctor.'

'I know. But even good doctors – oh! Look, there's Ted and Alice.' She jumped up, and the guests turned to see what had startled her.

Ted and Alice Tozer stood just inside the door. They were smiling broadly, and a wave of relief swept through the room. Joanna, who had hardly been able to eat a thing, left her chair and ran across to them.

'What's happened? How's Val? Is she going to be all right?'

'She'm fine,' Alice said, and began to cry.

As Joanna put her arms around her mother-in-law, Ted cleared his throat and said loudly, 'Sorry to take over your wedding, Jennifer, but I reckon everyone here wants to know our news. Me and Alice have got a fine, healthy grandson. He'm a little bit small, being as how he's a month ahead of time, but there isn't nothing wrong with him, nothing at all, and his name's Christopher Michael. And the best news of all – mother and baby are both doing well!'

The cheer that went up would have lifted the roof if it hadn't been replaced a few years earlier. There was an outburst of clapping, hammering of tables and stamping of feet that could almost have been heard, as Ted remarked later, back at Freedom Fields hospital itself. Travis jumped up and went to fetch another bottle or two of wine, and went round filling everyone's glasses, 'to wet the baby's head', as he said, and any other speeches were forgotten.

In the midst of it all, the door quietly opened and a young man stood there, taking in the scene with bemused eyes. He looked carefully around all the faces until his gaze came to the top table, where the bride and her party were seated, and then he paused.

Jackie Tozer turned her head as if it had been pulled gently by a string. She met his eyes and, for a second or two, she froze. Then she jumped up and ran down the hall towards him, almost knocking Travis over as he went back for more wine.

'Roy!' she cried, running straight into the young man's arms. 'Oh, *Roy!*'